PRAISE FOR
WILLIAM X. KIENZLE
AND HIS
FATHER KOESLER MYSTERIES

"As a storyteller, Kienzle surely ranks among the top talents working today."
Detroit Free Press

"Father Koesler is one of the best."
Richmond Times-Dispatch

"Father Koesler is on the case, thank God."
The Baltimore Sun

"There are few authors whose books a reader anticipates from the moment he finishes the last effort. . . . Add William X. Kienzle to that list."
Dallas Times Herald

"For perfect enjoyment you can always depend on William Kienzle. . . . A great delight."
West Coast Review of Books

CHAMELEON

William X. Kienzle

BALLANTINE BOOKS • NEW YORK

Copyright © 1991 by GOPITS, Inc.

Library of Congress Catalog Card Number: 91-6433

ISBN 0-345-36621-2

This edition published by arrangement with Andrews and McMeel, a Universal Press Syndicate Company

Manufactured in the United States of America

First Ballantine Books Edition: July 1992

FOR JAVAN

Acknowledgments

Gratitude for technical advice to:

Margaret Auer, Director of Libraries, University of Detroit
Rudy Bachmann, Ph.D., Clinical Psychologist
Ramon Betanzos, Ph.D., Professor of Humanities, Wayne State University
Sergeant James Grace, Detective, Kalamazoo Police Department
Sister Bernadelle Grimm, R.S.M., Samaritan Health Care Center, Detroit
Sergeant Charles Kelley, Firearms Inventory Unit, Detroit Police Department
Father Anthony Kosnik, S.T.D., J.C.B., Professor of Ethics, Marygrove College, Detroit
George La Berge, U.S. Postal Service, Retired
Irma Macy, Religious Education Coordinator, Prince of Peace Parish, West Bloomfield, Michigan
Walter D. Pool, M.D., Medical Consultant
Werner U. Spitz, M.D., Professor of Forensic Pathology, Wayne State University
Ann Walaskay, Head of Reference Department, University of Detroit
With special gratitude to Lynn Lloyd.

Any technical error is the author's.

CHAMELEON

1 "WHY WOULD A nun be on the make?"

"Wait a minute, I think I heard this one. But the way I heard it, the nun leaves the—whaddya call it?—the convent, the order, whatever. It's the middle of the school year, the wrong time for the job market, her being a teacher and everything. So, to tide her over, she gets a job as a hooker. And she does fantastic business.

"Her pimp can't figure it out. She isn't that great a looker, but she's bringing in twice the trade of any of his other girls. So, to learn how she does it, the pimp bugs her room. He hears her, usin' that tone of voice kindergarten teachers use—only she's talkin' to a john. And she's sayin', 'No, no! You're doing it all wrong. You're going to have to do it over and over again until you get it right!' "

"Very funny. But I wasn't joking."

"Whaddya mean?"

"Over there . . ." Under cover of his newspaper he gestured toward the far side of the lobby of the Pontchartrain.

"What?" The other man's eyes followed the direction of the gesture, but he could detect nothing out of the ordinary.

"Over there, Fred: sitting on the couch . . . near the lamp. She's doing her nails."

Fred pinpointed her. "Oh, yeah. What gives you the idea she's a nun?"

1

"That's about as uniformed as they get nowadays. It's called a modified habit."

"That's a nun?" Fred was not buying it. Not yet. "Go on! I've seen pictures of them!"

"Lately?"

"Sure! On TV. Ingrid Bergman. Loretta Young."

"Fred, those are old movies. You find a nun dressed in an old-fashioned habit from head to toe now, she's in a nursing home or she's wacko or senile."

"Well, pardon *me*, Al; we can't all be good Catholics like you."

"Just read a paper once in a while, willya, Fred."

"Why? You can get all the news you need in a half hour on TV."

"Even so, you musta seen nuns on the news. They're always protesting nuclear power plants or war or they're feeding the poor or something."

"Oh, yeah, there's Mother Teresa. I know her. But she wears the habit."

"That's a sari. But I'll give you it looks like a habit. Haven't you seen any of the other nuns?"

"Al, if they're not wearin' a habit, how would I know?"

"Well, for one thing, the TV reporter identifies them."

"I guess I haven't been payin' that much attention." Fred sounded repentant. "But take that little lady over there. How'd you know she's a nun?"

"The veil mostly."

"That's a veil? Don't look like a veil to me. Not a nun-type veil. Where's that stuff they used to wear around their faces that pinched their cheeks and mouth?"

Al sighed deeply. He would not have made a patient teacher. "That's why I called it a *modified* habit. The veil sits back on her head, lets her hair show. It's supposed to remind you of what the wimple—the old veil— was like. Same with the rest of the habit . . . *uniform*

would be a better name for it.'' His tone made it clear
he intended the term to be derogatory. Continuing the
comparison, he added, ''And that starched white collar
is what's left of the . . . you know, the bib. There's even
a scapular.''

''A what?''

''That strip of cloth that hangs down fore and aft. It
covers her shoulders. That's why they call it a scapular.''

Fred was impressed. ''God, Al, I had no idea you
knew so much about nuns. I didn't know anybody knew
that much.'' Fred mulled over his newfound respect for
the religious insight of his companion. ''Okay, so she's
a nun. But what makes you think she's a hooker? I
mean, I got a problem with that. A nun a hustler?
Sheesh! That almost makes me sick to my stomach.
Maybe you're wrong, Al.'' Fred sounded as if he were
praying that his otherwise knowledgeable friend was
mistaken.

''Maybe, but I don't think so. When was the last time
you saw a nun who looked like that?''

''Geez, I don't know. The last time I can remember
seeing nuns, all they had was faces and hands. Everything else was covered up.''

''Okay, well, take my word for it: Nuns—even today's nuns—don't look like that. Doing her nails in
public? Come on! And look at the makeup: That's practically professional!''

''Yeah!'' As Fred studied the woman in earnest, he
began to appreciate her less as a possible nun and more
as a desirable object.

''Don't get me wrong,'' Al continued, ''nuns today
may dress like everybody else or with a hint of a uniform like that one, but they're usually kind of . . . well
. . . plain. Maybe a little makeup, but nothing like
that.''

''Nuns don't necessarily prefer Hanes, huh?'' Fred
smiled. He enjoyed women more than just about every-

thing else in life. He felt a growing excitement in the possibility that this fantastic-looking female might be a nun and a hooker as well.

"So, Fred, I may be wrong, but I think she's here to turn a trick. You and I, we travel the country often enough as sales reps to know what a hooker looks like, how she acts."

Fred was grinning. "Hey, Al, whaddya say we hit on her? I mean, if she's really selling, I'd be glad to do a little buying. Whaddya say?"

Al shook his head. "Frankly, Fred, I don't think we could afford her."

She held up her hand, examined the tips of the spread fingers approvingly, tucked the emery board into her purse, and checked her watch.

She tapped her fingers against her knee. Time was not a significant consideration. Her basic charge was computed by the hour, and she had no other business on her schedule tonight. Nevertheless, waiting, killing time, made her fidgety.

As she glanced around the lobby she spotted the two men obviously studying her. They were seated far across the room, but there was no mistaking their interest.

She was used to this sort of reaction. She was a strikingly beautiful woman and she knew it.

But there was something out of the ordinary about those two across the room. At least about one of them. One was looking at her with that familiar lust to which she had grown accustomed. But the other one wore an expression that could best be described as disgust. Now why would—then she remembered: She was wearing the habit.

She almost smiled. Instead, she carefully curled a lip.

It worked. In a few seconds the two men exchanged a few words and then left the lobby. She had it all to herself. Just right.

One of the problems with being unoccupied, as she

was now, was that it gave one time to think. She didn't want time on her hands. She didn't want to think.

That guy—the one who had been regarding her with such distaste—he reminded her of someone. Who?

Her memory searched the distant past. Way back to the days when she'd been a student at Sacred Heart school in Dearborn. Yes, that was it: Monsignor Hardy. He'd always reminded her of someone who had just smelled something repugnant.

More than once, no, frequently, she had been marched into Monsignor Hardy's office in the rectory. Little Helen Donovan had been bad, had broken some rule, had violated some rule not yet legislated, had given scandal. Little Helen Donovan needed to be lectured, and then, after what passed for a fair trial in the parochial school of old, punished.

But that was it: old Monsignor Hardy used to look at her just the way that stranger had tonight.

It didn't matter. She was not going to continue this line of work forever. For one thing, it was far too dangerous. You never knew what sort of client you were going to entertain. Often enough it was just an insecure guy after some variety or a thrill that he thought only a pro could deliver.

But there were the other times when the john was a certifiable sicko. She shuddered. Those dicey episodes were only too easy to recall and to painful to ponder voluntarily.

Then too, she had done well—very well—financially. She felt sure she was on the verge of a secure future no matter what happened. Then—when that magic moment arrived—she could quit. She wasn't certain when it would happen. But she'd know when it did.

He was walking across the lobby in her direction. Even if he had not been headed straight for her, she would have known. Moderate height, moderate build, balding, dark hair clipped tight to the scalp. But it was his expression that identified him. It was a singular mixture of self-confidence, embarrassment, bravado, and ingenuousness. She'd seen it all too many times.

He stood before her chair, looked down at her and asked, "Are you . . . ?" He seemed unable to complete the question; what if he were mistaken?

". . . Helen? Yes, of course I'm Helen. How many women did you think you'd find in the lobby wearing a religious habit?" She was peevish, but she tried to make the putdown sound lighthearted.

"Well, good," he said. "And I'm . . ." He hesitated. ". . . John."

"Of course you are."

"Well, shall we go up to my room or would you like a drink first?"

"No, no drink." She didn't want one at the moment and, for her own protection, she was doubly concerned that he not start drinking. Sometimes the meekest, mildest men became mean drunks.

They said nothing on the elevator. But after entering his room, she turned to him, smiled, and said, "Well, John, is there anything special you'd like?"

"What do you mean?" He came close to blushing.

"I'm not a mind reader, John. We've got only this three hours together. I don't want you to feel anything but perfectly satisfied. So I've got to know just what you have in mind. I mean, in addition to the basics."

He fidgeted with his tie, pulling it loose from his collar.

She stepped close to him, undid the tie, and began unbuttoning his shirt. "It's like a menu, John," she said. "You've got to place your order before the meal." She felt him quiver slightly.

"I . . . I knew I wouldn't be able to tell you," he said, "so I wrote it out." He fumbled in a pocket, brought out a folded piece of paper, and handed it to her.

She quickly scanned the paper, then looked at him.

"This sounds like it could be a lot of fun, John. But it's going to cost three hundred dollars more."

He stepped back abruptly. "What? Three hundred bucks! I'm just a haberdasher from Toledo. That's heavy! Heavier, lots heavier, than I expected."

She moved close to him again and fiddled with buttons. "John, you're already paying two hundred dollars for the religious habit. You want a memorable evening. And you can have one. But everything costs, John. You know that. You're a successful businessman.

"But, it's up to you, John."

It was clear she was not going to negotiate. If he wanted it, he would have to pay for it. He shrugged and helped her with the buttons.

Another satisfied customer. She seldom disappointed. In fact, all things considered and since everyone had different expectations and levels of enjoyment, she might well claim that she never disappointed. Not only was each success a personal satisfaction, it was good for referral business.

It was near midnight as she exited the Pontchartrain. It was snowing. Long since, the streets of downtown Detroit, as well as most of the rest of the city, had been abandoned by nearly everyone except drug dealers and users, the homeless, drifters, and muggers.

All things considered, she felt fortunate there was a cab on duty outside the hotel. As she entered the vehicle, the driver awakened. He half turned to appraise his passenger. A nun. Odd. Especially at this time of night. But cabbies quickly get used to all manner of humanity. "Where to, Sister?"

"Forty-eight hundred Grand River."

"Forty-eight hundred . . . that be near 14th, 15th?"

"That's it."

"You got it."

She was grateful for the warmth of the cab. The driver had kept the motor running while waiting for a fare.

He had little alternative. It was December 26, a frigid December 26. That near the Detroit River, with the force of its piercing wind, without heat a person could get hypothermia in a hurry.

"Forty-eight hundred," the driver mused aloud, "and 15th. That wouldn't be old St. Leo's, would it?"

"Uh-huh." She didn't want conversation; she hoped monosyllables would make that clear.

"Ain't much goin' on at old St. Leo's anymore." The cabbie had not gotten the message. "You know, I grew up around there."

She made no sound.

Her lack of response did not discourage him. "Yessir," he continued, "it wasn't even St. Leo's. Was a franchise or a mission or something like that. Called Guadalupe—Our Lady of Guadalupe. Only one or two white families there when I was growin' up. Hell—'scuse me, Sister—but Guadalupe doesn't even exist anymore. Hell, St. Leo's hardly exists anymore.

"Geez, we used to go from church—Perpetual Help services—over to the old Olympia. Hell, the Olympia is gone, too. Red Wings—Howe, Lindsay, Abel—the Production Line. Jack Adams, best damn coach in history. Jack was a good Catholic too." He looked at her in his rearview mirror. "I'm a Catholic, y'know, Sister."

"I would never have guessed." Her attention then abandoned him. She became lost in thought: Was now the time to quit?

"Geez, Sister, I'll never forget one priest we had at old Guadalupe: Father Paddock—a good man he was— gone, now, I guess. This was a pretty quiet neighborhood most times back then, except on Saturday nights. Then all hell would break loose. I remembered old Father Paddock telling me one day that he stopped one of the black guys in the parish and asked him if the neighborhood could keep the noise down on Saturday nights 'cause on Sunday he had to work and he needed some peace and quiet on Saturday nights to get ready for Sunday Mass. And this guy says to him, 'Father, if you ever was a black man on Saturday night, you would never want to be a white man again.' "

She didn't laugh. But then, nuns, as he remembered them, were a quiet lot.

She had thought that when it was time to quit, she'd know it. Now, suddenly, out of nowhere, she was overwhelmed by a growing certitude that this was it. It had nothing directly to do with tonight's trick. He had been easy enough. Even, pound for pound, a gentleman. No, her concern was that she had been pushing her luck. The odds, if you will. Countless occasions of extreme danger . . . she had been saved by something. Something beyond her power to control. What? Prayer? She smiled. Whatever it was, she sensed that it was running pretty thin lately. The last thing she wanted was to end up on a slab in the medical examiner's emporium.

"So, there we were, Sister," the cabbie rattled on, "me and this friend of mine helpin' this guy sell newspapers outside the Olympia. The deal was, after we helped this guy, he would move us inside where he told the ticket taker that we worked for him and we were gonna sell papers inside, and when they were all sold he'd see to it that we left. But"—laughter—"that wasn't how it worked, Sister. Nah, we'd go in, leave the papers on the floor inside, and then go see the show." He shook his head, pleased at the memory.

"This one night it was wrestling, with Primo Carnera. . . ." He looked at her in his rearview mirror again. "He was the former heavyweight boxing champ, y'know.

"Anyway, it was a pretty good show. A fake of course, but a good show anyway. Then, after all the matches were over, I started walkin' home all by myself. And then, under a streetlight, I see these two guys waitin' on either side of the sidewalk. Well, I decided to go right ahead and right between them. But when I got to them, the bigger guy—he was lots bigger'n me and black to boot—anyway, he steps up and says, 'What's your name, boy?'

"So I says, 'Teddy.'

"And he says, 'Well my name is Joe Louis.' And with that, he takes a swing at me—a roundhouse right.

"Well, I knew darn well he wasn't Joe Louis—but I knew what he was gonna do next. So I ducked and got the hell out of there so fast they couldn't have caught me, even if they'd been firing bullets. Man, I really moved."

Still no sound from the nun. Well, maybe she'd fallen asleep. Hell, it was late enough. Matter of fact, after this fare, he was gonna go home and get some sleep himself.

It's simply too late, she thought; *I'm too tired to make a hard and fast decision about quitting right now.*

But tomorrow, she'd give the idea a serious analysis. Yeah, that was it: Something as crucial as this demanded the light of day before any firm decisions were reached.

"Well, here we are, Sister."

For the first time since their brief journey began, she was conscious the cab was not moving. "Oh?" She glanced out the window and recognized the familiar old, dirty gray buildings that had at one time, many decades earlier, constituted one of Detroit's prestigious parishes. She rummaged through her purse. "Listen," she told the cabbie, "wait for me here. I won't be long."

"Wait?! Are you kidding?"

"No, I'm not kidding. I want you to wait for me!" Testiness crept into her voice.

"Look, Sister, I don't mind drivin' you to this neighborhood, but I ain't about to sit here like a duck waitin' for somebody to step out of the shadows and off me."

"What are you anyway, a lily-livered coward? Nobody's gonna hurt you, little man."

"No need to get on your high horse, Sister. I'm not arguing with you. I'm just tellin' you I ain't gonna wait for you, that's all."

She was furious, but said no more. She found her cash and peeled off just enough for the fare plus an infinitesimal tip.

He quickly tabulated the excess as she exited the cab. "Thanks a bunch, big spender," he called out as he peeled away from the curb.

"Go to hell, you little son-of-a-bitch," she murmured ineffectually as she watched him speed off.

It was bitter cold and her coat, while stylish, was not all that warm. She turned her collar up and pulled the lapels as high as they could be stretched. It gave her face and ears some little protection against the wind-whipped snow. She found her keys, turned, and headed for the darkened convent. God, it was cold! Her entire body shook.

She glanced up at the building, now entirely dark and deserted. She hadn't planned on staying there this night. But now that the damn cabdriver had left, she had no choice. How was she going to get another cab to come to this neighborhood at this time of night? But of even more urgency was her need to get out of this frigid weather.

As she walked toward the convent, she recalled the vast number of nuns who had traversed this selfsame pavement over the years. Hundreds, probably. Undoubtedly, none of those nuns had actively chosen to be missioned to St. Leo's. They had been sent. And they went. Obedience. There must have been in excess of twenty nuns here at any given time years ago. Now just one person inhabited this entire building. What a waste! How senseless!

Just the thought of the olden days when there were so many nuns living and working in buildings like this brought to mind the old joke—definitely dated now, when the legendary chockful-of-nuns convents of the past no longer existed—about the repairman—Protestant— who was called to a convent to repair electrical outlets. He was taken to the site of the main problem—the convent's living room. The nuns called it their common room. While he was working away, all the nuns entered the room to spend some quiet time before supper. Their order's Rule demanded that at this hour they assemble together in absolute silence. And so they did.

The repairman observed this for the full hour they were together. Finally, the nuns left the room for dinner. Shortly thereafter, the repairman finished his work and left the convent. He went directly to the rectory where he met the parish priest. "Father, I'm not a Catholic, but I want to take instructions."

"That's nice," said the priest. "But why?"

"I was just over at the convent doing some repairs," the man replied, "and I figure there must be something to any religion that can put twenty women in the same room and for a full hour not one of them says a blasted word!"

She didn't see him.

She would not have seen him even if she had been looking for him.

He'd been waiting in the shrubbery to one side of the convent steps. That gave him the cover of the bushes and the poor light further shrouded his presence.

As she passed by, he stepped out of the darkness behind her, gun in hand.

In one sweeping motion, he raised the gun to the base of her skull and fired.

She never knew what hit her. The bullet entered her head and tumbled in its unstructured path, tearing tissue as it went.

She fell in a heap like a marionette whose strings had been cut. She was motionless.

He pocketed the gun. Seizing her by the ankles, he dragged her, face down, toward the bushes. But the branches were too dense at the base to position the body beneath. He had not anticipated that.

He resumed dragging her, face downward, around the corner of the building and toward the rear of the large, front-lawn shrine. As he dragged, her head and arms flopped about grotesquely.

Here, out in the open, her body would be discovered earlier than he would have preferred. But there was nothing to be done about that now.

He pushed the body with his foot until it rested tight up against the slightly less than life-size crucifix. Under the circumstances, it was the best he could do. He looked about one last time and faded into the shadows.

2 SISTER JOAN DONOVAN was holding herself fairly well under control.

It was she who had found the body, the body of her sister Helen. Sister Joan had screamed repeatedly, piercingly, and in genuine horror. But that had been slightly more than two hours ago. Now, she was merely numb. And in her state of shock, she wondered vaguely why they wouldn't leave her alone.

The janitor, in the process of opening the church, had heard her screams, found her at the shrine, saw the body, and called the police. Since then, she had been subjected to a barrage of questioning, first from the church people, then from the police officers.

By now, she was convinced that it didn't really matter to any of them that she had suffered the loss of someone very near and dear to her. The police needed information and they were single-mindedly going to pursue every lead they could uncover.

She was seated in the front parlor of the convent. It was so chilly. The heat was on but so many people were entering and leaving by both the front and rear doors, too often leaving a door ajar as they came or went. She shivered, partly from shock and partly from the draft.

"Are you cold, Sister? Perhaps you'd better put on your coat. It is chilly in here."

"I'm all right." Joan focused on the woman nearby, seated on a chair that had been positioned between Joan

14

and the front window by an earlier inquisitor. "Who are you?"

"My name is Moore, Sister; Sergeant Angie Moore. There are some questions I've got to ask you."

"But I've already told the other officers everything I know about this . . . this tragedy."

Moore nodded. "I know. But I'm with the Homicide Division. We're going to be investigating this case and we'll need your cooperation."

"Oh . . ." Joan was unable to frame an objection.

"The deceased was your sister?"

Joan nodded.

"Her age?"

"She was thirty-eight . . . seven years younger than I."

"Her occupation?"

"She was . . . self-employed."

Moore shook her head. "She was a prostitute, wasn't she, Sister?"

"If you know, why do you ask?"

"A matter of getting it on the record." *And,* Moore added silently, *to see how you handle the question.* "Now, when your sister was found, she was wearing a religious habit . . . not unlike the one you're wearing now."

"It was identical to this. It was one of my habits."

Moore raised an eyebrow.

"She asked to borrow it—just for last evening," Joan explained.

"This was unusual?"

"It was the first time she'd ever asked for that."

"You didn't object? Wasn't it a rather odd request? Bizarre, even?"

"As a matter of fact, I did object . . . at first. But . . ."

"I should think you might object. But you did let her have it."

"Helen usually got what she wanted."

"Oh?"

"She'd stay on a request like a bulldog. Persistence was her long suit."

"She say why she wanted the uniform?"

"She said she was going to a masquerade party."

"You believed that?"

"Hardly. But the more I pressed her the more vague she became. She just kept after me until my resistance was worn thin."

"She picked it up last night?"

Joan nodded. "I left her the key. I was going to be out—I'm out frequently in the evenings. My job—"

"Which is—?"

"I'm the delegate for religious."

"And that means—?"

"I'm . . . uh . . . sort of an ombudsperson for members of religious orders in the archdiocese of Detroit. Mostly, I represent the other nuns here. So I have frequent meetings with individuals and groups, particularly in the evenings when all the aggrieved parties can get together."

"And you were at such a meeting last night."

"That's right." Without waiting for the next logical question, Joan continued. "I met with another nun—Sister Mary Murray—and the parish council at Our Lady of Refuge, Orchard Lake. There is some question about Sister's contract as religious education coordinator," she explained. "We met until midnight. I remember because the council president noted the time as the reason he wanted to end the meeting and take the matter up at next month's meeting."

She noted that the policewoman was taking notes employing some sort of shorthand. Joan was certain the sergeant would be checking every detail for corroboration.

"So," Moore continued, "you would have returned here at about . . . ?"

"It must have been near 1:00 A.M."

"Tell me—and please include every detail you can remember—what did you do when you arrived? You parked your car . . ."

"In the garage. There really isn't anything significant to tell. It had been snowing. In fact it was still snowing. I remember wishing I had worn galoshes. Our janitor always keeps the walks shoveled, but it had snowed after his workday, so he wouldn't have gotten to it until this morning. Anyway I walked from the garage around in front of the church and up the front walk. It was bitter cold and the snow was blowing, so I kept my head down and got inside as quickly as possible. And then I just went to my room and went to bed and fell asleep very quickly. I was awfully tired."

"You noticed nothing unusual coming into the house?"

"No, nothing. As I said, I had my head down and my eyes nearly shut against the snow. I could travel from the garage to the house blindfolded," she added.

Moore concluded that either the nun had noticed nothing untoward—whether or not the crime had been committed after she had retired—or she was lying. "But," Moore said, "you were the one who found the body."

"Yes. I was going over to the church this morning. There are only a few parishioners who regularly come to church on weekdays. And our pastor is out of the country almost as much as he's here. He's very active in the peace movement, you know. So, weekday mornings, I conduct a sort of a prayer service and distribute Communion. It's a paraliturgical rite, you see—"

"That's all right, Sister, you don't need to go into that. The body?"

"Yes . . . the body." As Joan recalled all too clearly discovering her sister's body, a feeling of overwhelming loss pierced her again. "It was much lighter at seven this morning than when I'd gotten home, of course. And it was no longer snowing. When I came down the steps, I noticed the indentation in the snow leading over toward the shrine. It was as if something had been dragged there. Perhaps a sledge of some sort. I went over to see what it was. And . . .'' Her voice trailed off.

"Was your sister lying faceup?"

Joan seemed to pull herself together. "No. The . . . body . . . was face down. But I knew—who else could it have been? I recognized her coat—it was very expensive—and part of the habit was exposed.''

"Then you turned the body over, faceup?"

"I had to be sure.''

"Then you screamed, and the janitor came and called the police.''

Joan nodded and lowered her gaze.

"Thank you for your cooperation, Sister.'' As Moore rose to leave, spontaneously she patted the nun's shoulder. "If we have more questions, we'll get back to you.''

Outside the building, standing between the front steps and the shrine, in the middle of methodical beehive-like police activity, was Lieutenant Alonzo Tully. More familiarly known to friends and co-workers as "Zoo.''

Tully was intent on absorbing every detail, no matter how seemingly insignificant, of this, the scene of the crime. In determining what had happened here, the testimony of this silent scene was the sole witness that could not and would not deceive. He and the others investigating this case might misread or misinterpret the evidence. But the evidence represented fact. It need only to be correctly understood and evaluated.

The body of Helen Donovan had long been removed, but the traces were still evident. There were too many footprints now in the snow, but it was still possible to distinguish the essential indications.

Only the slightest tracks had been left by the perpetrator in the ensuing snowfall. Evidently he had hidden in the bushes to the right of the front steps. As the victim passed, the perp had stepped out behind her. There was no sign of any struggle. The perp had shot her once, the preliminary examination suggested at the base of her skull, then dragged her body behind what the people of St. Leo's called their shrine.

Tully was not in any way a religious person, but he could not have mistaken the shrine. It was a slightly-less-than-life-size depiction of the crucifixion of Christ, with two additional figures standing beneath the cross. Tully's familiarity with Christendom's central mystery did not extend beyond the main character. The other figures were Mary, Christ's mother, and his disciple John.

No struggle. That was an essential clue in this infant investigation. That plus the fact that her purse had not been taken—or even rifled; it contained more than five hundred dollars in cash.

For police purposes, it was providential that the victim's sister had discovered the body and could not only identify the deceased but also confirm her line of work. Otherwise, they would have been bogged down trying to discover who this nun was and why she would be carrying so much cash.

But, a hooker! In all probability she had just turned a trick.

Several cops who knew of her testified that she was definitely in the higher financial bracket of whoredom. A Cass Corridor streetwalker would have had to turn tricks for weeks to clear what Helen Donovan made in one night.

No struggle. Did the perp sneak up behind her, unnoticed, as Tully initially concluded? Or, another distinct possibility, had she known her killer and, unsuspecting, put up no fight?

Sergeant Angie Moore approached. Together, she and Tully stepped out of the cold into the building's foyer. Moore filled him in on her interrogation of Sister Joan, the actual nun.

A few details, such as what a delegate for religious did, Tully had to take on secular faith. A "religious" in the Catholic sense of the term had a specific meaning that was lost on Tully. But he listened carefully. All Moore's information was absorbed into the practiced computer of his mind. There it would be stored and even much later he would be able to call it up.

No sooner had Moore completed her report than Sergeant Phil Mangiapane, also a member of Tully's squad, arrived on the scene.

Mangiapane was enthused. It was an emotion that came easily to him. "Zoo," he said, "we nailed her john of last night." He pulled out his notepad and flipped it open. "One Henry Taylor, a very scared haberdasher from Toledo. In town on a buying trip. We're detaining him temporarily at the Pontch. Right now, he's wishing he'd left town last night. Or, better, never come."

"How'd it go?" Tully asked.

"Pretty good. At first he flat-out denied he knew who we were talking about. Even after we showed him the picture we got from her sister. But when we showed him his hotel room number in Donovan's date book and produced the bellboy who not only noticed Donovan in the hotel last night but remembered her taking the elevator with Taylor after he picked her up in the lobby, there wasn't much he could deny."

"So?"

"He said that after she left, he went to bed. But then we got lucky. The same bellboy who spotted the two of them enter the elevator said that he saw Donovan leave the hotel at about midnight. He was sure of the time because he was just about to end his shift. He saw her climb into a cab—a Checker cab. Then who should leave the hotel—hat and coat on—but Henry Taylor.

"When we confronted him with this, Taylor said that oh, yeah, he forgot that after she left, he took a short walk outside for a few minutes."

"And the bellboy?"

"Didn't know where Taylor might have gone. He just saw the guy leave the hotel and then he went off duty."

"Did the guy drive here from Toledo?"

"Yeah."

"So he had his car at the hotel. Could he have known where she was going?"

Mangiapane shrugged. "If he did, only him and the Donovan girl know. And he ain't gonna volunteer anything like that."

"Okay," Tully agreed. "Granted, the chance is slim, but say he knew she was returning here. Or say he was able to get in his car in time to follow the cab here." He stopped, then shook his head. "No, if he did that, how could he have had time to get to the bushes and be lying in wait for her?" He looked at Mangiapane. "Did you get a make on the cab?"

"Not yet," Mangiapane said. "Checker's a big company. But it shouldn't be hard. We know the approximate time Donovan left the Pontch and that she ended up here."

"Wait a second," Moore said. "If it's this Taylor guy, how come he didn't take his money back?" Pause. "And also destroy the date book that had any reference to his 'appointment' in it?"

Mangiapane shook his head. He had not considered these discrepancies.

"Maybe," Tully said, "he didn't think he had any time to fool around after the gunshot." *Then why did he take the time to drag her body all around?* "Maybe he panicked and ran." *Same question.* "Maybe he didn't think of it. Maybe all he could think of was getting even with her." *For what?* "Revenge." *For what?* "And maybe"—he looked at both of them—"this isn't our best lead. But it's a warm body, it's possible, and we've got him.

"Who's on the cabbie?"

"Martin," Mangiapane replied.

"Good. How about Donovan's apartment?"

"The guys called just a while ago, Zoo," Moore said. "They found her register. Lots of names and numbers."

"Very good." Tully was pleasantly surprised that so many leads were paying off. "Number one priority after you wring this Taylor out, start on the johns. Few people can get sorer the day after than a john."

"We'll get on it right away, Zoo," Moore said. Then she added, "You know, in this city, it could have been just about anybody. A guy high on crack or ice, or anybody on the lookout for an easy mark—or just some kook with a gun sees a woman alone at night."

Tully sighed. "I know, I know. But one thing argues against that: whoever did it didn't touch her purse—and she had a bundle in it."

"He didn't see it?"

"Long straps. She wore it over her shoulder. He couldn't have missed it. No," Tully said, "I'm going for someone she knew. And a john is my first choice."

"On that theory, Zoo," Moore said, "it could have been somebody who knew her and disapproved of her being a hooker. There are a lot of squirrelly people in the so-called moral majority. Especially if someone like that saw her in nun's garb and figured that she might have been a hooker. After all, waiting around in a hotel lobby and being picked up by a john! Could get a righteous man's blood boiling. Or a woman's," she added.

"Good thought, Angie," Tully said. "And we've got someone right now who could fit that profile. Angie, make sure the sister, the real nun, gets a paraffin test."

"The nun!" Mangiapane could not conceive of a nun/ murderer.

"The nun," Tully affirmed. "She must have been plenty embarrassed by her sister's line of work. A stain on the family's reputation. A nun, known by friends and acquaintances as sister of a call girl. Let's just see if she's fired a gun recently."

"It may be too late to test, Zoo," Moore said.

"But possible. Do it right away, Angie."

Moore left, though she was not eager to put the nun through this test. But it was a homicide and there was little if any room for sympathetic feelings.

Tully turned to Mangiapane. "One other possibility comes to mind. But it would make our job so miserable I don't even want to think about it."

"What's that, Zoo?"

"A case of mistaken identity."

"You mean somebody meant to kill the real nun?"

Tully nodded. "Helen Donovan was dressed exactly like her sister Joan. Wearing Joan's habit even. They're the same build. You saw Helen's picture and you saw the real nun. They look enough alike to pass for sisters even if you didn't know they were related. Say somebody wants to kill Joan. But the one who shows up dressed like Joan, looks like Joan, is headed for where Joan lives, is Helen."

"Okay, but one thing, Zoo: If somebody's lying in wait for Joan, how does he know she'll be coming back so late at night? Or, as it turns out, so early in the morning? Most of the nuns I've known get to bed kind of early. Why would anybody figure a nun would be coming home at midnight?"

"The answer to that came out when Moore was interrogating Joan. The nun says her department business keeps her out late almost every night. If someone was stalking her, he'd know that."

"Geez!"

"Yeah. It's one thing to off a hooker. And quite another thing to intend the murder of a nun. If that's the case, we're in for some long days and nights."

"Geez!"

3

"IT'S GOOD FOR you."

Father Robert Koesler chuckled as the thought came to him from a far distance in time.

Irene Casey had used the phrase jokingly when he and she worked at the *Detroit Catholic*. He was editor-in-chief; she was woman's editor and practically everything else, which is not unusual in thinly staffed operations.

In those days—now some dozen years ago—every time he would complain about something—a union meeting, a grievance session, an editorial deadline— Irene would advise, "It's good for you." The aphorism became an in-joke with the two of them.

He thought of it now as he shoveled snow. He had been pondering the odds of a heart attack when people his age—the early sixties—got unaccustomed to strenuous exercise. There was nothing wrong with his heart. But one did read about the hazards of occasional heavy labor, particularly for those people who led a normally sedentary life, as did he. And especially in a Michigan winter when anything from balmy temperatures to ice and snow could occur.

He had forgotten how much he enjoyed shoveling snow. All those years he'd spent as pastor of a suburban parish, physical labor had been a spectator sport for him, as janitors and janitorial substitutes had performed all chores from landscaping to snow removal.

This, however, was different. It had become common

practice for Detroit priests, even pastors, to move on from one parish to another after a certain but not fixed number of years. When his time came, he felt a strong impulse to return to a city ministry. St. Joseph's parish, near the heart of downtown Detroit, had opened up through the pastor's retirement at just the moment Koesler's option came due. Now he was in his seventh month as pastor and sole priest in residence at St. Joseph's.

Along with the ancient structures he'd inherited—church, rectory, and home for janitor and family—was a conscientious Italian gentleman who would have qualified as a sexton but that he did not need to dig graves. He certainly was much more than simply a janitor. He was electrician, plumber, horticulturist, and, frequently, early morning Mass server.

But Dominic—no one called him Nick, or even Dom, for that matter—was, like all else on the corner of Jay and Orleans streets, ancient. He was susceptible to the minor aches and pains that can be doubly troubling for the elderly. Presently, it was a mild case of the flu. Koesler had insisted that Dominic remain in the warmth of his home and the care of his devoted wife.

But somebody had to move this snow. And unlike his former suburban parish, where there had been substitute janitors, there was no money allocated here for that—nor were there any volunteering parishioners. So Koesler shoveled snow. And if he wondered whether this exercise might kill him, he had only to remember the sage advice of Irene Casey: "It's good for you."

But, he thought, it might have been better had he been able to use the snowblower rather than the present shovel.

The blower had been a present he had won for Dominic from a reluctant parish council. Koesler would never forget the first morning Dominic used the blower. It brought to mind the experience of a previous janitor in a previous parish. After the first few swipes, the janitor, looking like a snowman, had entered the toasty rectory kitchen to announce, "I'm-a-not like-a that machine." But once he'd gotten the knack of turning the spout in any direction but directly at himself, all had gone well.

Koesler did not have to worry about the spout; he couldn't get the motor to start. It was an ongoing manifestation of his undeclared war on machines and tools. After some twenty tugs on the ignition rope, he decided that if this kept up he was about to leave his game in the garage and be physically unable to push either the blower or a shovel.

Maybe there was something to that warning about heart attacks. He was now perspiring freely. He had cleared a path from the rectory to the church and also the church's front steps, as well as the sidewalk from Orleans to the parking lot. That would accommodate the faithful few who attended daily Mass.

He returned to the rectory, showered quickly, and donned a cassock. As he descended the stairs to the first floor, he caught the aroma of fresh-brewed coffee. He smiled: Mary O'Connor had arrived. Business for this twenty-seventh day of December had begun.

Mary O'Connor, a widow, had, in a sense, come with him from the suburban parish to the central city. In suburbia she had been the parish secretary and general factotum. She was easily capable of managing all the necessary nitty-gritty of parochial life if only he would stay out of her way. He did and she did.

When he applied for St. Joseph's parish Mary was faced either with having to get used to an entirely new and different style of pastoring, or retirement. Neither alternative had she found particularly appealing. So when Father Koesler hesitantly asked whether she would consider working with him again downtown, her problem was solved. Her only continuing concerns were the daily drive between Dearborn and Detroit, and getting used to how this antique parish functioned. She decided to live with the former and gradually solve the latter.

All that shoveling, plus his failed attempts at getting the blower started, had reduced Koesler's routine to rubble. He had time only to duck briefly into the kitchen, acknowledge Mary's presence, and hurry over to church.

He had practically no time for any last-minute preparation for the day's brief homily, but this day he didn't need much time. It was the feast day of St. John the Evangelist, one of Koesler's favorite saints. Author of the fourth Gospel and three touchingly simple Epistles, he was self-identified and known as "the disciple whom Jesus loved." John alone, of all the apostles, stayed with Jesus at the cross to the end.

And yet, what an odd and controversial conclusion to his own life. Tradition has it that he was the only apostle to escape literal martyrdom. Yet he is considered a martyr, since legend has it that the Roman emperor Domitian had John plunged into a cauldron of boiling oil from which he miraculously emerged alive. If this really happened, one wonders why Domitian didn't try it again. Maybe there was some sort of Roman law forbidding double jeopardy. Maybe pardon was a reward for escaping death. Maybe it never happened.

In any case, Koesler determined to develop a three-minute homily on John as a very old man constantly urging his disciples to love one another. When they complained about this repetition, John assured them that, "It is the word of the Lord and if you keep it, you do enough."

The fervorino on love went over well with Koesler's tiny but devout congregation.

By the time he finished Mass, Koesler could almost taste the coffee Mary O'Connor was keeping hot for him. It was not yet midmorning but already he felt as if he'd put in a considerable day.

Cold cereal, a banana, and coffee would constitute

breakfast. As he began eating, Mary joined him, pouring herself a cup of coffee. This was unusual. Ordinarily, he breakfasted alone while Mary continued to prepare St. Joseph's books and records for the twenty-first century.

"Did you hear the news?" Mary asked.

Koesler looked up, startled. They did not often discuss current events unless it was something of truly pressing importance. "No, I guess not." He'd heard the eleven o'clock news last evening, but that had contained nothing that Mary would consider vital. "I haven't started the *Free Press* yet and, seeing my duty, I cleared snow instead of listening to the radio. Something important happen?"

"Sister Joan Donovan's sister was murdered."

"The delegate for religious? I didn't know she had a sister." This though Koesler had been around long enough to be extremely familiar with the archdiocesan structure and personnel.

Mary sat down opposite him, cradling her cup. "My impression is that not many people knew. According to the news report, her sister was a high-priced call girl."

"No kidding!"

"The report I heard said she was killed at St. Leo's convent . . . at least that's where they found her body."

"Wait a minute: Sister Joan lives at St. Leo's. Everybody knows that. Was her sister visiting her?"

"I don't really know. The report was kind of sketchy and I'm not sure of all the details. I guess the body was found sometime this morning—not too long ago; there's nothing in the paper about it." A playful expression crept into Mary's eyes. "It's times like this that I wish I knew somebody who knew somebody in the police department so we could find out what really happened."

Only gradually did what she was saying dawn on Koesler. "You mean—" He smiled as he shook his head. "Oh, no!"

"Just think, we'd be the only civilians in this area

who would know what the police know." Her suggestion was made mostly in jest.

"You make much—much too much—of my contacts
with the police, Mary. Just because I know a few names
in the department doesn't mean I can get any special
treatment."

He was being unassuming.

He had, in the course of several homicide investigations, collaborated with the Detroit Police Department,
and over the years he'd become fast friends with the
head of the Homicide Division. In any case, it was the
furthest thing from his style to bother an extremely busy
police force just to get a little gratuitous information.
But she was teasing, and he knew it.

"Did the report you heard have any other details?"
he asked.

"The only other thing I remember is the address of
the victim."

"Which was?"

"Thirteen hundred Lafayette."

Koesler's eyes widened. "That's right in our back-
yard."

"That's probably why I remember it."

The area in the immediate vicinity of St. Joseph's
church comprised a potpourri of cultures. On its northern side were a string of small businesses and a run-
down residential area. Many of the houses were vacant.
But between the church and the Detroit River were a
series of high-rise apartments, some of them swank. In
the latter group was 1300 Lafayette.

Parishes in that area, principally Old St. Mary's and
Sts. Peter and Paul, as well as St. Joseph's, more or
less scrounged for members. But, of all the churches in
that general location, St. Mary's and St. Joseph's were
the most popular. Although Holy Family had its own
faithful circle.

Still, it was difficult to distinguish who of those attending the various Masses considered themselves parishioners and who were regular free-lancers.

Thus the mere fact that the deceased had lived in St. Joseph's neighborhood and, being the sister of a nun, probably was a Catholic, was no indication that she had actually joined any of the parishes. Koesler would have to wait until the dead woman's photo was inevitably published in the papers to see if he recognized her. "I guess I'll have to wait till I see her picture in the paper before I can tell whether she looks familiar . . . or ever attended Mass here," Koesler said.

As usual, Mary O'Connor had a better idea. "Why don't you attend the wake? Then you can get a better idea than any newspaper picture can give you. Besides," she added, "I'll bet Sister Joan would be grateful if you showed up."

"As usual, Mary, you're absolutely right. I'll do it. Sister probably could use a few extra friends just now."

Mary rose and moved to the hallway leading to the front offices. "I guess this means you're not going to call your friends in the police department." She was smiling.

"Absolutely not. For one thing—though realistically there's not much chance of its happening—I don't want to be anywhere near police headquarters or even in the consciousness of any of the officers when they investigate this case. The murder of the sister of a nun is just the sort of case that I might get roped into. And, in the immortal words of the late Samuel Goldwyn, when they get going with this one, I want to be included out."

4 A VAGUE SENSE of frustration rather than obligation prompted Lieutenant Tully to attend the wake for Helen Donovan.

There being no other surviving close relatives, Sister Joan Donovan had made all funeral arrangements. A central west side funeral home was selected, mostly because it was handy to St. Leo's where the Mass of Resurrection would be offered.

Joan had expected some sort of opposition to her request for a Catholic burial. Helen's Catholicism had been virtually nonexistent since she had escaped from parochial school. Joan was reasonably sure she'd be unable to locate anyone who had seen Helen inside a church—any sort of church—for a goodly number of years.

But the nun had been most pleasantly surprised and relieved when, far from official prohibition, retired bishop Lawrence Foley had assured her that he himself would celebrate the Mass. And that was doubly providential since St. Leo's pastor was somewhere in Central America. Foley solved her problem of having to find a priest to fill in during the pastor's absence.

Tully was unaware of all that Joan had feared and accomplished in the brief time since her sister's murder. He was aware that Catholic Church law might deny Church burial under stated circumstances such as in the case of a lapsed Catholic or a suicide. But what sort of burial rites Helen Donovan was accorded did not concern him. What did bother him was the lack of progress in her homicide investigation.

The paraffin test had established nothing. The result was negative in the case of both Sister Joan and Henry Taylor. But then, in both instances, the time was marginal. If either had fired a handgun, proof might have surfaced in the test. On the other hand, so many hours had passed since the shooting that any trace on the subject's hand could have faded from recognition. So in the end there was no proof of anything. The lapse of time might have ruled out a positive result.

Or it was just as possible that neither of them had fired a gun.

As it happened, there was no cause to further detain Taylor. Cautioned that he might be needed to answer more questions, he was released, to return to Toledo undoubtedly a chastened husband, firmly resolving never again to stray. Until the next sales trip.

Nor had there been any breakthrough in hunting down the johns listed in Helen's book. Most of the men were easy enough to locate. Many of them were considered prominent in anyone's roster of Detroit's movers and shakers. Noted figures from the business, political, entertainment, and sports worlds had been among Helen's clientele. Some members of Tully's squad took special delight in any investigation that legitimately called for the grilling of powerful and pompous men. Gratification aside, the interrogation of all Helen's clients had turned up nothing. Not even any additional likely leads.

Of course, that segment of the investigation was not yet complete. But with all these dead ends, hope dwindled that any breakthrough was in the cards, at least from that direction. So, uncertain of what he might accomplish, or even what he was looking for, Tully had come to the wake.

It was a small funeral parlor—too small. Tully had no idea why this mortuary had been selected. Whoever was responsible seemingly had not anticipated this mass of people.

Tully tried to study each individual he could isolate in the throng. The room was too congested for him to see everyone. In the far corner, clustered at the rear of the room, were five, maybe six women who shared Helen Donovan's line of work. He knew them from his years on the vice squad. They spied him at about the same time he spotted them. They smiled and nodded recognition. Though Zoo was on the opposite side of the law, they were not hostile. In their dealings, Zoo, as they all knew him, was always fair, frequently even tolerant.

A good bit of the reason they had clustered together was the nature of this crowd. Most of the other mourners appeared to have some sort of religious affiliation. Many of the men wore clerical garb. Most of the women were attired in a hint of a habit. Many of those in civvies seemed so familiar with those in uniform it seemed safe to assume that nearly all of them had some sort of religious status.

In such a gathering, Tully was, for the most part, a stranger at the gates of paradise.

Then he saw him.

This room wherein Helen Donovan was lying was actually two rooms. The divider wall had been opened up. So there were two doorways. Standing just inside the other doorway was a priest Tully recognized. Koesler—Father Robert Koesler.

Tully and Koesler had been associated in a couple of previous investigations. Tully's verdict on Koesler as a sleuth; not bad for an amateur. Tully's guess for this moment: The guy must feel right at home in this crowd.

He did. Koesler knew just about everyone there, with the major exception of a small group of women at the rear of the room. Considering their clothing and makeup and given the fact they were much more likely to be friends of the deceased than of anyone else in the room, they had to be ladies of the evening and not ladies of the Rosary Altar Society.

As for the others, as far as he could tell without a program, nearly all—if not all—the archdiocesan department heads were here, along with many of their personnel. It figured they would be here in respect for Sister's rank. As delegate for religious, she too was a department head. The nuns undoubtedly were friends from Joan's religious order as well as from other orders who knew her through her office as a delegate. Koesler didn't know many of the nuns. He hadn't expected to.

According to the obituary in today's paper, the rosary was scheduled to be recited at 8:00 P.M., which, by Koesler's ever-present watch, was just fifteen minutes away. He decided to wait until after the rosary to offer his condolences to Sister Joan. Meanwhile, he casually studied some people in the crowd.

The first person he focused on was Larry Hoffer. Most likely, Koesler's eye fixed on Hoffer because the gentleman was fidgeting. But then, Hoffer always fidgeted, usually jingling the coins in his left trouser pocket. Wherever Hoffer happened to be, his nervous habit always created the impression he wanted or needed to be somewhere else. So it was this evening.

Well, why not, thought Koesler. Hoffer's burden of responsibility was great. He headed the Department of Finance and Administration, with ten subdepartments clustered in the archdiocese's downtown headquarters, the Chancery Building.

Hoffer, seated just two rows behind Sister Joan, whispered periodically with a man Koesler didn't recognize, probably one of Hoffer's assistants.

"It just doesn't make any sense, Pete," Hoffer was saying, "no sense whatever."

"Well, not any financial sense, I'll grant you," Pete Jackson replied. Jackson headed Parish Finances, one of Hoffer's departments. "But you've got to consider the history."

"Why? History is yesterday. We're not living then. We're living now."

Jackson sighed. He didn't want to get involved in a debate with his boss, but he'd been drawn into the discussion and now he was forced to differ with Hoffer. It wasn't that Jackson was playing devil's advocate; he spoke conscientiously. "Larry, history is real to the people who lived it. You can't blame them for wanting to hold on to it. The people we're talking about don't have much else to hang on to."

Hoffer's leg was bouncing almost imperceptibly to the rhythm of an unheard nervous beat. He quieted the motion with the hand that had been jingling coins in his pocket. He turned slightly toward Jackson, his voice sufficiently muted that it blended into the low murmur in the room. "Do you know the actual financial condition of St. Leo's?"

Jackson could have been offended. As director of parish finances, one of his jobs was to be current with regard to the status of parishes, particularly those in dire straits, such as St. Leo's. However, for sake of the argument Hoffer's question was couched in hyperbolic rhetoric. Jackson took no offense.

"Yeah, sure, I know," he said. "They're lucky to pull in a hundred dollars in the Sunday collection."

"And they've got practically nothing in the bank." The bank to which Hoffer referred was an archdiocesan facility. When the late Cardinal Edward Mooney had reluctantly accepted his appointment to Detroit, finances had been crippled by the great depression. Well-to-do parishes, such as St. Leo's, were at that time lucky to pay the interest on their loans. There was little hope of reducing the principal. In perhaps his greatest coup, Mooney got his parishes out of the banks and into the chancery, thus unquestionably saving them from disastrous fiscal fates. To this day, the chancery is, in effect, the parochial bank for each parish.

"Plus," Hoffer continued, "they have only a handful of parishioners. And the number dwindles every year."

Jackson shrugged. "They die."

"It's a cinch they don't move." It had to be anyone's guess how many Detroiters continued to live in the city for the sole reason that they lacked the resources to get out. But the percentage had to be high. "And those buildings! Those huge, massive buildings! They've got to be maintained, heated, repaired. With what? St. Leo's hasn't got enough money to make the repairs that are crying to be made. God! I wish these buildings had been built on wheels: We could roll them out to the suburbs where the people are." The latter statement had been Cardinal Mooney's oft-quoted wish.

Jackson knew that the problem, far from being as simplistic as his boss was making it, was actually quite complex and many-layered. He also knew that they were talking about St. Leo's in particular only because Sister Joan lived there and was, as much as she was able, committed to the parish. And they were attending this wake service on her behalf. The two men could just as easily have been discussing any number of inner-city parishes.

There was a pause in their whispered dialogue while the two considered what had been said.

Finally, Jackson turned. "Larry, if this game were yours to call . . . if you didn't have to answer to anyone else, what would you do? Would you really close all these parishes?"

"In a minute."

They fell silent. But Jackson knew that this hypothetical question to his boss involved a condition contrary to fact.

Jackson—and almost everyone in the archdiocesan administration—knew that the ultimate leader, Cardinal Mark Boyle, was doing all in his power to keep these troubled parishes open. And that, in this stance, he was meeting determined opposition, not only from Larry Hoffer but from many Catholic movers and shakers in the Detroit metropolitan area.

In the end, Jackson was confident that the Cardinal Archbishop would prevail. If only because everything the Catholic archdiocese of Detroit owned—land, edifices, facilities—was held, by civil as well as ecclesiastical law, in the name and person of the archbishop. So these troubled parishes probably would remain open.

Unless the Cardinal changed his mind.

Koesler was unsure whether it was his imagination, but he thought that from time to time he could hear the loose change rattle inside Larry Hoffer's pocket.

A peculiar and somewhat annoying habit. Koesler wondered why no one ever seemed to bring it to Hoffer's consciousness—see if the habit could be terminated. On the other hand, Hoffer was so high on the administrative ladder in this archdiocese, who would have the standing to correct him?

The Cardinal, of course. But he was such a gentleman—a gentle man; it would be completely out of character for him to be so personal.

Koesler had never met Hoffer's wife. But surely, he thought, she must be aware of this peculiar habit—much imitated in jest by underlings. Why hadn't she corrected it? Subservient to her lord and master? Afraid of him? Deaf? Maybe *she* rattled coins in *her* pocket.

Koesler's attention was diverted by a person who had just entered the room, brushing by him as if he weren't there. The newcomer marched—yes, that was the word for it—marched up the narrow center aisle to the fourth row from the front, where he took a sharp right and marched past a series of hastily withdrawn knees. He lowered himself into a folding chair that had obviously been saved for him by an assistant.

Father Cletus Bash, director of the Office of Communications.

The Office of Communications dispensed information, provided one asked the right question. It produced ambitious television programming—although reception depended on one's TV set's ability to pick up a less than powerful signal.

More than anything, the communications office was a public relations operation, and Father Cletus Bash was the designated official spokesperson for the archdiocese.

No such office had existed in the local Church until the 1960s. At that time, having been newly established, it took neither itself nor its function very seriously. While other major organizations, such as the auto companies, financial institutions, and the like, were very concerned about their public image, the Catholic Church, by and large, was content that God knew all was well. In a system where the Pope gave the word to the bishops, who passed it on to their priests, who preached it to the laity, who did what they were told, whatever image was projected by this efficient procedure just didn't seem very important.

Then, once more due to the Second Vatican Council, things changed. Now, under regular siege not only by the ACLU but even by Catholics who could be and were critical, the Church began to get serious about its image problem. Accordingly, the Office of Communications steadily grew in importance. But the growth of the office was no match for the self-importance of its official spokesman, Father Cletus Bash.

He had two lay assistants who kept him informed and did menial tasks. They were made to understand that they were not to approach even the neighborhood of becoming spokespersons. In this department one alone talked to the media. One alone appeared in close-ups on TV newscasts. One alone spoke on the record for radio reporters.

It brought to mind one of Detroit's most famous priests, Father Charles Coughlin, whose name in afteryears was scarcely ever mentioned without the descriptive phrase, "Controversial radio priest of the thirties." Now it was, "Father Cletus Bash, official spokesman of the Archdiocese of Detroit."

If this distinction got to be a bit tiresome—and it did, for everyone but Bash—Father Koesler, a tolerant person, tended to understand and forgive. What he understood particularly were the difficult years Cletus Bash had spent as an army chaplain during the Korean War. And especially the injury he had suffered when, his group under fierce bombardment, a shell had exploded nearby. Of the men in that area, Bash alone had survived. In a series of operations, surgeons were able to form what, for that time, came close to being a bionic man. Still, he had little movement in his left arm. And he had lost the sight in his left eye.

But he came back. And if he was somewhat more macho than most of the other priests of his generation, he had, thought Koesler, some right to be.

Yet most of the other priests, as well as all who had to deal with Bash, would have agreed that Koesler understood and forgave a tad too much.

"Kind of warm in here, isn't it?" Bob Meyer commented.

Bash nodded curtly. He looked around the room. "Too small. Way too small. That's why it's so hot. Too many people crammed in here. This whole affair has been badly run. Shows what happens when you let amateurs run things."

"Amateurs?" Bob Meyer had been assistant director of communications for many years, through the terms of several directors. He had survived partly by keeping most negative opinions to himself.

"The nun," Bash elaborated, "Sister Joan. She's handled this thing badly from the beginning."

Amateur? thought Meyer. My God, she's the dead woman's sister, the only close relative! Who else would anyone expect to make final arrangements?

That's what Meyer thought. What he said was, "It is a small mortuary. Perhaps she should have picked one of the major parlors."

Bash shook his head. "No, not a larger home. A smaller crowd." Was he the only one who saw the big picture? Was there no one else who thought clearly?

He would have fired Meyer shortly after meeting him except for Meyer's extended tenure, which gave the assistant a unique background. He knew where all the bodies were buried and whose closets the skeletons were in. He knew every inch of the maze of bureaus and departments in the archdiocese. Besides, Meyer was good at nitty-gritty and detail work. And Bash, dealing with the big picture, had little time to go around crossing t's and dotting i's.

"I'm sorry, Father," Meyer said. "I thought you said the room—the funeral home—was too small."

"It is too small—for this crowd. The thing is, the crowd shouldn't be here. There shouldn't be this much of a crowd."

Not infrequently, Meyer found Bash confusing. This was such a time. "The crowd shouldn't be here?"

"This whole story should have been buried. It doesn't do the image any good to have a nun with a sister who's a prostitute. And not just any nun: a department head."

"Oh."

"No one—or practically no one—knew Sister Joan even had a sister, let alone one who was a whore. Then she gets herself murdered and everything hits the fan. If this story had been killed, no one would have been the wiser. This would have been the proper size mortuary for this funeral because almost no one would be here." There was exasperation in his tone. The tone of an irritated teacher dealing with a backward student.

Meyer's more practical judgment told him to let the

subject drop and to simply agree with his boss. His curiosity betrayed him. "But, Father, this was a homicide, with far-reaching complications. Helen Donovan wasn't a streetwalker or an ordinary lady of the evening. Some of her clients are among the most prominent men in southeast Michigan. The police haven't named any names, but the gossip columnists are having a field day with rumors and innuendo."

"I could have killed the story!" Bash spoke so forcefully that, for a moment, the low murmurs stopped, and there was complete silence in the room. Heads turned toward Bash and Meyer. But only momentarily. Then the whooshing sound began again.

Bash's statement startled Meyer. Partly because of its force, but more due to the presumptuousness and arrogance it revealed.

"The story should have been handled by us in the first place," Bash said, returning to a semi-whisper. "Why didn't we get the story?"

Meyer was tempted to just tell the truth: that this was not at any time an archdiocesan story. It was a homicide. It deserved to be where it had landed in the beginning—in the secular news media.

But the desire for longevity won out. "It just got away from us, I guess."

"The nun," Bash said. "She should have come to us at the outset. How in hell are we supposed to keep our fingers on everything newsworthy that happens in the diocese if we can't even trust our own department heads to channel everything through us? How many times at staff meetings have I warned the department heads of what can happen when we are not on top of all media events!? Well, this is what happens! You can well bet your bottom dollar they're going to hear about this incident as a prime example of how fouled up things can get."

Meyer breathed a prayer of thanksgiving that assistants were not invited to staff meetings. He wouldn't have to witness Cletus Bash browbeating some pretty nice people. The ironic thing was that due partly to Bash's pomposity and partly because the people he would be talking down to were some fundamentally decent human beings, they'd probably not challenge any of his ridiculous opinions.

Well, come to think of it, thought Meyer, I didn't challenge him either. Never mind that Meyer studiously avoided confrontation in order to maintain financial security and a considerable investment in a retirement fund. In the end there was no question about it: Bash got away with too much—far too much.

Koesler, like the others in the room, had no idea of what Bash and Meyer had been discussing.

Meyer it was who had saved a place for his boss. This came as no surprise to Koesler. He had met Meyer often enough to know it was almost impossible to get a firm opinion from the man. He was all questions and very few answers. That he would arrive at a place like this early enough to save a seat for his boss was to be expected. Meyer had made a science of kowtowing. Koesler found that sad.

But, Koesler wondered, what could Clete Bash mean by saying he could have killed a story? *What story?*

No one who read the local papers, watched local TV, or listened to local radio could be unaware that Father Cletus Bash was, for starters, the official spokesman for the archdiocese of Detroit. Indeed, faithful readers, viewers, and listeners could be forgiven for being fed up with Bash's intrusion when it came to news stories. It was as if there could be no Catholic news or Catholic reaction to news unless Cletus Bash did it or said it.

But what could he have meant by saying that he could have killed a story? Surely not this story. He must have had reference to some other story.

Koesler dismissed the whole business.

He would have been distracted in any case by a sudden stirring in this overly crowded and overly warm room. Archbishop Lawrence Foley was making an entrance. There was no possible doubt about that whatever.

Foley had a distinct—nay, unique—way of clearing his throat. He would half bury his chin in his clerical collar, cover his mouth with a closed fist, and clear his throat with a series of rumbling sounds.

The cough was the result of a combination of causes, including nearly fifty years of cigarette smoking, inveterate tea drinking, and, eventually, sheer habit. While he had quit smoking some ten years ago, his hack sounded as authentic as if he had just walked off a tobacco plantation.

Five years ago he had retired as archbishop of Cincinnati. The stated reason for his retirement was his age—seventy—and ill health. Both reasons were real enough, but the more pressing issue was that in some Curial circles he was considered "soft" on such issues as homosexuality and abortion. Foley wasn't really an advocate of either practice. He just loved everybody—including sinners and those considered by highly placed authorities to be sinners. The longer he lived, the more accepting and nonjudgmental he became—attributes not at all prized by the present administration in Rome. However, a few years before, Rome itself had been burned by the reaction of American bishops when a liberal West Coast bishop had his local authority shredded by some bureaucrats in Rome. Not wishing to be twice burned, yet not willing to endure any hint of doctrinal deviation, Rome had applied considerable pressure as Foley neared compulsory retirement age.

The archbishop, a loyal churchman despite his humanistic leanings, complied with Rome's wishes. He retired, but stayed on in a private Cincinnati home as bishop-emeritus. However, despite his striving to maintain a very low profile, his popularity remained strong. He was invited to meetings of such fringe groups as former priests, and women who demanded ordination. Often, he attended. The good man had great difficulty refusing invitations, particularly those from people who were hurting.

Pressure was applied again: this time, to leave Cincinnati and the people with whom he'd built a long-standing, mutual love affair.

Obediently, he packed. But where to go? He prayed. His prayers were answered almost ideally by an invitation to reside in Detroit.

Detroit had become known throughout the country and the entire Catholic world as an "open" diocese. The Second Vatican Council had hit Detroit harder than any other U.S. diocese and certainly no less forcefully than any other diocese in the world.

Rome was not enthused by the Detroit Syndrome. But there was some substantial if subtle differences between Detroit and Cincinnati. Detroit's archbishop, Mark Boyle, was a Cardinal, a "prince of the Church." That, plus Boyle's popularity among his confreres, had earned him the first elected presidency of the newly formed U.S. Bishops' Conference. Even Rome had to take these facts into consideration.

There were also differences between Boyle and Foley.

Larry Foley's conscience and conviction led him to more or less sympathize with the spirit of the fringe and outlawed groups with whom he dealt. Mark Boyle, on the other hand, seldom if ever swerved from the *vera doctrina*, the true doctrine as interpreted by Rome.

Boyle's great virtue—or flaw, depending on which side of the fence one sat—was his ability to co-exist with those whose opinions he did not share. Without shouting, "Off with their heads!"

Thus Boyle got along with Foley as well or better than with just about any other bishop in captivity. They had been friends for years; it was only natural that Foley had considered Boyle's invitation to reside in Detroit as heaven-sent.

With this background, Koesler understood why Archbishop Foley would receive mixed reviews from the people in this room. Many of them had the "bureaucratic mind" that disapproved of Foley as a maverick, while others appreciated him to the extent of loving him.

Among the latter was Sister Joan Donovan. While making no effort to conceal the details of her sister's life and death, she had, with anxiety, let her wish be known that her sister receive a Catholic burial.

Archbishop Foley had been the first—and, actually, the foremost—to respond to her appeal. He told Joan it would be an honor for him to preside over the Mass of Resurrection and burial. Thus Sister Joan joined the long line of those beholden to him.

Foley was here to lead the rosary. To that purpose he now made his way toward the front of the room where a kneeler had been placed before the bier.

The archbishop gave new meaning to fragility. Thin as a pipe cleaner, he was slightly stooped. Although he bore a generally dour face topped by wispy white hair, it was his eyes that distinguished him. They were blue and danced with merriment.

Even the soft whispering gradually ceased as Foley shuffled to the front of the room. As he reached the casket, Sister Joan stepped forward and joined him. For several moments they stood gazing at the remains of Helen Donovan. Foley had spoken words of consolation at the time he'd agreed to preside at the funeral, so there was no need to go into that again.

"She was very beautiful," Foley said finally. He had never met Helen Donovan in life.

Joan nodded. "She looks quite natural. I was told the bullet entered the rear of her head and didn't come out. So I guess there was no extensive damage in the front to . . ." She choked back a heavy pressure in her throat.

". . . repair?" Foley supplied.

"Yes, that's right."

Foley joined his hands as if in prayer. "Now that I've finally seen her, I am amazed how much she resembles you."

"Oh, she was much prettier."

"No, not really. She's lovely, of course. But then, so are you."

"Oh, come now!" Joan touched the bishop's arm. It was as if she were holding naked bone.

"No, no. You are both lovely ladies. Now, if an old coot like me can't get away with passing a compliment with no strings attached, who in God's green world can?"

Joan smiled briefly. "You know, Bishop, she and I were never close. That surprises me now that I look back on it. We were the only children in our family, both girls. You'd think we would have appreciated each other, shared things. But aside of my hand-me-downs we shared almost nothing. I got excellent marks in school—that sort of challenged her. I did well in academics; she did not. But she did better in almost everything else."

They fell silent for a few moments.

"Your sister is grateful to you now," Foley said. "Grateful that you've gone to all this trouble to have her buried properly."

"Oh, do you really think so? I've been wondering whether I'm doing all this for her or for myself. For a long, long time she couldn't have cared less about the church or religion. What difference would this ceremony make to her now?"

"Well, m'dear, I've always thought that when we die, we will be judged by love. I am so very, desperately grateful that when I go, I will not be judged by any fellow human—no matter how understanding and forgiving that person may be. No, your sister's been judged by the only one who goes on loving us no matter what we do. Keep in mind the words of St. John, 'God is love and he who abides in love abides in God, and God in him.' Forgive the sexist pronouns, m'dear.''

Strange, thought Joan, *he hasn't said anything I didn't know. And yet I feel so much better, so very much better.*

''And while we're at it,'' Foley added, ''we might remember some other words from Scripture: 'It is a holy and wholesome thought to pray for the dead.' Will you join me on the kneeler? I promise I won't get fresh.''

Joan almost laughed out loud.

As they knelt, most of those in the room followed suit. Archbishop Foley led the group in the glorious mysteries. To even slightly old-fashioned Catholics, the rosary, particularly in this setting, was a consolation. To others, the whole thing was a mystery—not joyful, not sorrowful, not glorious. Just a mystery.

The rosary completed, Foley creaked to his feet, said a few more words to Joan, patted her hand, and shuffled toward the exit.

The others waited, either out of genuine respect or in deference to his rank. Then nearly everyone participated in a mass exit. Koesler, intent on speaking to Joan, felt like a salmon swimming upstream.

By the time he reached the front of the room only a few people remained. They were clustered around Sister Joan. As he knelt briefly before the casket, he was struck by Helen's resemblance to Joan. They were not twins, but they very definitely were look-alike sisters.

As he prayed that Helen be at peace with God, he wondered how two lives so joined in consanguinity could have developed so differently, as Helen and Joan had drifted apart in every conceivable way.

When he finished his prayer, he stood at the rear of the small group offering condolences to Joan. She noticed him standing there awkwardly and broke away long enough to thank him for attending. It was a perfunctory greeting. Koesler was certain that later Joan would not even remember his presence. But that was understandable. It was not at all uncommon for the bereaved to be distracted, even unaware of what was taking place. The death of a loved one may be the ultimate shock.

As Koesler turned to leave, none of the original crowd, outside of the few with Joan, remained—except the ladies who did not represent the Rosary Altar Society. They were in the doorway talking to a black man with an engaging smile.

Koesler knew the man from somewhere. As usual in such situations, he began reflecting on parishes he had served. Frequently, priests' contacts with laity took place on the parochial level. This was an easy case to check; he had had relatively few black parishioners during his priestly ministry to date. He hoped to correct that imbalance through old St. Joseph's parish.

But, if not a parish, then where? Of course: Lieutenant Tully. What was that nickname some used? Oh, yes: Zoo.

Koesler was tempted to classify their association as having "worked together" on a couple of cases. But that would be a somewhat grandiose description. Let's keep things in perspective, he thought: Tully was the cop. And from what Koesler's close friend Inspector Walter Koznicki had said, Tully was the inspector's most valued officer in the Homicide Division. From the amateur's point of view, Koesler would agree at least with the fact that Tully was totally dedicated to his work.

And Koesler? Over the past decade, Homicide had investigated some cases with decidedly Catholic angles. He had merely clarified some facets of Catholicism that had cleared the way for the police to do their job.

In the periphery of his vision, Tully caught Koesler looking in his direction. He had been waiting for that. Graciously he terminated his conversation with the women and stepped forward into the nearly empty room toward Koesler. For Tully, Koesler represented an oasis of familiarity in a desert of foreign identities.

They greeted each other cordially but their mutual greeting was more pro forma than personal.

"For just a second there, Lieutenant"—Koesler's sole use of nicknames was confined to colleagues who were friends from childhood—"I was surprised to see you here. Then I recalled that this is, after all, a murder investigation. So why wouldn't you be here?"

"Uh-huh. Good to see you again. And you? Did you know the deceased?"

For just an instant, Koesler reacted as if he were being interrogated. "No, not at all." Then he relaxed. "I do know her sister, Sister Joan. I was afraid there wouldn't be many showing up for this wake so I was going to add my body to the few. Obviously"—Koesler's gesture encompassed what had been a packed room—"I was mistaken."

"You weren't the only one surprised. What attracted this crowd?"

"Oh, I think certainly the fact that Sister Joan is the head of a department in the archdiocese. A few of the people here tonight are also department heads, and a lot of the others work in the various departments."

That makes sense, thought Tully. "And you know all these people?"

Koesler nodded. "Most of them. Certainly all the department heads. Not everyone who works under them."

"Interesting. The elderly gentleman, the one who led the prayers, he a department head?"

"No, he's a bishop. An archbishop." Koesler had had this perception many times before. There was no shorthand to explain the trappings of Catholicism—its law, doctrine, morality, liturgy, etc.—easily and simply. "He's retired."

"Retired? Then why's he leading the prayers?"

Koesler didn't immediately grasp the thrust of Tully's question. "Leading prayers?" Then, "Oh, I see. Well, priests, bishops, even if they're retired, don't stop praying or even leading prayers. They can continue doing as much or as little as they wish and as the Church law allows, liturgically if not parochially. Most of them want to be rid of administrative work. But most of them still want to be with people—want to be of some service to people."

"Makes sense, I guess." Once again Tully felt overwhelmed with the amount of detail in Catholicism—in all of organized religion, for all he knew—and how little of it he understood or was aware of. At this point Koesler was his only guide to a vast unknown area that might be important to this case. He fervently hoped there was no connection. Mostly, he hoped this homicide was not a case of mistaken identity. For if the real intended victim was the nun, Tully could be drawn into this maze of Catholicism he so little understood. "You're not goin' on vacation anytime soon, are you?"

Koesler chuckled. "It seems as if I just got to my new parish," he said. "No, I don't think I'll be going anywhere soon."

"New parish?"

"St. Joseph's—old St. Joseph's downtown."

"Near police headquarters?"

"Uh-huh."

"Nice."

5

"THE CUT ON your lip looks okay now, but I don't know about that bruise on your cheek. You could end up with a mean shiner."

"How many stitches, you figure?" Arnold Carson asked.

Dwight Morgan, right index finger about an inch from Carson's face, began counting. "Three . . . four . . . five. I figure five or six. Hard to tell, Arnie. There might be some more inside your lip."

Carson tenderly touched his lower lip. "It hurts." He ran his finger inside the lip. "At least all the teeth are still there."

"You gonna sue?" Angelo Luca wanted to know.

"The cops?" Carson said. "I been down that road. No future in it."

"Geez, I feel like it's my fault," Luca said.

"Forget it," Carson replied. "It ain't your fault. You just saw the write-up in the paper. I'm glad you told us about it."

"But, geez," Luca insisted, "if I'd just kept my mouth shut, you wouldna got roughed up."

"Forget it," Carson insisted. "It's just the price we have to pay every once in a while." He spoke with all the pride a martyr might express.

In this instance, as in so many others, he did consider himself a martyr—a martyr for the good cause of truth, justice, right, and the One, Holy, Catholic and Apostolic Church.

51

Arnold Carson, a U.S. mail clerk in his early fifties, was, much of the time, an angry man. It had been Carson's good or bad fate to convert to Catholicism just before the time when, in his opinion, Catholicism was converting to Protestantism.

Carson had been born into a committed Episcopal family. In his youth, he had been an eager participant in all manner of church functions, youth programs, etc. He had even considered the priesthood. But he was not an achieving student. He received and accepted excellent advice from teachers and counselors to lower his academic sights.

When he graduated from high school, Carson became a member of the postal service, first as a part-time flexible employee (PTF), then as a regular employee. Almost by accident he had found his niche in life.

He felt at home, compatible, with things that had specific answers, bottom lines, absolutes. He didn't admit it to anyone, but he liked addresses. When he worked as a carrier, all he had to do was line up envelopes in numerical order, find the house with the matching number, and the job was done. Stamps were comforting too. One had either sufficient or insufficient postage. And the good old scale would provide that answer. Sufficient and one put it on its way to delivery; insufficient and one returned it.

It was that philosophical attitude which disenchanted Carson with regard to the Episcopal Church—all of Protestantism, for that matter, revealed by his investigation: Too many questions did not have absolute answers.

For instance: Could one be married more than once, more than twice, in the Episcopal Church? It depended.

Then, in 1960, at age twenty, he had stumbled onto Catholicism. Catholicism was crammed with absolutes and comfortable numbers. One God, two natures, three persons, four purposes of prayer, five processions in the

Trinity, seven sacraments, nine first Fridays, ten Commandments, twelve promises, fourteen Stations of the Cross, and so forth.

Could one marry more than once in the Catholic Church? Of course not. Not unless the petitioner could prove to scrupulous curiosity that a previous marriage was so null and void that it had never happened—or unless one's spouse died.

Carson searched and studied and investigated and questioned until he thought he had found heaven without benefit of death.

Home! Home was the compulsive, home from insecurity.

Then what to his wondering soul should occur but Vatican II. He couldn't believe it: They had a perfect system and they fixed it.

Carson didn't take it lying down. He studied the new monster to the best of his limited ability.

Maybe Martin Luther was right! Maybe "Father Martin," as he was respectfully treated by the hated new breed, was a saint! What happened to the ordinary magisterium? What happened to actions and thoughts that were evil to their very core? What the hell was situation ethics? What in hell was liberation theology? What happened to the enveloping, mesmerizing Latin? When did nuns start wearing miniskirts? Where did the priest's lifetime commitment go? What happened to all the goddam absolutes?

Carson had found heaven on earth, and as a result of a four- or five-year meeting in Rome it had been demolished.

Arnold Carson was not amused.

Indeed, he was fighting angry.

He could have taken several tacks. He could quit Catholicism by a simple act of will. Or he could join one of the organizations spawned by and because of Vatican II, organizations for conservatives upset by the council and determined to, in effect, save the Church from itself.

There was Catholics United for the Faith (CUF). Most of the members of this organization were reasonable people, though vigilant and active. They actually pretty much played by the rules set up by the hierarchy.

One program the Catholic Church has wrestled with for the past slightly more than one hundred years is what to do with an infallible Pope when he's not being infallible. Which is most of the time. Infallibility was defined and adopted (some would say rigged) by the First Vatican Council in 1870. Since then, arguably, there has been only one infallible pronouncement, and that was Pius XII's regarding Mary's Assumption into heaven.

All the other thousands of pronouncements by Popes and Popes-with-bishops fall into the category of the ordinary magisterium, or ordinary teaching office of the Church. What to do with that?

Liberal Catholics tend to regard papal pronouncements as being extremely important messages from a unique and well-informed source. Only for a most serious reason would such a Catholic eventually disagree with the Pope. But such disagreement is possible.

Not so in the eyes of CUF, or, for that matter, Church law. In effect, if a Catholic disagrees with the ordinary magisterium, he's not excommunicated; he's just wrong. And he is advised to go away and pray a while until he sees the light.

Arnold Carson gave CUF a shot and found it inadequate. All very well to write letters to newspapers, call radio talk shows, and argue at meetings. But Carson found such comparative inaction frustrating. He had always believed one had to hit something to get its attention.

So Carson joined the Tridentine Society, so-named for the Latin word for Trent, as in the Council of Trent,

Catholicism's legislative response to the Reformation. Trent (A.D. 1545-1563) was the precursor to Vatican I.

The Tridentines were so much in sync with Carson's makeup that in no time he became their leader. Under him they became, though small, yet, as they say in sports parlance, a force to be reckoned with.

Arnie Carson was not the type of general to position himself at the rear of the troops and send orders to the front. He was always in the vanguard—as he had been this evening at the funeral home.

On short notice, only Carson and his two most faithful lieutenants, Dwight Morgan and Angelo Luca, were able to assemble less than peaceably outside the Ubly Funeral Home, wherein Helen Donovan's wake was to be held.

The Tridentines had carried hastily and crudely made signs communicating the general theme that the archdiocese of Detroit equated whores and nuns. And that Cardinal Boyle's message to his flock was to "Live it up and whore."

They had done their very best to be obnoxious to the clergy and religious, who tried without much success to ignore them. Father Cletus Bash had phoned his civic counterpart, the spokesman for Maynard Cobb, mayor of Detroit. That intercession had attracted several blue-and-white police cars whose officers had orders to find some lawful way of moving the troublemakers out.

Thus when the small contingent of hookers arrived and gave as good as they got, the Tridentines—mainly Carson—transformed picketing to a contact sport, in which the police joined. The result: Morgan and Luca heeded the police invitation to "Drag ass outta here!" Carson chose to challenge the order and thus capped the evening in Detroit Memorial Hospital with a banged-up cheek and a cut lip.

Carson had been stitched up and left in the cubicle for a while to make certain there were no unforeseen complications. He now sat on the gurney, feet dangling over the side, as his companions offered moral support.

Carson moved gingerly, stretching his legs to touch the floor.

"Maybe you shouldn't be getting off the bed so soon, Arnie," Morgan said.

"Yeah, there's no hurry; why don't you wait a while?" Luca agreed.

Carson slid back onto the gurney. "Maybe I will wait just a couple more minutes or so. You know, if I get a concussion or something like that, I will sue. Did you get the badge number of that cop that hit me with his nightstick?"

"Geez, no, Arnie," Morgan said. "I couldn't get close to him. The other cops were holding me down."

Actually, Morgan and Luca had obeyed promptly each and every police order and thus had been nowhere near Carson, who had conducted a doomed offensive against a superior force.

"It's okay," Carson said. "I remember the creep. I could identify him if I have to. And if I end up with any kind of serious injury, you can bet I will."

"You were great, Arnie," Luca said.

"We did okay. The big thing is you can't let these people get away with stuff like this."

"Yeah," Luca agreed. "They say—and of course it wasn't in the obituary—that this hooker hadn't been to church in ages. No way she should get a Church burial. She's just an unrepentant whore who is roasting in hell now. But her sister's a nun. And a big shot in the diocese. So all the rules be damned; the whore gets a Church burial."

"By a bishop, on top of everything else," Morgan added.

Carson started to shake his head. Then he thought better of further scrambling his facial wounds, and gently massaged his temples instead. "Yeah, a bishop!" He almost spat the word. "A retired old geezer who should be dead already. Instead, he finds a comfortable home in Detroit.''

"It's Cardinal Boyle's fault," Morgan said.

"Uh-huh. The Red Cardinal," Carson said. It was a pun popular with Detroit conservatives, particularly the Tridentines. The color peculiar to a Cardinal is the most brilliant red imaginable. But when traditionalists called Boyle, "the Red Cardinal," they meant "red" as a synonym for Communist. That Boyle was nowhere near in the neighborhood of being a Communist would not deter Carson, who could think of no more entrenched enemy than the godless Communist.

"He should go back to Russia," Luca said.

"Do you think it was Boyle who gave permission for the whore's funeral?" Morgan asked.

"Good question," Carson observed. "I wouldn't be surprised if it went right to the top with all that publicity. That's a very good question. Dwight," he turned to Morgan, "why don't you draft a letter to the Holy Father and tell him that a known prostitute who hasn't seen the inside of a church since she was a kid gets a Christian burial in Detroit with a bishop presiding."

"Oh, boy!" Morgan brightened. "That's a great idea."

"We've done it before and nothing happened," Luca groused. "I don't think even the Holy Father is gonna get tough with a Cardinal."

"Don't sell the Holy Father short—not this Holy Father," Carson said. "If we keep him advised about what's going on in Detroit, eventually he'll act. I'm positive he will."

"What's he gonna do," Luca asked, "excommunicate a Cardinal?"

"Maybe not," Carson admitted, "but how about if he kicks him upstairs?"

"Huh?"

"Calls him to Rome," Carson explained. "Puts him in charge of something not so important—ceremonies or something. Especially after that goddam council, there's gotta be a lot of Curia offices that don't do much anymore. It would serve Boyle right. After all, he had a lot to do with the council. Let him stew in his own juice."

"I still don't think it'll work," Luca repeated.

Carson stretched out a hand and let it drop on Luca's shoulder. "Don't worry, Angelo, something is going to happen very soon that will make you very happy. In fact, it's already in the works. And we won't have to wait for Rome to act."

Luca looked into Carson's eyes hopefully. "What? What, Arnie?"

"I can't tell you, Angelo. I can't tell anybody. But when it happens—or when it keeps on happening—remember, you heard it here first."

Morgan's curiosity also was piqued. "What are you talking about, Arnie?"

"Yeah," Luca said, "for God's sake, if you can't tell *us* who can you tell?"

"We're with you, Arnie," Morgan said. "You know that. Is it you who's doing whatever it is you're talking about? You need help. Who else could help you like we could? We want to help!"

Carson smiled smugly. "All in good time. As far as you guys are concerned, pretend I didn't say anything at all. And you keep what I said to yourselves . . . got it?"

"Got it," Morgan said. "But . . ." His brow furrowed. ". . . we don't know what you said."

"Keep it that way! Swear?"

"Yeah."

"Yeah."

An attendant leaned into the cubicle. "You okay now?"

"I think so," Carson said.

"Then you better go on home. We need the space."

They left, Carson wondering if he had said too much.

⑥ SISTER JOAN WAS the last to leave the funeral home. She had waited until all who lingered after the rosary had offered condolences. The funeral director had assured her that all would be ready for the 9:30 prayer service tomorrow morning at the funeral home followed by the fifteen-minute drive to St. Leo's for the 10:00 A.M. Mass. She donned her coat and boots and started the drive home. The drive that would be repeated tomorrow morning with her sister as the main attraction, the star of the show.

Helen would like that. She had always conducted herself as the star performer in whatever was going on. It could be sports or amateur theater or dating, whatever: Unbashful Helen was the whole show. And so it would be tomorrow. *For the last time*, thought Joan, and choked on the unspoken word *last*.

She must get her mind off Helen and her horrible sudden death. She tried to pay attention to the neighborhood through which she was now driving.

This was easy. She was traveling up Trumbull past Tiger Stadium, whose one and only remaining attraction was the Detroit Tigers baseball team. Once upon a time, the Detroit Lions football team had played here also. The footballers had moved out to Pontiac.

This spot marked the site of professional baseball from shortly after its inception in Detroit before the turn of the century. It was almost hallowed ground. To the baseball purist it *was* holy ground. Here Babe Ruth and

Ty Cobb and Ted Williams and Al Kaline had all excelled in this game that they loved so well.

Sister Joan was not a baseball aficionado, nor was she particularly drawn to sports, but she could appreciate the historical distinction of this stadium.

It was eerie to drive these brightly lit streets, now so barren and deserted. The snow, while it still covered the sidewalks, had been mashed into slush in the streets. In another four months these streets would be alive with people participating in the national pastime in Detroit. Trumbull Avenue and Michigan Avenue and Kaline Drive and Cochrane Street would be teeming with happy folks doing a happy thing.

But that would be later. Right now it was difficult to focus on a happy thought. Her mind was filled with the image of her only sister in a casket. And Helen's soul . . . ? Joan tried to focus on the words Archbishop Foley had spoken. Words of hope and promise and understanding and forgiveness in a judgment of love.

As she thought back on the events of this evening at the funeral home, she recalled the voice that had spoken so loudly, jarringly. What was it he had said—something to the effect that he could have killed the story?

She hadn't had to turn around to know whose voice it was. Cletus Bash. She'd heard Father Bash often enough at meetings to recognize the voice and the arrogance it contained. She assumed Bash did not approve of the publicity resulting from her sister's murder. She was at a loss to know how it possibly could have been handled any differently. Regardless, she was convinced that the primary cause of Bash's irritation was that he'd been denied yet another opportunity to be featured on camera for the evening news. She was sure she and the others would hear about this again and again in memos and at staff meetings. She could barely wait.

The thought of Bash brought up another memory of this evening—at the very end of the wake service. She could visualize the scene as if she were a third party looking on at the event.

She had been standing with a small group of her nun friends when someone approached to talk to her. It was hard now to place who this person was. But something told her she should remember.

Of course: It was Father Koesler. And she had greeted him almost as if he were a stranger. She winced. How could she have been so thoughtless! She had to blame it on exhaustion, distraction, preoccupation—the whole darn thing.

She would make it a point the next time their paths crossed to apologize and explain why she had been so distant. She was sure he would understand.

She was home, or very nearly there. Fortunately, she didn't have to get out of the car to open the garage door. One of the very few luxuries of St. Leo's was an automatic garage door opener. She pulled in through the open door, parked the car, got out, and exited the garage, starting the door on its downward path as she did so. Pulling her coat collar up tight, she started on the short walk around the corner to the front door.

As she reached the center of the metal fence and angled to take the next few steps to the front door, she recalled that this was exactly what her sister had done just a couple of nights ago. Helen had gotten out of the taxi at this very spot and taken these same steps. The last short walk of her life.

Joan shivered. It was only partly due to the cold.

The streetlights cast shadows everywhere. She tried to quiet her imagination. It was playing tricks. She thought she saw shapes that, as she approached them, dissolved. Her pace quickened.

She was halfway up the steps when it happened. She knew: This was not a phantom of her mind.

Someone was in the bushes behind her. She distinctly heard the snapping branch. She caught the movement out of the corner of her eye.

She froze, not knowing what to do. Hurry toward the door? She'd never make it before he did whatever he wanted. Turn and confront him? Beg? Plead? What good would any of that do? All this took only a fraction of time to pass through her mind.

Next it was a voice. A voice shouting.

Later, asked what the voice had said, she could remember, but was embarrassed to repeat it. Suffice that it got the job done.

No sooner had the young man stepped from the bushes than, from behind one of the statues of the shrine, Sergeant Phil Mangiapane shouted a warning in the universal language of the street.

As he explained later, had the youth not at least lowered the gun immediately, Mangiapane would have fired. But the young man was so startled that instead of his lowering or dropping the gun, it flew out of his hand as if it had wings and a mind of its own.

In seconds, the sergeant had the man cuffed.

After trying to calm the nun, Mangiapane removed the keys from her trembling hand, opened the door, shoved his prisoner into the convent, and phoned for assistance.

It was hours before Sister Joan was able to bring her shuddering and shaking under some sort of control. Sleep was not even a remote possibility.

But it was less than half an hour before Mangiapane had the man at headquarters, with his rights read, and in the process of being booked on charges of assault with intent to commit murder and suspicion of murder in the first degree.

7

THIS WAS DIFFERENT and Sergeant Phil Mangiapane decided he liked it. Frequently he was the
butt of many of the jokes cracked by members of his
squad if not of others in the Homicide Division. The
jokesters were lucky Mangiapane had an active sense
of humor and was able, to some degree, to take a joke.
For the sergeant was a big man who worked out with
weights as part of a general fitness regimen.

Now, the morning after his dramatic arrest of the
man who almost shot Sister Joan Donovan, Mangiapane
was the toast of the division. By actual count—the sergeant was keeping track—at least one officer from each
of the other six Homicide squads had dropped by to
congratulate him. Heady stuff.

But something was wrong. Something was missing.
Mangiapane hadn't pinpointed it but Sergeant Angie
Moore had. She noted that Zoo Tully hadn't been in
yet. She knew he was in the building. At least he had
been when she got in this morning, just before she'd
learned that it was Mangiapane who'd become a hero.
On her way to work she'd heard the news on her radio
that the nun had been saved by "courageous and daring" police work. Somehow she had never connected
those adjectives to the big Italian with whom she
worked.

As far as the media were concerned, the apprehension of the man who tried to kill Sister Joan had effec-
tively solved the mystery of who had killed her sister

Helen. Clearly it had been a case of mistaken identity. He had meant to kill the nun but got her sister instead. The killer had returned to the scene last night, tried to correct his mistake, and was foiled by "courageous and daring" police work. To cap the climax, the police said the perpetrator had confessed to both crimes.

When she entered headquarters, she passed Tully in the corridor. They exchanged greetings, as they normally did. Then when she reached the squadroom she found that she was sharing space with a celebrity.

She was genuinely happy for Mangiapane as his fellow officers congratulated him. She too had been quietly tabulating the visitors. Her mental toteboard tallied with Phil's: at least one from every squad in Homicide.

Indeed, it was as a result of her keeping tabs that she became aware of a significant absence: Tully.

That was strange. Zoo always took proprietary interest in his squad. Whenever there was merit to be recognized, usually Zoo Tully was the first to offer praise. But so far he was a no-show.

Evidently, it had not yet registered with Mangiapane that his boss had not joined the happy group. Moore was not going to bring it up. If the absence augured something negative, there was no point in prematurely raining on Phil's parade.

Not long after Moore concluded that there was something ominous in Tully's nonappearance, in he came.

He deposited some files on his desk, looked around the room, smiled, and said, "Congratulations, Phil. Can I see you a minute?" With that, he walked out of the room.

Mangiapane's elated demeanor was tempered by doubt as he followed Tully into one of the interrogation rooms. Moore's suspicion of she-knew-not-what deepened.

"Sit down, Manj," Tully said.

Mangiapane sat. Tully remained standing. "Tell me about it."

"What, Zoo?"

"When did you decide on the surveillance?"

"Hard to say, Zoo. It sort of bothered me from the start. The more we questioned the johns, and getting nothing on anybody, the more I was convinced that whoever killed Helen wasn't trying to kill Helen: He was trying to kill Joan. It just made sense. Helen was wearing a nun's habit. You couldn't see it under the coat but you could see the nun's veil on her head. Helen was entering Joan's residence. It was dark, lots of shadows there. Plus the two women look a lot alike. I thought, what would I lose?" Mangiapane broke into a large grin. "I just froze my ass off, is all."

"You didn't have authorization."

Mangiapane's smile dissolved. "I know, Zoo. Actually, it came to me when I was driving home after work last night. It was just a hunch. And I played it." Mangiapane's voice took on a feisty tone. "And it worked, Zoo. It worked."

"You didn't get authorization."

"You weren't handy when I got the idea."

"What if something had gone wrong? What if that kid had turned on you and fired? You were performing surveillance with no order. The department couldn't have backed you. The insurance wouldn't have covered you."

"I know that, Zoo. There wasn't any way anybody was going to get the drop on me."

"It could have happened. And there's another thing: When Inspector Koznicki hears about something like this, he doesn't want to talk to *you* about it. He wants *me* to fill him in. And how in hell am I gonna do that when I don't know what the hell is going on because you didn't keep me informed—because you played your hunch!"

In a less assured voice, Mangiapane said, "It worked."

"That's another thing, Manj: Did it?"

"Huh?"

"I just checked with ballistics. It's not the same gun. The lab guys said they had to get the slug from the medical examiner. That's why it took so long this morning. Helen Donovan was shot with a .38. The kid last night had a nine millimeter."

Some color left the sergeant's face. He hesitated, then said, "Zoo, there's guns everywhere out there. The guy probably ditched the gun he used on Helen 'cause he thought he got the job done. It happens all the time, Zoo." Mangiapane's tone became almost pleading. But it wasn't Tully he was entreating. Fate? "Guys use a gun and then throw it. Somebody else uses it and throws it. It happens all the time, Zoo."

"I know. I know."

"Besides, Zoo, the guy confessed. All by the book. I read him his rights and no sooner do I get done than he spills it about Helen. I mean, what do you want, Zoo? *The guy confessed.*"

Tully was meditative. "Yeah, that kind of bothers me too."

"Huh?"

"I talked to the kid a while ago." Tully consulted notes he'd made earlier in the morning. "David Reading, white, male, five-feet-seven, 168 pounds, high school dropout, no previous record." He looked at Mangiapane. "Not a very intelligent young man, but able to read a newspaper. That's one way he could have known about Helen's murder: He read about it."

"Zoo, he confessed!"

"Uh-uh. He didn't know what kind of gun was used in the killing."

"That's not all that unusual, Zoo. Like you said, the kid's not sharp. Just because he found a gun or bought it or however he got it, doesn't mean he's a ballistics whiz. He knows if you load it, point it, and pull the trigger, you can kill somebody. All he needs to know."

"Uh-huh."

"And, Zoo, he confessed."

"He's also kind of happy."

"Huh?"

"You didn't notice that? How would you feel if you were spending your first day in jail accused of assault with intent, and murder one?" Considering the question rhetorical, Tully continued. "Little David Reading, on the contrary, is a pretty happy fella. For the first time in his life, he's important. People want to talk to him. They're interested in what he has to say. And we haven't even released his name to the media. And we won't till he's arraigned. But, like I said, he does read the papers. At least some of them sometimes. He knows he's gonna be the main attraction. He's happy about it all, Manj. Does all this cast any doubt on the matter?"

"Wait a minute, Zoo!"

He didn't wait. "This wouldn't be the first time, Manj. We've had lots of nuts who confess to crimes as a matter of course for lots of different, sick reasons. And frankly, this guy strikes me as one of them."

"Wait a minute, Zoo! I feel like you're putting a full-court press on me. I admit it's possible for it to be the way you tell it. The kid reads about the murder, or he sees the report on TV. He sees the amount of press the killing gets. He knows the nun still lives in the same convent. He decides to pull a copycat killing. So he sneaks around the corner of the convent. He knows she's usually out late. In any case she would have been out late last night at the wake service for her sister. She comes home, he pops out of the bushes, and I pop out from behind my cover and the thing is over.

"But here's where your case breaks down, Zoo. According to your scenario, he wants publicity. He wants to be star of the show. The only way he can get that is to get caught. And he didn't know I was there. He didn't know he was gonna get caught. And if all he wanted to do was confess, he could've confessed the earlier killing without the second one." Mangiapane leaned back, more content now.

"We're dealing with hypothesis, Manj. He didn't know he was gonna get caught, I'll give you. Maybe he would have turned himself in if you hadn't been there. Maybe he would have killed the nun and then come in to confess it this morning.

"All that we're gonna have to figure out.

"This much is for certain: The next time you go off on your own without consulting with me, I'm gonna have your ass before Walt Koznicki has mine. Is that clear? I mean is that *crystal* clear?"

"Yeah." Mangiapane stood and, face impassive, was about to head for the door.

"One more thing, Manj."

"Yeah?"

"You did a good piece of work."

Mangiapane left smiling.

Tully began pacing in the small room. It was completely possible that this case had played out just the way Mangiapane figured it. Just the way Mangiapane *wanted* it to be. Guns could be found just about anywhere in this city. Adults had them for protection. Crooks had them for crime. Kids had them for toys.

David Reading could have found or bought a gun and used it to kill Helen Donovan. Having shot her, for a reason yet to be satisfactorily explained, he could have disposed of it. If one killing was all he intended, he more than likely would have gotten rid of it.

Then he finds out he's killed the wrong person. Maybe goes back to where he ditched the gun, but it's gone. Someone else has it now. Again, it's not that hard to find or come by another one. He goes back to finish it off the way he'd originally planned it.

He wouldn't expect Joan Donovan to have police protection. And in that assumption he was correct. Unless a targeted person agrees voluntarily to stay in an inaccessible and remote place, no police force could come close to guaranteeing safety. An enclosed, controllable space may be protected. A person out in the open is beyond protection.

It was very bad luck for David Reading and a stroke of extraordinarily good luck for Mangiapane—and for Sister Joan—that he happened to be on the scene to foil and apprehend the would-be killer.

As far as Tully was concerned, it was bad news and good news all in one lump.

At the outset, Tully had hoped that Helen's killer was one of her clients and that the john could be identified. The matter, then, would be a platter case.

As it happened, the initial investigation did not turn up any really good leads. But it was still better than the worst case scenario: mistaken identity. That would have thrown the investigation into a completely new and much broader plane. In which case the police would not be looking for someone who had it in for a hooker. Lots of people fit that category.

No, if it were mistaken identity, they'd have to find someone who was after a nun. Another kettle of fish.

The bad news was that the way it was now working out, it apparently was a case of mistaken identity. The good news—so good Tully could scarcely trust his luck—was that Mangiapane had caught the guy responsible for the attacks on Helen and Joan.

So why was he so reluctant to look on the good side? Why was he looking a gift horse in the mouth? Why couldn't he shut the file on this one?

It wasn't the different guns used. It wasn't the readiness of David Reading to confess to everything. It wasn't the unlikely luck of having Mangiapane on the scene at the moment Reading is about to repair his mistake. All those disparities could be explained. Indeed, Mangiapane had just gone through a sometimes tortured logic to explain them away.

It was something else. A hunch. Intuition.

Tully shrugged and quietly snorted. Police work was

not based substantially on hunches and intuition, but on cold, hard facts, reality that could be argued in a court of law. And the coldest, hardest fact they had presently was one warm body caught in the act of attempted murder and freely confessing to murder in the first degree.

So what if it didn't feel right? Time to process David Reading and get on to the next homicide. He knew that in Detroit he wouldn't have long to wait for the next one.

8

"MAY I GET you something to drink?" the waitress asked.

"Yes," the Reverend Mr. Quentin Jeffrey answered, "I'll have a Beefeater martini, extra dry with a twist."

"Very good. And . . . miss?"

"Just some coffee—decaffeinated," Grace Mars, Jeffrey's companion, said.

The waitress left to fill their orders.

Eyes accommodating to the dim interior lighting of Clamdiggers Restaurant, Jeffrey looked about the room.

Quentin Jeffrey, now in his late fifties, was a permanent deacon of the Roman Catholic Church. Indeed, he was head of the archdiocese's permanent deacon program. Years previously, he had founded, established, and headed his own public relations firm. In his early fifties he'd sold the firm, becoming enormously wealthy in the process.

He and his wife traveled and, in every way possible, relaxed after the hectic life they had hitherto led. Then, long a faithful Catholic, Jeffrey became interested in becoming a permanent deacon.

The permanent deacon belonged to a diocese or religious order just as did priests. The deacon was ordained to do everything the priest does sacramentally except absolve from sins and offer Mass.

It was no exaggeration to say that Quentin Jeffrey was an invaluable catch for the Church. He had been eminently successful in the secular world. Indeed, on the

71

local scene, as well as in circles beyond, Jeffrey was prominent, a celebrity. That he had chosen the diaconate for his later years added a healthy measure of cachet to a program that had not been widely used in recent centuries.

He had become a deacon in order to work with people on a spiritual level in a parochial setting. He had neither sought nor wanted to head the entire program. But when Cardinal Boyle asked him to take charge of it, he had accepted the responsibility. He considered his commitment to serve in the archdiocese of Detroit to be open-ended. Whatever the archbishop wanted of him, as long as he felt himself competent, he would do.

Then, tragically, his wife contracted pancreatic cancer. Jeffrey took a leave of absence to care for her around the clock. The leave was not of long duration. The cancer advanced quickly and decisively. In a few months, it was over. He returned to his duties in the archdiocese a changed man.

Before he lost her, he'd never quite gauged how much of his life he had shared with her, how much he had depended on her. The loneliness was more profound because where he'd been whole, now he was half.

But life went on. And one of life's small pleasures was taking his secretary out for a pleasant dinner. It was a reward he gave himself with some regularity. He had no idea how much Grace Mars looked forward to these evenings. He only knew that she was darkly beautiful, an efficient worker, a reliable confidante, and an agreeable companion.

They made an eye-catching couple. He, well-dressed, well-groomed, with leading-man features and sculpted salt-and-pepper hair. She, with dark hair and dark eyes, deep dimples, even teeth, and tight skin. The fact that they obviously enjoyed each other added to the comfortable image they projected.

They were consulting their menus.

"What do you think, Quent?"

He looked up in mock surprise. "In a place like the Clamdiggers, what else? Clams."

She laughed softly. She knew he didn't like clams. He disliked all seafood. He was the proverbial meat-and-potatoes eater.

In honor of her reaction, he chuckled. "Okay, we'll get serious," he said. "The New York strip has a nice ring to it. And the lady?"

She glanced once again at the menu. "I think I'll have the Caesar salad."

"That's it?"

"Uh-huh."

"No wonder you're fading away to nothing." The exchange gave him an opportunity to appraise her figure openly. Her modest dress hinted subtly at the delights beneath.

The waitress returned with a martini and a coffee. Yes, they were ready to order, and they did.

"I must say I'm relieved that they caught that guy," she said, turning to one of the more popular topics in the metropolitan area. They had just begun discussing the arrest of David Reading as Jeffrey was parking the car.

He smiled. "Did you feel threatened?"

"I think every woman feels she is in some jeopardy when some nut is out there killing females for no reason."

"Actually, I don't think the police have determined whether or not the man had a reason . . . at least as far as I've been able to follow the story."

Grace shook her head. "It happens so often in this city. Guns, guns, guns, and killing. Sometimes it is completely senseless. Sometimes it's revenge or intimidation or even accident. But when a couple of women are murdered by the same person, I think all women, especially those of us who work in the city, feel . . . well . . . vulnerable."

Jeffrey was thoughtful. "Yes, I suppose that's so.

Well, at any rate, he didn't murder two women; they got him before he could shoot the second one. Good piece of police work."

"You didn't go to the funeral." It was a statement rather than a question; both she and Jeffrey had arrived at work on time this morning and she knew the funeral had started only an hour later.

"No, I went to the wake last night. Crowded—but good company for Sister Joan."

The waitress brought Jeffrey's salad. Grace's Caesar salad would be served along with Jeffrey's entree.

"Speaking of the wake and funeral"—Grace seemed appalled—"did you see that memo from Father Bash? I put it on your desk. About how all major stories must be channeled through the information department? Wasn't that incredible?"

Jeffrey slowly chewed and swallowed some salad, taking his time about responding. "I beg your pardon in advance, Grace, but Clete Bash is an asshole."

Grace blushed, though she knew he was. "He *is* a priest!" She smiled.

"Excuse me, a *reverend* asshole. Even *he* must know there's no way of dictating a story like this. He's just got a burr under his saddle because Joan's picture was on TV and Clete Bash was nowhere to be seen."

"You make it sound as if . . . as if he wants the spotlight all the time."

"That's it exactly, Grace: Bash wants to be *important*. I don't think he has the slightest inkling of what an information office ought to be. For Clete it's merely a springboard for his ego. Sometimes I wonder how far he'd go to inflate his vanity. Without that collar, he'd probably be in a breadline."

"Quent!"

"Okay, check that: His war record might get him through the door somewhere. But, mind you, he'd be out on his ear in no time once they found out what kind of card player he is."

The waitress brought their entrees.

"I don't want to seem presumptuous, Quent," said Grace, after the waitress left, "but shouldn't that job have been yours? I mean, with your success in public relations, you seem a natural for the Office of Information."

"Bash was already in place when I came on the scene."

"Even so—"

"Our Cardinal Archbishop is not known for firing his employees, or haven't you noticed? Except for more than adequate cause. And extreme ego needs doesn't seem to be on his list."

"Do you think the Cardinal knows?"

"What do you mean?"

"I mean, for instance," Grace explained, "I'll bet the Cardinal didn't get one of today's memos from Father Bash."

"Oh, I see. Yes, you're right there: Clete knows who's dealing. Of course, he plays the sycophant to His Eminence. But my impression is that Cardinal Boyle does not get to work early every morning just to set a good example. He knows what's going on. He knows what sort Bash is. Unfortunately for the rest of us, the Cardinal is able to live with a man like that in his administration."

"I guess that is unfortunate."

"The way to survive someone like Bash, Grace, is to have as little to do with him as possible."

"Even me? After all, I'm only a secretary."

"Grace, you have my complete and flat-out permission to act as if Father Bash has suffered a sudden and barely-provided-for death."

They both laughed, and finished their dinner with small talk on more pleasant topics.

Ordinarily, Grace took the bus home from work each evening. Making allowances for the—at best—erratic dependability of Detroit's public transportation, it was a simple, direct ride from downtown to the far west side of the city.

But on those evenings when she dined with Quentin Jeffrey, he invariably insisted on driving her to her apartment house. Sometimes he would accompany her to her door; other times he would remain in his car but wait until she had entered the building.

Grace tried to read some sort of message into these variables. When he stayed outside the building, did that mean that he was tired of her company? That this would be their final evening together?

When he entered the building, did he want to come into her apartment? He always declined her invitation. Was entering her building a metaphor for entering her body? She had to admit that, remote as it seemed, she enjoyed the fantasy.

Things were far less involved, at least on a conscious level, in Jeffrey's mind. He was aware of no special reason for either procedure. It was merely that he was invariably concerned for her safety. He would never leave until she was at least within the protective walls of her building. Sometimes, for no perceptible reason, he felt particularly ill at ease about the neighborhood— an unfamiliar car, the front door left slightly ajar, something, anything. At such times, he would walk her to her door. She would invite him in. He would politely decline the invitation. Sometimes he felt quite strongly that he should accept. But he felt even more strongly that he didn't want to complicate things.

Tonight when they arrived at her apartment building, he parked the car and wordlessly accompanied her up the walk and the stairs to her apartment. For the first time, he took the key from her hand, unlocked the door, and pushed it open.

Later, she couldn't say why she did it. Maybe because this evening at dinner he'd seemed to share his feelings with her more openly than ever before. Perhaps it was his unique gesture of taking her key and opening the door.

Whatever the case, as he opened the door, she slipped her left hand to the back of his neck and kissed him gently on the lips.

Startled, he pulled back. She immediately sensed that she had misinterpreted the signs. She dropped her hand and moved back, only to be clasped firmly in his arms and pulled forward and upward. The kiss that followed was passionate.

Still locked in their embrace, they began moving through her door, when, without warning, a resident of an adjoining apartment opened his door and stepped out to retrieve his afternoon paper.

For an instant, all three were immobile in mutual embarrassment.

The man swept his paper from the floor and stepped back inside his apartment so hurriedly he almost stumbled. For Jeffrey, the moment was past, the magic gone. But not for Grace; Jeffrey had to peel her arms from his back.

"Come in, Quent, come in," Grace pleaded. "It doesn't matter. He went back inside. He can't see us now. It's all right."

"No! Excuse me, Grace. I don't know what—I'm sorry. My fault entirely. I'll see you tomorrow."

He stepped away quickly and hurried down the stairs and out of sight.

Grace stood where he'd left her. She waited until she heard the outside door open and close.

He was gone. But not the memory.

She entered her apartment, closed the door, leaned back against it, and closed her eyes.

Her imagination began to film a movie. Her neighbor was expunged. She and Quent, still locked together, moved into her room. They kissed, more and more deeply. They moved, as if in adagio, into the bedroom, where their passion overflowed.

Afterward, he held her as, completely relaxed, they basked in each other's silent company.

Grace held the image all evening in happy contentment.

Quentin Jeffrey did not share her reverie fantasy. Immediately after starting his car, he turned off the heater. It was cold, but he was very warm. *God*, he thought, *I've forgotten what it was like.* He didn't linger for any possible reappearance by Grace Mars. He quickly pulled away from the curb.

And then, as was his wont, he assessed the situation.

He had let his testosterone run rampant, even if only for a few moments. He thought he had convinced himself after his wife died that there simply was no outlet for passion in his life anymore. And now an unguarded moment had put the lie to that conviction.

The good news was he'd been able to extinguish the fire before it became a conflagration. At the very least, an affair with Grace Mars surely would contaminate the atmosphere at work. He'd seen that happen so often when he'd been in business. Sex between workers, especially between employer and employee, even if not actually in the work arena, usually led to disastrous consequences.

He hoped that his letting down the protective layers, even so briefly, would not jeopardize the genuine friendship, as well as the business relationship, that had grown between them. He didn't think it had.

He had been driving with his mind in neutral. He shook his head and opened himself to the present.

There was something scheduled this evening. What was it? A gathering of some sort. Of course! How could he have forgotten poker with the gang? No wonder; after what had just happened—and after what had almost happened—he might well have forgotten his name.

But the game was set to start at 10:00. Later than usual. Perfectly acceptable; he could easily lose himself in a card game. And tonight he needed to get lost.

Here he was now, parked in front of his own home without a clear notion of how he got here. Force of habit, perhaps. There was still almost an hour before the game. Time to go inside and relax a bit.

He left his outerwear in the foyer closet. The thermostat had been programmed to have the house warm for his projected arrival. He poured a generous glass of Glenlivet neat, and slumped into his recliner chair.

He slid a mouthful of Scotch around in his mouth. Cleaning his teeth, he explained to himself. Also permeating his taste buds with that singular, satisfying piquancy.

He contemplated the glass. Martini for dinner and now Scotch. He didn't used to mix his beverages like this. He didn't used to drink this much.

Was his drinking becoming a problem? He didn't think it necessary to admit that. He used to drink with Maryanne, his late wife, but almost always in moderation. A little wine before and with dinner occasionally. A nightcap. Nothing like it was now.

His attention turned to the end table across the room. On it rested a photo of the two of them. It was a posed portrait taken many years ago at a happy time of life. They had health, security, fulfillment, and, most of all, each other.

Now she was gone. And he was left with . . . what? A bottle?

He felt an urge to go over and turn the picture face down. He couldn't bring himself to do that; he loved Maryanne too much. Though she was gone she was still a part of him.

And it was this dichotomy, her presence and simultaneous absence, that was tearing him apart.

If only she were alive. Sitting in this room. Now. They would be listening to music, and reading—he the newspaper, she a book. From time to time one would read aloud to the other and they would discuss what they were reading. One of them would say something silly. They would both laugh.

It was so quiet in this house. Not a sound. With the storm windows in, even the noise of the rare passing car was so muffled as to be almost unheard. So quiet. No one to talk to. Not even a companion.

He rose from his chair and walked slowly to the liquor cabinet. He refilled his glass. Not even any ice. He studied the glass again. It was going to be one of those nights when he drank himself to sleep.

No poker tonight; by the time he finished his second glass of Scotch he would be in no condition to play the game up to his usual standard of concentration. Odd; he considered himself capable of driving, but not of playing a game—albeit a game he considered an extension and measure of life.

He dialed the familiar number at St. Aloysius church and left his regrets for the evening on Clete Bash's answering machine. It was his best shot. Bash would be sure to check his messages before the game. Never can tell when the media might want some information or, better yet, a statement.

He sank again into his recliner.

He was lonely. Terribly, terribly lonely. And it wasn't just conversation he needed. If there were any doubt, the earlier events of this evening were a pretty clear signal.

Grace Mars was a desirable woman. She loved him. He knew that, even if before this evening he had not consciously acknowledged it. If it were not for canon law, if he were free, she would marry him. He could live very well with Gracie.

His mind was fogging.

Just a few months ago, his doctor had explored his drinking during a regular checkup. They had agreed he was not an alcoholic. Not yet. But his drinking had intensified, and the doctor had warned that this periodic compulsion to drink to the point of unconsciousness could lead to lost time spans—blackouts.

When he was in the mood to be brutally honest with himself, he had to admit that just maybe this had already happened once or twice.

If he were not careful, it could happen tonight.

With deliberate resoluteness he poured the remaining Scotch down the drain and, a bit blearily, turned on the television. It was a game show that, on top of what he had drunk, soon lulled him to sleep.

Before slipping off, he resolved that things would be better tomorrow. Things always looked more hopeful in the light of day.

9 CHRISTMASTIME TRADITIONALLY BRINGS a bumper crop of suicides. People plagued by depression find that depression intensifies when they are isolated amid the surroundings of the joyful majority who give and receive gifts, wax sentimental over the seasonal music, party and make merry with relatives and friends.

Fred Stapleton was not one of the depressed minority. Now in his early sixties, he was satisfied with his work as a psychologist in private practice. He was happily married to a former nun. Irma, their only child, a gifted pianist, who was a high school junior at the internationally famed Interlochen Music Academy, was home for the holidays. Fred enjoyed adequate to good health.

Yet Christmas was a difficult time for him. Fred Stapleton had been a Catholic priest, and as much as he missed his prime calling, he missed it most in this season. And this even though he'd been an inactive priest now for almost as long—seventeen years—as he had been a functioning priest—twenty years.

Tonight, his wife, Pam, an excellent cook, had served roast beef, one of his favorite dishes. He had only picked at it. She knew why. But there was nothing she could do about it.

Now, seemingly satisfied, he sat in his favorite rocker, puffing on his pipe. Pam was chatting with Irma about the future and her plans for after graduation next year.

They were aware that Fred had long since been lost in his own thoughts.

Irma broke off her conversation with her mother and turned to her father. "Daddy . . . *Daddy!*" She had to repeat it several times before she got his attention.

"Uh . . . yeah . . . what is it, honey?"

"You're on your own private planet again."

"Oh. Sorry."

"Won't you join Mother and me in the land of the living?"

"Sorry again. Are you going to play for us? Play for your supper?"

"Later, Daddy."

Fred shook his head. "Can't be later, sweets; I've got a meeting to go to."

"Tonight? A patient?"

Pam answered. "No, CORPUS."

"Dad! You don't have to go tonight. They have so many meetings. What's the harm in missing one?"

CORPUS was an acronym for Corps of Reserve Priests United for Service, an international organization of former priests who, though married, want a return to their ministry.

"These meetings are important, Irma. And they're getting to be more important by the year. By the month. By the day!"

"Dear," Pam said, "this group is very, very important to your father. You've got to understand that."

"Daddy, it's been . . . what? . . . seventeen years since you were a priest. You're a successful doctor. I know you're good at what you do. You help people. Isn't that enough? You don't need to be a priest anymore."

"You don't know. You weren't a priest for twenty years. You don't know what it's like."

"You make me think you regret leaving. That you regret marrying Mother. That you're sorry I came along."

"Don't be silly, honey. You know that's not true."

"If you hadn't left you wouldn't have had me. I wouldn't have happened."

Fred smiled briefly. "You'd be in pure potency."

"Well," Irma said, "once and for all: Are you sorry you stopped being a priest?"

"No, I'm not sorry, honey. But you're not getting the point. Just about every priest who leaves really wants to stay. Most of us left to get married. As if the two were incompatible . . . as if marriage and priesthood were mutually exclusive."

"You sent me to a Catholic grade school," Irma interjected, "and I didn't see any married priests."

"Ah," Fred responded, "but that's because you happen to live in this country and because you're a Latin Rite Catholic. If you'd been living anywhere that the ancient Oriental Rite has been functioning you'd have found married Catholic priests. You can even find Catholic priests with wives and families here in this country."

"Where?"

"In parishes where married Protestant ministers have converted to Catholicism and have been ordained to the Catholic priesthood.

"The point I'm trying to make, honey, is that in the first place there's no reason—Biblically, historically, or just about any other adverb—for us not to be married and still function as priests. And on top of that, they need us. They need us desperately."

"If they need you so much, how come they don't know it?"

"Irma," her mother admonished, "don't be flip. Your father is very serious about this!"

"Just playing devil's advocate," Irma said. "Daddy always says I'm good at that."

"You are good at it," Fred said. "Sometimes I wish you weren't quite so good. 'How come they don't know about it?' They know about it all right; they just won't admit it."

"But, Daddy, if they won't admit it, they won't admit it. What's the use of your struggling, going to meetings, trying to convince them, if they're just so stubborn they won't admit they need you?"

Fred Stapleton hesitated, lips compressed in a thin line of anger and resolve. "There are times," he said, finally, "when you have to do something you would have sworn you'd never do—if only to get their attention." As he spoke, there was an aura of foreboding about him that was completely out of character for this ordinarily gentle and compassionate man. Neither Pam nor Irma could bring herself to break the spell.

Finally, Fred tapped out his pipe in an ashtray, rose, and announced, "It's time. I'm going to the meeting." He softened as he studied his daughter. "You will give us a concert before you go back to school, won't you?"

"Sure, Daddy."

In a few minutes mother and daughter were alone, gazing at each other wordlessly.

"I'm worried about him, Mother," Irma said finally.

"So am I. He just hasn't been himself lately."

Irma hesitated. Then, "I've never asked you, even though I've wondered from time to time. But I have wondered. . . ."

"What? You know we can talk about anything you want to. What is it?"

"Well . . . what was it like when you got married? I mean . . . did you feel guilty about marrying a priest? Did Daddy?"

Pam smiled warmly. "I certainly didn't. I don't think your father did either. I'm sure he didn't. I'd left the convent long before we married. We fell in love slowly . . . oh, so very slowly." She obviously cherished the memory of their earliest days of a growing love.

"Our greatest hurdle," Pam explained, "was his priesthood, of course. He'd been a priest twenty years. It was all he'd ever wanted to be from the time he was a small child. He loved his work. And he loved what his vocation had become just a little less—as it turned out—than he loved me. It wasn't a matter of feeling guilty. It was a matter of feeling loss.''

"Seems like a case of seasickness and lockjaw simultaneously, to use the metaphor Daddy uses so often.''

Pam winced. "I guess so.'' True enough, Fred did use the phrase with some frequency. But she'd always found it in poor taste.

"So,'' Irma persisted, "how did he settle the dilemma? Or did you do it for him?''

"Oh, no. My only contribution was to urge him to stay functioning as a priest.''

"You did?'' This came as a genuine surprise.

"Oh, absolutely. I could see down the line in the years ahead where that could be an insurmountable problem. I never wanted him to feel that I had put any pressure on him to leave the priesthood. I knew the way he felt about his vocation he would surely miss being a priest. And he has. So it had to be his decision. His alone.

"With me on the side of his remaining a priest, there wasn't anyone even suggesting that he leave and marry me. No one but himself.''

"So it was his choice?'' Irma asked.

Pam shook her head. "You don't understand, dear. It's what your father was trying to tell you before. What he regrets is the Church's inability or refusal to understand that there's no contradiction in being a priest and, at the same time, being married.''

"I think I understand, Mom. He's very comfortable about having married you . . .''

"And having you for a daughter,'' Pam interjected.

Irma smiled. "Yeah. That's neat. So he's okay about all that. The problem is with the Church. He should be able to be a priest now—saying Mass and everything.''

"Think you've got it?''

"I think so. But I've got to think about it some more.''

"Good." Pam began massaging her forehead.

"Headache? Let me do that for you."

Pam smiled. "Know what you can do for me, dear? Maybe you could play something nice and soothing."

Irma gave it a moment's thought. "Sure." She moved to the spinet and the beautiful strains of Franz Liszt's "Liebestraum" filled the room.

Pam relaxed, rested her head against the chair, closed her eyes, and let the memories flood over her.

Her daughter's query had brought to mind those fateful days after she and Father Fred Stapleton had first met.

He was an attractive man, talented, handsome, well read, with an infectious sense of humor—and off-limits. On neither's part was it love at first sight. She taught in the parochial school attached to the parish of which he was pastor. As a nun, she had taught for many years before leaving the convent. She was a gifted teacher.

Father Stapleton took an active interest in his school and, naturally, in its teachers. Of all the teachers, religious and lay, he managed to find more time for Pam Baldwin than for any of the others. She was such a good teacher, and attractive and fun—and off-limits.

Their relationship grew, as most authentic love does, gradually. By the time they realized they were, after all, an ordinary couple who wanted to spend the rest of their lives together, it was too late to turn back. If Pam had made the slightest suggestion that he leave the priesthood so they could marry, he would have started the process immediately. On the contrary, however, her resolve that he remain an active priest was far stronger than his.

So when the decision was finally made, it was his entirely.

In terms of staying in good standing with the Church, they were fortunate. Fred left at a time when the Pope happened to be lenient in granting laicization.

Pope Paul VI had inherited the legacy of his predecessor, John XXIII. The inheritance included the Second Vatican Council. There are those who believe Paul didn't know what to do with it. Laicization, a modern phenomenon, at least in its frequency, was a case in point. Pope Paul vacillated from year to year in granting the request.

Laicization is the tortuous, complicated, and lengthy process by which a priest is "reduced" to the status of a lay person. And then some. Catholicism teaches that, "Once a priest, always a priest." But in order to function—say Mass, absolve, marry, bury, etc.—the priest needs "faculties"—permission of his bishop, in the case of a diocesan priest, or of his religious superior, for a religious order priest.

The bishop giveth as well as taketh away.

Permission to function is withdrawn if, for any reason, a priest's superior punishes him with a penalty called "suspension." Should a priest "attempt" marriage without having been granted laicization, he is automatically excommunicated, in addition to being forbidden to function sacramentally.

There were times when Pope Paul's policy would grant laicization for good cause; times when he tightened the restrictions by granting it, say, only to homosexuals; and times when he would not grant it at all.

In Fred Stapleton's case there was good and bad news. The good news was that at the time he applied, permission was being granted quite liberally. The bad news was that, outside of emergencies, such as when someone was in danger of death, Fred would never again be able to function as a priest.

They were married in the Church by a priest who was a mutual friend.

Fred continued teaching while he earned the degrees necessary for a psychology practice. Irma was not planned but she was made very welcome.

Fred became a very competent and popular psychologist-counselor. His clientele included many celebrities of the Detroit metropolitan area. Often he was quoted in the media, and his photo would appear in the paper or on TV. The Stapletons lived comfortably, though not lavishly. By Pam's standards, all was well—with the notable exception of Fred's attitude toward his enforced laicization. And that attitude had blossomed and hardened through the years.

In the beginning, laicization had been an O. Henry sort of gift. Fred thought Pam wanted everything to be kosher. Pam thought Fred would be distressed were he excommunicated. Neither assumption, as it turned out, was true. But each hesitated to talk about it. So Pam endured the months of delay and uncertainty and Fred endured the endless questions of the MMPI test.

Because he was put in the posture of a beggar, that which he sought—permission of the Church for him to function as a layman without the obligation of reciting the breviary daily, and a dispensation from his promise of celibacy—took on heightened desirability.

It was only after the permission had been granted and they were married that Fred could calmly and in clearer focus assess the "favor" the Church had bestowed. In the light of reexamination, it didn't appear all that beneficent.

As a result of his research into the history and rationale of clerical celibacy, Fred grew increasingly certain that he and others like him had been robbed. He could and should have it all. So, when CORPUS was founded and established in Minneapolis, Fred became a charter member.

Pam was far less enchanted with the organization's purpose.

Due to their status, Fred and Pam became familiar, and in many cases friendly, with other inactive priests and their spouses. By and large, thought Pam, these were excellent men. And, because it was so often true, she came to expect priests' wives to be strong, intelligent, capable women.

In Pam's eyes, CORPUS took a suppliant stance. *Dear Church: Have you looked lately? You're running out of priests. Have you noticed the current median age of your priests? Dear bishops and Pope: Unless you are theologically and historically naive, you know there is no legitimately compelling reason for mandatory celibacy in your clergy. And here we are, thousands of well-trained priests, waiting on the sidelines to go in there and win one for Mother Church.*

What galled Pam most about CORPUS was that there was seldom any sort of *demand* on the part of its members to return to a fully functioning ministry. Rather, she felt the group was willing, almost eager, to settle for some—any—small crumb of their once full ministry.

In short, she felt that good men were demeaning themselves by pleading for something each of them believed was due them by right.

But she sensed Fred's dedication to the organization and the cause. So she kept her feelings to herself, pondering them in her heart.

So lost in these thoughts was Pam that she was unaware that Irma had concluded "Liebestraum" and had added the unsolicited encore of Schumann's "Träumerei."

Irma had turned on the piano bench and was looking at her mother. Pam had no clue as to how long this had been going on. But now, conscious of Irma's gaze, she said, "Thank you, dear; that was marvelous. Just what the doctor ordered."

"You didn't hear a note I played."

"Oh, but I did. I found it so soothing I got lost in my own reverie. It helped, dear; honest it did."

Irma wore a concerned expression. "Mama, would you do something special for me?"

"Of course, sweetheart."

"Would you make sure Daddy doesn't do anything foolish?"

Pam was startled. "What?"

"He scared me tonight when he was talking about doing something he never thought he would do. It wasn't so much his words as his tone of voice. I was almost afraid of him. I've never felt like that before."

"You've got to have more confidence in your father, dear. Of course he wouldn't do anything foolish. Just put that out of your mind."

Pam would not mention it to her daughter, but Irma had put into words the exact fear that increasingly plagued Pam. She could not nor would she worry her daughter. But Fred *had* changed in subtle ways. Pam was concerned. She would do her best to make sure Fred did nothing foolish. She shivered as she prayed that even now it was not too late.

10

CARDINAL MARK BOYLE offered Sister Joan condolences on the death of her sister.

The Cardinal's speech pattern, on almost all formal occasions, brought to mind a technically and carefully worded textbook. And so it was now. In her mind's eye, Joan saw the Cardinal's words framed in hearts and flowers mounted on an antique greeting card.

The others at today's meeting murmured their agreement with Cardinal Boyle's expressions, which he had tendered immediately after opening the meeting with a prayer.

That is, at least most of them concurred.

That business completed, there came the shuffling of papers and scraping of chairs. This was a regularly scheduled meeting of "the staff," which included the heads, leaders, directors of almost every bureau or department in the archdiocese. It was an unwieldy group of some thirty people. Three were women: Sister Joan; the director of continuing education, Joan Blackford Hayes; and Irene Casey, present editor of the *Detroit Catholic*. Of the men present, almost half the number were lay.

It had not been that way in the beginning.

Father Koesler, as editor of the *Detroit Catholic* when these staff meetings first began, could testify that in the beginning there had been present only about a dozen people, all of whom were clergymen. In time, the number grew as departments were either added or recognized. And, reflecting the profound vocation shortage, more and more departments were headed by laypeople.

The staff meeting had two basic functions. Each department head reported in writing what his or her agency had accomplished in the past month. And each department head detailed future plans.

The chief topic of today's meeting was to be Catholic schools of the archdiocese, with emphasis on the ever-shrinking number of parochial grade and high schools.

There had been a time, up to the early 1970s, when almost every parish had its own parochial school. That was an era when teaching sisters were plentiful and some public school services were made available.

Then, in the wake of Vatican II and a judgment of the U.S. Supreme Court, both these staples of parochial education were made unavailable.

The Sisters vanished. Many left the convent for lay careers and/or marriage. Some remained in the religious life but opted for church positions other than teaching.

And simultaneously, few, very few, were entering religious life.

In 1971 the Supreme Court ruled that any use whatsoever of public funds for private education was unconstitutional.

The virtual disappearance of these two essential resources might imply that the parochial school system would collapse. It hadn't, but it was leaning more steeply than that tower in Pisa. That it was still even limping along was a tribute to Catholics dedicated and sacrificing to keep it going somehow. In the meantime, it was draining the budgets of those parishes still subsidizing schools.

Today, it was Father Cletus Bash's turn to chair the meeting, albeit with deference to Cardinal Boyle, who never left any doubt who was in charge.

Boyle's position as archbishop—sweetened by the title of Cardinal—gave him overwhelming power in the local Church. All the property in the archdiocese was held in his name. Church law gave him authority in the archdiocese second only to the Pope. In addition, Detroit was the metropolitan see in the state of Michigan, which gave Boyle some degree of clout over the other six dioceses in the state. Someone said it: Bishops in Rome were a dime a dozen; a bishop in his own diocese was a power to be reckoned with.

Father Bash called on the various departments one by one. Each director had previously submitted a one-page report for the month. Each director was expected to read all the others' reports prior to the meeting. Typically, few had done their homework. For those few, now, as Bash paged through one sheet after another, this was their opportunity to ask questions or comment concerning the reports. Instead, most everyone was blearily one or more pages behind Bash in trying to digest all the proffered information. There were few questions.

Bash was brusque and slightly caustic, as always. "I see everyone has pored over the reports as usual and, as usual, conditions among all departments are so good there aren't many questions."

A precious few were slightly entertained, the rest merely grumbled in muted tones.

"We now turn to the main topic for today's meeting," Bash proceeded unmindfully. "Our schools and our school system. For this part of the meeting you need only state your opinion—no advance work needs to have been done. So we can count on the meeting livening up."

More grousing.

"For greater clarity," Bash added, "we will not be discussing any of our colleges or universities, and we'll reserve comment on the central highs. Let's begin with our parochial grade and high schools. Anyone?"

Monsignor Del Young took the floor and hung on

tight. A throwback to a former time, he'd been superintendent of Catholic schools in Detroit for twenty years. Ordinarily, he would have moved out of that specialized job long ago. But he was so comfortable as superintendent on the one hand, and fearful of becoming a pastor on the other, that he fought the notion of a transfer each time the issue was raised.

It was not all that unusual for a priest in special work to want to remain there. Over the years, attending conventions, regional and national meetings, it was natural to become acquainted with almost everyone in the field. The continuing phone contact and correspondence tied them all together in a tidy subculture. It got to be cozy. The routine was reassuring.

Even so, a diocesan or secular priest such as Del Young had attended a diocesan seminary in order to become a parish priest. That's what diocesan seminaries produced. Thus, even if parting from a superintendent's position could be sweet sorrow, it shouldn't have been that hard. That parting with a preferred job could be painful is easily understood. Still, he would be moving into the position he had ostensibly started out to hold in the beginning—the office of a parish priest.

The final phenomenon contributing to Monsignor Young's durable dalliance with the superintendent's job was that the priesthood had become a buyer's market. This state of affairs had been generated by the priest shortage. Bishops needed—in growing desperation—warm priestly bodies.

At one time, Detroit priests were moved about the diocese when they received a letter from the chancery which invariably began, "For the care of souls, I have it in mind to send you to . . ." Where followed the name of the parish the priest would move to and serve in.

No longer. Parishes advertised in the priests' newsletter, and priests applied for the position—or did not.

There were exceptions, but considerable choice on the priest's part was the rule, not the exception.

So Monsignor Del Young wanted, and was able, to hang in there. Because he'd had the job for as long as many could remember, he feared getting into a parish where his authority would be unaccustomedly diminished, and particularly at age sixty-five, ten years from mandatory retirement, he was not about to be receiving a "For the care of souls . . ." letter.

Del Young could see only one possible fly in the ointment: What if they closed the schools? He would be superintendent of nothing.

As the first speaker in this morning's staff meeting, Monsignor Young spoke long, ardently, and with some eloquence on behalf of everything from self-sustaining schools to those whose income was minuscule.

Everyone in the room knew whence Del Young was coming and took all he said with huge doses of salt. Because, after he finished, there was still the matter of what to do about parochial schools. About one thing there was no doubt: parochial schools were in trouble. In some cases, lots and lots of trouble.

Sister Joan Donovan was next to raise her hand. She was recognized by Father Bash.

"I'm afraid we're slowly creating an elitist school system," Joan said. "For the past twenty years schools have been closing. First there was a trickle, then a torrent closed; now we're back to that trickle."

"We still have the fifth or sixth largest school system in the country!" Monsignor Young interjected.

"We know that, Monsignor," Joan replied. "My point is that it has come down to the issue of affordability alone. Costs are skyrocketing, and as we keep pulling our belts tighter it's going to be more and more obvious the Catholic schools are going to be found exclusively in the suburbs for little white boys and girls."

Young's face was reddening as if he were slowly choking on his clerical collar. "The reason the costs are skyrocketing—to use your word, Sister; I don't agree with such a blanket statement—the reason for the costs is the disappearance of the teaching nun. I should think the delegate for religious would not only know that, but be in a position to do something about it."

Joan smiled as she might have at a slow pupil. "Monsignor, that was a different day."

"A different day," Archbishop Foley mused. "Ah, remember when it was a mortal sin not to send your kids to the Catholic school?"

No one responded. Regarded as redundant and without clout, Foley was present at this meeting for the same reason he was residing in Detroit: Cardinal Boyle had invited him. Few others paid him much mind.

"It's not just a different day," Young snapped. "It's all your nuns abandoning their vows, their orders, their schools."

"Monsignor," Joan replied, "even if we had back all the Sisters who have left, we still wouldn't be able to staff the school system we once had. By now, too many would be retired, too many would have died. It's not just the Sisters who have left. And before you bring it up," she added, "it's not the ones who have gone into other apostolic work, nor even the girls who are no longer entering religious life. And, finally, it's not the teaching orders of men who, as good teachers as they are, never constituted the staple of Catholic primary education.

"It's a new day for women in the world. Not all that long ago, Catholic women found complete fulfillment as wives and mothers, keeping the house and kids orderly and clean; cooking, washing, repairing, doctoring, being understanding and supportive. Or they found completeness in the convent and in the community of other nuns, teaching in a parochial school—for nothing really, since their entire tiny salary went directly to their religious orders.

"Look about you, Monsignor. Women are prime ministers, rulers, doctors, successful authors; leaders in science, banking, law. Granted, women are still victims of injustice and discrimination. They still do not have complete parity with men by any means. But they are worlds ahead of where they were.''

"All this from a lady whose sister was a hooker.''

Bash spoke so quietly that only a few heard him. His murmured comment elicited a few feigned chuckles, but nothing wholehearted.

Though she could not make out what Bash had muttered, Sister Joan, aware that he'd said something and probably something shabby, was momentarily disconcerted. "I'm afraid I've lost my train of thought,'' she apologized.

"Like it or not, look at it as a bad thing or good, it *is* a matter of money.'' Father Bash, who, as chair, did not have to be recognized, picked up the theme. "We understand completely that without the generous sacrifice of teaching nuns the Church would not have had the courage to start the parochial school system. And now, they're gone. For whatever reason, maybe for the reasons Sister Joan mentioned. They want to be presidents, regents, tycoons, priests. . . .'' He smirked, knowing well that of all the prospects for equality with men, priesthood was undoubtedly the most remote.

"Whatever the reason for their no longer supplying the basic element in parochial education,'' Bash continued, "the fact is they're gone. And it's simply going to be survival of the fittest. If that means—and I agree it probably does—that eventually the only parochial schools will be suburban—then, so be it. If we Americans can't understand that, who can? Survival of the fittest. Capitalism. A reflection of our country.''

Archbishops, even when separated from their archdioceses, can develop the habit of speaking without benefit of recognition. "Capitalism!'' Archbishop Foley's shoulders seemed to sag as he spoke quietly and deliberately. "What in the world has capitalism got to do with Christianity?"

"Excellency . . ." Bash's tone was that of the adult who deigns to speak from his level to that of a child, ". . . my point is that we have to face facts and make the best of reality. Realistically, the city of Detroit has experienced 'white flight' for decades now. And it was mostly white Catholics who built these huge churches in the city—and white Catholics who supported them.

"For whatever reason—it's immaterial here—we never have made much headway with the blacks. The Catholic Church endured in the city because Catholics were there. They are no longer there in any significant number. But they didn't evaporate. They've relocated to the suburbs and there they've built new schools and they support them. Supply and demand. Demand and supply. Capitalism. Whatever you want to call it, Catholic schools will close in the city because there are too few Catholics there to support them. They'll be alive in the suburbs because that's where the Catholics are."

Bash wore a pleased smile. The archbishop's teacher had completed his pupil's lesson.

Those present no longer waited for an official recognition by the chair. Sister Joan spoke up. "That's simplistic, Father Bash. The core city schools that remain open may have a majority of black and non-Catholic students, and the tuition *is* high, but the parents are sacrificing tremendously to pay that tuition. They value that quality education easily as much, maybe more, than the people who sacrificed and built those schools."

"Ah, yes, Sister," Bash replied, "but it is not only white flight that's taken place in Detroit; It's economic flight now. Of course there are a few—a very few— areas in the city that are still fairly affluent, notably the riverfront, but most of the people who still live in the rest of the city are there because they can't afford to move out.

"Sister, my point is that it's not only Catholics—white or black—that are moving out; it's almost anyone who can afford to. As all of these people leave there won't be any possible support for the high cost of maintaining a parochial school. Parochial schools in the city are terminal."

Sister Joan regarded Bash. She'd never had the impression that he was particularly effective in the public relations arena and surely he was ineffective as a communicator. With his hubris and his macho facade he might have done well somewhere in the secular world, but, try as she might, she could think of no reason whatever why he should have become a priest. *Brash Bash.* It was difficult to say. She almost laughed aloud.

"I think there is something that can be done about the schools." The Reverend Mr. Quentin Jeffrey seemed almost disinterested, as if he were the only speaker so far who had no particular ax to grind. "I'm not sure any of you want to go in this direction, but . . . we might play on suburban guilt feelings."

"Guilt feelings?" Monsignor Young echoed.

"Uh-huh. White flight, or the odyssey of white *and* black affluence to the suburbs has been mentioned. What has not been addressed is that those who have fled—at least those among them who have sensitive consciences—are well aware that in moving they were abandoning the city. In other words, many of them have guilty consciences."

"That's true." Sister Joan nodded in agreement. "Priests who are responsive to social justice and the like preach about the need for Christians to identify with victims—victims of injustice, victims of indifference and abandonment. And many of these priests speak specifically of our literal neighbors suffering in the city. Sensitive Catholics must feel some sort of guilt, especially about the separate and unequal educational opportunities of suburban and city children."

"Exactly," Jeffrey continued. "There are precedents

galore. Cities 'adopt' other cities. Adults 'adopt' children in other countries, without ever seeing the kid. They just send money. This would be a case of a well-to-do parish with a parochial school 'adopting' a hard-pressed school in the core city.''

"That would never work. Before you came on the scene"—Father Bash tried to belittle Jeffrey by insinuating seniority—''there was an effort to link city and suburban Catholic schools by having an interchange of kids.''

"You mean," Jeffrey said, "having the suburban kids attend the city schools and vice versa?''

"Exactly.''

"Whose idea was that?''

"The core city people.''

Jeffrey snorted. ''That's an idea whose time not only has not come, it'll never come. A good number of parents with school-age kids moved to the suburbs for the express purpose of escaping from city schools. For good measure, add the fear that their deteriorating parochial schools in the city were likely to close. They're not going to return to the city or send their kids—not by a long shot.

''But their conscience still bothers them. So they don't send their kids; they send money. They 'adopt' a parish school and help subsidize it.''

"It won't work!'' Bash repeated himself. "If you were a priest instead of a deacon"—Bash tried to diminish Jeffrey by pulling rank—''and if you were in one of those suburban parishes, you'd know that most of those parishes are strapped for money. Go on out to the trenches sometime and ask the pastors out there if their people have enough money to support two schools! You'll find out soon enough there isn't any money.''

Jeffrey smiled and slowly shook his head. ''Father Bash, there's always more money. Money has a peculiar talent for self-multiplication. How many times do workers go on strike while management claims it's made its best and final offer? 'There isn't any more money anywhere.' Then the strike goes on, hurting everyone. Finally, management miraculously 'finds' more money.

"Or a family wants some luxury—a high-priced car, a summer home, a cruise—but they can't afford it. Happens all the time. You know it as well as I. When the family gets around to wanting whatever it is badly enough, voila: They come up with it. All it needs is a decent piece of P.R. work."

Bash hit the ceiling. "Decent P.R.! Are you intimating that my office lacks professionalism? Are you suggesting that we are incapable of carrying on an effective campaign? I resent such insinuation, sir! I resent it deeply!"

In his heart of hearts, Bash was intimidated by Jeffrey. Quentin Jeffrey had been a recognized success in the public relations field. It was awkward for Bash, who had no formal training or experience, to function while a professional looked on and conceivably evaluated his performance. Bash could bulldoze his way through almost any situation. But, inwardly insecure, he was cowed by Jeffrey's talent, experience, and proven ability. So Bash reacted to his deserved inferiority complex by striking out at the better man.

Quentin Jeffrey was unruffled. He really didn't care whether or not his suggestion was implemented. He considered it good advice. But he was keenly aware that it would not be easy to make it work. It would require diplomatic and adroit handling. Something the ham-fisted Bash was incapable of.

Cardinal Boyle did not like his people to engage in confrontation. Some carping was unavoidable as he tried to steer a middle course, faithful to the mind of the Church while permitting as much freedom and initiative as possible. But here at a staff meeting was not the place for angry recrimination.

"Gentlemen, gentlemen!" Boyle said. "Now I am sure that Reverend Mr. Jeffrey did not mean to impugn the abilities and accomplishments of the office of communication. Mr. Jeffrey's suggestion is worthy of consideration. And I am sure it deserves further examination. In any case, Father Bash, nothing that Mr. Jeffrey said need trouble you.'' The Cardinal smiled as he toyed with his pectoral cross. ''You must develop a tougher hide, Father Bash. These are troubled times.''

''Yes, Eminence.'' When it came to the Cardinal Archbishop of Detroit, Cletus Bash was the quintessential yes man.

Larry Hoffer's hand was raised. Bash thought that a good sign: The meeting was returning to order as decreed in Robert's Rules of Order.

''Mr. Hoffer.'' Bash recognized.

By leaning heavily on his right elbow, Hoffer was able to get his left hand in his pants pocket and jingle coins. ''I feel as if I ought to apologize for what I'm about to say, but as director of finance and administration, I must see things in dollars and cents and very little else.''

Jingle, jingle.

''I can't help remembering how things were when I was a boy. The recollection was jogged by Archbishop Foley's recalling a time when Catholics had to confess a mortal sin if they were not sending their children to a Catholic school. At that time, I was going to a parochial school—so my parents were spared that embarrassment.''

Particularly from the usually dour Hoffer, that was a humorous line. For that very reason, no one laughed. They couldn't believe he would be treating this matter lightly. They were waiting for the other shoe to drop.

''Earlier in this meeting,'' Hoffer proceeded, ''Monsignor Young referred to the virtual disappearance of the teaching nun. I put that together with what Archbishop Foley said and came up with a picture of the school I attended. And all the nuns. Sisters I still remember. Rarely if ever did a layperson teach in a parochial school. Whoever came up with the teaching nun, it was, indeed, an ingenious idea. She gave of herself completely, selflessly. She is a golden memory for all of us old enough to have attended that kind of parochial school.

"And that is gone. We all know that. Now, I don't pretend to understand all of the complex reasons it's gone. I am concerned only with the aftermath, the consequences of the loss of the teaching nun.

"Even if we were able to bring back the nuns in anywhere near the numbers we once had, I doubt that we could keep our schools open regardless. The cost of everything else has risen so much—there's the age of the buildings, their desperate need of repair and replacement; there's utilities, insurance, supplies; the cost of attaining a teaching degree now. All that overhead would have to figure into the tuition we'd have to charge.

"Still, if we had the nuns, it might be worth a try. But . . . we haven't got them. When you lack food, you lack a meal.

"What we have now is what Father Bash and Sister Joan—from different perspectives—have agreed on: Our city schools are in desperate need of subsidization. Deacon Jeffrey suggests that our suburban schools should do the subsidizing. There's merit in that approach, except that most of our suburban schools are already draining an increasing percentage of their parishes' income. Deacon Jeffrey cites the remarkable power of money to seem to multiply. But not infinitely. And that's what would be needed for our schools to survive: money raised to infinity. Because the cost will continue to rise dramatically, and there is no end in sight."

Hoffer left off with no attempt to state any sort of conclusion to his argument. There remained a prolonged and expectant silence. Then, for the first time, Irene Casey spoke. "So . . . so what do you propose, Larry?"

Hoffer did not reply.

"You can't mean you're recommending closing all our parochial schools!" Irene pressed. "City *and* suburban?!"

"That," Hoffer said, "is exactly what I am recommending: Close them before they eat us alive."

From the reaction this statement received, it seemed evident that no one present had ever considered the possibility of eliminating the entire parochial school system.

In the hubbub that ensued, Monsignor Young finally made himself heard. "You don't understand! You don't understand, Mr. Hoffer! You don't understand how interdependent some of our parishes and schools have become. Some pastors have told me that their parishes were almost inactive—lifeless from Monday through Friday—before they built their schools. Then a real community was formed. You don't understand this!"

"That's not my concern," Hoffer replied. "I have no way of speaking to that point. My job is to deliver to the Cardinal the best advice I can give him as his chief financial resource person."

Monsignor Young—along with others—was coming unglued. "But . . . but, Mr. Hoffer, don't you see, if you close those schools, you might as well close those parishes!"

"As a matter of fact," Hoffer replied, "there are quite a few parishes that are in the same situation as the schools. They should be closed."

"What!?" was the reaction of almost everyone, especially Monsignor Young. No parishes, no schools. Superintendent of nothing. Ten years to go and no niche for him. That would not do. That very definitely would not do.

From this point on, the dispute grew heated. Father Bash lost his prerogative of directing this meeting. In fact, with all the wrangling, he was shouted down several times.

The feverish dispute ranged widely. Some contended that, after all, without the nuns and the clear-cut dogma and morality of the past, what was the use of having Catholic schools anymore? Or, Catholic schools were needed more than ever today when public education, generally, had been intimidated from teaching religious values by the Supreme Court.

The dispute went so far afield as to include the shrinking number of priests. With that in mind, maybe it was a good idea to circle the wagons more closely and close a few marginal parishes. Or, looking at the same diminishing priest supply, it was absolutely imperative to keep the parishes open. Where in the world were the desperately needed candidates for priesthood going to come from if the kids hardly ever even saw a priest?

And on and on it went.

One of the few who did not dive into this cacophony was Irene Casey.

Technically she was not a department head. But, as editor of the *Detroit Catholic*, she felt she needed to be familiar with the background of what was going on and what was being planned by the archdiocesan administration. Besides, her predecessor, Father Koesler, had always attended these meetings. She had made her case before Cardinal Boyle, and because it seemed a reasonable request and also because Boyle genuinely liked her, he had approved.

In all the meetings she had attended since her initial invitation to join the group, Irene had never witnessed anything like this.

These were very angry men and, in two instances, women. A few of them were saying things she was sure they would regret having expressed. Even occasional interposings on the part of Cardinal Boyle could not restore either Robert's Rules or civility.

Mrs. Casey felt the slacker for not joining in the various arguments. But confrontation, for her, was more a matter of necessity than choice. Besides, the debate had begun to take on abusive tones as well as including personal insults. It seemed to Irene that she detected a vituperative quality which barely sheathed an undertone of violence that disturbed her deeply.

A Steve Allen song came to her mind: *This could be the start of something big.*

11

THE HOFFERS LIVED in a rambling old house on Birchcrest near the University of Detroit in Gesu parish, which was staffed by Jesuits.

They'd lived at this address for most of their married life, raised five children, who were now all married and moved away; they themselves had no intention of moving. The neighborhood was racially mixed but stable—such stability being rare in the city of Detroit. There was a tad more danger than in the average suburban neighborhood—or at least that was the created impression. But there were neighborhood watches, block parties, a form of Welcome Wagon, and interested and interesting people.

Georgeanne—friends called her Georgie—Hoffer had served beef burgundy, one of Larry Hoffer's favorites, for supper. The two were now seated in a very lived-in living room. She was reading a book, her reading glasses barely bonded to the tip of her nose. He was reading the *Detroit News*, the city's afternoon newspaper. Curled around her feet like a small white muffler was Truffles, her dog.

One might have referred to Truffles as *their* dog, except that the poodle belonged to Georgie. Larry tolerated the animal. His philosophy regarding pets was, If you're going to have a dog, have a big dog; if you're going to have a little dog, have a cat. But Georgie loved the little mutt—who understood completely that he was his mistress's dog—and that was good enough for Larry.

The softly playing radio was tuned to WQRS-FM, the

area's classical music station. The station, at this moment, was torturing its listeners with a Béla Bartók chamber piece. Larry was preoccupied enough to pay it no mind. Georgie, having missed the introduction, did not know who had composed the piece, and was enduring it to the end solely to discover who had perpetrated this insult to the human ear. At long last, as was inevitable, it ended and the announcer identified it.

"Bartók," Georgie said. "If I'd been paying attention before it began, I'd have switched stations."

"Um."

"Well, they've got it out of their system, I hope. Maybe now they'll stick to the big guns."

"Uh-huh."

She couldn't see his face behind the paper. From the sounds he was making, she knew that he was awake and probably not paying attention. There were ways of finding out whether his mind was here or elsewhere. "Did you come across the item in the paper yet about how Mayor Cobb is going to move all the bodies out of Gethsemane Cemetery so he can enlarge City Airport?" She'd invented that.

"Uh."

"Yes. He's going to replant them in the salt mines under the city and create our own version of the Roman catacombs."

No response.

"In time he thinks it will increase tourism."

Still no sound.

She tried another tack. "Peter"—their eldest son now happily married and living in upstate New York—"called today. He's getting a divorce and coming back home to live."

Slowly the paper was lowered. He looked at her quizzically. She was smiling. He smiled. "Was I that far away?"

"Afraid so."

"Sorry."

"Was the *News* that absorbing?"

He crumpled the paper in his lap. "Not really. Well . . . I shouldn't say one way or the other. I haven't been reading it."

"You certainly gave a good imitation."

"One of those times when you find yourself reading the same item over and over with no comprehension."

"Anything wrong?" She became slightly apprehensive. After many satisfying years of living with each other they had grown finely tuned to the smallest signs. There was, for instance, nothing particularly noteworthy in his not paying attention to what he was reading. It happened often enough to nearly everybody. One becomes distracted and preoccupied with something—anything—and cannot concentrate on whatever is going on at the moment.

But there was something different tonight.

Georgie had been merely playful, toying with him by making up outrageous items to see what it would take to get his attention, to draw him back to reality.

But even after he shook off his reverie something was still not quite right. It was nothing anyone else would catch. But, sensitive to his every mood, she knew something was troubling him.

He hadn't answered her question. She repeated it a fraction more urgently. "Anything wrong?"

"Nothing of any importance." He paused, then realized the futility of trying to hide anything from this beloved woman. "Well, there was that meeting this morning. . . ."

"The staff meeting?"

"Yes. The special topic for discussion was the parochial school system."

"Oh?" They had discussed the topic before, more frequently recently as he and his department were drawn into bandaging this hollow giant in terminal condition.

"So many of them—the staff members—want to hold

on to the schools—even more the parishes. I think perhaps a majority agree on saving the system.''

"But it's impossible," she said. "We've talked about this before. How about Cardinal Boyle?''

The furrows in his forehead deepened. "I can't read him on this one. Ordinarily I'm pretty good at figuring out which way the wind is blowing. But not on this issue.''

"And that's critical, isn't it?''

"Absolutely. It's not that the department heads are window dressing, as they are in so many other dioceses. The Cardinal really listens to us and weighs the evidence we bring him. But in the end, he is the Cardinal Archbishop of Detroit. By law he runs everything. We go with his decision. That's all there is to it.''

Georgie thought a few moments. "If the staff is divided and you can't read the Cardinal, this thing really is up in the air.'' She now understood in more depth what was troubling him.

"If my figures are accurate, it won't be up in the air forever. The schools will close—if not now, eventually. I can see the argument that it is somewhat less painful if they go slowly, one by one. But at the same time, they're depleting chunks of money just struggling to survive.

"Some of the public schools are in almost as much trouble as we are. But they can turn to the taxpayers, and if they make a good case for their need they may get a millage increase. We have no chance there. We depend on tuition, fundraising, and parish subsidies.

"Our utility bills are high and we've got oil burners in our older buildings that have to be replaced. We've got leaky roofs and problems with asbestos." He seemed to be mentally tabulating an unending series of expenses while being too tired to continue enumerating them audibly.

After a few minutes of silence, Georgie spoke again.

"Dear, I think your problem is that you're second-guessing yourself. And that's not like you."

He reflected a moment. "You may be right. But there really is another side to this coin. We're talking about an institution—Catholic education—that began in this country in 1606. Almost four hundred years ago! And I'm recommending ending that institution." He smiled in spite of his depressed state. "Sort of like killing off the last dinosaur."

Georgie searched her mind to find facts that would support her husband's basic belief in himself and his oft-proven financial acumen. "Remember, dear, we talked just last week about the one incontrovertible reality that sealed the fate of our schools?"

"The nuns."

"Yes, the nuns. Or rather the absence of them. Whereas once nuns and teaching brothers accounted for almost a hundred percent of the staff of the parochial schools, now the figure is down to just above ten percent. And on top of that, according to what you told me last week, our lay teachers are getting about nine thousand dollars a year less than their counterparts in public schools. How can anyone hope to continue attracting quality teachers with that kind of inequity? The lay teachers we've got now are practically donating their services compared with what they could be earning in public schools. Pretty soon we won't have even the lay men and women teaching in our schools. I think it's been said best: Without the teaching Sisters no one would have given a serious thought to starting parochial schools. And without them now, there's no way for the system to survive."

His was a wry smile. "You're giving me back the figures and reasoning I gave you."

She returned his smile. "You convinced me of the rightness of your position. I thought if you heard your reasoning coming from someone else, that you'd be convinced all over again. Like I said, the trouble is you're second-guessing yourself.''

He nodded. ''You're right, of course. But I didn't realize it until just now. And there's something else, something that wasn't clear to me until just now.''

''What's that, dear?''

''The reason why I've been second-guessing myself. I don't know if I can put it into words.'' He paused to collect his thoughts. ''This is it. I think. I'm an economist—''

''And one of the best,'' she interjected.

''Thanks. I can put the dollars and cents together and come up with answers, answers I'm sure of. I can rely on the bottom line. Always have. But there's something different here. I caught it this morning at the meeting. I wasn't sure what it was. Just an added ingredient that emerged from some of the staff . . .'' He drifted off in thought.

After a few seconds, she asked, ''What is it? What possibly could make you doubt yourself?''

He smiled. ''Faith—ironically, faith.''

''Faith!''

''Yeah. The deacon, Quent Jeffrey, voiced the idea that money tends to stretch. It's an adman or PR approach. In reality, money doesn't stretch. If you're a bum and you've got sixty cents, you can get a cup of coffee. But no matter how much you want a steak dinner, you aren't going to get it with sixty cents. Jeffrey had to be talking about priorities.

''Suppose you and I wanted to add on to this house. Suppose we figured that we couldn't afford it—that we didn't have enough money to do it. But then we keep thinking and talking about it until . . . we do it. Seemingly, we've stretched our budget, we've stretched our money. In reality, the money was there, somewhere, all the while. You can't spend what you haven't got. We didn't stretch money; we changed our priorities.

''Jeffrey's suggestion might work if it were properly

implemented—which, by the way, I don't think our communications office could do. But it wouldn't work forever. Sooner or later, everyone would discover we were pouring money down a bottomless pit.''

"I don't understand," Georgie said. "What does this have to do with faith?"

"Just that I considered Deacon Jeffrey's solution iffy. '*If* this happens' and '*If* that happens,' then the system will be saved, or at least prolonged.

"That got me thinking about what some of the staff were saying during the argument that followed my suggestion to start thinking seriously about shutting the system down altogether.

"They were talking about how this was not a business or an office or a company or any other secular enterprise we were considering. These were *Catholic* schools. This was the *Christian* education of children.

"It got me thinking about when I was a kid in parochial school. There were tortuous moments. But then most kids can expect that as part of any schooling—part of growing up. And we learned a lot of things that had to be unlearned. But the formation, the discipline, the good habits, the respéct for authority, the early exposure to prayer—well, I don't think I could have gotten that whole range anywhere except in my parochial school."

"That's right, honey," Georgie said. "I can relate to that same experience in my own parochial training. But what about the money necessary to run the system?"

"That's just it, Georgie. As I listened to some of the staff—that sweet old man, Archbishop Foley—they seemed to be pleading with us to wait for . . . a miracle."

"A miracle!"

"Yes, a miracle. A miracle! This was God's work. Catholic education is God's work."

" 'God will provide'?"

"Exactly! If we can just hold on, not close any

schools or parishes, subsidize them until . . . until God solves our little problem. Georgie, I'm out of my element. I deal with currency. You can count it, bank it, know when it's turning a profit or when it's running out. I've worked at this all my life.

"But what if they're right? Money is my field. Miracles are their specialty. What if there's a miracle coming around and it doesn't get here until after I succeed in having the schools closed. I can't tell if they're right or not. What if they're right?"

Georgie could tell that he was agonizing over the problem. She was unsure of how to help him. She sent up a quick prayer for guidance. "Wasn't it someone in the Bible—was it Saint Paul in one of the Epistles?—who said something about each of us having special gifts, special talents that are complementary? Yes, I think it was Saint Paul: something about those who spoke in tongues and those who interpreted the strange words."

"So?"

"It's just as you said, dear: Miracles aren't your sphere of expertise. You're a financial whiz. And that's all your responsibility is: You give your boss, the Cardinal, your best effort to aid him in understanding what the financial situation is in the diocese. In this case, you tell him what's going on with his schools. Based on all you know—and that's why he hired you: to get the benefit of your financial advice—based on all you know, the parochial school system is in so much trouble it may well not survive. The Cardinal selected you and trusts you to give him this information.

"If someone else thinks there's reason to expect a miracle, that's their business. If you want to feel sorry for anyone, feel sorry for the Cardinal. His is the ultimate decision. He has to take all these facts, opinions, and hopes and decide what to do. Your job is to do your job." She sat back with a self-satisfied grin.

He considered what she'd said. "Sounds pretty good

to me, Georgie. But . . . I don't know. I'm going to have to think it over.''

Her worried expression returned.

He chuckled. "Now, don't look that way. You know you said just the right thing. You also know it takes me a while to absorb new ideas. That's the way it is. That's the way we are. Just give me a little while . . . to agree with you.''

They both laughed. She looked at her watch. "Just eleven o'clock.''

"Time to take Truffles out, eh?'' It was a day-ending ritual. He always took the little dog out for the final opportunity to get comfortable for the night.

"Be careful now,'' she warned. "There's ice out there. Some of the walks haven't been that well cleared. When you come in we'll have some cocoa. And I'll treat you to a back rub.''

"Well, now, you said the magic word. I was thinking of taking the beast out and never returning. But if you throw a back rub into the bargain, well, that certainly tips the scales.''

She smiled invitingly and affected a Southern accent. "Y'all hurry back . . . hear?''

He donned hat, coat, and scarf, attached the lead to Truffles' collar, and went out. Heeding his wife's advice, he negotiated the sidewalk with extra care.

She was right. As usual, she was right. But it would take a little time before he would be able to shake these guilt feelings. Similar scenarios had been played out in the past. It took him time to absorb her native wisdom. She was such a help in so many ways.

As he walked and the dog trotted, his thoughts turned to the priests who had attended this morning's meeting. From all that was said—and shouted—they were every bit as much agitated as he, if not more. But they had no loving wives in whom to confide, get it off their chests. They had no Georgie who not only could listen with love but had the wisdom to suggest the appropriate solution.

In all probability, they might be doubting themselves as much as he had second-guessed himself. What if no miracles were forthcoming? Would they accept the responsibility for wasting tons of precious resources over a dream? A dream that would never come true? They had no Georgie to tell them to cool it. Their job was to express their convictions on the matter—and they had.

In this, as in so many diocesan matters, the buck stopped at the Cardinal's desk. And, come to think of it, he too had no mate in whom to confide. Of all who most could use the companionship and wisdom of a good and loving mate, the archbishop was, perhaps, most in need.

He smiled as he contemplated Mr. and Mrs. Cardinal. The very name, Mrs. Mark Boyle, sounded alien, even incongruous.

While these thoughts engaged him, Truffles had done his duty. They turned and retraced their steps.

As he looked up the street toward his house, there seemed to be someone on the sidewalk. From a distance, the figure appeared to be standing just in front of his house.

That was strange. Was it someone waiting for him? Who? For what purpose?

It was always possible this could be a mugging. Suddenly, he wished the little dog were twenty times its size.

But it wasn't quite right for a mugging. Whoever it was, judging from the silhouette, seemed to be wearing an overcoat and a hat. Muggers don't get dressed up for an assault—at least no muggers he'd ever heard of.

If only the light were better. But the street lamp was situated several houses down from his and behind the man. What did they call that—backlighting? He approached cautiously, eyes straining to identify the figure.

Finally, when he was a step or two away, he could discern the man's features. "Well," Hoffer said, "I'll be . . . what are you doing here?"

The man said nothing. In the shadows, Hoffer could not see his right hand slowly moving upward until suddenly the gun was pointed at the underside of Hoffer's chin, only inches from his face.

There was an explosive sound as the gun was fired. Hoffer tumbled backward as if tugged by a chain. In seconds he was dead.

Truffles, frightened, began to yap. One quick blow with the gun's stock knocked the dog unconscious.

The man pocketed the gun and disappeared into the darkness.

Georgie heard the report, of course, as did her neighbors. Her first tendency was to assume it might have been a car backfiring. But if one lives in the city long enough, that innocent supposition quickly gives way to the reality of ever-present guns. In the probability that it was indeed a gun, most Detroiters had learned to duck behind something—anything. Which is what Georgie's neighbors did.

But Georgie knew Larry was out there. There was no hiding for her when her dear husband was out there unprotected.

She went to the front window, parted the curtain, and looked out, hoping not to see what she half expected to see.

Two bodies lay on the ground. She gasped, then screamed as she burst through the door, raced down the steps, and knelt to cradle the head of her dead husband.

Her neighbors heard her keening. One by one, two by two, they came to her.

The dog recovered. But he was of little use, an eyewitness who could tell the police nothing.

12 EIGHT O'CLOCK IN the morning. Not particularly early. But Zoo Tully had awakened much earlier.

He had awakened at 5:30. He'd tried to get back to sleep. It didn't work, and, as usual, the harder he tried the more sleep eluded him.

Shortly after 6:30 A.M. he gave up the struggle and slipped out of bed, careful not to waken Al. He managed not to rouse her through a shower, shave, and a hurried breakfast.

He was, of course, the first detective on his shift to arrive. There wasn't much to do. Things would not slip into gear until about 9:00 when the others on this shift arrived. So he had an hour, an hour to figure out what was troubling him.

He checked the list he'd run by his consciousness earlier while lying in bed in the darkness.

His relationship with Al? No, that wasn't it. In fact, seldom had they been happier together. Before Al, he'd been married to a very good woman. They'd had five kids. They would still be together if she hadn't been jealous of his job.

He didn't blame her. He recognized clearly that he was much more married to his job as a homicide cop than he ever could be to any woman. So his ex, now remarried and living in Chicago, was happier without him.

Oh, it was amicable. He visited his kids occasionally.

119

His former wife had made it clear that he could visit them anytime he wanted without the restrictions the divorce judge placed on visitation rights. He smiled. She was clever: She knew he would be so occupied catching the bad guys that he would seldom get to Chicago even to visit his children.

That was what was so great about Al. No games. She knew what the ground rules were and she went along. She felt almost, but not quite, as dedicated to her job as a social worker. They got on well together, were deeply in love, knew where each other's priorities lay, and—who knows?—might one day get married. No, the problem definitely was not Al.

The job: a multifaceted consideration. Over Christmas and since, there had been a veritable epidemic of flu—not "blue flu," the police version of a wildcat strike, but genuine influenza. It had hit Tully's squad particularly severely. The walking wounded had to shoulder the absentees' work loads as well as their own. That was stressful. There were the usual threats of layoffs. The city always seemed to be on the verge of bankruptcy. Somehow the police and firefighters—the ones without whom no city can get along—were always the most vulnerable when economizing measures loomed. Besides, no matter what extraneous forces were at work, he loved his job. That was a given. But there was something . . . what?

As was his daily custom, Tully collected the reports that had been filed by other squads during the previous day and night. Not every homicide lieutenant bothered with this. But then, by no means was every squad leader as completely dedicated as Tully.

The only difference in this morning's routine was that having come in so early, Tully was able to study the reports at greater leisure. Among the many reports—

From Squad Three: Wife kills husband.

Nothing particularly noteworthy about that. Officers quickly learn that the "domestic trouble" call can be the most dangerous of all to answer. Could be anything from a simple and fairly civil disagreement to murder with the attendant threat to the police when they arrive on the scene.

Now this was a little different. According to the report, the husband had a long history of drinking and abusing his wife. He should have waited a bit longer to start drinking last night. He came home dead drunk and fell into bed. She took advantage of the lull in being beaten. She sewed him within the bedsheet and whacked him to death with her high-heeled shoes. A platter case.

Tully had to smile. He wondered if the guy who wrote the report had heard the one about the wife who had beaten her husband to death. When the investigating officer asked her why she'd done it, she answered, "Because he called me a two-bit whore." Asked what she'd hit him with, she replied, "A sackful of quarters."

From Squad Five: A kid. Damn! Another kid. Twelve years old, black, on Conners near I-94. He was shoveling off the front walk of his parents' home. A car—late model Ford—passed by, didn't stop. Somebody leaned out from the passenger's side. An automatic weapon. Squeezed off ten rounds. Ten rounds as they just drove by! The kid likely was dead before he hit the ground. DOA at St. John's. No motive, no suspects. And, Tully added mentally, no hurry. Whoever shot the poor kid probably would be gunned down himself in time. In not a very long time. What a society!

The gang, such as it was, began to assemble.

First in was Phil Mangiapane. That surprised Tully.

Mangiapane sneezed, then blew his nose several times theatrically. Tully appreciated that Mangiapane was creating the groundwork for a few days' medical leave. Tully was not going to volunteer Mangiapane for any sort of disability. Nature would have to take its course, no matter how sick the sergeant was—or thought he was.

"Oh, hi, Zoo," Mangiapane said.

"Uh." Tully continued to study the reports.

From Squad Four: Victim, white, fifty-eight years old. Shot at close range in front of residence, Birchcrest north of Curtis, name Lawrence Hoffer, employee archdiocese of Detroit, head of finance and administration. No robbery. No apparent motive. No suspect.

It was as if a crucial piece of the jigsaw puzzle fell into place. That elusive something that had been troubling Tully no longer troubled him. He looked around the squad room. Mangiapane was again elaborately blowing his nose.

"Manj," Tully called out, "what was the gun used on the Donovan woman?"

Mangiapane thought. For the duration of this dialogue he forgot to blow his nose. "A nine, I think, Zoo."

"No, that's the caliber he used when he was after the nun."

"Oh, yeah. Lemmee think. Yeah, it was a .38."

"Did we get a ballistics on that one yet?"

Mangiapane turned and sorted through the files. "No, not yet, Zoo. But there was no 'urgent' marked on it. They don't usually get it in this soon."

"We need it. Hop over to the ME's office. I want the slug from a . . ." Tully consulted the report he was holding. ". . . Lawrence Hoffer."

"Lawrence Hoffer?" Mangiapane wrote the name in his notepad.

"Yeah. He got it last night. The ME will have the record, the body, and the slug. I want that slug now."

Mangiapane's face screwed into an expression of great reluctance. "Geez, Zoo, can't you send somebody else? I'm in no shape to spar with Willie Moellmann."

Tully did not look up from the report he continued to study. "If anything, Mangiapane, you are a prime candidate to see a doctor. Judging from that cough, maybe soon you'll need the ME."

"Aw, Zoo . . ."

"Besides, if you're lucky, maybe Moellmann won't have Hoffer. Maybe one of the other docs will have him."

Pouting almost like a child, Mangiapane began shrugging his huge frame into his coat and scarf. With a full head of dark hair, he never wore a hat. Which omission might have contributed to the severity of his present cold.

As the sergeant was about to leave the squad room, Tully called out one final order. "Manj, when you get the slug, I want you to take it directly to ballistics and see if they can make a match with the one that killed Helen Donovan. I want the test done now."

"Now?"

"Not even this afternoon."

"Now."

"That's right."

Mangiapane left headquarters, but not willingly. He cursed himself for not following what would have turned out to be his better judgment and calling in sick. He had been sure that with his coughing and sneezing, his red nose and stuffy head and chest, he would be treated with kid gloves at work. He might have been sent home. Which would have made him feel more justified in babying himself. At very least he had counted on staying inside all day.

Instead, here he was, monkey in the middle. Two of the most thankless jobs he could imagine were trying to hurry both the medical examiner and ballistics. Moellmann would subject him to verbal abuse, sarcasm, and humiliation. Ballistics would grouse about the burdens of the job and note that every cop wanted every report yesterday and just why did he think his case was so much more urgent than anyone else's.

All the while, Mangiapane would know that on the other side Zoo Tully would not hear of failure.

Which left Mangiapane in the middle, enduring Moellmann—who, after exacting his satisfaction, would surrender the bullet. To be followed by a bout with ballistics that could be won only through dogged determination and perseverance.

In the end, it took Mangiapane until nearly noon to get the job done. At that, he had almost gone past Tully's deadline of "this morning." Personally, Mangiapane thought he'd done yeoman's duty in completing both tasks in the space of a single day. Yet he knew that Tully would expect no less.

And so it was.

All the time Mangiapane had been gone on his rounds, Tully had been occupied with assignments, interrogations, and trying to stretch his decimated manpower.

Thus, when Mangiapane returned with his Mission Impossible report, Tully acted as if the sergeant were delivering the daily paper. Tully received the report wordlessly and gave Mangiapane another assignment, one which, fortunately, would not require his leaving the building. Mangiapane undertook the new assignment with the private resolve that he would spend the rest of the day on this one.

Tully took the report to his desk and, using the special talent that allowed him mentally to shut out every distraction, proceeded to study the findings.

He did not know, nor could he decide, whether the report spelled good or bad news, or some combination of the two.

There was no doubt: The gun that had killed Helen Donovan had been used again to kill Lawrence Hoffer. The kid Mangiapane had caught was trying to be a copycat killer.

Tully had to admit Mangiapane was taking it like a trooper. He had not apprehended the murderer of Helen Donovan after all. Still, he had prevented the murder of Joan Donovan. But it was hardly the coup he had been savoring.

Unknown to Tully, Mangiapane had not seen the report. So intent was he on getting the job done before noon, he had returned directly from ballistics with the unsealed envelope containing the findings. He did not yet know that his heroic proportions had been halved. But he would.

Now what have we? Tully wondered.

What we have is a series of questions.

Given: Somebody killed Helen Donovan, a hooker dressed as a nun, her sister. Why? Did the killer intend Helen as his victim? Or did he mistake Helen for Joan?

For a while it was thought one David Reading had killed Helen in a case of mistaken identity, then had returned to the precise scene of the crime and tried to correct his mistake by killing Joan, the real nun, but was intercepted by Mangiapane. There was even a confession—a confession Tully had distrusted from the outset. Now the confession was worthless. Reading would be tried for attempted murder, but that was it.

Of course it was possible that whoever had killed Helen had pitched the gun after the murder. And that somebody else had picked it up—and that that somebody had killed Hoffer. That was possible, but Zoo thought it entirely improbable; Zoo Tully's years of experience, his every instinct, his gut, told him that whoever owned the gun used to kill Helen didn't pitch it after the murder. He kept it. And used it to kill Lawrence Hoffer while David Reading was locked in the slammer. Zoo believed that, and he would operate under that assumption unless and until the facts proved otherwise. But he didn't think they would.

Now, the most immediate questions. Did the guy who actually killed Helen want her? He didn't come back to get the real nun. Would he have if Reading hadn't decided to be a copycat?

The guy who killed Helen also killed Hoffer. What's the connection? Was Hoffer one of Helen's clients? Her pimp? There had to be a connection. But what was it?

Joan Donovan and Lawrence Hoffer were both employed by the archdiocese of Detroit. That much Tully had learned from the investigation into the crimes against Joan and her sister as well as the report he'd read this morning on Hoffer's murder.

But there was something more. Tully played out his memory as though it were a word processor.

The evening of Helen Donovan's wake. Talking to Father Robert Koesler. Something about how well-attended the service had been when neither Tully nor Koesler had expected a crowd. Why the crowd? Ah, yes: Koesler had had the solution. Or, at least as far as Tully was concerned, what Koesler had said made sense: Sister Joan Donovan was a department head, as were many in the crowd. And many more worked for those department heads.

Now the question: Was Larry Hoffer a department head as well as Joan? That surely would be a connection.

He turned back to the report on the Hoffer killing. There it was: employee archdiocese of Detroit, *head of finance and administration*.

It was a connection. Was it *the* connection? How many other department heads were there? What, if any, connection might they have with Joan and Hoffer? Was this the beginning of open season on Catholic Church department heads? Or was it merely a coincidence?

Since the guy who killed Hoffer appeared to have failed with Sister Joan, would he be back for a second big try?

In any case, the thing Tully had most dreaded in the beginning of this investigation had come to pass: He was smack dab in the middle of the rigmarole of the Catholic Church. He who understood so little if anything about even mainline churches. And the most complex of them all, as far as he could tell, was the Catholic Church.

Tully had a sneaking hunch that the answers he was looking for—or might be looking for—were buried in that maze of ecclesial panoply and bureaucracy that was Catholicism.

Tully's next thought was much more than a hunch; it was a certainty. If this was indeed a "Catholic" case, he needed a guide to get him through this most unfamiliar territory. And he knew just who this guide was going to be.

He opened the yellow pages to the section listing churches, found "Catholic," then found St. Joseph's downtown, and dialed.

He hoped Father Koesler hadn't been kidding when he said he wasn't planning a vacation.

13 IT HAD BEEN about ten that morning when Irene Casey called Father Koesler. Larry Hoffer's murder had badly shaken her and she wanted to talk with someone. Koesler was the someone she'd selected. Did he have a little time for her?

If he hadn't, he would have made time. Irene Casey was one of his favorite people.

When he had left the *Detroit Catholic* he had recommended that Irene succeed him. Cardinal Mark Boyle had concurred. That was how Irene had become one of the earliest, if not the first, of her sex to be editor-in-chief of a weekly diocesan paper.

Over the years Koesler and Mrs. Casey had remained fast friends. With her lively sense of humor and unfailingly thoughtful kindness it would have been difficult not to like her.

Under her leadership, the *Detroit Catholic* was very much a middle-of-the-road publication, which supplied her with enemies on the right as well as on the left. These enemies were not unlike those Cardinal Boyle attracted. Koesler felt strongly that none of these people understood or appreciated either Irene or the Cardinal.

When Irene arrived at St. Joseph's rectory, Koesler ushered her into the spacious kitchen. It was not the most appropriate room in the house in which to entertain. But it was the warmest area in this old, old building, and it was a very cold day.

As soon as they entered the kitchen, Irene, familiar

with the room from previous visits, began to make coffee. It was not so much that she yearned for coffee—although the warmth would be welcome; it was just that she felt it necessary to beat Koesler to the punch. As often as it occurred to her, she wondered why he consistently made such atrocious coffee. It wasn't that difficult to make good coffee, but somehow he always found a way to botch it.

When they were finally settled at the kitchen table with their coffee mugs, she began filling Koesler in on what was happening backstage in the archdiocese. Little of what she told him was news to Koesler. His contacts were not identical to but were easily as good as hers. As Irene talked, he wondered again at all the confidential information this lady had. She knew where nearly all the Church skeletons were buried. But she would undoubtedly take all that juicy gossip to her grave rather than publish any of it. No wonder she had endeared herself to Cardinal Boyle.

Then she gave Koesler a blow-by-blow account of yesterday morning's staff meeting. As she launched into the account, he offered a quiet prayer of thanksgiving that he no longer had to attend those meetings.

He was not surprised at the opinions expressed at the meeting. He could have predicted the position taken by each of the speakers.

Sister Joan was committed to the core city—enough to live there, which was a major step beyond those who expressed concern while staying so far removed they could scarcely find the city. She was sure to fear the elitism that would mark the closing of inner-city schools while the financially more secure suburban institutions stayed open.

And Clete Bash was the type who would see nothing wrong with that.

Everybody knew that Monsignor Del Young was holding on for dear life to Old Faithful. He had to be superintendent of something. Odds had it that if Del survived until retirement, he wouldn't give a damn what happened to the system after that. Or anything else for that matter.

Koesler also could have foretold the fine public relations touch contributed by Quent Jeffrey. He probably could make his approach work. Whereas Clete would fumble it without doubt.

And what else could a money man conscientiously recommend other than cutting the losses and closing the marginal schools that had no choice but to drain the coffers of everything in sight?

The single item that did surprise Koesler was Larry Hoffer's suggestion to close down the entire parochial school system. In all his private ruminations as well as the bull sessions with his confreres, Koesler had never given serious consideration to closing everything. He would have to think that one over.

Irene described in detail the ruckus that followed Hoffer's proposal.

The shadow of a smile crossed Koesler's lips when she described Cardinal Boyle's futile attempts to mediate for moderation. Koesler could remember watching that process innumerable times. Boyle twisting his bishop's ring, toying with his pectoral cross, inching forward in his chair, clearing his throat, gaining the floor, achieving peace for the moment, only to see all his efforts gurgle down the drain.

"I've seen some unruly meetings," Irene concluded, "but nothing like this. Some of them—some of the priests even—went . . . berserk! That's the only word for it!"

"Yes, but Irene, couldn't you almost expect something like that?" Koesler countered. "I mean, that is a volatile topic. Larry Hoffer scarcely could have said anything that would ruffle feathers more than suggesting that we abandon our school system."

"You weren't there!"

"No, but your description was graphic. I might just as well have been there.

"Irene, I don't know; there may come a day when the parochial school system will be a mere historical oddity. And maybe that time is now—or soon—I just don't know. I must confess I've never given any serious thought to what it would be like having no parish schools. But I think when it happens, or *if* it happens, that they're all closed, the finale will be not a whimper but an explosion. So I guess I can't get overly excited that Hoffer's proposal was greeted as you describe it."

"Okay. But the point is, I remember thinking at the time that the emotion that came out in that room was close to violence!"

Koesler smiled briefly in disbelief. "You mean you thought they were actually going to fight? I mean, physically?"

"A couple of times, I thought some of them were close to doing just that!"

"Irene, I don't think—"

"And then," she interrupted, "I had this premonition that something violent, something terrible was going to happen. I really did!"

Koesler could tell that she was on the verge of tears. "I see," he said, "and then . . ."

"And then this had to happen. Larry was . . . was . . ."

". . . murdered." Koesler could tell she couldn't bring herself to say the word. "But what about—"

"What," she interrupted again, "what if the murder was caused, or occasioned, or triggered by something said at the meeting?"

"Irene . . ." Koesler touched her hand gently. "Irene, come on! You and I know these people. They're priests and nuns and dedicated laypeople. They're Church people. They may have their disagreements, and sometimes those disagreements may be deeply felt. But they're not . . . I mean, I've been at these meetings too, before you, and I've seen how deeply they feel, how much they have invested of themselves in their work, how affected they are when their territory or interests are threatened. But they wouldn't . . . not one of them would. . . ."

"Then how do you explain it? I thought we were done with this horror when the police caught that David Reading person. After Sister Joan's sister was murdered and Sister was almost murdered herself . . . that was so horrible. But it was over. It was done. They caught the killer. Now . . ."

"Irene, they *did* catch the man. It *is* over. Believe it. This is tragic; there's no doubt about that. But it's not connected. As much as we'd like it to be otherwise, living in this city has its dangerous aspect. There's no getting around it. Larry was probably the victim of a random mugging. A mugging that went too far. It's tragic. But it could have happened to anyone. It just happened to be Larry Hoffer."

Irene seemed to be drawing some consolation and reassurance from Koesler's explanation. "Then you don't think . . ."

"Not for a moment. And you shouldn't either. Of course we're saddened by this thing. That's natural. But we've got to go on."

"I . . . I guess you're right. It's just that I witnessed . . . I saw how angry some of the people at that meeting were. And most of the anger was directed at Larry. And then when I heard this morning that he'd been killed . . ."

"I guess it was only natural. You were sort of primed to link the two, the argument and the hostility, with what happened to Larry. But, think a bit. Who? Which one of those people at the staff meeting could have done it? Can you think of a single person there who might actually be capable of murder?"

Irene gave it brief consideration. "I . . . suppose not.

But then I never focused on any specific individual. It was just so coincidental.''

"That's it, Irene: coincidence. An eerie coincidence. Natural.''

Mary O'Connor stepped apologetically into the kitchen. "Excuse me, there's someone on the phone for you, Father.''

"Did you get a name?''

"Yes, a Lieutenant Tully with the police department.''

Koesler did a quick appraisal of Irene Casey. She seemed more at peace than she had been earlier. He wasn't sure his words had completely calmed her but they had been a help. No doubt about that. He felt he could accept the call. So, thanking Mary and excusing himself to Irene, he picked up the phone near the refrigerator. Irene could not help overhearing Koesler's side of the conversation.

"Yes, I remember Lieutenant . . . yes, at the funeral home.

"You want to come here? Well . . .

"Well, I was going to ring some doorbells. The Lafayette Towers complex . . . 1300 . . . just check in with some of the people who live in my parish. There hasn't been much evangelization carried on in this parish in recent years and . . . yes, evangelization . . .

"Well, it's a kind of recruitment . . . I guess I could postpone it for just this afternoon if you think I can be of some help, but I don't—

"Sure. Okay. I know you're practically next door. But could you delay just a few minutes? I'm with somebody now and . . .

"Okay. I'll see you in a little while.'' He hung up.

"You're having company? Now?'' Irene asked.

"Lieutenant Tully. He's with the Homicide Department. He wanted to see me. But don't feel you have to rush off. He won't be here for a few minutes.''

"No, no, we're done. It's okay. You've been a big

help," Irene responded. "Actually, just being able to talk to someone, express my fears, did the trick, I think."

Thanks a heap, thought Koesler. *Nothing I said helped.* It was the talking cure again. Koesler had seen it work any number of times, especially in confession— or the sacrament of reconciliation as it was now called. "Well," he said, "if you're sure . . . really, there's no hurry."

Irene rose, left the table, and went directly to the cupboard.

Koesler smiled. "What in the world are you up to, Irene?"

"Just going to make a pot of coffee before I go."

"No need for that, Irene. I can do it. No trouble."

"No, you're going to have an important visitor and you'll want to serve him some coffee. Or at least offer it to him. I can get it done in a jiffy."

"Well, if you insist. Thanks."

Some day, thought Irene, the right moment will come to tell him about his coffee. Maybe even teach him how to make it. For now, she was reluctant to expose her friend's culinary failing to a stranger.

She made the coffee and left, confident that she had saved Father Koesler from embarrassment. And the policeman from a taste worse than gall.

14

"GOOD COFFEE," TULLY observed.

"Thanks." Koesler saw no reason to explain that someone else had made the coffee. The fact that Irene Casey had brewed it was irrelevant and immaterial, as the movies had them say in court.

Mary O'Connor had admitted Tully just a few minutes ago. She'd led him to the kitchen, whose comparative coziness Koesler preferred on a cold and windy day such as this.

A few initial questions from Tully elicited the fact that the kitchen, cozy as it was, was not what he would term secure. The secretary, the janitor, or any number of others might drift in at any time. So, at the officer's insistence, the two had repaired to Koesler's office, where the wind whistled through the closed but drafty windows.

Tully simply acclimated himself, a skill he had cultivated so assiduously he had become adept at it. As for Koesler, he hovered over his coffee for warmth.

"Father," Tully began, "I'm going to tell you something that hasn't been made public just yet: The gun that killed Helen Donovan was also used to kill Lawrence Hoffer."

"What?" Few things surprised Koesler anymore, but this certainly did. "I thought you arrested the man who killed Helen."

"So did we. That's what we thought. But there was a hole in that case. Not big enough to drive a truck

135

through, but a hole anyway. The same gun was not used in the murder of Helen Donovan and in the attempt on her sister. Of course it was always possible, for lots of reasons, that he might have used different guns. But it isn't likely he actually did.''

"But I thought the man confessed!''

Tully shrugged. "It happens. There are people out there who confess to things they didn't do.''

"I don't understand.'' Koesler looked pained. "I thought it was all over.''

"That would have been nice. But it didn't work that way. Now, Father, what I've told you so far is being released to the news media. But I'm going to tell you more of the details, facts that won't be given to the media. I'll have to ask you not to reveal them.''

Koesler did not reply.

"Father?'' Tully pressed.

"Oh, oh, certainly.'' All he could think of was that he had just assured Irene Casey that this madness was over. What would she think now? Then another thought occurred. "But why are you telling me, Lieutenant?''

"Because we could use your help on this case, and for you to help us you've got to know what we're working with.''

"But why not tell the media everything? Wouldn't that help in apprehending the man?''

Tully noted that Koesler had used the masculine noun in referring to the perpetrator. Did Koesler know something? Through the confessional? Likely it was no more than the natural tendency to link men rather than women to murder. Nonetheless it was noted. But to Koesler's question. "The problem with that is that it encourages copycat murderers, like what probably happened with David Reading, the guy who almost got the nun.''

"Oh, very well then. Certainly. I'll keep what you tell me in confidence.''

"Good. By the way, I checked out using you and letting you know what we've got with your friend Inspector Koznicki. He gave me the green light. So it's official.''

"Certainly.''

Koesler had given up all thought of drinking his coffee. He was now clutching it for survival. If this conversation was going to go on much longer, he was going to need a coat. Maybe a hat.

Tully leaned forward. ''About the only hard information we've got so far has to do with the weapon. We know the gun used to kill Helen Donovan was a .38 caliber. We know because we retrieved the slug. More on that in a bit. The gun we took from Reading was a nine caliber. The theory was that after Reading killed Helen, thinking she was Joan, he had no further use for the .38 so he got rid of it. Then, when he found out he'd missed his target, killed the wrong woman, he couldn't recover the .38, for whatever reason. Unfortunately, that explanation was suggested to Reading during interrogation, and he agreed to it as part of his 'confession.' That's when we thought we had everything wrapped up.

''Then came the murder of Lawrence Hoffer. I suspected there might be a connection because both Joan Donovan and Hoffer were part of the administration of the local Catholic Church. And that proved to be correct. We compared the slugs that killed the Donovan woman and Hoffer and—they matched.''

''And,'' Koesler said, ''at the time Larry was killed Mr. Reading was already locked up.''

''Correct. Now, let me tell you something about the ammo used 'cause it tells us quite a bit about the killer,'' Tully said.

''The bullets were 158 grain, half-jacketed, flatnosed, down-loaded .38 caliber. Does that have any significance for you, or mean anything special?''

Koesler shook his head.

''Not familiar with guns?''

Koesler shook his head again.

"Okay," Tully said. "This kind of bullet is ordinarily used for target practice. Particularly because of its flat nose, it makes a nice, neat round hole in the paper target. That way it's easy to see where all the bullets hit the target even if more than one bullet hits almost the same spot. Okay?"

Koesler nodded.

"Okay. Now, when this kind of bullet—one with all the specifications I mentioned—is fired point-blank into, say, a person's head—the way Donovan and Hoffer were hit—something very specific happens.

"Because it's down-loaded, it's not likely to exit the body, the head. Because it's half-jacketed, it holds together; it doesn't expand when it hits its target. Because it's flat-nosed and doesn't exit the body, it causes one hell of a lot of damage." Tully looked expectantly at Koesler. "See?"

Koesler pondered for a moment. "Not really."

"Okay." There was no good reason why a priest inexperienced in ballistics should grasp the significance of what the perpetrator intended. But he had hoped Koesler's deductive powers would be sharper. Still, Tully reminded himself, he had sought Koesler's input because of his familiarity with things Churchy, not because he might be able to interpret a murderer's mind.

"What this comes down to," Tully explained, "is that, one, the killer wants to finish his victim with a single sure shot. So he uses a flat-noser that will do a maximum amount of damage in the victim's head.

"Two, it's down-loaded, so it will remain within the victim—so we'll have no trouble finding the slug.

"Three, it's half-jacketed, so it holds together and we'll be able to easily make the ballistics comparison and identify the slugs as coming from the same gun." Tully stopped and again looked expectantly at Koesler.

"So," Koesler said, thoughtfully, "the killer is being careful to make certain that you are able to recognize when it is he who is operating. Other people would be able to use a .38 in the commission of a crime, in a murder. But he alone owned and operated the gun that killed Helen and Larry."

It was Tully's turn to nod.

"And if there were a copycat killer around," Koesler continued, "he would know from what you released to the news media that you had proof from ballistics that the same gun was used to kill Helen and Larry. And since only the police knew what ballistics showed, there was no point in trying to copy the murder."

"And . . ." Tully prompted.

"And . . ." Koesler repeated, then thought for a moment. ". . . and you are also sending a message to the killer that you understand what he is trying to tell you in his peculiar selection of the bullets he's using."

Tully thought there might be hope for this man.

"This," Koesler continued, "reminds me of some of the other homicide cases I've been involved with." Pause for further thought. "Now, I don't want to appear ungrateful that you bothered to take me all through this . . . but I'm still in the dark about how I can possibly help you."

Tully looked away as he spoke. "We know a murderer has struck twice in a very definitive pattern. He may prove to be—if he is not already qualified as—a serial killer. With the murder of Lawrence Hoffer, it becomes far more likely that his first intended victim was Joan—not Helen—Donovan. The only connection, as far as we are able to tell just now—for want of a stronger connection—is the rank Joan and Hoffer hold in the Church structure. Quite frankly"—he looked at Koesler—"we don't know where he goes from here.

"He may be done. If he is, what he has accomplished is not at all clear. And I get the impression, from the pains he's taken to help us recognize the slugs, that he wants to make his purpose clear—very clear."

"So, where does he go from here?"

Tully paused. Koesler deemed the question unanswerable.

"Does he go back to first base?" Tully asked finally.

"You mean Sister Joan Donovan? Is it possible the poor woman's life is still in danger?" Koesler asked. "After all she's gone through?"

Tully shrugged. "If it's a case of mistaken identity, then he killed the wrong woman. The 'right' woman is still out there. Alive. Or . . ."

"Or?"

"Or . . . something else. What? We don't know. And this is where you come in."

"I don't—"

Tully cut in. "I find myself in a tightly specialized territory: department heads in a Catholic Church structure, the administration of the archdiocese of Detroit. I might as well be in the middle of a maze."

Koesler could see the difficulty. This structure—"the staff"—with which he was so familiar could easily intimidate one who was a stranger to it. "What can I do?"

"For starters, give me a map so's I can feel a little more at home in this maze."

Koesler smiled. So absorbed had he become in the business at hand that he no longer felt the cold. "Okay. For starters, here's the basic chart." He opened a desk drawer and drew out an 8½ × 11 brochure consisting of just four pages.

"And that . . . ?" Tully asked.

". . . is a phone directory fo archdiocesan department numbers, along with the business phone numbers of just about everybody who works in the administration."

Tully looked interested. He slid his chair closer.

Koesler looked up from the brochure to see Tully separated from him only by the width of the desk. He turned the brochure around so it was facing Tully. The priest opened the brochure and began to explain as he ran his finger through the listings. "Now, these are—"

"You can read upside down?"

Koesler grinned. "A leftover of my days as editor of the *Detroit Catholic*. They were still using Linotypes back then, and when they put the type in the galley it was upside down and backward. If you wanted to find something before they ran a proof of it, you had to get used to reading things upside down. It's not a skill that comes in handy every day, but now and then . . ."

"Um," Tully said, creating the impression that Koesler's explanation was more than was needed to understand a marginal accomplishment.

"Anyway," Koesler proceeded, "the important part is right here . . ." He outlined the area with his finger. "All the archdiocesan departments are listed in alphabetical order, with the exception of the first listing."

"The Cardinal's office," Tully read. "The big boss comes first. Makes sense."

"Yes, outside of the Pope himself, the Cardinal is the big boss. Now, the abbreviations in the parentheses are simple. Opposite the Cardinal's office you see (C2), which means the Chancery Building, second floor. The other abbreviations are (G), the Gabriel Richard Building, just on the southwest side of Michigan Avenue and Washington Boulevard—"

"Yeah, I know where it is."

"Sorry."

"No, no; don't leave anything out," Tully insisted. "Anything you can think of, say."

"Okay. The only other abbreviation besides the Chancery and Gabriel Richard Buildings is SHS, which stands for Sacred Heart Seminary. Know where that is?"

"Chicago Boulevard?"

"And Linwood. That's it."

"Good God," Tully exclaimed as he ran his finger

down the columns, "there must be . . . seventy-three offices!"

Koesler was smiling. "The bureaus do tend to grow like Topsy. But it's not as complicated as all that. You're counting each and every office. There aren't that many actual departments. Just count the listings that are flush with the left margin."

Tully did. "Twenty-two. Not much better."

Koesler shrugged. "There's no helping it. That's how many there are. And I must confess, I don't know a great deal about many of these offices."

"That's okay." Tully studied the listings for several minutes. "I can get my people to call on all the offices listed here and get that straightened out. For now, tell me what you can about the people who head these departments."

"A big order."

"But you know them."

"Pretty well."

"Well, take the ones who got us started on this: the nun and Hoffer."

"Sister Joan Donovan? Right. She belongs to a religious order, the Sisters, Servants of the Immaculate Heart of Mary—or IHMs. They're a teaching order. And that's what Sister Joan did, for many years: taught. Then things began to change. Because of a Church council called Vatican II."

"Okay. I've read about that. What happened to her?"

"Like lots of other nuns, she stopped teaching and went into another line of work. In her case, Joan got into parish ministry—working in a parish, doing a lot of things priests used to do back when there were lots of priests."

"Holding Sunday services?"

"Not Mass. Sometimes when there's no priest around, nuns or even laypeople conduct prayer services. But Mass is much more than that for Catholics. Only a priest can offer Mass. But Sister Joan did lots of other things, like counseling and visiting the sick and, of course, some office work too.''

"But how did she get to be . . . what?"

"Delegate for religious?"

"Yeah."

"Appointed. Kind of elected. But basically appointed. The powers that be recognized that she was popular with many of the nuns. They realized that she'd have to be effective as, in effect, their representative. Then, for formality, the Cardinal appointed her to the position."

"She could have made some enemies among the nuns?"

"Enemies?"

"It's not a friend who wants to kill her."

"Oh, I don't think that's very likely."

"Okay, how about Hoffer?"

"That's something else. Assigning a job like his to a layperson is a very recent phenomenon. In the not-too-distant past, positions like that were always handled by priests. Probably not as well as they are now," he added.

"Not as well?" Tully was surprised. "The priests weren't trained for specialized jobs?"

Koesler pondered the question before responding. "Sometimes yes, sometimes no. When an academic degree was called for, priests were sent away to get the appropriate certificate. Social workers, for instance, got an MSW. Or priests who were assigned to teach in the seminary were sent to graduate school, although sometimes in a field that didn't interest them.

"Or take my case: I was named editor of the *Detroit Catholic*. No academic degree was required, so I got none. Matter of fact, after my appointment was published, a priest friend called and asked if the archdiocese had spent a penny getting me ready for the job. I had to admit he was right in his assumption—not a cent.

Then he said''—Koesler chuckled—'' 'Well, it won't be your fault when you flop.' ''

The faintest trace of a smile crossed Tully's face.

"Even more peculiar," Koesler continued, ''—and you may find this hard to believe—but in most of the special assignments, the priests didn't want them in the first place.

"You see, all these men I've been talking about, they all went to a diocesan seminary to become parish priests. That was their choice. If they had wanted to be social workers, if they had wanted to be teachers, they wouldn't have gone to an institution that exclusively turned out parish priests. If I had wanted a career on a newspaper, I'd've gone to Marquette or the University of Missouri. I would have gotten a job at a newspaper.''

"Seems like a funny way to run a railroad.''

"We did what we were told. But back to Larry Hoffer, God rest him—''

"Excuse me," Tully interrupted, "but before you get into that, could we have another shot of that coffee?''

"Certainly.'' Koesler rose and picked up both mugs. "I'll be right back.''

Fortunately, Irene Casey had made more than enough for refills. Thus saving Lieutenant Tully from a memorable but awful experience.

15

WHILE TULLY WAITED for Father Koesler to return with the coffee, the lieutenant let his concentration relax a notch.

He studied the room. Real wood paneling with meticulous detail. This was an old, old house. He reflected that Koesler, and, he supposed, all priests—at least the ones Koesler called parish priests—lived where they worked. Not many people did that anymore. In a situation like this, the demand on one's time went on around the clock.

Although he himself did not live where he worked, Tully thought wryly, he worked where he lived. And it was to her everlasting credit that Alice recognized that and tolerated it. All too frequently, he took his work home with him in the form of reports, assignment rosters, or just a preoccupation with a case he happened to be investigating. Had he been required to punch a time clock, in all truth he scarcely ever would punch out.

Tully was a dedicated cop. None could deny that. In fact, very few officers cared to match his dedication.

Yet, as he thought on it, he figured that most priests would have to be as dedicated to their calling as he was to his. The very condition of working and living in the same space, especially in a service occupation where people sought help at any hour of the day or night, demanded close to total dedication.

He'd never before looked at it in this light. But then,

to date, he'd seldom thought about priests. If he were a prayerful man—which he most definitely was not—he would have prayed that he would never again get involved in a homicide case that had any religious overtones whatsoever. Immediately after that nonprayer, Koesler returned with two steaming mugs of—blessedly—Irene's coffee.

"Now, where were we?" Koesler said as he settled into his chair. "Oh, yes: Larry Hoffer, God rest his soul." He took a sip of coffee, set his cup down, and thought for a minute. "Larry was a good example of what seems to be happening more and more these days. A growing number of men and women are turning to some sort of Church work after they retire from their secular careers. More men than women—although I think that will even up as women's careers more nearly match men's. The problem, of course, is that the Church can't match the salaries and benefits offered out in the world.

"Anyway, Larry Hoffer had a brilliant career in the comptroller's department at Ford Motor Company. When he was nearing retirement, he decided he wanted to do something for the Church before finally retiring.

"Needless to say, he was a great catch for the Detroit archdiocese. Cardinal Boyle hired him immediately. Of course we couldn't match what he earned at Ford. But he wasn't so much interested in the final buck as he was in contributing his talents to the Church.

"Fortunately, the position of head of finance and administration was open when Larry offered his services, and he moved right in. He's done a magnificent job, as everyone knew he would. Until . . . until . . ."

"Was he married?"

"Yes. Poor woman. I didn't know her but I will certainly pray for her. Come to think of it, Larry's situation is very much like Quent Jeffrey's."

"Humm?"

"Quentin Jeffrey. A deacon—head of the deacon program."

"A deacon? The Baptists got deacons, as I recall." Tully's comprehension was threatening to disintegrate. "This may be more than my mind can handle."

Koesler could sympathize. "Lieutenant, it seems confusing because we're dealing with the bureaucratic Church. It gets simpler as it gets down to just people."

"We are, unfortunately, where we've got to be," Tully said. "Whoever killed the Donovan woman and Hoffer, if he's messing with department heads, may know as much as you do about the top echelon. He sure as hell knows more than I do. Continue, please. What about deacons? What about Jeffrey?"

"Deacons go back a long way. All the way back to the Bible. When the infant Christian Church began to grow, the apostles found that they couldn't do it all. So they appointed 'seven holy deacons.' The rank goes back that far! For centuries, men—and men only—in their progress toward priesthood were ordained to the functions that, in earlier times, had been full-time jobs in the Church. In the ceremony called tonsure—a cutting of hair—" Koesler explained, "the man became a cleric.

"Then," Koesler continued, his explanation interspersed with subexplanations, "followed four 'minor' orders: porter (janitor), lector (reader), exorcist (caster-out of demons), and acolyte (a server at the altar). The 'major' orders were subdiaconate—which included the obligations of celibacy and daily recitation of the monastic hours of prayer, or the breviary; diaconate—the first step into the sacrament of Holy Orders; and finally, the priesthood.

"The order fell out of practical use some centuries ago. Until very recently, nobody remained a deacon. It became merely a step you took on your way to becoming a priest. Then we started running out of priests, and what was called the 'permanent diaconate' was re-established. Now, in the post-conciliar Church, the diaconate has also been made available to men who choose to remain in that office, without intention of progressing to priesthood.''

''Why would the Church do that?''

''Because a deacon can do almost everything a priest does—baptize, preach, witness marriages—everything except saying Mass and absolving from sin.''

''But what's the advantage? For the deacons, I mean: If they can do *almost* everything, why not just become priests?''

''Deacons can be married.''

''Oh.'' Tully almost asked a follow-up question but thought better of it.

''Now,'' Koesler continued, ''what got me started on Quent was the similarity between his background and Larry Hoffer's. Both men were significantly successful in their lay careers. Larry a financial wizard prized by Ford, and Quent with his public relations firm, Jeffrey, Smith and Allan . . . maybe you remember them?''

Tully thought briefly. ''Yeah . . . didn't they do a lot in politics?''

''Uh-huh.''

''I remember: Jeffrey used to sit in on WJR on election nights predicting the results. He was pretty accurate. Good-looking dude.''

''Still is. But the election business was only part of what he did. Then, like Larry, he decided to leave the public arena and devote his talents to the Church. So he became a deacon. And because he was so talented, the Cardinal asked him to guide the program. Even though it goes all the way back to the Bible, for us, now, it's a relatively new game.''

''And,'' Tully tested his understanding of the matter, ''Jeffrey became a deacon and not a priest because he was married.''

''That's about the size of it. But now, unfortunately, he's a widower.''

Tully raised an eyebrow.

"His wife died of cancer a while back. It was tragic."

Tully mulled that over. "But he'll probably marry again. He's still young and he's still a good catch."

"No, he won't marry again."

"You seem pretty sure of that."

"He can't marry again. Church law makes it impossible for men who are deacons or priests to marry. In so many words it just says clerics in major orders cannot contract matrimony."

"But you just said—"

"There is no second marriage allowed after one becomes a deacon or a priest. There is no marriage allowed for men who are going to become priests."

"Say again?"

"Young men who go to a seminary to become Catholic priests know that they will never be permitted to marry if they go on to ordination. If a priest marries, he is no longer authorized to function as a priest. If a man is unmarried when he goes into the permanent diaconate, he never will be allowed to marry. Some men who are ordained in Protestant faiths, like Episcopalians and Lutherans, and who are already married, are allowed to become Catholic priests if they convert to Catholicism. They may remain married, but, like the permanent deacons, if they become widowers, they are not allowed to remarry.

"Now there are some extenuating circumstances, for instance if there are small children involved who really need a mother as they mature. But there are none of these extenuating circumstances in Quent Jeffrey's case. He will never be permitted to marry again. But of course he knew that going in."

Tully decided to ask the follow-up question he had rejected a moment before. "Just what do you guys have against sex and marriage?"

Koesler's first impulse was to laugh at the provocative exaggeration implicit in the question. But on quick reflection, he decided to take Tully's question quite seriously on face value. What was the saying—If only we could see ourselves as others see us?

"One could argue," Koesler said, "that we haven't got anything against sex and marriage. People who have gone through our matrimonial court trying to get a judgment that will declare their marriage null and void could assure you that we are extremely serious about marriage. As for sex, the teaching is that it finds its place within marriage."

The two regarded each other, each knowing Koesler's argument could be considered extremely shallow.

Nonetheless the priest forged on. "But I suppose you're referring to the laws regarding marriage for the clergy."

"That's what I had in mind."

"Lieutenant, I can only tell you what my experience has been. I attended the seminary in the forties and fifties. I became a priest in 1954, which was eleven years before that famous Church council was concluded. I spent the maximum number of years— twelve—preparing for the priesthood. All of us in the seminary wanted very, very much to become priests. It was made crystal clear that among the requirements was that if we were ordained we'd never marry. It was something you accepted and stayed in or rejected and left. It was no surprise. Adding credibility to the whole thing was the fact that in those days almost nobody left the priesthood. A priest who left and got married was looked on pretty much as a notorious sinner."

"But I got the impression lots have left and married."

"True. Another result of that remarkable council. Lots of the guys became convinced the rules of the game had been changed. There was a new way of looking at the priesthood, the laity, the Church, and marriage. As a result of this new vision they had, they couldn't see any good reason why they couldn't be married and still be priests.

"But the Church didn't see it that way. If they were determined to marry then they couldn't function as priests. Not that everybody who left did so specifically to get married. But most did."

Tully thought that over. "But why the rule? Ministers get married. Rabbis get married. Why not priests?"

"That is truly tough. It's been a long while since I studied the history of celibacy. Jesus, of course was not married. But tradition tells us that all the apostles with the exception of John and Paul were. As I recall, there were a few attempts at getting an unmarried clergy early on, but it never took hold. After a while there was a problem with married priests willing their church properties to their children—thus taking some extremely valuable properties out of the hands of the Church. But it was not till the twelfth century that the Church simply made a law rendering each attempted marriage by a cleric in major orders invalid. And it's been that way ever since.

"But let me have a question, Lieutenant: Why this interest in married and celibate priests? What's it got to do with your investigation?"

"Okay. A big part of what I'm lookin' for is conflict, a grudge, resentment—things, emotions, that could become motives for violence, for murder. I thought I'd find something here, and I think I have. These guys who had to quit the Church . . ."

"Wait," Koesler interrupted. "If you're talking about priests who get married, they don't leave the Church. They may leave the priesthood, but they are not forced to leave the Church."

"Corrected."

"It's a common enough mistake."

"Okay," Tully said, "but they do have to quit bein' priests if they get married . . . right?"

"In effect, yes. They are not allowed to function as

priests—do what they'd done as priests—unless there's some sort of emergency.''

"The point I'm getting at," Tully explained, "is that they could be pretty sore about that. You tell me that bein' priests is just about the only thing they ever wanted to do. Then this council happened and, if I've got you correctly, the rules of the game changed.''

"A lot of people perceived it that way."

"You?"

Koesler hesitated. "Yes."

"Now, through no fault of their own—at least they can look at it that way—they can't be priests anymore. Just because they want to be married.''

"Some of my former confreres certainly see it that way."

"Then they could be pretty angry about this. Angry enough, maybe to want some sort of revenge.''

"I find that hard to imagine. Besides, why would anyone who felt that way strike out against two innocent people like Sister Joan and Larry Hoffer? They didn't have anything to do with the Vatican Council or the laws that create a celibate clergy. Or even the laws that allow some of the clergy—deacons and converted ministers—to marry and still function as clergymen.''

Tully drained his cup. "Who are they going to shoot, the Pope?''

"It's been done."

"Let me put it this way: If they were to shoot the Pope—kill him this time—would it change the rules?''

Koesler did not need to reflect on that question at all. "No, probably not. Another Pope would most likely not change a thing, especially on the question of a celibate clergy.''

Tully shrugged. "Then it might make some sort of sense to get a kind of revenge wherever somebody could. It might make some sort of sense—to a very disturbed mind.''

In the silence that followed Tully's statement, the ticking of the grandfather clock could be clearly heard.

Tully was again reminded how very old this structure was.

At length, Koesler said, "In all fairness, Lieutenant, former priests are not the only Catholics with an ax to grind. Particularly if you're looking at this from the viewpoint of a disturbed mind."

"That's what I want to hear. Go ahead."

Koesler paused. Then he said, slowly, "There are so many, I'm ashamed to say. And yes, the council brought out most of them." He sighed. "There are those thousands upon thousands of parents who had a dozen or so children—if you go back far enough, and it's not that far—because sexual abstinence was the one and only acceptable form of birth control. Then, in the fifties, the Church approved the rhythm method, which didn't work all that well in many cases. Nowadays, while abstinence and rhythm are still the only officially accepted methods of family planning, only the Pope, the bishops, and very few others believe this."

"So?"

"So, all those people who had kids every nine or so months or suffered with the guilt of serious sin if they used birth control could be extremely angry. Once again the rules of the game changed, and changed drastically, for their children and grandchildren.

"Then—holy cow, there are so many! Like all those people who became converts to Catholicism before the council! I gave instructions to a lot of them. They became members of a Church that changed like the ground moving beneath them. They accepted doctrines and moral directives—in some cases with a lot of reluctance—only to see them subsequently questioned, reexamined, and reinterpreted by responsible theologians. They could be very angry.

"Many Catholics in the archdiocese of Detroit are angry specifically with the archdiocese of Detroit. Our archbishop lives in the eye of a hurricane, and his space is shrinking all the time. Some wish he would cut through all the red tape and allow inactive priests to function again. Or officially expand the permissible means of family planning. Or admit that there may be circumstances—rare but potential—for a licit abortion.

"Or, on the other side, they want the Cardinal to discipline outspoken priests and nuns. They want him to enforce the most restrictive interpretations of Church rules, laws, and dictates. They want everything returned to where everything was before the council and the sixties happened. And, as someone remarked, that's about as possible as getting toothpaste back in the tube. But they want and demand it anyway. And they can get very angry when it doesn't happen."

Koesler paused. Tully could guess that the priest was struggling with some sort of difficult decision. He decided to help resolve the quandary. "Remember, Father, this is a homicide investigation. I need every bit of information I can get. Maybe even to save some lives that might be taken if we don't get this perpetrator soon."

Koesler decided. "You're right, of course." He then related what had happened at the staff meeting, leaving out no detail that Irene Casey had narrated, and including his own insights on the outspoken players in that scene.

"So," Koesler concluded, "you can see that tension is running pretty high, even—I might say especially— at the top level of administration in the archdiocese. It is strange that the crisis in that meeting was triggered by what Larry Hoffer proposed. Now, I think it far-fetched to suggest that Larry's proposal to, in effect, end parochial education in the archdiocese was the cause of his being murdered. Unless it might have been the straw that did it.

"My reason for telling you of the meeting was only to fill you in on the level of tension and crisis going on in the Church. If you're looking for reasons and suspects for the murder of Larry Hoffer and the apparently mistaken murder of Helen Donovan, there are lots of reasons and lots of potential suspects."

"Amen," Tully added uncharacteristically.

Tully now had many more leads, ideas, and questions than when he had walked into St. Joseph's rectory just a short time ago. Expressing gratitude and reserving the option of more questions as they arose in the investigation, he left Koesler to his ringing of doorbells and—what was it?—evangelizing.

Father Koesler donned hat, coat, and boots. On the surface, it seemed odd that one would go out recruiting on a Saturday—particularly on New Year's Eve. But it was St. Paul who said the work of the Lord must be done "in season and out of season."

16 ARNOLD CARSON STOOD at his "window" behind the long counter. He was among the few not bleary-eyed this Tuesday morning after the New Year's holiday. His postal uniform reflected the care he gave it—cleaned, pressed, even a touch of starch. Carson was inordinately proud of his employment: the United States Postal Service, the best of its kind in the world. If it were not for Catholicism—the genuine, pre–Vatican II version—the postal service might qualify as his religion. At least the post office was faithful to its origins, unlike what had happened to his faith.

But that wasn't the fault of Catholicism. An enemy had done this. Everything had gone along swimmingly until that old sick Pope John XXIII got elected and convoked the council. Arnold Carson shrank from indicting any Pope—even John, who'd started this downhill slide. After all, Popes were infallible. Even when they weren't using the extraordinary cushion, they had the ordinary magisterium, which meant they were right.

The rationalization that Carson found for Pope John was that he had not lived much beyond the opening of the council. Had he survived just a few years longer, he surely would have seen where all this was leading and he would have called a halt.

As it was, those rotten theologians and liturgists got hold of the reins during that confused period when a successor to John was being elected. Those wolves calling themselves "experts," those thieves stole the council, led the bishops—even poor mixed-up Pope Paul VI—astray. As much as Carson disliked John XXIII, it wasn't his fault.

This was Carson's logic. He was comfortable with his rationalizing and conclusion.

It also gave him the impetus, courage, and mostly perseverance to do what he could to get the Church back on track. No easy job. He was only one person, one of the faithful. But by damn, he was part and parcel of the Church Militant—not to be confused with the Church Suffering (purgatory) or the Church Triumphant (heaven).

As he stood at his station (it was still called a "window" in memory of what it once had been), he could have served another customer. Instead, he busied himself by taking inventory of the stamps and cash in his drawer, for which he was accountable. Several times, the next-in-line made a move toward him, but on noticing it, he discouraged the person with a brisk shake of his head. It gave him a feeling of power. He liked that.

Three-and-a-half more years. Three-and-a-half years till retirement. He already had his thirty years of service in. And he would soon be fifty-five years of age. The magic formula.

He remembered well the late fifties, America's last decade of innocence, as some put it, when he first became a postal employee. It was rugged at first, deliberately so. As a PTF (part-time flexible employee), he worked at the whim of his supervisor, who could call him in or not with no regard for him whatsoever. His task more often than not was coolie labor such as unloading trucks filled with heavy sacks of mail. Gradually he learned the scheme of sorting routes, to which there was a science. Then he joined the National Association of Letter Carriers. From that time it was mostly a matter of seniority. That and careful planning served to fit a shrewd man into just the position he desired.

One might become a clerk or a carrier; there was no difference in pay. In any case, one had to wait in the seniority line to be offered either position. If offered the unwanted job, one could refuse up to three times.

Most chose one or the other job, depending on whether one preferred outdoor or indoor work. Some avoided clerking for the sole reason of not wanting to be held accountable for the stock. If either stamps or cash were missing or unaccounted for, the deficit was taken out of the clerk's pocket. Which as a considerable responsibility, especially for those weak in math or completely lost without a hand computer, into which one could inadvertently press the wrong number and end up with a financial headache.

Yet it was this very responsibility that attracted Arnold Carson into becoming a clerk. First, he was quite competent in math. Then, he enjoyed the absolute assurance of numbers that led to an inevitable and dependable answer. Finally, he gloried in the veneer of power the clerk could exercise over customers. At first blush, it appeared the clerk served the customer. But if one were as hungry for power as was Carson, little things could effect a slight reversal of roles. The customer wanted commemorative stamps? Carson had an assortment of five different issues, but offered the customer a choice of only three. The customer was uncertain which class to use in mailing books, say? Carson could mentally set a brief time limit for the customer to make that decision, without offering any help or recommendation. There were various opportunities for petty power to be plucked from service, and Carson was dedicated to finding as many as possible.

Carson noticed that the waiting line was lengthening markedly and turning customers into a surly mob. He liked that. But reveries have their place. One must be careful not to attract unduly the attention of a supervisor. There was a knack to appearing occupied while daydreaming. And Carson had mastered it.

"Next!" Carson intoned.

An insignificant little man, diminutive and apologetic in every way, stepped up to Carson's window. Slowly, the man extracted a handwritten list from his coat pocket. With some sheepishness, he carefully smoothed the paper flat and hesitantly pushed it over the counter toward Carson.

Carson took it all in impassively. The man was a Jew, obviously. One of the Christ-killers. As far as Carson was concerned, Hitler had to be defeated, otherwise the world would no longer have been safe for democracy— not to mention Hitler's antagonism toward the Church. But, give the devil his due, he'd had the right approach to the "Jewish Question."

As he picked up the offered list, Carson reflected that if he were a bank teller instead of a postal clerk, this might be a holdup. At least that's the way it always happened in fiction. But this was not a bank and this probably was not a holdup. If it were, Carson's only regret would be that his gun was at home.

It was very neat script. Probably written by the Jew's wife. Carson's imagination took over. They probably lived in Southfield. Many Jews, after more or less abandoning the city of Detroit, had moved north into the well-landscaped suburb that now boasted several synagogues. In a moment he would know for sure, because the little man had begun to write a personal check. That would necessarily reveal his address.

Carson began to punch into the computer the individual charges for the stamps requested by the customer as he was making out his check. Ten 30¢ stamps, five 20¢, ten 5¢ ten 3¢, and ten 1¢. Carson totaled the order, looked at the bottom line, and smiled. God was good. "That will be," he announced, "four dollars and ninety cents."

The man began to fill in the amount on his check.

"You can't use a check," Carson said.

The little man looked up from his writing with a bewildered expression. "Can't use a check?" he repeated. "Can't use a check? Why not, please?"

"The amount has to be at least five dollars or you can't use a check."

"What's the amount again, please."

"Four dollars ninety."

"Four dollars ninety. Five dollars. Ten cents?" The tone was incredulous.

"A rule is a rule." Carson well knew that when the amount of difference was so minuscule, he had the discretion to waive the rule. But that was not his style. You keep the rule and the rule will keep you. Lower the standard for one and it becomes worthless for all. The Catholic Church he knew and loved, briefly, used to be like that. Then, among other evils, the Church got into situationism, and the whole thing fell apart.

Besides, it was especially savory to insist on the letter of the law from this member of a race that carried the curse of being responsible for the blood of Christ. That's what Pontius Pilate said when the Jews persisted on calling out for the crucifixion of Christ: "His blood be upon you and upon your children."

Of course saner souls knew that the Vatican II statement on the Jews refuted all that nonsense. But, as has been observed, Arnold Carson did not validate that Church council.

The customer, his partially completed check now useless due to Carson's strict judgment, began checking the money in his wallet and searching through his pockets for change. He spread the total amount on the counter. "Three, three-seventy-five, four-twenty-five, four-fifty, four-sixty, four-sixty-five. That's all I got, Mister."

"Seems you're short both ways. You want to write a check? Then you gotta buy more stamps." From Carson, this represented compassion beyond the call of virtue.

"I don't know," the customer said, searching his

pockets in vain for just a few more coins. "I don't know. That's all the stamps she said to get. Mama says our budget is tight like nothing. I better not." The man looked intently at Carson. He was confused. He needed a drop of mercy, not strict justice. "Please, mister: ten cents!"

Should he take $4.65 worth of stamps—and hope that the lack of the additional fifteen cents worth wouldn't upset Mama's plans? If so, he could always make another trip and come back later—

"Move on. You're holding up the line. There are people in line who know what they're doing. You're keeping them waiting."

The little man was about to make one more plea but decided against it. He could read the self-satisfied, taunting look, the affected superiority in his antagonist's smug smile. He concluded that while Carson probably was not German, he would have made a typical Nazi.

The customer turned and left. He had failed the simple mission his wife had given him. He would have to go all the way home to find out what Mama had in mind next.

Carson, exceedingly pleased with himself, fixed his gaze on the slumped shoulders of the departing would-be customer. He, Carson, had won another one for Jesus Christ. And he hadn't even needed his gun.

Before Carson could call for the next customer, he heard his supervisor's voice behind him. "Arnie," he stage-whispered, "take your lunch break now."

Without a word, Carson placed the "closed" sign at his window and retreated to the inner room. There he found five other postal employees brown-bagging it, one of them Jerry Hessler, a continuing thorn in his side. Carson was not surprised; Hessler often lunched at this time.

Carson preferred to eat in peace—much better for the digestion. So he would just as soon not have had to contend with Hessler. However, if it be God's holy will that he do battle during lunch, his loins were girded, figuratively, and off to war he would march.

Hessler waited until Carson began to eat his egg salad sandwich. It was Friday and, although Catholics long ago had had the law of abstinence from meat on Fridays lifted, Carson still observed the restriction. So, indeed, did all the members of the Tridentine Society, as well as a few other Catholics, though the latter for far more rational reasons.

"Hey, Harry," Hessler called across to one of his friends, "did you hear they're raising the urinals higher on the walls in the Vatican?"

"No." Harry knew where this was going. "Why's that?"

"To keep the Cardinals on their toes."

Everyone laughed, even the neutrals. With the exception of Carson; he felt like smashing the remainder of his sandwich in Hessler's face. But even Carson could recognize that, on the one hand, the provocation was not yet outrageous enough and, on the other, that Hessler would keep it up until the provocation was sufficient.

The six employees resumed their meal. They had all been through this routine often enough to know that the war was strictly between Hessler and Carson. It did not pay either to intervene or take sides. Eventually the two men would be shouting at each other, and a supervisor, hearing the noise, would come in, restore order, and clear the room.

"Hey, Harry," Hessler called out again to his straight man, "did you hear that the Pope announced that the Church has just discovered a first-class relic of Jesus Christ?"

"No kidding. I thought he ascended into heaven."

"He left part of himself on earth."

"What?"

"His foreskin."

The laughter was a bit more hearty. Again Carson restrained himself.

He bit into his sandwich and chewed it until the laughter subsided. Then he spoke, almost offhandedly. "I didn't hear about that, Hessler. But I can understand how they could have found the relic."

"Why?" Hessler taunted. "Because your Jesus Christ was a Jewboy?"

"No, not really. Because, unlike yours, his was big enough to find."

No laughter. A little sniggering. It was heating up for personal attacks early on. Not much longer to wait for the yelling and shouting.

Carson had scored. Hessler's beet-red face attested to that.

Hessler was a member of no faith and had no faith. He would have been labeled an atheist or, at very least, an agnostic, if he'd bothered to consider faith in any fashion whatsoever. But he did not. He merely despised all organized religion and particularly hated religious fanatics. And of these, Arnold Carson ranked at the very top of Hessler's list.

"I wouldn't talk about a little pecker if I was you, Carson," Hessler said. "At least I'm married and I got three kids. Which is one wife and three kids more than you got. Carson, you gotta take your hands off your pecker sometime or you're gonna be dead and there won't be any little Carsons around to bore the hell out of everybody."

Laughter, albeit strained.

"I've seen your kids, Hessler. . . ." Carson leaned forward. "Two of 'em look like the garbage collector and the third is a dead ringer for your brother. Cute little bastards."

He had reached Hessler. Veins were bulging in the big man's neck. "Why don't you go screw the blessed Virgin Mary?" Hessler almost screamed across the small room. "Amateurs like you should start with a whore!"

That did it.

Carson hurled what was left of his sandwich at Hessler. It disintegrated in flight. Most of it fell to the floor. Some of it hit some of the bystanders. But the battle was joined and for the first time in their hostilities it was going to go beyond verbal abuse.

They charged at each other. Even before they met near the middle of the room, the bystanders were cheering and urging them on.

Hessler was so much bigger than Carson that this did not promise to be a long, drawn-out affair. If there had been an opportunity to wager before the battle, Hessler would have been the unanimous pick of the small fight crowd.

But there was no way to measure Carson's inspired wrath. He was not simply drawn into a fistfight, he was off on his own private crusade.

The first blow went to Hessler. In an unconventional move, he swung both arms in an inward arc, smashing Carson on either side of the head. Hessler had used this tactic before to paralyzing effect. Ordinarily, after this somewhat premature coup de grâce, Hessler's opponent folded, ears ringing as if a demented hunchback were swinging bells inside his head.

But bells were not ringing in Carson's head. Rather, he heard a thundering angelic choir chanting, "God's will! God's will! God's holy will! Flatten this heathen!"

Carson was all over him. It was as if Hessler were trying to fight off a swarm of angry bees, and just about as effective. In only a few seconds, Hessler had irretrievably lost the initiative and was reeling backward.

Hessler fell heavily onto the table at which just seconds before he'd been eating. The table, near splintering, collapsed under the weight of the two men, who tumbled to the floor in a heap. Instantly Carson, flailing away like a frenzied windmill, was on top, punishing Hessler mercilessly. Carson gave no quarter.

At this point the bystanders intervened, if for no other reason than to save Hessler's life. With great difficulty they pulled Carson off. Even then, it took their combined strength to hold him back from attacking Hessler again.

For Hessler, dazed, breathless, and bloodied, the fight would have been over and done with and lost at that point but for one final strategy. As he scrambled to his feet, he drew a knife from his pocket, and flipped the blade open. The sight of the weapon and its size so startled the men that all, even Carson, involuntarily stepped back.

For Carson, the retreating step was instinctive. Instantly regaining his holy mission, Carson prepared to dive back into battle, knife or not, when a shout from the doorway froze him and everyone else in the room.

The supervisor's attention had been drawn by the sound of the table shattering under the two combatants. Now, eye caught by the impressive knife in Hessler's hand, he shouted several furious obscenities that stopped them all in their tracks.

"Hessler!" the supervisor roared. "Get rid of that knife! This minute!"

It was over, at least for now. Hessler closed the knife, pressing the dull side of the blade against his thigh, and slid the weapon into his pocket. Later, in a more composed moment, he would recognize that the fight would not be resumed. He'd been in lots of fights before, against men of just about every size, although not many his size or better. But this jerk Carson was a madman. If the guys had not pulled Carson off, he might have bitten off one of Hessler's ears or his nose. Carson was that crazy!

The supervisor got the two men into separate offices, told them to cool it, then called the police.

It was standard procedure. Because the post office is

a federal agency, the structure a federal building, and the workers federal employees, the local police lacked jurisdiction in a matter such as this. However, the police served the essential function of getting the two combatants out of the building and away from each other. From that point on, postal inspectors would handle the case.

Due to the seriousness of his offense—wielding a deadly weapon—Hessler would appear before the sectional center, where the process of firing him would begin. Eventually, using every grievance procedure available to him, he would survive with a lengthy suspension. All would be duly noted in his work record.

As for Carson, the onlookers testified that Hessler had begun the altercation with remarks aimed at riling Carson. They further affirmed that it had been a fair fight until Hessler pulled the knife.

Carson's file was clean. In fact, he had an exemplary record. No one could think of a single rule he had ever violated.

So Carson was issued a letter of warning and given a one-month suspension. And that was bargained down to ten days.

Actually, Carson was pleased with the outcome. For one, word quickly spread that he had taken Hessler apart. And hitherto, Hessler had had the reputation as a virtually invincible bully. Thus, Carson now became known as a force to be reckoned with. His reputation as a latter-day David who smote Goliath was enhanced.

For another, he could use the ten-day suspension productively. He needed the time to make further refinements in a plan he hoped would save the Church in Detroit and the world from itself.

17

LIEUTENANT TULLY WAS paging through reports turned in by various members of his squad at various times. All concerned the same case, the investigation into the presumed serial killing of Helen Donovan and Lawrence Hoffer.

After notifying and getting the approval of Inspector Walter Koznicki, Tully had assigned every member of his squad to interview the people who headed departments in the archdiocese of Detroit. Each resultant report contained a plethora of information. In scanning each one, Tully concentrated on the responses to such questions as, "Can you think of any enemies you personally have?" Or, "Are there any persons you can think of who are opposed to the work of your department?" Or, "Can you think of anyone who is opposed to the policies of the archdiocese of Detroit?"

In the responses, a pattern was forming. Almost no one named anyone who might qualify as a personal enemy. In response to the other questions, quite a few were mentioned. Tully was jotting down names that kept recurring throughout the reports. There were quite a few.

His talk with Father Koesler had helped. Tully felt slightly more confident wandering through the hitherto totally unfamiliar territory of Church administration. Not completely at home by any means. But not in a totally foreign field either.

Seated across the desk was Sergeant Angie Moore.

She had been the latest and last of his squad to turn in a report. Tully studied the result of her investigation, frequently cross-checking it with the other reports.

"Zoo, be honest," Moore said. "I drew the meanest bastard in the lot, didn't I?"

Tully smiled. "Seems like it. But how would we know beforehand? It wasn't on purpose."

"But he was, wasn't he, Zoo? I mean the meanest?"

Tully maintained his relaxed and engaging grin. "Judging by the other reports, I'd have to say he ranks. No; give the devil his due: You got the meanest."

"I thought people in public relations were supposed to be pleasant, nice."

"So did I. But there's always the exception—"

"Well, he proved the rule okay," Moore interrupted. "It'll be a long time before I forget Father Cletus Bash."

"I see he's the only one interviewed who admits to having a personal enemy or two."

"Is he the only one?" Moore had no access to the other reports; this was the first she knew that none of the others had acknowledged any enemies. "I guess I'd put him down as paranoid, except that after spending an hour with him I expect his enemies are probably not imaginary. They could be for real."

Tully studied silently for a few moments. "It says here," he referred to her report, "that among his own enemies and those he listed as opposed both to the Church and the Church in Detroit are guys named Stapleton and Carson. Those are two names that are pretty familiar. They show up repeatedly on the other reports."

"Do they? That's interesting. That's why I looked into their background a little bit, because Bash mentioned them three times. No one else got that kind of billing."

"You did? Good. What did you find?"

"A lot on Carson. Not all that much on Stapleton.

"I went over to the *Free Press* library and went through their records—through the automated, the semi-automated, and even back through the envelope files," Moore continued. "Carson goes back to the early sixties. Whatever he did before that couldn't have been very newsworthy: They didn't have any prior clippings on them."

The early sixties, thought Tully. What was it? Something Koesler had been talking about. Yeah, that council that changed everything. Tully concluded that whatever it was Carson had done to make the news probably had been a reaction—his reaction—to that council. "Wasn't that the Vatican Council in the early sixties?"

Moore was surprised. "Gee, Zoo. I didn't think you paid any attention to religion. But, yeah, that was when the council was going on—early sixties."

"Go on." Tully was all business.

"Okay." Moore rummaged through her tote bag. "I got some readouts and made some notes. Here we go. The early reports on Carson aren't all that inflammatory. I think they were included in his file based on hindsight. I think that after he got to be a newsmaker, they went back to find some sort of things, no matter how innocuous, that he was involved in earlier. But it notes that he was among the earliest members of a group called Catholics United for the Faith. It seems to be a pretty popular movement. Most people know it by its initials, CUF. Then he went on to a more extreme group called the Tridentines. That's when he begins to get some individual attention in the media."

Tully remembered Koesler's explanation of the right-wing reaction to the council. Without that briefing, this would not have made a lot of sense.

Moore looked up from her notes inquiringly as if asking whether she need go into detail about these groups. Tully caught the subtle query. "Go ahead."

Moore shrugged. If he thought he understood all this,

it was all right with her. But she was at a loss to know how he did it.

She resumed. "It was just a little while after he joined the Tridentines that he became the group's leader."

Moore, a lifelong Catholic, well remembered the aftereffects of the council and the turmoil that had ensued, particularly in this archdiocese. Cardinal—then Archbishop—Boyle was elected the first president of the National Conference of Catholic Bishops. He had been extremely active and influential in that Vatican Council. And he saw to it that the changes and developments ordered by the council were implemented in his archdiocese.

That was by no means the reaction of other bishops and archbishops. One of those changes involved encouraging the laity to get more deeply involved in everything from parish life to policy-making on an archdiocesan level. People reflecting the spirit as well as the letter of the council took this bit and ran with it.

Meanwhile, CUF, not to mention the far more militant Tridentines, were generally opposed to the letter of the council. The less easily defined "spirit" of the council was, in the eyes of the right wing, an abomination.

Thus, in those early days there were many public meetings and gatherings sponsored by and starring, for want of a better designation, Church liberals. At most of these meetings, the right wing was conspicuously present, frequently and vociferously led by Arnold Carson.

Without the presence of Carson, along with his faithful few followers, these meetings would have been peaceable and calm on the whole. With Carson and crew present, they frequently degenerated into angry confrontations and occasionally even some measure of violence and reaction.

Moore attempted to explain all this briefly to Tully.

He accepted her explanation, knowledgeable about part but by no means all of the history.

"See," Moore continued, "once Carson got to be the leader of the Tridentines, he was bound to make news. From the very nature of the organization and the fact that it existed just when it did—when all the changes were taking place. So"—she glanced again through the notes and readouts—"there were some arrests, lots of charges of 'police brutality,' and plenty of media coverage for Arnold Carson.

"In the seventies"—Moore continued to finger through her notes—"there was a Catholic 'Call to Action' meeting. It was a national meeting hosted by Detroit. Sort of a put-into-practice-what-we-learned-from-the-council. Carson and some of his friends showed up, carrying a banner hailing Boyle as the 'red' Cardinal—in effect calling him a commie. Which in Tridentine terms is about the bottom of the barrel.

"Then there's a note about the time he pushed a priest down the steps of a church—"

"Wait," Tully cut in, "some violence? An arrest?"

"The priest didn't press charges. But here's the funny thing: The priest was Father Fred Stapleton!"

"The one who—?"

"The same. Carson shows up almost any time you'd expect a right-wing reaction. He was part of a protest when Martin Luther King was here. And if there's any kind of peace march, he's out there buzzing and opposing it. I mention this just to show that he's an all-purpose fanatic. But mostly he's a religious fanatic."

"How about abortion?" Tully asked.

"You got it. Almost any time there's either a prochoice or pro-life rally, or—as happens most often—both at the same time and place, he's there."

Tully massaged his right eyebrow. "But no violence," he mused.

"Outside of that one incident where he shoved the

priest. Maybe he's mellowed out. If he's been active this long, he must be getting on in years.''

"He's close to retirement. You're right about that, Zoo—but he's hardly mellowing. The night of the wake for that hooker, Helen Donovan, he and a couple of buddies were harassing some of the mourners. It got sticky when some hookers showed up for the service.''

"Wait a minute . . . I was at that wake.''

"It must have happened before you got there, Zoo. Some uniforms were called and cleared them out. Took Carson to the hospital.''

"A fight?''

"Just some pushing and shoving. Carson ended up with a cut lip. Nothing major. No arrests. No charges.''

"I don't know,'' Tully said. "There's not much physical going on in what you found. Sounds like he talks a good fight.''

"Wait, Zoo. I phoned the postal branch where he works. He's not working there anymore.''

Tully looked at her inquiringly.

"He's been suspended by the post office. He's appealing the penalty and it'll probably be a minor punishment that could be reduced.''

"What did he do?''

"Got in a fight—a no-holds-barred fight with a co-worker.''

"Um.'' Tully made a relieved sound, as if he'd found the missing piece to a jigsaw puzzle.

"I got this from one of the guys who witnessed the fight. It began when this guy named Hessler started riding Carson about religion. Things like accusing Carson of getting horny over the Blessed Mother.''

"Sounds like a sweet character.''

"He's the town bully, Zoo. Big guy. Make maybe two of Carson. But he kept at it until Carson blew his cork. Then Carson tore into him. Now I'll quote this guy I talked to. . . .'' Moore read from her notes. " 'I never saw anything like it,' he said. 'Arnie'—that's Carson—'Arnie didn't stand a chance.' " She looked up from her notes. "Not only is Hessler twice as big as Arnie, according to my witness, he's a brutal slob with a real mean disposition. He's been in lots of fights, usually with smaller guys. He doesn't just win his fights, he punishes the other guys—beats 'em up. This guy said he was really scared for Carson. Hessler wasn't just having fun picking on a smaller guy like he usually does; Hessler was mad." She quoted again from her notes. " 'Cause when he was givin' it to Arnie—with his mouth, that is—Arnie was givin' it right back to him. Pretty good, too.' " She looked up from her notes again. "But when Hessler made that crack about the Blessed Mother, Carson tore right into him."

As Angie looked down at her notes again, it was hard to tell whether she was quoting verbatim or acting out what she had been told. " 'Well, Hessler starts by givin' Arnie this rap on the ears. I seen it before: Once Hessler does that, the other guy is in the ozone. I thought old Arn would fold right there. And since Hessler is really sore, I thought we'd be pickin' Arnie up with a blotter. But would you believe it? Arnie plows right in like Hessler had kissed him instead of paralyzing him. Arnie was . . . he was . . . *inspired*.

" 'To make a long story short, we had to pull Arnie off Hessler or so help me, he woulda killed him. He really woulda.' "

Moore looked up, pleased with her notes of the account. "Now, does that sound to you like a guy who has mellowed out?"

Tully, pleased also, shook his head.

"Carson's supervisor called 911 and a couple of uniforms got them out of there and filed a report. Of course it's not our jurisdiction."

"The report our guys made corroborate the story you got?"

Moore nodded. "But not as colorful."

"It couldn't have been. It was a bare-hands fight?"

"It was in the beginning. But let me go back to my source." Angie had really gotten into the spirit of the affair. So much so that Tully could easily envision the scene as she half quoted, half extrapolated from her witness's account of events. " 'It was after we got Arnie off Hessler that the guy came up with the shiv, a big one. Then I was really scared. Not only for Arnie. For the rest of us, too. Hessler was like an animal fightin' for his life. He woulda cut anybody. Lucky for us that was just the time when the super came in and broke it up.

" 'But you know the funny thing? Even after Hessler pulled the knife, Carson wanted him. I mean there was four of us holdin' Arnie back and even after Hessler showed us the knife, I had to work as hard to hold Arnie back as when we pulled him off. You know how sometimes there's a fight and you pull the guys apart and hold 'em? And they're really not puttin' up no fight to get back in it; all you gotta do is just keep your hands on the guy so the other guys get the idea the guy really wants to get back in the fight? Well, that ain't the way it was with Arnie: He really wanted to tear Hessler apart. Even when the SOB was holdin' a knife. Could you believe that?' "

As she triumphantly wound up her vivid recital, it was impossible to know whether the last question was hers or had been voiced by her witness.

"So the other guy had the weapon," Tully said.

"Our guy's report corroborates that," Moore affirmed.

"Well," Tully said, "the main thing for our purposes is that Carson seems to have the killer instinct. Your source sounds convinced that Carson would have gone all the way, given the chance."

"Oh, yeah, Zoo. No doubt there. Although he did seem to think it was somewhat out of character—in that Carson had mouthed off lots of times in the past, but this was the first time, in my guy's experience anyway, that Carson had actually become physical, violent, and even deadly.''

"God, I wish we knew if Carson owned a gun! But . . . okay for now. Real good work, Angie. How about the Stapleton character?''

She withdrew a much smaller packet of notes and readout sheets from her bag. She held the packet aloft as if performing a show-and-tell.

"Not nearly as much with Stapleton as I found on Carson,'' she said. "All I found in the *Free Press* library was a few items. There was a story dated June 1974 noting that quite a few priests were quitting the priesthood at roughly the same time. Stapleton was among them. But the story didn't highlight him. The lead was given to a priest who was head of the justice and peace department of the Detroit Church. Stapleton was just mentioned as one of the others who was leaving.''

Head. The word caught Tully's attention. Another head of another department. Could that have any bearing on the present investigation? "Angie, what was the name of that guy—the head of the Church department?''

She had to page backward to find the item. "Burke . . . Father Pat Burke.''

"Anything on him?''

"I don't think so. I knew him back then. Matter of fact when I was a kid in parochial school, he was the assistant pastor in the parish. I had a crush on him.''

"Where is he now? Do you know?''

"Not really. After he quit the priesthood, he moved out of state. Arizona, I think. As far as I know, he's still there.''

"Check it out, will you?''

"Sure, Zoo.''

"Now, let's get back to Stapleton.''

"Well, with Fred Stapleton, the only prior notice I could find before that story about all those priests leav-

ing was the one we talked about earlier—when he was
shoved down the church steps by Arnold Carson. That,
by the way, is a real coincidence, don't you think?''

"Uh-huh. And I don't like coincidences. They smack
of blind luck and we deal in facts. Whether we find
anything or not, we'd better check on whether there's
any connection there.''

"Connection?'' Moore asked.

"Where does Stapleton fit in? As far as the Church
is concerned.''

"You mean . . . ?'' She didn't finish her thought.

"Well, liberal, conservative? Left wing or right?''

"Oh, Stapleton is a liberal.''

"And Carson is a conservative.''

"Off the globe.''

"Ah,'' Tully observed, "that would explain the pushing incident.''

"Yes. Stapleton and Carson were always on opposite
sides of just about everything.''

"Just about,'' Tully observed.

"What are you getting at, Zoo?''

"They've got some common ground now.''

"Common ground?''

"They've both been listed as being opposed to prac-
tices and laws of the Church.''

"Oh, yeah, Zoo. But the things that Carson can't
stand just couldn't be the same problems Stapleton
has.''

"Maybe not. But suppose they agree to bury the
hatchet for the duration so they can get the Church's
attention. Suppose that's the purpose of this crime
spree. Suppose they find they have the same goal for
different reasons. We can't overlook the possibility . . .
or any possibility, for that matter. This is growing into
one slippery case.'' Tully might have added that it was
the sort of case that he most appreciated. One that called
on every skill he possessed. "But, go on, Angie. What

else about Stapleton? Besides the pushing incident and the resignation report?''

''Well, there were quite a few items either featuring him or mentioning him.''

''Oh?''

''He's a psychologist. Kind of prominent, at least locally. Every so often you see him on one or another local TV news program. You know how the news anchors get into pop psychology and they get local authorities for 'expert' commentary. Well, Dr. Stapleton is there pretty regularly giving his opinion. He's also quoted on radio and in newspapers along the same line. His picture's been on TV and in the papers pretty often.''

''Ever give expert testimony in court?''

''Well, yeah, a few times.''

''In homicide cases?''

''Once in a while. Although, evidently, not in any of your cases. I think most people in the metropolitan area would be fairly familiar with Stapleton. In fact, from the number of times their pictures have been in the media, I'd guess that Carson and Stapleton are equally recognizable to a lot of people.'' She stopped, almost embarrassed. She did not want to make her point too plainly. But it was evident that while Carson and Stapleton would qualify as local celebrities—at least in the sense of being easily identifiable—Tully had paid no attention to them.

It was one more indication of the measure of dedication Tully gave to his work. To a significant extent, as far as he was concerned if a news item had no relevance to his work it was not news. Some might call such an attitude tunnel vision. Others, dedication. Whatever one called it, Tully was near totally absorbed in his work. His former wife had discovered this truth early in their marriage and thought she could fight this intangible enemy. She spent a few years of her life in this doomed struggle. Tully's present-day companion recognized and understood his priorities early on and was able to handle being a very strong but definite second in his life.

Anyone who had eavesdropped on this present conversation would have come to the same inevitable conclusion Angie Moore had reached: Alonzo Tully did not pay much attention to the passing parade. It was almost as if he did not want extraneous information crowding out the things he needed to know to do his job as well as or better than any comparable officer.

Tully's unexpected grasp of the effects of Vatican II on current Church affairs was a case in point. From some source, presently unknown to Sergeant Moore, he had been briefed on the council and its impact on Catholicism. Still, there was no indication that Tully had mastered more than he needed to know to further the investigation of this case.

At any rate, Tully clearly did not seem embarrassed, defensive, or even concerned that a couple of otherwise famous faces were foreign to him. "Stapleton: rich?" he asked.

"Comfortable. I talked to a few people who knew him well—therapists, priests, ex-priests. Stapleton does a lot of charity work, mostly at old Trinity parish in Corktown. He's married, got one daughter who's going to school at that music academy up north—Interlochen. That must cost a bundle.

"Oh, and one more thing: He belongs to CORPUS."

"What the hell is that?" Tully was growing irritated at the continuing confusions he found in Catholicism.

"It's an organization for ex-priests who want to be able to function clerically again. They meet, put out a publication, lobby bishops, even the Pope."

"Mostly talk?"

"I guess so. But Stapleton's been very active in the group."

"So? It seems harmless enough. If all they want to do is get their preacher's license back, what's the problem? I don't see why he's on Bash's shit list." He seemed puzzled. "He was even mentioned by some of the other department heads."

Moore didn't reply immediately. Finally, she said, "Well, I can't speak for the others 'cause I didn't interview them—but I'd be willing to bet they agree. My man, Father Bash, doesn't consider either Carson or Stapleton as physical threats. Of course he undoubtedly didn't know about Carson's all-out fight yesterday at the post office. So I think he could be mistaken about Carson.

"Anyway, I think Bash sees Carson and Stapleton as . . . well . . . just troublemakers. And if you saw things through . . . what?—institutional eyes—that's all they'd be. As you know"—although she didn't know *how* he knew—"that Vatican council stirred up lots of controversy. I get the impression the institutional Church desperately wants everything to calm down. And people like Carson and Stapleton won't let that happen.

"That's my impression. People like Bash would like to see Carson and Stapleton just go away—or at least shut up. But neither one of them seems to want to do that. So they are seen as people opposed to Church rules and regulations. And from that point of view, they are.

"Of course Bash sees them as personal enemies. But I don't think it would take anybody long to become a personal enemy of Father Bash."

They both laughed.

Quickly returning to seriousness, Tully said, "Let's keep as tight a rein on Carson as possible. I don't see Stapleton as a violent type. And I wish to God that we could keep that nun in a jar."

"Sister Joan? You think somebody's still after her?"

"It would tie things up neatly, wouldn't it? She's still the first base that nobody's touched yet."

"There's no way we can keep her under surveillance.

She's determined to continue doing her job. And her job drags her over the whole metropolitan area.''

"Uh-huh.'' *Damn! It could almost drive a man to prayer.*

18

"WHERE'S FATHER BENZ?"

Cardinal Mark Boyle finished chewing the morsel of lamb before answering. "There is a gathering of his priest friends at the seminary this evening. I gave him the night off."

"Good." Archbishop Lawrence Foley was pleased to be able to spend the evening alone with his friend. Benz, secretary to the Cardinal, was a nice enough young man, but he was from a different era, two or more removed from these two old bishops. Without the young man, who, courtesy demanded, should be included in the conversation, the older men were free to retreat as far as they liked into history. And they would.

Foley lived in a condominium on Detroit's far east side. He could have lived virtually anywhere he wished, but he wanted to reside in the city, though not in an area inhospitable to strolling the streets, and not in a rectory. He had reached an age where he would deal with people and the clergy in particular only when he wished. Not when they wanted him. Retirement, he thought, should have some privileges.

But this night—for he would stay over till morning—he would spend with his old friend Mark Boyle.

Boyle, at sixty-nine, was slightly more than five years Foley's junior. They had met some forty years before in Rome when both were students. Both had been ordained—Foley for the diocese of Miami and Boyle for the diocese of Cleveland. As brilliant seminarians, both had been selected by their respective bishops to attend graduate studies in Rome. Foley majored in canon law, Boyle in theology.

Even as young men, they had enough in common to become friends. They were English-speaking United States citizens, at the peak of their youth; roommates, expected to achieve much by their appointment to graduate study—and they were strangers together in a foreign land.

Building on that, they formed an abiding friendship that had grown stronger and deepened over the years. Each was of Irish descent, as were so many American bishops. They both had become auxiliary bishops, Foley in his native Miami, Boyle in his native Cleveland. Foley had risen to the rank of archbishop when he was named ordinary of Cincinnati. Boyle was named archbishop of Pittsburgh, then archbishop of Detroit, then named a Cardinal by Pope Paul VI.

The two vacationed regularly together, usually in Florida, where Foley had so many friends and contacts. They golfed together, neither well, both mostly for exercise. They could spend evenings together chatting knowledgeably about many things or in companionable silence.

The pièce de résistance having been finished, Mrs. Provenzano, Boyle's housekeeper, removed the dishes and served coffee and sherbet.

"Delicious lamb," Foley said to Mrs. Provenzano, who smiled and, thank God, was still able to blush at a compliment.

"She was a genuine find," Boyle said after the housekeeper had left them. "She has only two rules by which to live: no beef and no chicken."

Foley chuckled. "The martyrdom of today's bishop, stuffed to death with rubbery chicken and leathery beef cooked by the ladies of the Rosary Altar Society on the occasion of parish confirmations."

Boyle smiled. "Of course they are well-meaning

people, but they surely need an injection of imagination. The beef is usually sliced thin enough that one can get by without having to consume very much. But whichever doctor it was who pronounced chicken a healthy food never tried the parochial mass-produced variety.''

Foley began toying with a spoon.

''Still miss cigarettes?'' Boyle asked.

Foley studied the Cardinal. ''Now what would make you say a thing like that?''

''Something to do with your hands. Toying with a utensil instead of handling a cigarette.''

''Doesn't happen much anymore. But after a good dinner and with coffee . . .'' Foley shrugged.

''Still?''

''There was a time, Mark, me lad, that I could not envision being on the telephone, getting through the daily mail, a hundred other daily tasks such as getting up in the morning or going to bed at night, without a cigarette. It's down to this, after a good dinner. That's not so bad, is it now? Nice bit of deduction though.''

''It just occurred to me. You used to say that you thought much of your reason for smoking was to have something to occupy restless hands.''

''True as far as it goes, but a bit of a simplification. There's the nicotine, an addictive drug. But speaking of deduction, has anything new come up in the police investigation?''

''Into the death of Larry Hoffer? Not that I'm aware of.''

''What do you think? Isolated instances? Coincidence? Or is there a connection between the murders of that poor woman and Hoffer?''

Boyle finished the sherbet and carefully wiped his lips. ''I feel very strongly that they are related. And that's why I'm concerned about Sister Joan's welfare. I believe that whoever killed Larry also killed Helen Donovan thinking she was her sister. And the guilty party is still at large, probably looking for an opportunity to attack Sister Joan.''

"It's hard to hide, particularly in this day and age.''

"I've talked to her about going away. A vacation, study, virtually anything to get her away from here, somewhere where she could be safer.''

"She won't go?''

Boyle shook his head. "She's politely refused every offer. I get the impression she feels some sort of debt to her sister. She is certain the killer was looking for her and that her sister was in the wrong place at the wrong time. With Sister it is the whole thing. That her sister was dressed in Joan's habit. There's a sense of desecration in a religious being attacked. In many ways, Joan feels that in death if not in life she is her sister's keeper.''

Foley was tempted to fiddle with something, anything: spoon, knife, whatever. But having had his subconscious raised, he deliberately interlaced his fingers and rested his hands on the tabletop. "But, why?'' he asked. "What possibly could be the connection between Larry Hoffer and Sister Joan—given the assumption that she was the real intended victim?''

"I've thought about that a great deal. Almost obsessively.'' Boyle sipped his coffee. It was excellent; Mrs. Provenzano had experimented with the blend until she was satisfied. "I keep returning to the recent staff meeting—the last time they were together. Sister Joan as one who had escaped the grave, and Larry Hoffer at his final meeting—though none of us knew it at the time. I've even seen it in a dream. I can hear the angry voices, most of them directed at Larry. And I wonder: Could anyone at the meeting . . . a staff member . . . could any one of them . . . ? But then I dismiss the questions as impossible speculation. Besides, such questions are better asked—and answered—by the police.''

"They need help!'' Foley's tone was forceful, urgent.

"Help? The police? From whom?''

"Us!"

Boyle looked startled. "You're not serious."

Foley was very serious. "These are officials of the archdiocese of Detroit. If there were only one victim—Larry Hoffer—we might suppose his enemy could have been . . . anyone. It's not hard to suppose that he's made enemies during his long career. He was, after all, a financier, and money is a common enough motivation for enmity, hatred, violence . . . murder.

"But that is true only if Hoffer were the only victim. It does not in any way address the selection of Sister Joan as a designated victim by the same killer. Whoever is doing this is doing it for some religious reason. Oh, I know to the police that might sound like a contradiction in terms. But we could list hundreds of examples through history when people were murdered for reasons connected to religion."

"Well, I can assure you, Lawrence, that I am not going to volunteer my services, such as they are, to the Detroit Police Department." A smile threatened to break through, but Boyle held it well in check. "Of course, if you . . ."

"Come, come, Mark," Foley interrupted, "you know I wasn't referring to a couple of old fogies like us! I meant one of your priests. You must have someone who could guide the police through the morass of Church bureaucracy."

Boyle's smile did break through. "There is someone. I don't think you've met him yet. Father Robert Koesler."

"He has some special training?" Foley was surprised that any priest would spring immediately to mind as a liaison with a homicide department of a major city such as Detroit. If anyone had challenged him to come up with such a priest in Cincinnati, he would have been hard-pressed to do so.

"Not training, Larry; experience."

"This . . . this Koesler: He's done this sort of thing before?"

Boyle nodded. "It's uncanny, but it certainly has happened before. I've had occasion to speak with him about it, of course. I'm convinced a good deal of his involvement is not by design. He certainly is not in any way trained in criminology. But he has been called upon by the police to do just what you suggested: help them find their way through Church avenues and paths that seem to be an added mystery to the police."

"Do you . . . assign him to this duty?" Foley found this difficult to comprehend.

"He seems to gravitate to this role quite independently of anyone's commissioning him."

"Well," Foley said, "he certainly seems made to order for what I had in mind."

"Shall we repair to the study?" With the meal ended Boyle thought Foley would be more comfortable in the well-upholstered study.

Boyle rose from his straight-backed chair fairly spryly. Foley had a considerably more challenging time of it. But he managed. Boyle did not offer assistance. He knew Foley would prefer to be independent.

The study was exactly that. Just about every inch of wall space was lined with books that were read, consulted, treasured. Cardinal Boyle spent many a contented evening alone with his books, studying.

The two settled into comfortable chairs. Boyle offered a selection of liqueurs. Foley, claiming an advanced stage of fatigue, declined. They sat in silence for several minutes.

Foley was first to speak. "Have you given much thought to the future . . . to the future of our Church?"

"Certainly. It won't be long."

"No, it won't. Pretty soon all the priests—even the Pope, *in nomine Domini*—will be too young to remember what the Church was before Vatican II." Foley shook his head. "That is if there are still any more priests."

"I'm not inclined to be that pessimistic, Larry."

"God will provide?" Mockingly.

"Yes . . .", Boyle drew out the word, "but not magically."

"A married clergy?"

"I think it inevitable. We already have the beginnings of it with the sizable number of married Protestant clergy that have converted and are now functioning."

"The transition is going to be difficult."

"No doubt. But it has to happen."

"There are going to be some angry Catholics. Some very angry Catholics."

"There are already some very angry Catholics." Cardinal Boyle had had firsthand experience.

"But it works." Foley resettled himself in the chair as if fighting off tiredness. "We've known it all along. Martin Luther, among others, was right. It is not only possible but beneficial to have a married clergy. The Protestant clergy—just about every sort of clergy but Latin Rite Catholics—have proven the naturalness of a married clergy. And now the converts among ministers and Protestant priests, they're doing all right. And I almost forgot that other phenomenon, our brother priests who marry and then become Protestant—even Orthodox—priests. Quite a display of proof there. It is as you yourself just said: inevitable. Yes, yes, yes: We are going to have optional celibacy—the day after I die."

Boyle chuckled. "Thus saving some poor woman from becoming Mrs. Lawrence Foley."

" 'Mrs. Foley . . .' Even the name sounds peculiar. In that context," he clarified. "The first and almost the only Mrs. Foley that comes to mind is my mother."

"Besides, Larry, it is not as smooth a picture as you paint."

"Oh, I don't know."

"There's the problem of divorce among the clergy."

"I suppose," Foley admitted. "You don't have divorce when you have an unmarried clergy. But then, divorce seems to be part of life—a tragic part of life. Something we would better understand if some of us had to go through it."

"You're mellowing, Larry."

"I've mellowed, Mark."

"Another problem you've skipped over: the convert clergy with their wives and families, many of them, are not being accepted by all parishioners, even though the parishes they are assigned to are carefully selected."

"Transitional, Mark, transitional. Our people are so used to the unencumbered priest that it's going to take a while for them to adjust." Foley cocked his head toward the Cardinal. "What is it with you, Mark? Are you merely playing *advocatus diaboli* or do you have serious reservations about a married clergy? You did say it was inevitable."

"Inevitable, true. But . . . somehow . . . I regret the loss of what we had. It was, I think, nobly unique."

They sat in silence for several minutes.

"Admirably unique," Foley agreed at length.

"The seminary training," he continued, "so strict and unyielding, yet the system formed men—good men, responsible, leaders. But," he sighed, "that's pretty much gone already."

Boyle nodded agreement. But then he amended Foley's statement. "The mere change to optional celibacy may or may not have its effect on the training for priesthood. But, in any case, it will no longer be necessary to produce that challenge to human nature, the asexual macho man."

"Yes, yes, yes. No more *Going My Way*, or *Bells of St. Mary's*, or *Keys of the Kingdom*, or Father Flanagan of *Boys' Town*. It's probably just as well that Bing didn't live to see this."

Boyle smiled.

"But, more seriously," Foley said, "and more positively: It will do away with our caste system. To be truthful, that has been a problem for me for longer than I like to think. It was that universal and mandatory celibacy that created a separate class in Christian society. Priests were not 'ordinary people.' They were 'above' the laity, not just because of their function in the Christian community but in the nature of their membership in the Church. Because of celibacy, the clergy were in a more spiritual, and ergo a superior, form of Christian life."

"You're right," Boyle agreed. "It is more neoplatonic than Christian."

"Strange," Foley picked up the theme, "how much of our life is structured by celibacy. It's not just a single life. My god, single people are looked upon more often than not as 'odd,' somehow failures at the sexual game. But with the distinction of celibacy—dedicated virginity, consecrated singleness—we are looked upon as different kinds of creatures. Mark, when you were a child, did you ever wonder whether priests and nuns went to the bathroom?"

Boyle chuckled. "I think when we were children that would have qualified as an impure thought."

"You know," Foley said, "I'll bet most of our people think that an unmarried clergy goes back to the beginning of Christianity. Whereas, you know that, despite some early attempts at celibacy, we had a married clergy for about the first half of our history."

"The Second Lateran Council, A.D. 1139," responded Boyle, thus proving that the books in this study were used. "It was almost a textbook of simplicity in legislation. The First Lateran Council prohibited the marriage of clerics in major orders. And that did not do the job. So the Second Lateran simply pronounced such marriages invalid. And that is pretty much how things stand to this date."

"That was a sad period for the Church, if memory serves."

"Indeed it was," Boyle agreed. "The tenth and eleventh centuries were shot through with weak Popes and clandestine clerical marriages or, more often, a very common concubinage. The time was ripe for an uncompromising move in one direction or another. Either the Church would have to abandon its effort to form a universally celibate clergy or come up with the sort of legislation that, as it happened, was promulgated."

"Went for broke. Isn't that the way of it?" Foley's question was rhetorical. "In almost every crisis, historically, there was always a minority who could be depended upon to react and save celibacy. If they'd followed the will of the majority, more than once celibacy would have been discarded." He paused. "Just as it was nearly discarded as a result of the Second Vatican Council. But," he added wryly, "I surely don't have to tell you. You were among the shakers and movers of that council."

Boyle nodded as he recalled the seemingly endless meetings, the maneuvering, the lobbying. "There's no doubt about that. Although few beyond the council participants were aware of what was going on, imposed celibacy was a burning 'behind-the-doors' topic at the council. But pressure—pressure from that dependable entrenched minority—kept the topic off the formal agenda."

"So now, here we are," Foley summed up, "with the law of imposed celibacy, living right alongside a married clergy. Add to that priests becoming an endangered species, and it can't be too far off before we will have optional celibacy."

"Ah, yes," Boyle said, "that is the question: when? It's the question I doubt anyone has an answer to. When? Pope John, who began it all with his convocation of the council, with his call for a change in canon law, with his *aggiornamento*, with his openness to change . . .

even he could not bring himself to make this reformation. On occasion, he even said as much: that with a stroke of his pen he could put an end to enforced celibacy. But he said he simply could not bring himself to do it.

"Then his successor, Paul VI, two years after the council's conclusion, put another nail in the coffin with *'Sacerdotalis coelibatus,'* which just repeated the standard explanations and dismissed all the arguments against obligatory celibacy."

"So we are faced with a law that hangs by a single thread: tradition. A tradition that, as a law, is less than half as old as Christianity itself. But you know, Mark, you and I are not the only ones who are familiar with the background of this law. What of those who demand an immediate answer to 'When?' and those who insist 'Never'?"

The Cardinal shook his head and stifled a yawn. It was getting late, especially for two elderly men who had had a busy day. "I don't know. I simply do not know. But the situation puts me in mind of an earthquake waiting to happen."

"Huh?"

"California, for example. The earth gradually, ineluctably, grinding in opposite directions, but the motion being encumbered by massive buildings. The stress keeps building as the earth continues to creep apart and the buildings sit there like Band-Aids—until, with unimaginable force and destruction, the quake occurs.

"That is what I am reminded of: We are moving toward great change in the Church, even greater than we've experienced as a result of the council. Celibacy is only one area where this is happening. The movement toward optional celibacy—a married clergy—is inevitable. And it's being advanced by people who are tired of waiting, who know it will happen, and who demand that it happen now.

"But the opposition, that powerful minority of convinced conservatives, is digging in its heels."

"There will be an explosion," Foley concluded.

"It seems destined."

"The law could be changed."

"And," Boyle added, "Californians could tear down their buildings and get out of the way of the earth's movement. Of course, it would be far easier to change the law enforcing obligatory celibacy. But that's no more likely than respecting the movement of land."

"The Holy Father could do it all himself."

"But he gives no indication that he will. And those who demand change recognize his intransigence."

Foley was unable to repress his yawn. "Well, Mark, it seems we've settled most of the Church's problems, if not the world's. Time to retreat so we can fight another day."

Boyle agreed. So, leaving some lights on for the return of Father Benz, they retired for the night.

Neither bishop thought to relate what they had discussed to a motive for murder.

19

"A PENNY FOR your thoughts."

"They're not worth that much."

"They are to me." Pam Stapleton was sitting on a sofa with her husband.

"Oh," Fred said, "I guess I was thinking a dozen things at the same time." Pause. "I was remembering parties like this when I was a priest. Usually everybody was married-and-there-with-spouse except me. And when it came to being seated for dinner, it was boy-girl-boy-girl until it came to me. Odd man out."

"Did it make you feel like a fifth wheel?"

"No, oddly, it didn't. It was like that was how it was supposed to be. Of course, nine-tenths of the time I was in uniform: the clerical black suit and roman collar. And everybody deferred to 'Father.' Actually"—he smiled at the memory—"it was quite nice."

"I never had that sort of experience."

"You didn't?"

"I was in the convent, remember? By the time 'Father' arrived at his parishioners' party, 'Sister' was working over tomorrow's lessons plans. And by the time 'Father' was enjoying his after-dinner drink, 'Sister' was fast asleep."

They laughed quietly.

"And now, here we are at a party together," Pam said. "Only now we aren't with parishioners."

"True. Every husband in this room is a former priest

or seminarian. And a goodly number of the wives are former nuns.''

''A lot of good men and good women.''

''Yes. What a waste!''

Pam patted her husband's knee affectionately. ''Don't think about it.'' She knew this had all the ingredients for a difficult evening. Their daughter, Irma, had urged them to go to the party even though it would reduce by one the number of evenings they could spend together as a family before her return to school after the Christmas holidays. Irma was just grateful that it was a party they were going to and not a meeting of CORPUS.

But Pam knew better. She had not shared her reservations about this party with her daughter. No sense in spreading gloom. Besides, it was entirely possible nothing untoward would happen.

Nonetheless, she was hypersensitive to her husband's potential reaction to what he inevitably would encounter this evening.

A return to the active ministry had grown to become an obsession. What had begun as a harmless enough second-guessing of his decision to leave the priesthood and seek laicization had evolved into a matter of mental self-flagellation.

Her fears seemed warranted when she took stock of those who showed up tonight. While some—albeit a minority—of the women had never been in religious life, every man present had once been either a priest or a seminarian who had not reached ordination. The solid majority had been priests. Every one of these men, to Fred's way of thinking, should be as concerned as he about the state of the Church and the injustice involved in their being forbidden to use their priestly powers. And of course few if any of them spent much time thinking about it. None of them cared as much as Fred. And therein lay the possibility of a problem.

''You know,'' Fred said, ''I may be wrong, but have

you noticed that these get-togethers are different from
the parties we go to where the guests are laypeople?''

"How's that?"

"Think about it. Remember the Christmas party we
attended a little more than a week ago? The one sponsored by the State Psychology Society?''

"Yes.'' Pam let her mind's eye recreate the earlier
party. The crowd at the psychology bash had been more
stylishly dressed than the group here tonight. But the
earlier party was formal. Outside of that and, of course,
the fact that nearly everyone tonight had an explicit and
strong religious background, while religion was not the
long suit of the psychologists and their spouses, she
couldn't anticipate what Fred was suggesting.

"Well,'' Fred continued, "we've been here almost
an hour. About an hour after we arrived at the psychologists' party, nearly all the men had gathered in the
kitchen around the drinks. And nearly all the women
were seated in the living room.''

"Okay,'' she said, "I remember. So?''

"Well, just look at this group. No oil and water here.
The couples are still together, talking to each other with
no apparent need to separate the men from the women.''

With this perspective, Pam felt as if she were assess-
ing the guests with new eyes. And as she recalled past
gatherings, more than less they conformed to this
general pattern. Secular—for want of a better term—
assemblies did tend to split up according to sexes. It
seemed that men wanted each others' company, leaving
women to themselves.

Or was it women's topics of conversation? Did they
talk about babies? House decoration? Clubs? Fashion?
Was that why men isolated themselves in the kitchen?
Which came first, the chicken or the egg? Did men
make the first move to talk about work or sports or
other sorts of "male" conversation, thus leaving the
ladies to shift for themselves? Or were the men bored
silly and ran away to preserve their sanity?

Whatever, it did not seem so with gatherings like the one tonight. She wondered why. This tended to be a singular mix of older people, most of whom had married comparatively late. Many were thus childless. As for those who were parents, most had only one child, and the ages of those children varied widely. Almost none had grandchildren, though most were easily old enough.

Pam's speculation was silent. Fred's was not.

"I think," Fred said, "the people at parties like these are mostly of very strong character, especially the women. Much stronger women than average, don't you think?"

"I guess so," Pam agreed tentatively. "I haven't thought much about it. But now that you mention it, I guess I've never met any former priest's wife whom I didn't like. At least there are so few I don't get along with well that a negative experience is most rare."

"See what a great support group we'd make for each other if the Church would be reasonable and let us function again."

"Wait a minute, Buster. . . ." Pam quickly decided to be playful to lighten the subject. "When you are beating a path back to a former life, let me tell you, I don't want back in a convent—and I don't think that any other former nuns here tonight want to jump back over the wall."

"Right you are, my dear. And I know of no organization that proposes such a reentry. If any of these women wants to get back into religious life it would be as a priest."

"Again, count me out."

"Noted. But some do. And they ought to be able to."

"Hey, you two, you're not allowed to have a nice time alone. You gotta join the rest of us and be bored." One of the male guests had peeled himself away from the small group he'd been with and joined the Stapletons on the sofa.

"Oh, come now, Cass," Pam responded, "you are constitutionally unable to be boring. That's why you're such a successful insurance agent."

"Shh!" Cass Hershey held a prohibitive finger to his lips. "There may be somebody from the IRS here." He looked about mock-furtively. "As a matter of fact, there probably is. They're everywhere."

Pam was glad Cass had joined them. He didn't attend many of these gatherings so she didn't know him well. But on the infrequent occasions they'd been together he was always lighthearted, full of fun, finding humor where others did not. Right now, given Fred's preoccupation, Cass Hershey seemed just what the doctor ordered. So, instead of responding to his implicit invitation to join the others, thus risking a potentially embarrassing situation, she decided to try to draw Cass into their own conversation.

"Fred was just remarking," Pam said, "what strong women the wives of ex-priests seem to be."

"I'll say!" Cass enthused. "It's certainly true of Debbie. Wanna see my bruises?"

"Cass"—Fred's tone carried nothing but good humor—"don't you ever get serious about anything?"

"Work. Yes, I consider that to be serious business. Involving incidentals such as food, clothing, and shelter. But . . ." Cass hesitated. ". . . even then, sometimes you can't get away from the light side of life, even at work." He did not seem inclined to elaborate.

This line of conversation was just what Pam thought was needed. "Go on, Cass, tell us about it," she encouraged.

"It wasn't all that much, but it's a true story, a slice of life." Hershey had been sitting relaxed against the back of the sofa. Automatically, as a storyteller will, he sat up and leaned forward. "Remember Noel Parker?" He directed the question at Fred.

Fred searched his memory. "No, I don't think so. Should I?"

"He was a priest. Left recently. I recruited him for Massachusetts General."

"How old is he?"

"Mmm . . . mid-thirties, I'd say."

"Too young. I wouldn't know him."

"Doesn't matter. I just thought you might. He's a bright young man. Went through our training phase with flying colors.

"Part of the training is memorizing a spiel, then personalizing it. We usually approach owners of successful small businesses, and the first contact is by phone. The object is to give the prospective customer a variety of reasons that might make him want to consider our services. So you trot out every attractive credential you can muster.

"Noel is pretty new at this, so he was kind of anxious. After all, you get only one crack per client. If you sign him up, it could mean thousands of dollars. If you blow the initial contact, that's it forevermore.

"Noel himself told me about one of his first calls. No sooner had he started the conversation—remember he'd never actually met this guy—than he could sense that the potential client's attention span was not gangbusters and that the guy thought this was a waste of his valuable time. So Noel was understandably nervous. But he launched into his spiel. He mentioned that, along with other credentials, he held a doctoral degree from the University of Michigan. To which the client replied, 'Who gives a shit?'

"Noel just laughed, God bless him, and plowed on. After citing a few more credentials, Noel said he'd been a Catholic priest for ten years. And the guy says, 'Now that interests me.' And Noel was at least inside the door."

They laughed. Pam's laughter was a mixture of equal

parts of genuine appreciation and gratitude that Fred had been amused and distracted.

"So you see, Freddie, all is not bleak and serious, even in the very serious arena of earning a living.

"But why am I telling you that?" Cass went on. "You look to me like you're having a ball. A solid practice—and I see your handsome mug in the paper and on the tube with some regularity."

Fred instantly grew solemn. "I'd give it all up in a minute to get back in the functioning priesthood."

"You're kidding!" Cass exclaimed.

"Not for a minute. And I'm sure that underneath it all, the guys feel the same way."

Cass smiled amiably. "Speak for yourself, kiddo."

Pam squeezed into the conversation. "Just before you joined us, I was telling Fred that I, for one, didn't want to go back into the convent, nor, for that matter, forward into the priesthood."

"Sounds nice and normal to me," Cass commented.

"Do you mean to tell me," Fred said, "that you didn't want to become a priest?"

"Of course I did. Nobody twisted my arm. But that was a different day."

"No different than today. Don't you miss offering Mass, the Sunday liturgies, all the things you could do for people as a priest?"

"Fred, that was a long time ago."

"But don't you miss it?" Fred persisted.

"It was too long ago. Okay, yes, every once in a long while I remember how it was—and parts of it were very worthwhile. Some of it was even fun. But it was a long time ago, Fred. Loosen up."

"It can be ours again, Cass. We're making progress. Have you heard of CORPUS?"

"Sure."

"Well?"

"Well, I've heard of it."

"You don't belong, do you?"

"Ever see me at a meeting?"

"You could still belong."

"I don't."

"Why not?"

"Why?"

"Because," Fred explained, "it's our best . . . our most practical way of getting back into the ministry. Sure, it's a small, gradational step. But it's going to work. Lots of other men, converts from the Protestant ministry, are married Catholic priests now."

As Fred spoke with deepening emotion, his voice rose. Gradually, other conversation in the room quieted, then ceased. Some few in the group were aware of Fred's intense commitment to CORPUS. Others were learning of it for the first time.

Pam, aware—as her husband was not—that nearly everyone had tuned in to the interchange, was deeply ill-at-ease. "Fred," she said, touching his arm, "don't you think—"

But it was Cass who interrupted. "Is that what this is all about, Freddie? You want to function as a married priest. And to do that you'd be willing to crawl to Rome and beg to be allowed to do some of the things a deacon can do. God! Some of the things laypeople can do now! Well, you can count me out of that one."

"I thought you said you wanted to be a priest!"

"I did. What it comes down to is why we—you and I—quit the priesthood. That's what it comes down to." Cass, fueled by Fred's fervor, was becoming emotionally involved in the debate. "You left in order to get married."

"Of course."

"And I did not."

"You didn't!?" Fred was surprised. While he had not canvassed all former priests by any means, the overwhelming majority of those who had talked about it had pinpointed marriage as their primary reason for leaving.

"No, I didn't," Cass repeated, "and neither did you."

"I should know my own mind." There was irritation in Fred's tone. "I know why I resigned. It's the same reason everyone in this room did."

"Is it now? Think of all the priests you knew when you were growing up, when you were in the seminary, after you were ordained—all you knew before the council. Can you think of one or two—if that many—who left for whatever reason and got married during that time?"

Fred did not immediately reply. Then, "If you're saying the dam broke after the council, I wouldn't argue that."

"That's not quite the point. How about us? You were a priest for . . . what?"

"Twenty years."

"Twenty years. A career, by God. Well, what was it with us? We were priests for ten, fifteen, twenty years; celibates, enjoying days off together, spending vacations together, the epitome of male bonding. What happened? After five or ten or fifteen or . . . twenty years, we woke up one morning and said, 'Hey, wait a minute . . . there's girls!'? Is that the way you think it happened?"

"Of course not—"

"Left to get married! With me, it was just about the exact opposite. Debbie was one very ill lady. She'd drifted off sick leave and lost her job. It was tight, but she was making it on a combination of worker's comp and help from my priestly salary. It was no time to leave the security of Mother Church and get a job out in the cruel, hard world.

"Don't you see, Fred, it was the worst possible time to leave, at least for me. I didn't leave to get married. The only thing that changed for me when I left was that I was out of a job. Okay, so we were now a legitimate couple. We didn't have to worry any longer whether we would meet anyone we knew in the infrequent times we dared go out together. But by the single act of resigning, we went from a nice cozy security to insolvency.

"We didn't leave to get married, Fred. If we had, we'd have done it long ago, when we were much younger men. When the juices were really flowing. When we were young priests, we—all of us—met any number of great women who would have made terrific wives. So did all those priests who preceded us. They lived and died celibates. And we will not."

"I wouldn't argue with you, Cass, about the women we met when we were young. Most of them were fine Catholic women and most of them were already married. And there's something else you're overlooking: Before the idea of leaving occurred to us, it had already dawned on nuns. Typical. Women got the idea first. After they left, when they were free to marry, it was only natural that we would be attracted to such fine, strong women. Our backgrounds were almost identical. We shared a deep commitment to religion, to Catholicism. And they were free to marry. They were not already attached."

"Nice argument, Fred, but it won't wash. One of the results of Vatican II—for me, the major achievement—was the questioning attitude that remained after the council was concluded. All we ever did as kids—and adults—was learn and take orders. We never questioned. But when we finally did, we found out there weren't all that many good answers around.

"We went back to our origins, and asked things like where and when did the cultic priesthood come from? When did the successors of the humble Apostle Peter get all the trappings of a king? When did they get to be infallible and why? Where did a mandated clergy come from and why?

"For a lot of us the answers of old weren't good enough. For ten, fifteen, or twenty years, it was worth the sacrifice of being celibate. And then it was not. We didn't leave and get married because our hormones suddenly got to be too much for us to control. We left because we saw the Church in a new light. And the changed Church we now saw was not worth the sacrifices it still demanded.''

Hershey delivered the argument with a flourish. The by-now attentive audience almost applauded.

But Fred Stapleton was not vanquished.

"Cass"—Fred had his eyes on Hershey, but he was openly addressing the entire gathering—"we have lived our entire lives intimately bound up in the Church. You can joke about it, but we don't call it 'Mother Church' for nothing. Especially us, Cass. Think! Remember! If not all of us, then a very high percentage, came from devout Catholic families who treasured the priesthood. That's certainly where the idea of becoming a priest began for us. We were altar boys and we memorized the Latin euphonically. We served Mass for every kind of priest imaginable—old, young, thin, fat, devout, irreverent, fast, slow, saints, and sinners. And all the time, that's what we wanted to be. That's what we wanted to do.

"We spent up to twelve years in the seminary while we made up our minds and the faculty made up its mind about us. We were ordained. It was the culmination of our dreams. We spent years of committed service as priests before, for whatever reason, we left . . . so far, a fair enough picture?''

"So far.'' In all honesty Cass couldn't fault the narrative even if, in the light of the council, it was, he thought, a bit simplistic.

"As a matter of self-examination,'' Fred continued, "why do I want to return to the active ministry? Lots of reasons—but then no one does anything for a single reason.

"Why do I want to function as a priest again? Because the same things that attracted me as a boy draw me now. I love the cultic priesthood and I really don't care where it came from or why. I miss the miracles only a priest can work in counseling sessions. And, believe me, as a practicing psychologist, I can clearly tell the difference between purely psychological therapy and the opportunity to soothe a troubled conscience by making contact with God's love. I love and miss all of the small day-to-day miracles a priest performs.

"But mostly, 'Mother,' as we call the Church, whether sarcastically or fondly, is in trouble. She doesn't even realize how much trouble she's in. Soon there will be so few nuns the vocation will be little more than a memory, and a dusty memory at that. The median age of priests is so high now and there are so few remaining active that 'burnout' vies with retirement and death in thinning the ranks. Seminaries are virtually empty, especially when you contrast the few enrolled with the need for many times that number.

"Lots of reasons are given for the drastically low number of seminarians. But part of one reason—a large part I think—is us. You said it yourself, Cass: The priests we knew before the council remained active into the next life. When we were kids and we thought of becoming priests, we subconsciously put our ambition in the context of permanency. Young men today cannot overlook us. We were good priests and now we function as priests no more. Young men don't have to argue about why we left. All they need know is *that* we left. If we found the priestly life that difficult, that impossible, they think why should they get involved. Why should they make the sacrifice? For what?

"Finally, 'Mother' is in trouble because she can't or won't see any of this. The Church needs us. She needs our experience, our expertise, and our presence. The Church needs our unique contribution. But 'Mother' believes she can get along quite well without us. Here is a 'Mother' who thinks she can get along without some of her most completely trained and most needed children. Not only would it be a joy to return to the active ministry, it would go a long way to repay the debt we owe the institution that nourished our religious lives since we were children.

"Cass, in the final analysis, we must save the Church from herself."

The hush in the room was remarkable. What had begun as a lighthearted party had evolved into a debate between two of the most successful people at that party. Hershey and Stapleton had started their adult lives as simple parish priests. Abandoning that, the former quickly rose to the top of the local chapter of Massachusetts General Insurance. He was now impressively wealthy.

The latter, while not in Hershey's financial stratum, was prosperous, but beyond that, he was respected, well regarded in his field, and, at least on the local level, a celebrity.

Among the listeners to their debate, an aura of agreement seemed to flow from one to the other. When Hershey scored a point, though there was no literal movement in the room, one could sense that the majority had been convinced. Only to feel the conviction shift as the other made his point.

Stapleton, with his emotional appeal to affection—even love—that everyone here at least once had for "Mother Church," had the upper hand at the moment.

"Fred," Hershey came back, "it's a mighty strange 'Mother' you want to save from herself. Take the two of us, her children, for example. Me first.

"I left the priesthood in about as filial a way as any mother could expect. I didn't cause any sort of ruckus; no press conferences, no public statement of any kind. I didn't make any demands about eventually getting a pension, even though I had worked for the Church better than ten years. Now, just about any conscientious organization you can think of gives an employee a vested right to some sort of pension after ten years of employment. Fortunately, I don't need one. But other guys do, and they're not going to get it. If big bad businesses can care enough for their employees, you'd think a mother would be at least as decent to her children.

"Instead of rewarding us for our service, 'Mother' excommunicated me. Not for leaving the priesthood— no, for getting married.''

"No," Fred interrupted, "that was because you didn't get laicized."

"Which," Cass returned, "brings us to you. You went through the process, and almost as luck would have it, you got it. You were laicized. So, although you, like me, got married, you are not excommunicated. But what did 'Mother' demand as a price for granting the dispensation?

"I've read the rescript and I'm sure you have too."

Fred winced inwardly. He knew what was coming.

"In return for keeping all the rules and going through the whole demeaning process, 'Mother' threw some new rules and regulations at you. I can't hope to re- member them all, but here's a few:

"Outside of being able to absolve someone who is in danger of death—something, by the way, that even I in my state am empowered to do—you cannot exercise any function of a priest. You can't preach a sermon. You can't take any part in a liturgy anywhere your 'condi- tion' is known. Like you had leprosy and people would be shocked if they knew about it.

"Almost anybody in any parish can be delegated to distribute Communion. They're called 'extraordinary ministers of the Eucharist.' You, who gave Communion almost every day of your life for twenty years, you can't even be an extraordinary minister.

"You can't do anything in any seminary in the world. Not only are you barred from teaching theology, you can't even teach a language in a seminary. You can't teach in Church-related colleges. You can't even teach in Church-related schools unless a bishop specifically okays it, and even then, you can't teach religion there.

Of course, the bishop just might—and that's a heavy-duty 'might'—let you teach religion as long as it wouldn't cause scandal. Once again, you are the leper.

"Your marriage has to be the sort that used to be performed in a rectory rather than a church. It has to be performed as if everyone involved is ashamed of what's happening.

"You are supposed to move out of the locale where you were a priest to somewhere where no one has a chance of knowing that once upon a time you were a priest. Again, a bishop can dispense with this atrocity.

"And finally—and most damaging to your whole argument—it's final. You can never go back. As excommunicated as I am, I haven't been put in your category. Were I to be divorced or—God forbid—become a widower, theoretically I could function as a priest again, though they'd probably try to send me to Ethiopia. But you: You're *laicized*. You played by all their rules. And because of that, you're out for good."

Stapleton was quick to respond. "You're exaggerating. For one thing, nobody—at least nobody I know—enforces those rules totally. And for another, that ban on laicized priests returning can be changed by the Pope at any time."

"Okay, Fred, the Pope can do anything he damn well pleases, but this Pope is not likely to do that. And whether or not the rules are enforced is beside the point I'm making—which is that there is no earthly reason why you cannot give Communion, or teach religion, or why you should have to get married like an ecclesiastical leper. There's certainly no logical reason why you should be specifically banned from functioning as a priest again. The point is: 'Mother' is being vindictive, nothing more, nothing less. 'Hell hath no fury,' etc. And I don't think it's worth it, saving a vindictive 'Mother' from herself. Let her founder, I say."

"It's worth it, damn it! *She's* worth it!" Stapleton was becoming charged. Something he rarely did. "It won't be easy. That I admit. Something drastic has to happen—is happening—that will get the Church's attention.''

"There isn't anything extreme enough to get this institution's attention. What could do it, Fred? What could do it?''

Stapleton hesitated. He seemed to be struggling inwardly with a decision. "It can't be told yet. But it will be eventually, and then you'll see. All of you. You'll see for yourselves.''

With that, Stapleton nodded to his wife, who long ago had known the evening was going to end early. She went to collect their coats. Then, after murmuring a farewell as well as an apology to the host couple, she rejoined her husband as they left and headed home—in silence, as it turned out.

The party slowly revivified as the guests gradually recovered. Most of them split into small groups and proceeded to debate the issues that had been raised by Hershey and Stapleton.

Meanwhile, Debbie Hershey joined her husband. "That was some tussle.'' Debbie carried two highballs. She handed one to Cass.

"You said it. How did we get into that anyway?''

"Don't you remember? You went over to try to get them to join the rest of the crowd.''

"Yeah, that's right.'' As he sipped his drink he became aware that his throat was sore. "Instead of getting the party together, we damn near broke it up.''

"You know, Cass, we've been together a long time. But I've never heard you talk about the Church like that.''

Hershey shrugged. "I never think about the Church, I guess. Certainly not as a mother in need of my presence.''

"Well, Fred Stapleton certainly does. He made that crystal clear tonight.''

"That's got me puzzled, Deb. He was never like he was tonight. Not all the time I've known him."

"I hardly know the Stapletons. They don't usually come to get-togethers like this."

"I know. I thought these gatherings were just not his cup of tea, or that he was too tired. But from what I saw tonight, I'll bet he spends every free moment he's got on this CORPUS thing."

"It sure sounded like that."

"I know some people in that organization. They're committed, but not like Fred." He shook his head. "I can't figure it out. He was a few years ahead of me in the seminary but I knew him pretty well. Quiet, thoughtful; he seemed a dedicated student. But just about the opposite of a rabble-rouser. The kind of guy who would make a good priest—or, for that matter, a good shrink. As often as I see him on TV or hear him on radio or read about him, I've always felt good for him. Good that he found this psychology gig. He seemed a natural." Brow furrowed, he shook his head again. "But . . . after this evening . . ."

"I know; there were a couple of times tonight when I thought you two might come to blows."

"Did you? It didn't cross my mind. But now that you mention it, there was something . . . I don't know what. You're right: There was a hint of a time bomb—just below the surface. Way, way out of character for Fred Stapleton. Way out of character. Like someone else had taken over. And then at the end, when he said something about getting the Church's attention . . ." he looked at her searchingly. "What the hell was that all about?"

"I don't know, honey, but it sounded kind of ominous."

"Yeah, something's going on with Fred. But what?"

20

"FIVE CARD DRAW, gentlemen," the Reverend Mr. Quentin Jeffrey announced. "Jacks or better to open, and one-eyed jacks are wild. Let's ante."

Father Koesler scarcely ever attended poker games. Early on, he had learned that conversation, idle chitchat, was not welcome at the poker table. And Koesler did like to chat. What better to do when priests get together socially? Something that happened too rarely these days. Almost more importantly, he hated to lose. He hated it to the point of fearing it. And that was not the proper attitude to bring to the poker table.

So why was he here tonight?

Cletus Bash had asked him to come. Almost pleaded with him. Father Bash was having a difficult time gathering sufficient numbers.

No trouble getting Quent Jeffrey, of course. Poker was second nature to him. Everyone knew that. But all the other dependable regulars seemed unavailable. Bash could have played two-handed with Jeffrey but, in all candor, Bash knew he was no match whatever for Jeffrey. Safety in numbers, he figured.

All this was a conclusion Koesler easily reached. Another measure of Bash's desperation was that the fourth player tonight was Monsignor Del Young.

While the monsignor had an overstocked purse and didn't mind losing at games of chance—which he did with determined regularity—he, too, was an irrepressible conversationalist.

Koesler was unable to guess how many clerical prospects Bash had contacted earlier. The number must have been astronomical if the best Bash could do was himself, Bob Koesler, and Del Young. It was next to impossible to tell how frustrated Bash felt. He was, normally, quite surly and sharp. Those words exactly described him tonight. But then, they probably would have defined his disposition even if he had had greater success in lining up more dedicated players. The few times Bash could have been considered as being ebullient, as far as Koesler could recall, were those occasions when his high profile was being featured in the local media, clearly identified as the archdiocesan spokesman—read best-informed person in captivity.

Bash spoke. "Someone's light."

Koesler glanced at the table top. Three white chips lay where they had been casually tossed. "Del," Koesler said softly, "I think you forgot to ante."

"Me? Did I? That was careless. Sorry." He pitched a white chip onto the center of the table.

The cards were being dealt noiselessly, expertly, one at the time, five to a customer. Koesler marveled at Quent Jeffrey's dexterity. While card games were not Koesler's favorite pastime, he'd seen his share of dealers—mostly fellow clergymen—although he'd never joined any of the guys in a Las Vegas vacation, nor had he witnessed any truly professional players. Nonetheless he thought Jeffrey must come close to the professional norm.

Jeffrey did not bother looking at the cards as he dealt. Rather, he studied the faces of the other players. Particularly Del Young, who picked up and appraised each card as it was dealt. Neither Bash nor Koesler touched a card until all were dealt.

Following Jeffrey's lead, Koesler scrutinized Young as he picked up the cards and fitted them into some sort of order in his hand. To Koesler's surprise, it did seem possible to tell whether Young was experiencing good or bad cards by little movements of an eyebrow or cheek muscle. Young's was the antithesis of the storied poker face.

Koesler wondered whether he himself betrayed his hand, bad or good, in the same way. But he decided that he played so seldom it wasn't worth worrying about.

Everyone studied his cards in silence.

"I'll open for two." Bash dropped two red chips into the small pot.

"All right here." Young contributed two red chips.

Wordlessly, Koesler and Jeffrey did the same.

Jeffrey picked up the deck and looked expectantly at Bash.

"Three," said Bash. Jeffrey dealt him three, again studying the face, not the cards.

"One," said Young.

"Three." Koesler.

Jeffrey: "And the dealer takes three."

Each player having discarded, picked up, and studied the newly dealt cards.

Koesler's hand had not improved. He'd started with two tens; that was still the best he could do. It was a hopeless hand. One had to have at least a pair of jacks to open and Bash had done that. Thus Koesler was defeated without leaving the gate.

Jeffrey waited, looking at Bash, who had opened so it was his move.

"Check," Bash said.

"Well, I guess I'll open with five." Young carefully deposited five blue chips in the pot.

Koesler, his hand already defeated, had studied Young as the monsignor had picked up his one card. Both eyebrows had reacted. It was a safe guess that he had gotten his card. Koesler threw in his hand, as did Jeffrey. Had Jeffrey also spotted the reaction?

"I'll call you, Del," Bash said as he dropped five blue chips in the pot.

Nothing happened. Something should have.

"Del," Jeffrey said, "what have you got? Clete called you."

"Oh!" Young exclaimed. "Yes, of course." He spread his five cards on the table as he declared, "Full house. Kings over eights."

"Damn!" Bash muttered, and pitched his cards face down on the table.

"Well," Young said happily, "looks like my night."

All things are possible, thought Koesler. But the likelihood of Del Young's having a "night" of luck was so remote as to be ludicrous. There was his tendency to bet impetuously, which was definitely not the mark of a winner. Then there were the dramatis personae of the evening. On his best day, Del Young could not gamble successfully against Clete Bash. And Quent Jeffrey was way out of both their leagues.

As for himself, the difference between Del Young and Koesler was that Koesler knew his limits—and they were very narrow. Indeed, it had been at Koesler's insistence that the stakes were reduced for the evening. White chips were worth twenty-five cents. Red chips were worth fifty cents. And blue chips were valued at a dollar. Usually the stakes were much higher.

But, as always, Koesler's highest hope was to break even. While he did not mind contributing to charity, his favorite charity was neither Bash nor Jeffrey.

Clete Bash gathered the scattered cards and began to shuffle them.

"Anything new on the murders?" Young asked, making conversation. And then clarified, "I mean poor Larry Hoffer and the Donovan woman."

"Not that I'm aware of," Koesler said. "I've tried to keep up with the news but it seems the police investigation is proceeding without any breaks in the case."

"I wish they'd hurry up," Young said. "I'm getting

nervous. There's somebody out there who seems to be hunting down officials of the diocese.''

"And you're one of them,'' Bash said as he shuffled. He was poking fun at the monsignor.

"All well and good for you to feel secure—at least tonight,'' Young retorted. "After all, we're playing on your turf. You don't have to get home after this is over.''

They were gathered in the common room on the Chancery Building's seventh floor. Bash's living quarters were on the ninth floor. In former times the priests' residence rooms on the building's ninth and tenth floors would have been almost all occupied, and the common room well populated at this hour. However, these were lean times. Having a chancery full of resident priests at the expense of help in parishes would have been a senseless luxury.

"Five card stud,'' Bash announced. "First and last card down. Ante two.''

Each pitched two white chips in.

Bash dealt the first card to each player face down, the second face up. Each glanced at his secret first card. Only the player himself knew what he held, while everyone knew what the second card was.

"King bets,'' Bash said, referring to Young's face-up card.

"Well, it does seem to be my night,'' Young said. "King bets one.'' He pitched in a red chip. Everyone else followed in kind. Bash dealt the next card to each face up.

"Well, well; a pair of kings.'' Bash referred to that portion of Young's hand everyone could see. "Kings bet.''

Young was so pleased he almost twitched. "My goodness! Did I say this would be my night? Well, kings will bet five.'' And he slid five blue chips onto the table center.

In three cards, Koesler had nothing. With only two

cards remaining to be dealt, he would have to come up with at least a pair of aces to beat what Young had showing, let alone what might be the monsignor's hole cards. Wisely, he folded.

"I guess I'll see you, Del," Jeffrey said, "and raise you five." He pushed ten blue chips into the pot. Young answered his raise.

Bash, whose hand resembled Koesler's, folded. It was between Jeffrey and Young. Bash dealt another card, face up, to each of the remaining two players. In addition to his two kings, Young now had a ten of hearts showing.

"Kings still high," Bash, as dealer, announced.

"So they are," Young agreed. He peeked again at the hole card, as if it might have changed spots since his previous look. "Well, then, kings will just chance another five."

Jeffrey regarded Young with quiet amusement. He pushed ten blue chips into the pot. "And five," he said.

Everyone looked more closely at that portion of Jeffrey's hand showing. Two, seven, and eight of hearts. A flush? With one card yet to be dealt, it seemed the only possible hand that could beat Young's. Interesting, even for Koesler.

Silently, with some temerity, Young pushed another five chips into the pot.

"All right, gentlemen, the last card. Down and dirty." Bash dealt Young, then Jeffrey, each the final card, face down.

Young slipped both hole cards to the table's edge in proximity to his ample stomach, lifted the corners, and contemplated the completed hand that only he could see. He continued to contemplate until Bash said, "Del, what'll it be?"

"Eh?" Young realized a decision must be made. *Be bold.* For Jeffrey to have a flush both hole cards had to be hearts. The likelihood of that . . . not high. Young decided to smoke Jeffrey out. "We'll just up things to ten." And Young let ten blue chips drop one by one to the table. It could have been a dramatic gesture, except that he didn't quite carry it off.

Amazingly, as far as Koesler was concerned, Jeffrey only now turned up the corner of his final card to see what it was. Cool. He paused only seconds before pushing twenty blue chips forward, and said, "Your ten and ten more."

Everyone looked at Young, who betrayed surprise. He had been certain his ten-dollar bet would clinch his winning hand. Now this. He picked up his hole cards and studied them again. Whatever they had been they still were. No one pressed him. This was a fairly steep pot, worth thinking about.

Finally, Young exclaimed, "You're bluffing!"

Jeffrey smiled and shrugged.

"There's one way to find out, Del," Bash said.

That was true. Young had three choices: He could raise the bet again, hoping to call Jeffrey's bluff. He could call Jeffrey and end this hand one way or another. Or he could fold, in which case Jeffrey would not have to reveal his hand. He would take the pot.

Young, hand trembling slightly, added ten more blue chips to the pot. "Let's just see what you've got there, Quent."

Gazing steadfastly at Young and again not looking at his cards, simply aware of where they lay, Jeffrey turned over a five and a nine of hearts to go with the two, seven, and eight of hearts.

A flush.

Wordlessly, Jeffrey raked in the fat pot.

Young, rallying quickly, said, "Well, a little setback, but a good hand anyway." Although there was no need, he exposed his hole cards, revealing he'd had two pair: kings and tens. Good but not good enough.

It was Young's turn to deal. He began gathering cards. "Say, Clete, how about some refreshments?"

"So early?" Bash said.

"I'll go along with Del," Jeffrey said. "Missed supper tonight. I could use something, something solid."

"Okay," Bash said. He got up, went to the refrigerator, and began rummaging through it.

Koesler was elated at this break. Time for conversation. He hadn't dared hope for a recess this early.

"I still say they should at least have some suspects by now," Young said in what seemed a non sequitur.

"Suspects?" Jeffrey said.

"Suspects," Young repeated. "Suspects in the murders of Larry Hoffer and what's-her-name, uh, Helen Donovan."

"They've got the kid who tried to kill Joan Donovan," Jeffrey said.

"Not the same," Young said. "The one who wants to kill diocesan officials is still loose out there."

Bash was assembling cheese-and-cracker snacks. With his back to the others, he said, "They do have a couple of suspects."

"They do?" Koesler noted the self-satisfied tone Bash did not attempt to hide.

"How do you know?" Young was not an instant believer.

"I've got sources in the police department. But it's privileged information," Bash cautioned. "The media doesn't even have it yet. But when they get it, I'll be ready for backgrounding."

"Well," Young said, "for Godsakes, man, who are they? Who are the suspects?"

"It's privileged. I can't reveal it," Bash said.

"For Godsakes, man, we're not going to tell anyone. For Godsakes, we're . . ." Young paused. He was about to say they were all priests and disciplined in the ultimate secret of confession when he remembered that one of their number was a deacon and not empowered to hear confessions. After the slight pause, he concluded ". . . we're all men of the cloth."

"Okay." Bash put the dishes holding cheese and crackers respectively on the table. "Remember, this is only in the investigative stage. But the cops are looking into . . ." He paused for effect. It worked; he had their undivided attention. ". . . into Arnold Carson and Fred Stapleton." He smiled triumphantly.

"Stapleton!" Koesler exclaimed. "Fred Stapleton? There must be some mistake."

"No mistake," Bash responded. "What'll anyone have to drink?"

"Pass here," Jeffrey said. "The cheese and crackers should hit the spot."

"Nothing here either." Koesler made a sandwich.

"How about a beer?" Young said.

Bash returned to the fridge for beers for himself and Young.

"I hadn't thought of it before," Young said, "but Carson is not a bad bet. Good God, how many times has he taken the lead in protests? Why for heaven's sake, he's forever in the papers and on TV."

"Before Vatican II, nobody ever heard of him," Bash said. "But after the council . . . well, the guy never lets up. He's forever up on the ramparts protecting Mother Church."

Young nodded. "And now Mother Church may need protection from Arnold Carson."

"Who's Fred Stapleton?" Jeffrey asked. "Not the psychologist!"

"The very same," Bash affirmed. "Don't forget, he is an 'ex.' "

Jeffrey smiled briefly. "I guess I had forgotten or at least overlooked the fact that he'd been a priest. But that was a long time ago. Now I tend to think of him as a psychologist. And a good one. At least very popular. He's always being asked to give his opinion in local cases. He's in the media more than just about any other local psychologist. What in the world would make him a suspect?''

"Not because he's a shrink," Bash said. "Because he's an 'ex.' ''

"Come on . . .'' Young had drained half his glass in a chugalug. "There are hundreds of ex-priests around here. All of them suspects?''

"It's because of his work for CORPUS. He's become a militant," Bash said. "And some say he is verging on becoming extreme.''

"Fred? Extreme?" Koesler was astonished. "That doesn't make sense. Fred is one of the sanest, most reasonable men I've ever known.''

"About your time, wasn't he, Bob?" Young asked.

"A year or two behind me, as I recall," Koesler said. "But I know him as well as I knew most of my classmates. He really couldn't qualify as a violent person. Just the opposite.''

"Seen him lately?" Bash asked.

"Well, no," Koesler admitted. "It's been a while. After he left and got into the psychology field we sort of drifted apart. I referred a couple of cases to him but that's about it.''

"People change," Bash observed.

"Not Fred. Not that much," Koesler protested.

"You never know," Bash said. "Besides, I'm not up to arguing the point. I'm just telling you what I got from my sources. But I can tell you one thing: If the investigation of these guys leaks, I'll be more prepared for the press than anybody else in town. And we're talking national coverage, gentlemen, not just the local guys.''

"Refresh me," Jeffrey said, "what's CORPUS again? It rings a bell, but I'm drawing a blank.''

"A bunch of exes," Young said. "They want to get back in, fully functioning as priests—wives, kids, and all. Say, Clete, how about another beer?''

"You finish that one already?" Bash said. "You better slow up." But he went to the fridge and brought back another beer for the monsignor.

"Okay, I remember CORPUS now," Jeffrey said. "They've got just about all the arguments on their side: history, early tradition, and now the admission of converted married Protestant ministers. They've got it all. And they haven't got a chance."

"They've got one more thing you didn't mention, Quent," Koesler said. "We're running out of priests. They've got need on their side. There are thousands of inactive priests who want to become active again. They're completely trained. All that's required is for the Pope to open the door and a good portion of our desperate need would be solved."

"It's not going to happen," Jeffrey said. "The bottom line is canon law—and canon law holds all the cards."

"Quent is right, Bob," Young said. "The Church in Rome really got stung when these guys quit. It's been a constant source of embarrassment to the Church that these men resigned from an office that brooked no resignation. They took on a lifelong commitment and then left it. In effect, the Church told the world, This is the highest vocation known to mankind; only the best and brightest can qualify. And then thousands of the best and brightest leave. That hurt. And the Church is not going to forget about that. Nor is the Church going to let *them* forget about it."

"Now that I think about it," Bash said, "that's probably what would turn Fred Stapleton to violence: the sheer frustration of trying to accomplish the impossible." He nodded. "It makes sense."

"Maybe," Koesler said. "But I just don't see it. Carson, possibly. But not Stapleton. No," he shook his head, "not Stapleton."

"Come on, Bob," Young said, "you just admitted

it's been a while since you've had any contact with Stapleton. People change.''

"What is this?" Bash demanded. "Are we hosting a convention or playing poker?"

"Right! Where were we?" Young looked about him.

"Your deal, Del," Jeffrey said, and began gathering the cards to give them to Young.

"Any more beer in the fridge?" Young wanted to know.

"More than even you can drink," Bash answered. He went to get the beer. "Better be careful, Del. You're the designated driver for your car."

They laughed. Each of them was his own designated driver since each had come alone. Only Clete Bash would not be driving. And that only because he was already home.

As Del Young began shuffling cards with hazy determination, Koesler studied the group.

Three priests and a deacon. All four men were of a certain age, so they had much in common in addition to their vocation. They had each developed in the pre-Vatican II Church and all had been through the trauma of ensuing radical change. The only noteworthy thing about this group was how easily Quent Jeffrey had fit in with the priests.

The permanent deacon program produced deacons, not priests. With a preparation program of just a few short years, deacons were to priests what the ninety-day-wonders of World War II were to traditional military officers.

Added to that, the vast majority of permanent deacons were married. They quite naturally structured their lives around their families. Another sharply dividing feature from the celibate priests.

That had to be one of the reasons the Reverend Mr. Quentin Jeffrey fit into this group far more snugly than the average permanent deacon. He had been married.

Now he was a widower, his children grown and living their own lives.

Here they were—four bachelors. Three had consciously chosen the celibate life. One had backed into it unintentionally, as it were. A married clergy was on the way for the Roman Catholic Church—indeed, it had already begun—once the law of celibacy became optional. Koesler was certain of this. He had no idea how the Church could possibly continue without a sacramental ministry. And you needed priests to do the sacramental things.

Even now, there were "no-priest" parishes. On Sundays a nun or a layperson would lead a prayer service during which Communion would be distributed. But sometime before that prayer service, a priest had to offer Mass and leave behind him those consecrated wafers that were distributed at the Communion service.

There was just no getting around it: Priests were the only ones who could confect the Eucharist. And the Eucharist was at the center and heart of Catholicism. Koesler simply could not conjure up his Church without the Eucharist and the priest to confect the sacrament.

But clearly the Church was suffering already from a dearth of those priests. The only logical move had to be to get more priests through the method most often suggested: optional celibacy—a married priesthood.

But how would these married priests blend in with the remaining celibates? Would there be many remaining celibates? Any?

Koesler fully expected this radical move in his lifetime. One more gigantic change. These were interesting times.

His daydream was broken off as Cletus Bash almost shouted at Del Young, "Are you going to shuffle the spots off those cards!?"

Young, who had been shuffling the cards interminably, was roused. "Ah, yes, poker. Gentlemen, we'll play seven card stud; low in the hole is wild." After thinking about it, he added, "Also wild are twos, nines, and . . . uh . . . one-eyed jacks."

"Why don't you have fifty-two wild cards!?" Bash bellowed. "I'm out!"

"Before I deal?" Young said.

"I'm out!" Bash insisted.

Jeffrey laughed out loud.

It was then that Koesler realized that Jeffrey was merely tolerating this peculiar poker company. Much as a scratch golfer might temporarily put aside thoughts of a serious match when teamed with duffers.

As it happened, they played what passed for poker on and off until just after midnight.

Quent Jeffrey had won a ton. Clete Bash lost a small sum. Bob Koesler lost a bit more than Bash. Del Young was the evening's big loser, which surprised no one, including Young.

However, the monsignor had enjoyed himself, gotten a lot of gossip out in the open, and demonstrated once again his prodigious capacity for beer.

After convincing everyone that he was fully capable of driving himself home, Young proceeded to do so.

Monsignor Del Young was in residence at St. Benedict parish in Pontiac. It was a long drive from downtown Detroit. Fortunately, at that time of night, the Lodge Freeway and Telegraph Road, his thoroughfares of choice, were uncluttered. So his much-diminished reactive powers were not tested. But his need to empty his bladder grew with each passing mile. He did not see any restaurants still open, and he thought it unseemly for a prelate to relieve himself along the highway.

Thus it was with a relieved sigh that he turned from Telegraph onto Voorheis and then onto Lynn. Home at last.

He parked. The biting cold—an eighteen-below windchill—hit him hard after the comfortable warmth of his late-model Olds. He tried to walk quickly to the rectory, but found himself staggering slightly.

Then he saw him.

Young couldn't be sure at first. He wanted to believe his eyes were playing tricks.

He advanced no further. Fear cleared his mind of all alcoholic fog.

It was a man. He could make out the outline now. Trousers, some sort of short coat, a hat—looked like some sort of baseball cap. Not dressed for the weather. Dressed for what? Dressed to kill?

The man made no movement. He stood on the sidewalk just outside the rectory, blocking Young's access to the rectory, to safety.

Just where the others had been killed. Donovan on the steps of St. Leo's convent; Hoffer just outside his home. On the sidewalk.

Young was unsure what course to essay. All he knew was that he had been selected to be the next victim. But why? What had he done? *Why me?* he almost shouted. But he couldn't speak.

Then, suddenly, he could. "NO!" he yelled. Then he ran. He ran as swiftly as he could. He didn't dare look back. He gave brief thought to screaming for help. But what good would that do? It was near two A.M. Everyone in the neighborhood would be asleep. Besides, how eager would any of them be to come out into freezing cold in nightclothes. For what? To be killed for their trouble? He had to find safety.

The school! Somewhere on his key ring was a key to the school door. He hadn't wanted it, but the pastor had insisted he have it. It just might save his life now.

He made it to the school. So far so good. Miraculously, out of all the many keys he carried, his fingers found the key to the school. He didn't fumble. The key slid into the lock and turned smoothly.

He was inside.

For the first time, he dared look behind him. There was no one in sight.

Before anything else—he felt he was about to explode—he found the boys' lavatory and relieved himself. Next he called the police.

The remainder of that early morning was an explosion of sound and light. There were sirens, questions, first from the police, then from the media. There were flashbulbs, of course, and the sun guns of the TV people.

He told his story over and over again. He walked it through just as he had earlier run it through. There would be no rest for him until late that afternoon.

He did not miss the sleep. After a while, he began to relax and enjoy the whole thing.

He was a celebrity. He had met the killer and escaped. Heady stuff.

Meanwhile, a stranger from out of town was one very bewildered man.

He had come up north from Florida. He'd been out of work too long. So, leaving his family behind, he hitchhiked to the Detroit area, certain he could find work here.

His first discovery was that he had badly misjudged the weather. It was so cold. He was nearly frozen. And he was in desperate need of shelter in a foreign land.

Good Catholic that he was, he was sure he would not be turned away by a priest. If only he could find one. It was late when he began his search for a friendly rectory.

A clerk in a twenty-four-hour gas station, where he'd been left off by his latest driver, directed him to St. Benedict rectory. He'd gotten there at about the same time as Monsignor Young.

He'd been surprised—happily—that he should be so fortunate as to have a priest meet him on the sidewalk—

at that hour! Clearly, it was a most touching answer to prayer.

Then the priest had screamed at him! And began to run.

The vagrant could not figure out where this demented priest was running. He looked around to see if someone was chasing him. By the time he turned back, the priest had disappeared—there was no sign of him.

The vagrant found several packing cases in an alley and, somehow, survived the night.

The next day, a softhearted hash-house owner gave him a few hours' work cleaning up the basement and the alley behind the eatery. He was about to tell the owner of his singular experience in the wee hours of that morning, when he heard the news on the eatery's radio: A maniac serial killer, striking fear in Catholic leaders in the archdiocese, had almost struck again.

Good Catholic that he was, this news, quite naturally, interested him. So he stopped work to listen.

This killer had struck twice previously and would have killed again had he not been thwarted by the quick-thinking and courageous Monsignor Delbert Young.

Interesting.

The monsignor had arrived home early this morning when he was confronted by the alleged killer just outside the rectory. Somehow, the monsignor was able to elude the assailant and escape and call the police, who were even now conducting an investigation.

Interesting—and familiar.

The action took place at St. Benedict parish at 40 South Lynn in Pontiac.

Caramba!

What to do? He'd been in town less than a full day and already he was being sought as a serial killer. To lay low or not? With his luck, the police would find him, identify him as the one who was waiting for this crazy monsignor, and the next thing, he'd be in the electric chair. And if they didn't have capital punishment in Michigan they'd establish it just for him.

There was no choice. He sought out the police and finally made them understand what had happened.

His account was reluctantly, and shamefacedly, corroborated by Monsignor Young.

As Andy Warhol said, everybody would be famous for fifteen minutes.

21

AFTER THE EARLY morning clouds had dissipated, it had turned into a bright, sunny, if bitterly cold day.

Strange that it had been so cold for so much of December. Michiganians had January and the feared February to endure before even remote thoughts of spring could be entertained.

In his spacious, book-lined office on the chancery's second floor, Cardinal Mark Boyle was visiting with Archbishop Lawrence Foley. The Cardinal was somewhat restive. He had much work ahead of him. Archbishop Foley had not been on the schedule for this morning, but Boyle could not bring himself to refuse a request from his old friend.

They had talked about and chuckled over the Monsignor Del Young saga. Both had gotten nearly all their information from radio and TV. Neither had talked with Young as yet. The office of communications had circulated a lengthy memorandum that communicated little more than that its director, Cletus Bash, was on the job and that, to the extent that all archdiocesan departments would cooperate, the communications office would keep a tight rein on the story.

"Every time I think of it—" Foley was saying, "Jose Lopez running away from Del Young, and Del Young running away from Jose Lopez—I start to laugh all over again."

"No one could blame you." Boyle, smiling broadly,

sat back deeply in his extra-sized chair. He had settled in to talk to Foley for as long as the archbishop wished. Boyle did not want any body language to betray the fact that he was pressed for time.

"There are a few memories, over the years," Foley said, "that are so entertaining I hope I can recall them on my deathbed. I'd like to go out laughing. And Del Young's flight to safety is one of them."

"Then you'll have to have a prodigious memory. You're going to go on for ages."

"Not so sure about that. Though . . . why not? Live to a hundred and fool the actuaries." He paused, brow knitted. "But, more seriously, Mark, this whole incident, in my mind at least, seems to go back to the latest staff meeting, when so much anger and hurt feelings poured out as Larry Hoffer suggested closing the schools and—save the mark—parishes too."

"I know what you mean, Larry. My mind plays the same trick on me. It all seems to have stemmed from that. I think it is because, at the time, we did not know that Sister Joan, and not her sister Helen, was the first intended victim. It is difficult to realize that whoever killed two innocent people had been planning the crimes long before they were committed."

Foley shook his head. "There's a lot of anger out there, Mark."

Boyle snorted. "Tell me about it."

"No one needs to tell you. You've felt it. And it hasn't come to an end by any means. There are decisions yet to be made that are going to bring out a very emotional response."

Boyle's mood matched the somberness of Foley's. "I know that. But . . . decisions must be made, no matter how painful they may be. And, unfortunately, no matter how much pain they may cause."

"Then what will you do, Mark? I need to know for my own peace of mind. I know I'm on the shelf now. I've got no responsibility in this diocese—or any other, for that matter. But I feel as if I'm a part of what's going on here. And I know full well that this is only due to your kindness in including me in the decision-making process. I know the arguments pro and con closings.

"Emotionally, people treasure their spiritual roots. Even those who have taken the place of the people who sacrificed to build these churches and schools feel they would be lost without them.

"On the other hand, they were built to answer a need. Immigrants, ethnic groups, converts—there were so many that they built these huge ornate churches and gigantic schools. Now, most of them are gone, moved out to the suburbs. Those who are left to maintain this heritage are so few in number that it makes no financial sense to keep alive buildings meant to serve thousands but occupied now by less than a hundred. Indeed, for all we know Larry Hoffer may have given his life for taking a stand on this issue.

"But he couldn't have made a final decision. No one can make that but you. Have you made it? Can you tell me?"

Cardinal Boyle regarded his friend carefully. Bushy eyebrows pressed so closely together they seemed to form a single line, he seemed to be debating with himself whether to answer candidly.

"I have reached," Boyle hesitated; he usually spoke slowly as he searched for just the word or phrase he wanted, "what might best be termed a tentative conclusion."

"Tentative?" Foley repeated.

"Tentative, in that I have not closed my mind to cogent arguments from either side. Arguments that, if not changing my decision radically, might cause me to modify my approach to that decision.

"However, I don't want to communicate to my staff that I have reached a decision. Who knows how they would react? At very least, they most probably would cease contributing their thoughts on the matter in the belief that their opinions could have no effect. And, as I have suggested, I want their continued input. Their thoughts will, I feel, very definitely affect the manner in which we will proceed. There will be repercussions to my decision that I simply cannot foresee. One or another of the staff very likely will pinpoint such consequences and we will be able to address them before they descend on us out of nowhere.''

"I understand," Foley said, "and I agree with your approach completely. But, Mark, *will* you close the parishes? The ones too poor or underpopulated to support themselves?''

Boyle hardly ever answered a complex question with a single word. He saw too many sides of every issue to, in effect, oversimplify his response.

"Parishes may close," he said thoughtfully. "Some are dangerously close to collapsing in upon themselves—much as matter disappears into a black hole. But . . ." He paused for emphasis. ". . . I am not going to close any parishes or schools. Not in the core city nor in the suburbs. In any case, certainly not in the city.

"Some years ago, under enormous pressure, I agreed to close several parishes in a section of the city called Poletown. The ramifications of that decision have haunted me ever since. It may have hastened the death of a very fine priest. And, undoubtedly, it caused grave pain to many trusting people. And all for a will-of-the-wisp financial benefit to industry and the city. I vowed then that I would never repeat what I now consider a grave error.''

Foley leaned back into his chair, smiling as if relieved of a burden. "I applaud your decision, Mark. But not everyone will. Lots of people, mostly in the suburbs, will think you very foolish. Your decision will make no sense to them at all. And I fear they will make their disapproval known by withholding contributions.''

"I've thought of that," Boyle responded. "That is,

of course, possible. But I hope not. And this is precisely where the input of yourself and the others on the staff is so important. We are faced with a massive challenge to give witness to the suffering Christ. Somehow we must make it crystal clear that Jesus identifies with the poor.''

'' 'He had nowhere to lay his head,' '' Foley paraphrased Scripture. ''The first homeless Christian was Christ himself.''

''Exactly.'' Boyle's spirits rose. ''Our approach to our brethren in the city cannot be the threat of eviction or foreclosure. We must come to them with open arms and the simple question, 'What do you need?' ''

The intercom buzzed softly. Boyle picked up the desk phone, listened for a few moments, then hung up and turned to Foley. ''You have an appointment with Father Koesler? He's waiting in your office.''

''Is it that time already?'' Foley glanced at this watch, then struggled stiffly out of his chair. ''Appreciate the time you gave me, Mark.'' He clasped the Cardinal's extended hand in both of his. ''And appreciate being associated with you.''

''Not at all, old friend. It is our privilege to have the benefit of your experience and wisdom.''

Foley nodded, smiled gratefully, and shuffled out of the Cardinal's office. As he slowly made his way through the vestibule, the two female secretaries smiled at him. For them it was an unaffected reaction. Some in the archdiocese thought Lawrence Foley an anachronism. Others had discovered the richness of his wisdom and spirituality. Almost everyone liked him to some degree or another.

He took the elevator to the fifth floor where he and the auxiliary bishops had their offices. As announced, Father Koesler was waiting.

''Excellency.'' Koesler rose to his feet as the archbishop entered the office.

''Oh, you don't need to go to all that trouble. . . .''

Foley's waving hand motioned Koesler to be seated. "I'm not the Pope, just an old man on the shelf."

Koesler waited for Foley to be seated behind his desk before lowering himself into his chair. "I knew you weren't the Pope," he said. "But you're certainly much more than a casualty on the shelf."

Koesler had to admit the older man in some ways did resemble a drifter, albeit a clerical one. Foley's black suit always had a rumpled look, trousers that couldn't remember a crease, food stains here and there on the jacket. He wore a black shirt with a white tab insert at the collar to mark his clerical status. Only his bishops' ring and the small segment of gold chain showing beneath his jacket identified his rank.

"Well, Father Koesler, good of you to come in on such short notice."

"No problem, Excellency. I live downtown now . . . or at least on the fringe of downtown."

Foley nodded. "We've never met, have we, in the little more than a year that I've been here?"

"Not formally, Excellency. We've attended many of the same functions, where you'd have no reason to recognize me. But I'd have every reason to identify you. Mostly because usually you were presiding."

"And even if I weren't presiding, there's that funny hat I wear and that strange stick I carry."

Koesler chuckled. He was most appreciative of Foley's self-effacing humor. He'd heard it often enough in homilies and talks the archbishop had given.

"I asked you to come in, Father," Foley said, "because of something Cardinal Boyle said about you."

"I'm making a quick examination of conscience. And for the life of me, I can't think of anything I've done wrong—that he would know about."

Two could play at that self-deprecating game, thought Koesler.

"No, no, no." Foley smiled and shook his head. "Nothing you've done wrong. Something you've been doing above and beyond the call of your clerical duties.''

"Oh?"

"I have reference to your helping the police solve murders.''

"Hold on a minute, Bishop; I'm sure the Cardinal didn't say that. You're exaggerating?''

"A little. But you have collaborated with the police on occasion . . . no?''

"Well, y . . . e . . . es, a little bit. But mostly my contacts with the police have been a matter of chance. Bad luck or good luck. Being at the wrong place at the right time. Or vice-versa.''

"Whatever the cause, you have had occasion to contribute to police investigations.'' Foley gazed at the priest intently. "Specifically regarding homicide . . . no?''

"Well, yes. But I fear that you have the notion that I play policeman from time to time. And I assure you, I don't. Unfortunately, there are hundreds of murders in Detroit annually. Once in a great while, there is a distinctly Catholic cast to one of these killings. A missing monsignor, say, or churches being desecrated by murder—something like that. Sometimes I have simply happened to be at the scene when something like that occurred. Sometimes, since I have had contact with a few homicide detectives, sometimes I'm asked to provide an explanation of things Catholic that seem relevant to the investigation.''

"Relax, Father. I have no intention of accusing you of playing policeman. It's just that Cardinal Boyle mentioned, just as you have, some of the circumstances that got you involved in these investigations. Which set me to wondering whether you had been called upon to assist in the matter of Larry Hoffer and Helen Donovan. It seemed to me that these cases qualified as the type you get involved in.''

Koesler was not inclined to discuss his involvement

in these cases, any more than he had been interested in being asked by Lieutenant Tully to get involved. But he recognized the position Foley held in the Church and this archdiocese. Koesler respected Foley's rank and, without knowing him well, nonetheless liked the man.

"Lieutenant Tully—he's a Detroit homicide detective I've been associated with in the past—called on me a couple of days ago. The current police investigation is based on the hypothesis that the murders of Helen Donovan and Larry Hoffer are linked in that Ms. Donovan was mistaken for her sister Joan. And that this is the work of a serial killer who has some peculiar reason to target leaders of diocesan departments. Because, of course, that's what Sister Joan is and Larry Hoffer was.

"The point is, Excellency, that this hypothesis was formulated by Lieutenant Tully. And he feels, understandably, at a loss in the archdiocesan structure—Church bureaucracy. That's why he came to see me. He wanted me to interpret things. Well, I'd guess you would agree that's easier said than done. The deeper you get into the administration of a large diocese like this, let alone the Curia in Rome, the more you're apt to feel you're in the middle of a maze. Unless it's a part of your life, like me."

"Or unless you're part of the bureaucracy and the maze, like me."

Koesler smiled. "I suppose you would understand it better than most. Anyway, I tried to draw him a road map, as it were."

"I'm sure you did. Tell me, did this lieutenant say anything to you about how the investigation was going?"

"No, Bishop. It was pretty much a one-way conversation. I did most of the talking and explaining."

"There aren't any suspects, then." Foley made it a statement, not a question. And it was said with a trace of sadness.

"Well . . ."

"There are?" A touch of hope crept into Foley's tone.

"I didn't get this from Lieutenant Tully." Mentally, Koesler evaluated the source of his information. Cletus Bash claimed that the identities of the two prime suspects were given him as a matter of police security and secrecy. But the secrecy was aimed at the media.

"Frankly, Bishop," Koesler said, "my source is Father Cletus Bash. He got his information from press relations people with the city and the police. The information is, I believe, protected by neither a professional and certainly not a confessional seal. It would be a shame if it were leaked, primarily because of the damage it probably would do to a couple of men who have not even been charged with a crime."

"I fully understand, Father. I'd be obliged if you would tell me what you know. It will go no further."

Koesler shrugged. He was not at all happy with this dilemma that was not of his doing. If Tully had not sought his help, if Bash had kept his mouth shut, if Archbishop Foley had not asked for the information with such sincerity; if none of this had happened, Koesler could now be ringing doorbells in high rises, trying to augment his tiny flock.

"All right. First, I should make it clear that this information is second or third hand and that I have no idea, even if this information is correct, how seriously the police regard these men as suspects. But the two are Arnold Carson and Fred Stapleton." Koesler allowed the names to sink in while Foley tried to put faces on those names.

"Arnold Carson . . ." Foley's voice was barely audible, as if speaking to himself. "Arnold Carson . . ." a bit louder. "Isn't he the right-winger?"

Koesler nodded.

"Leader of the Tridentines, isn't he?" Foley pursued.

"Very good," Koesler said.

"I remember him," Foley said. "He's forever in the

media. Abortion—whether it's pro-choice or pro-life, he's there throwing his weight around, saying things calculated to get quoted. Yes, I can see him now. I've got a clear picture.

"And the other one. What did you say his name is?"

"Stapleton. Fred Stapleton." Koesler briefly considered offering some specifics but thought better of it. Let's see if the archbishop can come up with it, he thought.

"Stapleton," Foley repeated. "Let's see, he's in medicine, a doctor. Medical? No, a psychologist. That's it, a psychologist."

"And a former priest," Koesler added.

"Of course. That's why I remember him. He's a priest . . . or was one, I guess. He too is heavy in the media. Never met him but I've seen his picture many a time. I know I would recognize him if I ever saw him. But why in God's green world would he be a suspect?"

"He's a very active member of CORPUS. Are you familiar with that organization?"

"Certainly. But why should that make him a suspect? CORPUS is a pretty . . . I want to say 'tame,' but better make that 'gentlemanly' bunch. They just want to function as priests again. Always seemed logical to me," he added.

"I agree, Bishop. But as we've already noted, you're not Pope."

"Yes, I see what you're driving at," Foley said. "Just because we see no problem with bringing these qualified men back to practice doesn't mean it's going to happen. A right-wing minority, some highly placed Cardinals and bureaucrats and the Holy Father himself are very strongly opposed."

"Exactly. And that contributes to a certain level of frustration on the part of those men who are knocking on the door. Almost everyone I've met in CORPUS is extremely self-controlled. They tend to see the rightness of their cause and they seem to make a super virtue of perseverance. They're just going to keep knocking until the door finally is opened to them. And they're confident it will be one day. I can't say I'm that confident it's going to happen,'' he added.

"You may very well be right. The opposition to them is, I think, not a majority. But it is powerful. But, back to this Stapleton. Perseverance is not his long suit, I take it.''

"We were pretty close in the seminary, Excellency, but I haven't seen him for quite some time. I knew him as a patient, thoughtful person. But others, who are more currently acquainted with him, say he's changed. That his frustration is on the verge of—or already is—running over. Some even say they can picture him becoming extremist. I can't see that myself. But, again, it's been a while.''

"I see.'' Foley seemed lost in thought. Koesler did not intrude.

Abruptly, the archbishop looked sharply at Koesler. "I suppose,'' Foley said, "you're wondering what this is all about . . . my asking you to come down here and all?''

"Well, yes and no. I can easily see how you would be concerned about this business. We all are. You'd like all the information you can get. But others have better information than I have. For instance, the names of the possible suspects the police are working with; as I mentioned, I got those from Father Bash. In fact, that I could come up with the names was purely accidental. I just happened to be playing cards—which I very seldom do—when the subject came up. So, Archbishop, I can understand that you want as much information as you can gather. But, why me?''

"Well, I'll tell you. Ever since the Cardinal mentioned your . . . uh . . . avocation of assisting the police, I've been looking into the matter—quietly and unobtrusively, mind you. Now I don't doubt for an instant that your involvement in police work has come about just as you've explained: You've been drawn in by peculiar sets of circumstances—the right place at the right or wrong time sort of thing.

"However, after that I fear you are far too modest. Several times, or so I've been told, you've been much more than simply a source of information and authentication. Sometimes you have actually solved the case. Now don't be denying it," Foley quickly added.

"I suppose you might conclude that. I don't look at it quite that way. But I guess it's not worth arguing about. So even if we grant that I've contributed something of substance in the past, I'm still left wondering why you chose to call me in just now."

"Two reasons. This case, by its very nature, needs someone like yourself to cut through all the mysterious nooks and crannies of our creaky old Church. Secondly—and for me more important—I've had a premonition for some time now. The premonition is that Mark—Cardinal Boyle—is among the intended victims this murderer is stalking.

"Now, I know very well that there's no proof for such an idea. And you're probably telling yourself that it's just an old man's hallucination. But it's very real to me, Father. And I want to do everything in my power to make certain sure it doesn't happen. Do you understand?"

In his younger years, Koesler very probably would have pooh-poohed something as vague as a premonition. Just as he had once dismissed intuition as nothing more than a hysterical reaction. But no more. He was older and, thank God, somewhat wiser.

"I understand," Koesler said, "and I respect your premonition. But what makes you think that Cardinal Boyle could be in any danger?"

"To tell the truth, it came to me in prayer. I was saying my breviary the other day and came across the saying, 'Omnes scandalizabimini in me in nocte ista:

quia scriptum est: Percutiam pastorem, et dispergentur oves.' "

Isn't that nice, Koesler thought; *he still reads the breviary in Latin.* " 'All of you will be scandalized in me this night: because it is written: I will strike the shepherd and the sheep will be scattered,' " Koesler translated.

Isn't that nice, Foley thought; *he still remembers his Latin.* "Yes," Foley said, "I read the phrase and it transfixed me. It was as if the Lord himself were getting my attention. I don't have any idea how many times I've read that text—hundreds. But this time, it was as if I were seeing it for the first time. It was such a unique experience for me! I prayed long over this experience. And the more I prayed, the more I associated the text with the Cardinal. And it fits rather nicely with one or the other of those fellows you said were under suspicion by the police."

"How's that?"

"Well, both of them, uh . . . Carson and, uh . . . Stapleton, seem bent on stirring up a ruckus to get the Church's attention—though for different reasons, of course. Carson wants to go back to the thirteenth century, or at very least to the 1950s. And Stapleton wants to jump ahead into the twenty-first—or twenty-second—century. But to do either, they figure they've got to stir things up—get the attention of the Church.

"What better way than to strike down the chief shepherd of the diocese? Do that and the sheep will be scattered, dispersed, all shaken up. He will have gotten the Church's attention. Don't you see?"

"Yes, Bishop, I see. But if that were the intention of whoever is doing this, why bother with Sister Joan or, particularly, Larry Hoffer? How would they fit into this scheme?"

Foley's brow knit as he gnawed at his lower lip. "I don't know. This is not a full-blown theory, you know, Father, it's just a premonition. But a very strong one."

"Okay, Bishop, let me try to fill in the missing pieces.

"Suppose your premonition is accurate. Now, I agree that the murder of an ordinary, an archbishop and a Cardinal, would make the hierarchy wake up and pay attention. But what if these other two murders were simply a prelude to the gross act of attacking the archbishop? How much more terrifying this scenario would be. In effect, the attention of the sheep as well as the other shepherds would be attracted even before the perpetrator struck down the chief shepherd. What do you think?"

Foley regarded Koesler with seemingly greater interest. "See: There, I told you: You were being modest. You have got a knack for this sort of thing."

"Bishop, I'm only fleshing out your idea. We both easily could be as wrong as wrong can be."

"But what if my premonition and your added impressions are on the mark?"

"All right, what if they are?"

"Then that would bring me to what they like to call 'the bottom line,' the reason, the real reason, I asked you here."

"And that is?"

"That is that I very much want you to involve yourself in this case."

"But I am—or have been. I told you about my meeting with Lieutenant Tully."

"I know, Father, I know. And I've listened to you explain how you got involved in the past. You've been very passive up till now. You just happened to be in the right place at the right time. The present case is certainly no different from the previous cases. There you were, in your rectory, minding your own business, tending to your parishioners, when this Lieutenant Tully called on your knowledge of Church structure and the administration of this archdiocese. So you gave him what he was looking for—information. And now you're finished. There will be no further involvement on your part . . . unless, of course, you again just happen to be in the right place at the right time."

Koesler smiled. "I can't dispute your assumption. But why are you making me feel guilty?"

"I don't know why you're feeling guilty, but I'm glad you are. Because I'm asking you to get involved in this case. As involved as you possibly can be."

Koesler hesitated. "Bishop, I'd like to do what you ask of me. But what you suggest sounds rather pushy. And that's not my style."

"I want you to do it because I fear for Cardinal Boyle. I don't know how you feel about the man. . . ."

"That's easy. I admire him and I'm proud as punch that he's my bishop. I have no qualms whatsoever in representing him."

"Good. I'm glad to hear that. He is a good man. But hardly one who would go into hiding or even take any sort of precaution to protect himself. He'll go on with his duties, appearing regularly in public.

"I hope and pray I'm wrong. But if he is the next target, somebody has to do something to protect him. And since we can't depend on his being any help to himself, the best thing that can happen is that this case gets solved before anything does happen to him."

"Bishop, I want to put your mind at ease. I'd like to tell you I'll get actively involved. God save us, I'd even like to assure you that I will get in there and solve this case. But to be brutally honest, I don't have a clue as to what's going on here. I wouldn't even know where to start."

Foley rose from his chair, walked around the desk, and stood immediately in front of Koesler.

"God bless you, Father. I don't expect you to sweep the police aside and become a one-man force to single-handedly solve this case. Heaven forbid, I know that's impossible. All I'm asking is for your positive involvement. Now, I know you wouldn't know where to start.

But you've got a talent for this sort of thing and it's extremely important—a case of life and death, I believe, quite literally—that you try. I'm asking you to open yourself to the Holy Spirit. Because I am going to pray for you. I'm going to pray as intensely as I ever have. What you and I cannot do with our meager strength, God can accomplish through us. Will you, Father? Will you?''

Koesler sighed as his shoulders sagged in an I-can't-fight-this-any-further slump. ''All right, Bishop. I'll do what I can. But you had better be awfully darn good at praying.''

22

SERGEANT ANGIE MOORE was describing the case she had handled earlier in the day. "According to just about everybody I talked to, this guy was the life of the party. I mean, all the time. He was never 'off.' Helped around the neighborhood too. A regular Good Neighbor Sam. But before he'd go home, almost every time . . ."

"He'd booze it up?" Lieutenant Tully interrupted.

"How'd you guess?"

"I don't know. Maybe I've been over this territory too many times. When he's out, he's Dr. Jekyll. But when he goes home, he's Mr. Hyde. There has to be some potion he takes to speed up the change. My guess is it's not drugs or the neighbors would know about it and he'd lose his image real quick. So: booze."

Moore and Tully were seated in the otherwise empty squad room. Tully was struggling to pay attention. But what Moore was describing was a platter case, and besides, he was preoccupied with the Catholic affair—which was proving the opposite of a platter.

"Well," Moore admitted, "you're right. It was booze."

"And he had to get more and more 'cause he was building up an immunity."

Moore laughed. "Say, whose case is this anyway?"

"Sorry. Go ahead. I'll shut up."

"You seem to have guessed what happened when he got home."

Tully simply looked interested. He'd promised he wouldn't interrupt anymore.

"Okay," Moore continued. "He would beat his wife to a pulp."

"Witnesses?"

"Two teenagers. Their son and daughter. Sometimes they'd try to intervene, but then they'd get it too. He was a big son-of-a-bitch. After a while, they just quit trying. Sometimes she'd try to fight back but she'd only get hit harder."

"I take it things got reversed this morning. I mean, after all, the guy's dead."

"Yeah. But not the way you'd expect."

Tully showed some interest.

"Last night," Moore said, "he came home stone sober. Then, after a while, he got tanked and started throwing her around. The boy stepped between them, pleading for his mother. The guy almost killed his son. That did it: She told us she could have taken the abuse, even if it killed her. But not her baby. She decided to get out."

"Mother love."

"So this morning the guy gets up, goes out to start the car—to warm it up before he went to work. He turned the ignition on and blew himself into jelly."

Tully was surprised. "The wife wired the car?"

"That's the funny part. Right now, it looks like he did it to get rid of her."

"How—?"

"They got two cars. Last night when he got home sober he worked on the car his wife drove. Neighbors saw him. His foreman checked and found that he'd taken some explosives from work. That's it, Zoo: This morning he was so hung over, he started the wrong car."

He had to agree there was a different twist here. But it was still a "platter" case.

Sergeant Mangiapane cleared his throat. At some point he had entered the room and had been standing just inside the door. Neither Tully nor Moore had been aware of his presence.

"Yes, indeedy," Moore took the hint, "I got some work to do." She gathered up her tote bag and left the squad room.

Once again Tully was alone with one of his detectives. This time there was a genuine interest. Mangiapane was among the officers still investigating Larry Hoffer's murder as well as that of Helen Donovan.

"Got something?" From the manner of Mangiapane's entrance, Tully was fairly sure the sergeant did have some fresh development.

"Maybe." Mangiapane sat down directly opposite Tully.

Tully merely looked at him, waiting.

"You know that nursing home up in Pontiac? On Watkins Lake Road?"

"No, can't say that I do." Tully had no reason, by his lights, to be aware of the facility. It had never been involved in any case he had investigated. Until now, at least.

"Well, okay," Mangiapane said. He wondered from time to time about the comparative narrowness of Tully's interest. "There is one. It's been there almost thirty years. The reason I'm bringing this up is that my aunt works there. She's an RN."

Tully would not have been surprised should Mangiapane volunteer his aunt's medical education and achievements. Excessive detail was one of the boy's failings. Fortunately, he had more than enough virtues to offset the drawbacks. He had all the makings of a fine detective. One day he would be one of the best. As long as he paid attention.

Tully was about to redirect Mangiapane's attention to the case at hand when the sergeant returned to it of his own volition.

"I don't see Aunt Marie very often—Christmas, Easter, family get-togethers, that sort of thing. That's why I was surprised when she called me.''

"When was that?''

"Yesterday. Well, last night, actually. She said she'd been keeping up on this murder case in the papers and she knew I was working on it. She sort of brags to the patients and the staff when I'm on a big case.'' He smiled modestly. "She always wonders how come my picture ain't in the paper when I'm on a major case.''

There he goes again. "Manj,'' Tully said, "tell me why I should be interested in what your aunt thinks of our investigation of this particular case.''

"Sure, Zoo. Sorry.'' Mangiapane had been made aware of his tendency to digress. He tried to reform, but it wasn't easy. "What it was, Zoo, is that Aunt Marie has this patient at the nursing home. The old lady's not quite with it most of the time. But once in a while, she's . . . whaddyacallit?''

"Lucid?''

"Yeah, I think. Anyway, Aunt Marie heard her talkin' about her nephew and niece, who were religious. I mean the nephew is a priest and the niece is a nun. Catholics usually are proud of a thing like that, Zoo. So it wasn't unusual that she would brag about it. At least she did it a few times when she was . . . lucid.''

"I think we've gotten through the introduction, Manj. Has this story got a middle or an end?''

"Sure, Zoo. The thing is, her niece's name is Sister Joan Donovan.''

Tully leaned forward.

"And . . .'' Mangiapane paused for a perfect theatrical delivery. ". . . her nephew is Father Fred Stapleton. Or was.''

"Stapleton? Donovan. They're . . .''

"Cousins, Zoo. Forty-second, maybe, but cousins.''

"Now that is interesting.'' Mangiapane had Tully's complete attention.

"Aunt Marie remembered this when she read about

Sister Joan being an intended victim and how I saved her. My aunt had never heard of Stapleton—except from hearing this old lady talk about him. What she called me for was to tell me about the nun and how it was a coincidence that I had saved her life by collaring that jerk who tried to kill her. She just mentioned Stapleton because the old lady always mentioned them together. She had no idea both cousins figured in this investigation.''

"Interesting. Very interesting. Did you follow it up?''

"I went out to the nursing home this morning, Zoo. Aunt Marie was really surprised and happy to see me. She took me to this lady, but the old girl wasn't having one of her . . . lucid times. Batty as a bedbug, Zoo. She just sort of mumbles and drools. But—and this is the big thing—they've got her last will and testament on file out there. I guess it was made at one of the times she'd run out of drool.

"It turns out, Zoo, that these two people are her only living relatives. She was an old maid. She's left everything to them. And it's quite a pile. Her daddy was in on the beginning of General Motors—loads of stock. He built it into a pretty big fortune, and he left the whole shebang to his daughter. And she was no slouch: She invested her inheritance until it got to be several million dollars. She's using some of it—although she probably doesn't know what's going on—for her care now. Still, there's a bundle left for Donovan and Stapleton.''

Tully's eyes were animated. "Now that's very intriguing.''

Buoyed by Tully's growing interest, Mangiapane continued. "I asked Aunt Marie if the old lady knew that her nephew had quit the priesthood. She said she didn't think so 'cause even when she was rational she never mentioned that. She always calls him 'Father Fred.' Besides, even Aunt Marie didn't know Stapleton was out.''

"She didn't know?" Tully was surprised again. "Your aunt didn't know that Stapleton is a psychologist? Hell, he's practically a celebrity. And she didn't know?"

"No, Zoo. She don't pay much attention to current affairs." Mangiapane was surprised that Tully was surprised that Aunt Marie didn't read the papers or watch TV news much. Of all people, Tully, with his lack of interest in events that had nothing to do with his work, should appreciate Aunt Marie's information gaps.

"Okay," Tully said. "Go on."

"Well, I asked Aunt Marie what the old lady would do if she knew her nephew wasn't a priest anymore. She didn't have to think about it a minute. Right off she said the old lady would be mad as hell and would cut Stapleton out of her will."

"Just because he stopped being a priest?" Tully obviously found that hard to believe.

"That's the way it is with Catholics, Zoo . . . at least the old-time ones. They're proud as peacocks when a relative gets to be a priest or a nun. But let them quit and their names might as well be mud. Anyway, Aunt Marie says that's not likely to happen: The old gal hardly ever comes to anymore. And on the off chance she would be wide awake anytime that Aunt Marie was with her, she said she'd never tell her. The old gal'd go bananas. It could kill her."

"Either the nun or Stapleton ever come to see her?"

"Sister Joan used to come and visit. But she stopped a long time ago. I guess it just wasn't worth the effort. As far as Aunt Marie knows, Stapleton never came."

"Do the nun and Stapleton know about the inheritance?"

"Aunt Marie isn't sure. But back when the old lady was a bit more with it and used to talk about her nephew and niece, she'd say how proud she was of them and that she told them she'd leave everything to them. So if she wasn't dreaming, I guess they do know."

Tully thought about that. "Wait a minute: Stapleton's got a teenage daughter. He's got to have quit the priesthood long ago. How come his aunt didn't know about that?"

"If he never visited her when she was cookin' on all eight, it's possible. There's not much general publicity on a thing like that. Usually there's nothin' in the regular papers or on TV. And the Catholic paper usually just says the priest has taken a 'leave of absence.' So it could work out. They were never all that close anyway. The old lady wouldn't fuss about her nephew not comin' to visit. She'd just be quietly proud that he was what she thought he was. In time she'd die, he'd have half her money, and he'd be sayin' Masses for her way beyond her time in purgatory."

Tully knew better than to ask what in hell purgatory was about. "Wait a minute. He was a priest. Could he have kept all that money?"

"Oh, sure, Zoo. He was a secular priest. He didn't have no vow of poverty. He coulda kept the bundle."

For a moment, Tully thought of the only priest he knew to any degree. There was a fleeting image in his mind of Father Koesler living in a luxury high rise, fantastically wealthy. It was a ridiculous notion. But briefly amusing.

Tully realized to what supposition all this was leading. He wondered if Mangiapane did. "So, whaddya think, Manj?"

"What I was thinkin', Zoo, was that maybe this case ain't anything like what it looks like. Suppose Stapleton knows about the inheritance. He probably does if the old lady really did tell both of them about it. Then he knows that when she dies—which can't be far off—he and his cousin split a fortune . . . if they're both alive.

"But what if the nun dies in the meantime? Then Stapleton gets the whole enchilada. Of course, he could make sure she was dead by killing her."

"And the Hoffer murder?" Tully was gratified that his detective was reaching the same conclusion he had.

"Well, I was thinking, Zoo: Suppose Stapleton wants his cousin dead. With the contacts he's kept up with priests and nuns, it ain't hard for him to find out her routine, if he didn't already know it. So he either already knows or he finds out that she usually gets home real late at night. He waits for her outside St. Leo's. Somebody in a nun's habit who looks like her gets out of a cab and heads for the convent. It has to be her, doesn't it?

"And so he kills the wrong cousin. The cousin who would never have made it into the old lady's will because, far from being a nun, Helen's a prostitute.

"Now he finds out he's killed the wrong woman. Then I stop somebody from pulling a copycat murder. He develops plan B—or maybe it was part of his plan all along. He kills another head of another diocesan department. Right away we figure it's some sort of plot to knock off department heads for God knows what reason.

"Meanwhile he can go back anytime he wants and get the right cousin. Maybe after that he kills the old lady. Or if he can wait just a little while, she'll do him a favor. And then he's got it—the whole bundle."

Tully was tempted to call out a "bravo," but he didn't. "Good, Manj. Very, very good. I love it. It gets us out of all this mumbo jumbo about Vatican Councils and priests who can't marry and priests who are married so they can't be priests and people who are mad at the Church for a zillion reasons.

"Now we got simple greed. That we can deal with. Get on it, Manj. Start digging into Stapleton. Get into his financial records—debts and liabilities. His daughter's going to some ritzy music school. Look into that. I'll get the rest of the squad into other facets of the man's finances. This is it, Manj: Let's wrap it up before he gets back to the nun.

"And, by the way, it probably would help if he knows we're onto him. It may keep him away from the nun. So squeeze him, Manj; squeeze him."

"You got it, Zoo."

Both were elated. The conclusion of a very complicated investigation was nearing.

It was time for a celebration. But that would come later. Right after they caught the bad guy and delivered him for trial, conviction, and punishment.

23

ARCHBISHOP LAWRENCE FOLEY was surprised when he answered the door to find Father Ralph Higgins.

Higgins was an old buddy from Miami. He and Foley had been friends all through the seminary years. After ordination their paths separated. Higgins had been assigned to a series of parishes in the St. Augustine diocese—from which the diocese of Miami was created in 1958—until he had been named pastor of St. Agatha parish and finally pastor of Our Lady of Lourdes in Boca Raton. Foley, of course, after ordination spent only a brief time in parochial ministry before he was sent off to Rome for graduate studies, followed by a series of chancery assignments; then he became a bishop and ultimately archbishop of Cincinnati.

Even though their ecclesiastical careers diverged, they remained close friends. After Foley had moved on to Cincinnati, whenever he and Mark Boyle vacationed in Florida, they would stay with Higgins.

"Ralph! What a surprise!" Foley exclaimed. "What brings you here?"

"Like most things when you reach our years: a funeral."

Foley's demeanor instantly changed to one of concern. "Oh, I am sorry. Who was it?"

"A sister-in-law. Not terribly close. But at this stage in life, one of the last of the relatives. I thought I owed it to her memory—and, of course, to my brother, God rest him.''

"But, if I had known . . . I would have attended the funeral . . . we could have gotten together, done some things. Why don't we—I could get some tickets . . . the symphony, a show—?''

"No time, Larry. Another time. I just got in this morning. Leaving in just a couple of hours. Just couldn't be in town without seeing you, even for only a few minutes.''

"Well, that's great. Can I get you something, anything?''

"No, no; had supper. I can only stay a few minutes.''

Foley took his friend's coat, and they proceeded to the comfortable living room where Higgins was assaulted by a small but eager dog. He tried petting the animal but it wasn't having any. "Now I know how the early Christian martyrs felt.'' Higgins laughed.

Foley spoke sternly to the dog. "John Paul, come! Sit! Stay!'' The little spaniel mix bounced willingly to Foley and sat contentedly against his leg. "His manners are not the best, but he's an obedient little fellow.''

"John Paul?'' Higgins tilted his head. "You named him after the Pope?''

"It was the least I could do.''

They laughed.

"I'm so sorry you can't stay,'' Foley said. "Mark will be too.''

"Can't be helped. How is Mark, anyway?''

"Very fit, I'd say. Walks a lot. Stays healthy.''

"That's the secret, okay. The path to health is not to get sick. But try telling that to the oldsters in Boca Raton. And, by the way, Larry, when are you and Mark coming down? It's January, you know.''

"Just. I'd like to go. God knows these old bones don't react very well to all this cold and snow. But I haven't been able to convince Mark it's time for us to migrate. I wish . . . I fervently wish I could.''

"I wish you could too. After all, Larry, Florida is your home.''

Higgins never admitted it, even to himself, but he was jealous that Foley had chosen to live out his retirement in Detroit rather than in Florida. Quite simply, it meant that Foley's friendship with Mark Boyle was stronger than his attachment to Higgins. So much stronger that Foley would endure the bitter Michigan winters instead of basking in the warmth of the sunny South. In addition, Foley's roots were in Florida, not in Michigan, nor even Cincinnati.

"It's not just the warmth or the golf or the relaxation,'' Foley said.

"That's not bad for starters.''

"Yes, yes, I know, Ralph. But I'm worried about Mark. You've probably read about these two murders we've had here involving people in diocesan administration.''

"Even with all the murder and crime we've got in Florida, yes, Michigan murders regularly out-bizarre us. Yes, I know of them. But—''

"They're not solved. Not even close. And I have this feeling that Mark is on the list . . . on the killer's list.''

Higgins was genuinely shocked. "You must be kidding. Whatever for? Why would anyone want to harm the Cardinal?''

"I'm afraid it's not 'Why would anyone?'; it's more 'How many would?' You must be aware there are a lot of unhappy people out there suffering in one way or another from the effects of the council.''

"Sure. Although I don't think it's as bad where I am. By and large, most of our Catholics—at least the ones who still go to church—match the somewhat advanced age of the clergy. We are all precouncil people. So we tend to put as many of the changes as possible out of our minds as well as out of our liturgies.''

"Well, that's not the case up here, Ralph."

"I know. I know that. But for heaven's sake, Larry, you're talking about murder. That's a whole lot more than just being a disinterested, disgusted, or even an angry Catholic."

"It's strange, I admit, even incredible, but it seems to many of us—it seems to me—that's exactly what's going on."

"I find that hard to believe, frankly. But if that's what you people think, all the more reason for you to come on down. You know our routine for vacations. Nothing evil can happen to you down there."

"I know that well. That's why I've been trying to convince him to go. But I think he feels his place is here now while danger threatens. The Irish have a phrase, *an beárna baol*—the gap of danger. It's the spot where the bravest position themselves to take the brunt of any attack. You know Mark. You know he's not the type to run from danger. Just the opposite."

"Yes, I know. But even if you're right, there's nothing stopping you from coming down. Hell, you're retired. You can spend as much time as you want wherever you want."

"I can't leave him, Ralph. I know there's not much I can do to help or protect him. But I can't leave him. Not now."

Higgins shrugged. "If you can't, you can't. But we'll keep your rooms cool and ready." He was giving up reluctantly, bowing to inevitability. He glanced at his watch. "I guess it's time for me to be getting out to the airport."

"So soon? I was going to ask you about old John Gordon. Is he still helping you at Lourdes?"

" 'Helping'? That's a rather generous word for what John does at Our Lady of Lourdes. Actually, we try to talk him out of 'helping' us on the weekends."

"He's worse, then?"

"I'll say. His latest symptom is a kind of unconscious kleptomania."

"Kleptomania!"

"Stoles, altar breads, every now and again a chalice."

"Are you sure?"

"Uh-huh. He'll finish Mass, divest, and every once
in a while tuck a vestment or some such in his overnight
bag. I just go through the bag as a matter of routine
before I drive him back to the home. I retrieve the items
that belong to the parish or me. We never mention anything about it. But it's nerve-racking."

"Poor man." Foley shook his head. "It's just age,
I'm sure. Could happen to any of us—please God not.
How old is he now . . . in his late eighties?"

"Ninety going on a hundred. You might get a kick
out of what happened when we celebrated his ninetieth
birthday. Actually, it was a super turnout. Incredible
when you think he doesn't have any contemporaries left.
They're all dead now."

"Careful, Ralph, we may be the closest he has to a
classmate."

"I don't know about you, Larry, but I plan to be a
little bit more in control as we assail the seasons."

"Anyway, I interrupted: Go on with your story,
Ralph."

"Yes, well, there must have been a dozen, fifteen,
priests there to concelebrate Mass with the old man.
One of the guys was John Miller. You remember
him, Larry?"

"I think so. Good sense of humor. Used to be Gordon's assistant, wasn't he?"

"Uh-huh. Pastor himself now. Well, you know how
stooped over the old man is—almost doubled over."

"Yes, yes, the poor man."

"Well, we are all vesting before Mass, and Miller
came over to the old man and said, 'I want to get one

thing settled: Are you going to straighten up or are we all going to have to stoop over like you?' ''

Foley chuckled.

"Then, during the Mass, right after the consecration, he put the chalice down on top of the host. He covered the bread with the chalice. None of us saw him do it. Actually, we should have been paying closer attention. Anyway, just before the Lord's Prayer—''

"The minor elevation," Foley cut in. "Don't tell me: When it was time to elevate the host and chalice, he couldn't find the host!''

"That's it," Higgins said. "Hunted all over for it. Looked at us as if he'd just worked a miracle.''

They chuckled over that for several minutes. And that story led to another and another until they had used up an additional forty-five minutes.

Ralph Higgins glanced again at his watch. "Holy mackerel, wouldja look at the time! I've really got to move it.''

"What time's your flight, Ralph?"

"I'm on the 12:30 nightcoach.''

"You'll be okay." Foley glanced at his watch. "Just 10:30 now. Do you need a taxi? Or can I drive you?''

"No, no, Larry. Rented a car when I got in this morning. It's right outside.''

"Then you'll be fine. It hasn't snowed today so the freeways will be clear. And you don't have to worry about parking. They have shuttle buses at the rental places.''

Higgins struggled into his coat. "A few hours from now I'll put this mackintosh back in mothballs. You know, Larry, if you guys are worried about some nutty killer up here, you shouldn't be so free and easy about opening your door. There's no peep glass in your front door, and you didn't have the chain on when you opened the door for me. I could have been anybody.''

Foley chuckled. "I'm worried for Mark, not me. Who'd ever want to kill an old fuddy-duddy like me?''

"Anyway, take care, old friend."

"You too, Ralph. Safe home."

And he was gone.

Foley looked down at his dog contentedly wagging its tail and looking up at its master. "I've got to hand it to you, John Paul. You are a very well-behaved pooch. Now, you come in here with me. I've got my office to finish for the day. Fortunately, just compline, night prayers, to say. I'll just have time to finish before our eleven o'clock last run."

Foley shuffled back into the living room, John Paul at his heels, tail going a mile a minute.

The old man sat down in his favorite chair, picked up and opened the breviary, and tilted his head back so he could see through the lower part of his bifocals. Before he could begin compline, a compact ball of dog landed in his lap, nearly taking his breath away.

"Ungh!" he grunted. Dog and master looked deeply into each other's eyes. A long history of Irish humor crinkled the corners of Foley's eyes. Clearly, John Paul was singularly eager for the next anticipated event of the evening.

"You be patient now," Foley admonished. "It's not eleven o'clock yet—no matter what your usually accurate inner clock tells you. We've got a few minutes till I finish my prayers. Then we'll go for our walk, and then—and only then—your cookie."

At the word "cookie," the busy tail began beating a furious rhythm between the arm of the chair and Foley's thigh. The archbishop patted the dog until he quieted.

Foley opened the tattered old breviary and began. *"Noctem quietam, et finem perfectum concedat nobis Dominus omnipotens."* May the almighty Lord grant us a peaceful night and a perfect ending.

Yes, John Paul, thought Foley, a perfect conclusion for you comes down to a cookie.

Distractions! The bane of my prayer life from the beginning, he thought, and plowed on.

"Fratres: Sobrii estote, et vigilate: quia adversarius vester diabolus tamquam leo rugiens circuit, quaerens quem devoret: cui resistite fortes in fide." Brothers, be alert and vigilant, for your adversary, the devil, goes about like a roaring lion seeking whom he may devour: you must resist him strong in the faith.

He launched into the three psalms and further distractions. Distractions from his distractions.

While Foley's lips formed the words of the psalms, his mind recalled an old anecdote told by, among many others, Fulton Sheen. It had to do with a monastery in the Middle Ages. A serf was talking to the abbot about the contrast in their conditions. The serf complained about his life of endless hard work while all the monks had to do was pray.

"Praying is not all that easy," the monk said. "It is almost impossible to pray without distraction. I'll tell you what I'll do," the abbot added. "If you can pray the Lord's Prayer without a single distraction, I'll give you that beautiful horse over there."

The abbot had made an offer the serf could not possibly turn down. After all, all he had to do was recite the prayer aloud. He planned to play by the rules and have no distraction. But then who would know whether or not he was successful? And afterward, the horse would be his.

So the serf bowed his head, closed his eyes and began. "Our Father . . . who art in heaven . . . hallowed be thy name . . . thy kingdom come . . . thy will—by the way, do I get the saddle too?"

Foley chuckled, which disquieted the dog, who began to bark.

The archbishop glanced at the mantel. Eleven exactly. He shook his head. What a body clock!

"All right, John Paul: It's time. Let's go."

The dog bounded from his lap and beelined for the door. Foley went to the closet, struggled into his boots and coat, put on his hat, buckled the collar with its license tag around John Paul's neck, and out into the winter they went.

As was their custom, they commenced to walk completely around the small compact block. John Paul, as usual, sniffed at everything, paying special attention to trees, streetlights, and the fire hydrant. Foley, watching the dog's breath emerge as vapor, wondered why they were all still up here in the Winter Wonderland, as the Chamber of Commerce would have it. The dog at least had a coat that seemed to insulate it from the cold. But what of humans? Particularly those with skin that was thin and bones that were brittle?

He walked slowly, far too deliberately for the little dog, who covered twice the distance by running ahead and then returning, diving into snowbanks and finding his stubby legs too short for reaching the ground as he scrambled out of the drifts.

Foley smiled as he contemplated his dog and lost concern over nearly everything else. Maybe there was something to say for having all the seasons, as Michigan very definitely did.

He was feeling fairly carefree as they turned the final corner heading back to the condo. That was when the dog stopped and began to growl.

"Come now, you vicious puppy," Foley said in a gentle tone. "It's too late to go chasing cats."

That was when he noticed movement behind the large blue spruce. Whatever was back there was far too large to be a cat, or a dog for that matter. The motion continued as a man stepped out of the shadows. He was wearing dark clothes, and his hat was pulled low on his head. As he advanced toward Foley the streetlight picked up his features. John Paul, now barking furiously, appeared about to snap at the man's shins.

"Stop it!" Foley commanded. "Keep quiet! Come here! Sit! Stay!"

The little dog, obediently hushed, came and sat on

the sidewalk next to Foley. The archbishop peered into the shadows. "Why . . . what are you doing here?"

There was no answer. The man continued to gaze at Foley.

Without explanation it became clear to Foley. "You . . . you're the one, aren't you?"

Silence.

"But, why me? Whatever can this mean? What would I—?"

Still, silence. But as the man raised his arm slightly, the glimmer of the streetlight reflected sharply on the gun's metal surface.

"May I . . . at least let the dog inside? He's done nothing."

The hand continued its steady motion upward.

"Give me a moment, please." Foley turned his back and knelt on the sidewalk next to his dog, who looked at him wonderingly. The archbishop murmured one of the closing prayers of compline. *"Vigilemus cum Christo, et requiescamus in pace—"*

The quiet air was shattered by the roar of the gun. Foley pitched forward. He lay motionless. His years speeded the process of dying. It was over before he could reflect on another thought.

The dog, who had sprung straight up in the air at the gun's blast, barked furiously, then tentatively. Then he began to whimper, stopping only to lick the body of his master, who would never again reach out to comfort the small animal.

Later, much later, a night-owl resident of the condominium spotted the dog sitting near what seemed to be a pile of laundry. After a closer look, the resident raced to phone 911.

In order to remove the body they had to almost peel the dog from its master.

By then, the assassin was long gone.

24

THE GENERAL REACTION of the public to Archbishop Foley's murder could not have been foreseen. At the very least, it was not anticipated by Detroit's city government.

In death, the undeclared affection in which Foley was held during life overflowed. Messages of sorrow, disbelief, horror, and anger poured into the chancery. Condolences came from both the powerful and the ordinary of Florida, Cincinnati, Detroit, other parts of this and other countries as well as, of course, the Vatican.

Detroit's Mayor Cobb was forced to face yet another crisis.

Detroit's citizens, generally, were titillated by the murder of a hooker mistaken for her nun sister. They were puzzled and drawn into the speculation that accompanied the murder of a Catholic leader. Was there, as the police investigation seemed to indicate, a connection between the two killings?

But in these two murders, there was no consensus of emotional involvement on the part of the public.

That changed with the murder of a warm, kindly, harmless old man who had, in his own quiet way, charmed a frequently jaded city.

Editorials in the press, on radio and television typically excoriated the city that could not protect even the most gentle of its citizens. The movers and shakers demanded a speedy wrap-up to this investigation.

263

A decree went out from Maynard Cobb: Sew it up—now! Use whatever manpower necessary, but solve it—now!

Cobb's directive trickled through the chain of command, sometimes increasing, sometimes diminishing, the creative vulgarity of its original form.

Eventually, the order and commission reached Lieutenant Alonzo Tully. It was not the first time he had been picked to lead a special task force. He didn't like it now any more than he ever had.

It wasn't the department; it was city government. If you've got a pesky problem, throw money at it. If you've got a particularly offensive murder case, throw a large bunch of homicide detectives at it.

There was comfort in numbers. But a case like this was not cracked because it got buried under tons of cops. It was a lucky break, dogged police work, mainly the investigative know-how of a seasoned and dedicated detective.

But, no matter; the message was clear: The mayor wanted a show of force to indicate to his constituents that the city was doing all it could. Now the mayor could claim, in effect, It ain't my fault. Now the spotlight was on the department: You've got top priority; go get yourself a lucky break.

Mostly because he could trust them to do precisely what was required of them, Tully chose as his closest assistants on this, Angie Moore and Phil Mangiapane. Also—and of equal importance—they had been in on the case more or less continuously from its inception to date.

Moore, Mangiapane, and Tully were at a table in a Greek-town restaurant near police headquarters. Tully had just gotten the word from Inspector Koznicki about the task force and the lieutenant's role in it. The special force was being assembled at this moment but Tully wanted—needed—a quiet moment with two of his most trusted associates.

"Are they sure?" Moore asked. "I mean, did it go through ballistics?"

"You got doubts?" Mangiapane was being sarcastic.

Moore slowly shook her head. "Not really, I guess."

"There wasn't any doubt," Tully said. "But, yeah, it did go through. Ballistics is under the same kind of pressure we are. A .38 caliber wad cutter; same marks, same gun."

"Really rips my theory to hell and gone, don't it?" Mangiapane said.

"What theory was that?" Moore wanted to know.

Tully explained the discovered connection between the distant cousins—Fred Stapleton and Sister Joan—and their dotty aunt at Lourdes Nursing Home. "We were going to draw you in on this theory this morning, Angie. But, last night . . ."

"Sounds good to me," Moore said. "Like the kind of break we wanted. What's the matter with it?"

"Well," Tully said, "the original theory had it that Fred Stapleton was aware of the small fortune he was about to inherit and so was his cousin Joan Donovan. Only he wanted the whole fortune, not just half of it. He tried to kill the nun, but made a fatal error—literally—and got the hooker instead."

As Tully sipped his coffee he seemed to drift into his private stream of consciousness.

"The problem," Mangiapane explained, "was why would Stapleton go and kill the Hoffer guy."

"To cover his tracks," Moore replied. "And to throw us off the track. He would get us thinking that there was a plot to knock off officials of the Detroit Catholic Church. Our investigation would go off in that direction, while Stapleton could double back and get Donovan."

Mangiapane grinned. "Great minds . . ."

"The problem, of course," Tully rejoined the conversation, "is why would he go on? He only needed to kill Hoffer and his plan would be well off the ground.

He had us doing just what he wanted. We were running all over ourselves in the Catholic administration. He was free to go back after the nun. Why would he go and kill the old man?''

''Yeah, he already achieved his secondary objective,'' Mangiapane said.

A brief silence followed as the three either warmed their hands around their cups or actually sipped the strong coffee.

''Wait a minute,'' Moore said. ''I have an idea.''

''Let's hear it,'' Tully said.

''Supposing Stapleton found out—supposing, one way or another, he discovered that Manj was on to him. Right off the top I'm not sure how he would've known that. From the old woman, maybe?''

Mangiapane shook his head. ''She's a full-time looney tune.''

''Your aunt?''

''I don't think so, but I can check easy enough.''

''Another patient who overheard or knew?'' Moore persisted.

Tully rubbed the stubble he hadn't had the time to shave this morning. ''A possibility. A definite possibility. Make that a top priority, Manj. Get enough manpower to quiz everybody at the home. Stapleton might have found out from someone out there that the lady is your aunt, that she talked to you, that you had checked the old lady's will.

''If he found out—that's a pretty big 'if,' but possible—it just might be that he wanted to get us back on the original track by killing the old man.

''Good, Angie, very good. Get on that now, will you—both of you.''

Moore was up and moving. Mangiapane, gulping the remainder of his coffee, was only a step behind.

Tully caught the waitress's eye and pointed to his mug. She refilled it with regular coffee. He needed to be as wide-awake as possible.

It was always heartening to have something going for you during an investigation. And, in Moore's hypothesis, the Stapleton connection with his cousin was revived. But it was still on tremendously shaky ground.

The scenario from the beginning had been extremely flimsy, he had to admit. It was based entirely on hearsay.

Apparently the old lady was related to both Donovan and Stapleton. She had a fortune of some as-yet-undetermined amount. She was leaving whatever she had to the two; Mangiapane's reading of the will indicated that.

After that, what?

Did Stapleton need money that badly? Did he murder the wrong cousin? Did he kill Hoffer? If he did, was that part of the original plan, or was he winging it?

There wasn't a shred of proof. Deep down, Tully suspected that should this case work out just the way they were figuring it now, he might begin to believe in miracles.

He knew what he must do. And he didn't want to do it. He had to take one more dive into the murky administrative waters of the archdiocese of Detroit.

Father Koesler had never seen his archbishop in such a state.

As a result of heart surgery a few years before, Mark Boyle had slimmed down. He now took regular and extensive walks for exercise. Lately, he'd looked fine. Trim in his inevitable clerical suit, vest, and collar, with gold pectoral chain; thinning white hair smoothed over a noble head; his handsome Irish features topped a better-than-six-foot frame.

But today, though none of his physical characteristics had changed, he seemed somehow deflated, almost as if air had been let out of his body and it had shriveled somewhat.

He had phoned and asked Koesler to stop by. Yet now

as the archbishop greeted him, Koesler got the impression that Boyle was distracted and unsure why the priest was there. But he soon recovered, at least to the point of getting down to business.

"Good of you to come, Father, at such short notice." Boyle's formality remained unchanged.

"Certainly, Eminence. I'm sorry about Archbishop Foley. I admired him, and I know he was your good friend."

Boyle's eyes welled up. Koesler thought the Cardinal might actually weep. But he pinched his eyelids and quickly regained his composure.

"It was just yesterday that Archbishop Foley was sitting in this chair that you are using," Boyle said. "He was so alive. Though he was retired, he was still very active and alert. A great loss. And so tragic. But . . . that is not why I asked you here."

Koesler waited, saying nothing.

Boyle continued. "While we visited yesterday, I got a message that you had arrived for your appointment with him. He hadn't mentioned the appointment, so I knew nothing about it. However, I now wonder whether it might not cast some light on last night's tragic occurrence." His eyebrows arched as he looked to Koesler for any relevant information.

Koesler proceeded to recount most of his conversation with Foley, including the names of the two suspects high in the order of importance to the police investigation. The Cardinal listened attentively, fingers forming a pyramid that touched his lips, eyes never leaving Koesler's face, seemingly not even blinking.

After Koesler finished his narration, neither man moved or spoke for a few moments.

"What interests—troubles—me," Boyle said finally, "is why he was so concerned about this matter."

"The very same question I had, Eminence. I mean, we are all concerned about these murders, of course. But it wasn't at all clear to me why he was so anxious to the point of calling me in to talk about it. So, eventually, I asked him. The reason for his special concern was yourself, Eminence.''

"Me?" Boyle was startled.

"He was afraid that you were slated to be the next victim. No, it was more than apprehension; it was a premonition. That's what he called it: a premonition."

"He actually thought . . .''

"It came to him in prayer. The passage about striking the shepherd and scattering the sheep. Of course he'd seen that Scripture countless times in prayer and preaching. But the other day he read it again and, as he expressed it, it was as if he experienced some sort of revelation. Suddenly, the shepherd was yourself and the purpose behind these killings was—well, it wasn't clear to him. But it had to do with further confusing the faithful.

"In that hypothesis, it wouldn't so much matter whether the killings were being committed by someone like Arnold Carson or Fred Stapleton. The target was the atmosphere created by Vatican II. There was anger—in this case insane anger—about too much or not enough change engendered by the council.

"I tended to agree with him about the motive for the killings. But as for your being a target—or becoming a victim of this murderer . . . well . . . it was Archbishop Foley's premonition, not mine. However, I must confess, he was very persuasive."

"Worried about me . . . isn't that like him."

The archbishop should have used the past tense, thought Koesler. Foley was no longer among the living. He wondered if the reality of Foley's death had not yet reached the Cardinal's consciousness.

"There remains one final question, Father: Why would the archbishop call on you specifically?"

The question was a mild surprise to Koesler. While they had never discussed it, he knew the Cardinal was aware of his involvement in past homicide investigations. He thought Foley's reason for calling on him might have been obvious to Boyle. But then, on quick reflection, Koesler remembered that only yesterday he himself had not divined the reason Foley had called him in until the archbishop had explained.

So, with greater understanding, Koesler explained to Boyle. "Archbishop Foley had heard that I'd had some experience, at least some contact with the police in certain instances in the past."

"That's right, you have. And," he reflected, "I am the very one who told him about you."

"Archbishop Foley, to put it bluntly, wanted me to get rather actively involved in this case."

"Actively?"

"Eminence, I may in the past have been a resource for the police when there was a strong element of Catholicism or religion involved in an investigation. But the archbishop was entirely correct in assuming that I did not dive right in and volunteer my services. He wanted me to do so in this case. He said he would pray for me."

"And did you?"

"Did I . . . ?"

"Dive right in as he asked you to?"

"Eminence, that was just yesterday. I have been thinking about it. But to be perfectly frank, I haven't the slightest notion where to begin. I truly believe Archbishop Foley is in a much better position in heaven to have his prayers answered, but no manner of inspiration is getting through to me."

Cardinal Boyle swiveled his chair so that he was looking out the window at a once-posh Washington Boulevard. He was deep in thought. Koesler did not intrude.

At length, Boyle spoke. "Father, it is beyond my dominion to commission you or assign you the task of 'diving right in' as you put it. But I would like you to."

"You would?" During their association, Cardinal

Boyle had assigned Koesler to a number of diverse jobs. Strangest of all, given his lack of journalistic training, had been the assignment as editor-in-chief of the *Detroit Catholic*. But nothing could compare with asking him to, in effect, solve some murders.

"Does this surprise you?" Boyle asked.

"I'm flabbergasted."

"I had given some consideration to asking this of you. However, I don't think in the end I would have asked you if you had not told me of Archbishop Foley's request. I feel we owe this to him . . . to his memory."

"Well, I'm . . . impressed. I'd like to tell you that with a double episcopal commission, I am indeed about to dive right in. But I still haven't the foggiest idea of where to begin."

"We must trust in Divine Providence."

"Yes, Eminence, but—"

The phone rang. Boyle pushed the intercom speaker button.

"Excuse the interruption, your Eminence," came the unmistakable voice of the Cardinal's secretary, "but there is a call for Father Koesler. It's from a Lieutenant Tully of the police department. I wouldn't have disturbed you, but the lieutenant said it was urgent."

For the first time this morning, Boyle smiled. "An answer to prayer?"

Koesler picked up the phone. "Your place or mine?"

25

"THE TENDENCY NOW is to panic," Tully said.

He and Koesler were seated on opposite sides of the desk in the priest's office in St. Joseph's rectory. Tully had requested they meet here to avoid the intense traffic, noise, and confusion of police headquarters.

"Everybody wants this case closed yesterday," Tully continued. "So far, the news media have been having fun with the story. Now that the old bishop got killed they're acting like for the first time we got to get serious about this thing. A gentle old man gets killed for no apparent reason and right away they want a body on the gallows. The media reached the mayor, who makes a grandstand play of seeming to assign every cop in the city to the case. That's when everything hits the fan and there's a tendency to panic. But that's a blunder. So I want to have a very cool-headed conversation with you and figure a few more things out."

"I'll help any way I can," Koesler said. He had no intention of mentioning to Tully anything about his recent conversations with Archbishops Foley and Boyle.

"If you're going to be a help on this case, you've got to know most of what we know. And then I want to know everything you know," Tully added.

"First off, we had what I thought was an excellent lead that doesn't seem to be working out. Unless that lead gets hot again, there's no reason we have to go over it now. It's enough to say that that lead has nothing to do with the Church.

"Something you should know," Tully continued, "is how Foley was killed."

"It was different from the others? I didn't hear anything about that in the news."

"We didn't release that information. It was an execution-style killing."

"Execution-style? I—"

"The bullet entered from the top of the skull. The old man was forced to kneel and then he was shot from behind, like some poor sucker who crossed the mob. I don't know why the killer had to do that; as far as I can tell, the poor guy didn't do anything to anybody."

"Kneeling . . ." Koesler said, barely audibly. "I may be dead wrong, but I don't think the bishop was forced to kneel."

"Not forced—? Then what? Praying?"

"I think it's that exactly. I think the bishop asked to say a last prayer when he knew he was going to die. And it sort of fits the profile of your suspects."

Tully reacted as if he'd been stung. "Suspects? What suspects?"

"Uh-oh . . ."

"What suspects? What have you heard?"

"Only that two men are under suspicion." Koesler yielded before Tully's hard gaze. "Arnold Carson and Fred Stapleton."

"Where did you hear that?"

Koesler hesitated. "A priest."

"Damn leaks! We don't have the time to find them— now. Later. Okay, if Carson and Stapleton are suspects, why would that fit in with the way Foley was killed?"

"Only that they both are—it sounds kind of illogical when we're talking about a murderer—but they both are rather deeply religious, even at opposite extremes of the spectrum. I mean—as you said, Lieutenant—there was no reason anyone would want to turn this murder into an execution. Particularly since Helen Donovan and Larry Hoffer were not dealt with in that manner. That, plus the bishop's deep spirituality, makes it likely that he wasn't forced to kneel. He probably asked to do so—if he didn't do so instinctively.

"The thing is," Koesler added, "if what we're supposing actually happened, the request was granted. It's safe to assume that an ordinary killer, far from being inclined to grant such a request, would probably be anxious to get it over with and get away as quickly as he could . . . isn't that right?"

Tully nodded.

"So," Koesler said, "only someone with a rather strong confidence in prayer—a strong faith, as it were—would be moved to let the bishop have the time to pray. The killer would be risking detection the longer he held the bishop at gunpoint. It was, after all, right out in the open. Anybody could have happened along. As a matter of fact, if this morning's newscast was accurate, that's how the bishop's body was discovered, wasn't it? A passerby coming home late last night noticed the body on the sidewalk . . . no?"

Tully nodded again.

"Well," Koesler said, "to tell the truth, I can't imagine either Carson or Fred actually killing anybody—let alone a bishop. But if either were going to do it and the bishop asked for time to pray, I could easily imagine that either one would let him do it—no matter what complications that might cause."

"Okay," Tully said. "I guess that makes sense." More sense than the previously held theory that the murder had been a ritualistic execution, he thought.

This was working out rather well. Koesler had begun by making sense of nonsense. He might be of more help than Tully had anticipated. In any case, at this stage of the investigation, and given the pressure to close the case, Koesler was Tully's sole guide.

"Now," Tully proceeded, "let me spell out the basic

problem we've got here. What we've got is a serial killer. He has committed three premeditated murders. Well, make that two-and-a-half, assuming that he aimed for the nun but got her sister instead.

"We know it's the same person in each instance because ballistics tells us the same weapon was used in each instance. . . ." Tully's voice trailed off as a new thought entered the process of analysis. What was it Koesler had said—". . . *they both are rather deeply religious, even at opposite extremes of the spectrum.*" Was it possible . . . ? Granted, ballistics said the same gun was used in each killing; but there was no way of knowing whether or not the same hand had held that gun in each killing. What if . . . what if two different people—? Tully's blood turned cold: What if *more* than one or two people were involved? What if this was some sort of insane conspiracy, with a number of people involved? What good was it to check possible alibis when the one who had committed one murder could easily have an alibi for the next killing, which one of his conspirators had carried out?

Tully's head was buzzing. Granted the mayor had given the department carte blanche manpower-wise, but, still, did they have enough staff to follow such a widespread lead? Tully sighed. They'd have to; they'd have to have enough staff. They'd have to check this all out.

Tully became aware that Koesler was gazing at him quizzically. He smiled, grimly. No need to muddy the waters as far as Koesler was concerned . . . at least not yet. "Sorry," he said, "I got carried away with . . . well, never mind. As I was saying, we know it's the same person because ballistics tells us the same gun was used in each killing. He—the killer—also used the same kind of bullet—a slug that's usually used for target practice. Now the way the killer is using this bullet is up close and into the head. What that does is cause an awful lot of damage. So he's sure as sure can be that the one shot will cause death.

"It also makes it pretty easy for us to recover the bullets, compare them, and come up with the conclusion that"—he proceeded resolutely—"it's the same guy doing all the killing. That's common with a serial killer," he explained. "He usually wants it known that he's the same one killing more than one person."

Koesler was aware of the phenomenon of the serial killer wanting each of his murders correctly attributed to him. He'd read about it in newspapers and books. He'd experienced it in some of the cases he'd been involved in in the past. But Tully's refresher course was welcome.

"The challenge," Tully continued, "is to find the connection."

"The connection?"

"He's killing blondes, or prostitutes, or coeds, or alcoholic bums, or stewardesses. The secret, the link, is in the perp's head. He knows why he is choosing the people he selects to murder. Sometimes the connection between the victims is obvious and sometimes it's not. What we've got here is a pretty confusing puzzle."

Which could be even more confusing if we are dealing with more than one killer, was Tully's added unspoken thought.

"Why has he selected Sister Joan, Larry Hoffer, and Archbishop Foley, that's the puzzle," Koesler said, while wondering somewhat at the lieutenant's uncharacteristic distractedness.

Tully, having concluded that, single killer or multiple killers, the immediate problem was to discover the common denominator, the link, the motif, in these killings, addressed Koesler's statement. "That's it: If we could figure out the connection; if we could crawl into the killer's mind, we could unlock the mystery. If we knew why he selected the nun, Hoffer, and the bishop, we'd know whether or not he was done, finished."

"You're saying there may be more murders?"

"Anything's possible. There may be one or more than one still on his list. Or this may be it. But if this is it, then what was the point? Why these three? What statement was he—someone—trying to make? And on top of that, one of them—the nun—is still alive." Tully shook his head. "Very confusing.

"Now, what I want you to do, Father, is tell me all you can about these three people and their positions in the Detroit Church. Someplace in who they were or what they did is the secret. We've got to unravel that secret and solve it."

Koesler took a deep breath and offered a quick, silent, but fervent prayer that somehow, as he explained all this to Tully, the elusive secret might come to light.

"Okay," he said, "I'll start with Larry Hoffer."

"Any particular reason?"

"Mostly because he's the one I know least about."

"Why's that?"

"Because he's the 'money man,' and what I know least about in this world is money."

Tully almost smiled. He sensed Koesler's unease. But the matter was far too serious and important for any attempt at humor.

"As far back as I can recall," Koesler began, "the 'money man' has been a layman. There must have been a time when the job was handled by a priest, but I don't remember that—and I go back a long way."

"Wait," Tully interrupted, "can you be clearer about your 'money man'? I mean more specific? What's he in charge of?"

"Off the top of my head, I couldn't name all the departments. But, just a minute. I've got the directory. . . ." Koesler rummaged through the desk drawers. "Ah, here it is." He thumbed through the front pages. "Here we go: Finance and Administration—which is what Mr. Hoffer headed—encompasses the Building Office, the Business Office, Collections and

Disbursements, Computer Services, Archdiocesan Development Fund accounts, Development and Church Support, Human Resources, Parish Finances, Properties, and Purchasing. Which makes, let's see: ten departments spread throughout three floors of the Chancery Building.''

"A lot of responsibility," Tully commented. "Know anything about the man?''

"Not much, I confess. He became a member of the staff long after I stopped attending staff meetings . . . I used to attend the meetings because I was editor of the diocesan paper," he explained gratuitously.

"Anything you can think of might help." Tully returned to the topic at hand: "Happily married?''

"As far as I know. I've never met Mrs. Hoffer, and I knew Larry only slightly. A fidgety man.''

"Why do you say that?''

"He was sort of famous for rattling coins, keys, whatever, in his pants pocket. It was no more than a nervous habit, but it did give him away.'' Koesler paused reflectively.

"Anything?''

"Only that he controlled a lot of money and financial investments.''

"That's kind of obvious—from those departments he was responsible for . . . isn't it?''

Koesler reddened. It *was* obvious. "Of course. Sorry.''

"Don't be. Just go ahead. Anything you can think of.''

"Well, I've heard it said—no, it's stronger than hearsay—that he had some controversial opinions.''

Tully grew even more attentive.

"I suppose it was natural for someone in his position. I mean, he had the overall view of income and disbursements on the diocesan level. And it's no secret that financially we are limping badly, especially in the core city. Those huge, beautiful churches in those parishes are nearly empty and the school system is in trouble in just about the whole diocese.''

Tully understood more clearly than Koesler would have guessed. Catholicism, as far as Tully was concerned, was a white religion. What he had no way of gauging was the sense of community, belonging, and dedication that endured among those relatively few black Catholics who had established a sense of ownership over those parishes.

"The point is," Koesler said, "Larry Hoffer wanted to close not only the financially strapped parishes but the whole school system."

"What's wrong with that?" Tully asked, in keeping with his understanding of the situation.

Koesler hesitated. The question raised a topic too vast and too complex to adequately treat in depth. He saw no point in going into the parishioners' love for those parishes or the dedication with which their priests served them. But there was another facet that might prove relevant and interesting to the lieutenant.

"One thing that at least some people think is wrong with those threatened closings is that the people concerned—including the staff members who are responsible for parishes and schools—don't want them closed."

"I suppose that's natural."

"No, Lieutenant, when I say they don't want them closed I am understating. They *really* don't want any closings."

"Oh?" Tully found Koesler's emphasis not only interesting but provocative. "How much do they not want it? Enough to get violent about it?"

"I couldn't say that. I don't know. Most of the people we're talking about just are not violent people."

Briefly, Tully considered the possibility that Koesler was so naive he couldn't conceive of anybody as being a murderer. Then he remembered that the priest had been involved in previous homicide investigations. He must know.

"Could you be more specific?" Tully asked. "Who are these nonviolent people who are so opposed to the closings?"

"Well, for instance, Monsignor Young. He's in charge of Catholic education in the diocese. He's also nearing retirement. Close the schools and he's out of a job. He, and people like him, are very, very strongly opposed to closings. But I can't imagine any of these people getting violent over it."

"Okay." Tully thought it useless to pursue this topic—at least for now. Koesler had told him enough to establish a motive for someone perhaps wanting to murder Hoffer. At least Hoffer had his enemies. He wondered whether Stapleton and/or Carson could have been motivated by parish or school closings. Carson seemed unstable enough to be a fanatic over this. And Stapleton's profile appeared to possess the potential for fanatical violence.

Now if that could only be the emergence of a thread that would link up with the lives of the other two victims. It could be the jumping-off point of a motive for serial murder. And from that motive would emerge the perpetrator. Or, he reminded himself grimly, perpetrators. In any case, they were beginning to make progress.

With some enthusiasm then, Tully asked, "Now, what about the nun? Her personally, and her job?"

Koesler smiled. "Sister Joan I know pretty well. She became a religious in order to teach. But like so many other nuns, she's no longer doing what she started out to do. In her case, it was capability. I mean it wasn't so much that she chose to go into another field, like switching from teaching to social work or pastoral work. She was selected by her religious order, the other nuns and religious in the diocese and, eventually, appointed by the archbishop to become delegate for religious. As such, she is an intermediary between not only the various religious themselves but also between them as a group and the diocese. Sort of 'monkey in the middle.'

"She's not the first woman to hold that post—maybe the third or fourth. I'd have to check. But I can tell you a story that will put this in context.

"She came into the office as assistant to the delegate. The nun who was then delegate was not allowed to eat lunch in the chancery dining room with the priests and bishops. She had to eat in the kitchen—if you can imagine such a thing."

"Yeah, I think I can imagine what discrimination is like."

Once again, Koesler was embarrassed. "Oh, I am sorry. How stupid of me!"

Tully shrugged. "It's okay. Go on."

Koesler nodded. "Okay, back to my story.

"The first day Sister Joan was on the job in the delegate's office, her superior told her to eat lunch in the chancery dining room. Joan understood that this was a first, and that she would not be welcome. But it was an order, and nuns, especially, are used to carrying out orders.

"It was with fear and trepidation that she approached the dining room just after noon.

"When she entered, the table talk, which had been lively, ended. In the loaded silence that followed, she didn't even know what food she was serving herself from the buffet, and she was mumbling incoherently.

"Then, breaking the silence, Cardinal Boyle said, 'Sister, when you're ready, come and sit next to me.' And that was how the chancery lunch counter was integrated, as it were."

It was an interesting story, and Tully's regard for Boyle rose, but he was unable to draw from the account any conclusion that would be useful to the theory he was trying to construct. So he simply looked expectantly at Koesler.

"The point," Koesler said after a moment, "is that this is how the delegate for religious was treated. Even though the delegate's status is rather exalted in the Church."

Koesler saw that he was not getting through to Tully, so he attempted to clarify and amplify. "This job in this diocese was originally filled by a bishop, and later by a priest. At that time the position was termed 'vicar for religious.' Then, when nuns filled the position, the title was changed to 'delegate,' because a woman could not be called 'vicar'—a title reserved to the priestly caste.

"Not only was the title changed—and changed to one lower in rank—but the delegate was further humbled by not being allowed to eat in the dining room with priests. All the while, the vicar—or delegate, whichever title one wished to recognize—outranked most of the priests in that dining room.

"You see, Lieutenant, if you were to put that job in the context of, say, the administration of the president of the United States, the position would be of cabinet rank. It's not usually looked on in this way—but, if it were, she, Sister Joan, would be the highest ranking woman in the archdiocese of Detroit."

Tully reflected on that for a few moments. "I see," he said, slowly. "Well, then," he challenged, "is your Church as racist as it is sexist?"

It was Koesler's turn to reflect. "That's not easy to answer," he said finally. "I don't think the Church is racist—though you couldn't prove that by the number of black Catholics, let alone black priests or bishops. Generally, the Church has been on the scene and given witness in the civil rights movement. But I must admit that point is arguable.

"As for sexism, there can be no doubt we're guilty—and I must confess we're not doing much besides talk to remedy the situation."

After another moment's thought, Tully said, "You

are an intelligent man. You can see what's wrong. Why do you stay in?''

"In the Church? In the priesthood?''

"Uh-huh.''

"Because I love the Church and I love the priesthood. Even though I can see the warts and the blemishes, I still love it. I think if there weren't a Catholic Church, somebody would have to invent it. I guess I love it more for what it sometimes has been and what it someday can be. Let me ask you, Lieutenant, is everything perfect in the police department?''

Tully didn't need time for deliberation. "No." He smiled. "Okay, I get the drift. Back to the nun and her job: What, if anything, would she have to do with parishes and schools closing?''

"Nothing, directly, that I can see offhand. She is not in a position to close any of them, or keep them open, for that matter. I suppose if she were to successfully recruit hundreds of young women to become teachers in parochial schools, she would contribute mightily to the preservation of those schools. But that, I think, would be next to impossible—for anyone—now.''

"Okay. But would she have any influence on somebody else's decision to keep them open or close them?''

"Like who?''

"Like Hoffer. Supposing Hoffer decided to close some parishes or schools. Would the opinion of the delegate for religious carry any weight?''

"I'm afraid I haven't explained things very well. Larry Hoffer couldn't close a parish or a school no matter how much he might have wanted to.''

"Because?''

"Because, in ecclesiastical as well as civil law, the archbishop owns everything.''

"Everything?''

"All properties, lands, institutions, buildings— everything that belongs to the archdiocese of Detroit— and not, for instance, belonging to one or another of the religious orders—everything's in the name of whoever happens to be the archbishop of Detroit.

"So, for now, only Cardinal Boyle, as archbishop of Detroit, can close parishes or schools. But I must say this for Cardinal Boyle: He truly listens to the people he puts in charge of things. I can tell you from personal experience, when he appoints someone to a special job, he expects that person to do the job. But, at the same time, he does not abdicate his ultimate responsibility and power. So neither Hoffer nor Sister Joan would have the power or authority to effect a closing or extension of operation of any archdiocesan institution. But both of them could, and undoubtedly would, make their opinions known. And Cardinal Boyle would give those opinions careful consideration."

"Okay." Tully was zeroing in on what he considered the vital question. "We know what Hoffer thought: He wanted to close a number of parishes and maybe the whole school system. How about the nun? Would she have given the same advice to her boss?"

"I'm not sure. Possibly she herself doesn't even know. I did hear some talk that at the most recent staff meeting, when Larry proposed the closings, Sister Joan argued against closing. But that was a brainstorming session. Her constituents probably would approve of the closings. Rather than have some schools with no nuns or maybe at most one or two, consolidating would give the religious more voice, clout. I think, when push came to shove, they probably would have sided with Larry."

That's two, thought Tully. His infant theory was gaining strength. Suppose the thread that held these serial killings together was the determination to close parishes and/or schools. The next step then would be to identify others among the Cardinal's advisers who would counsel in favor of the closings. It might not be much of a handle, but it was better than nothing, which was precisely what he had been looking at before this talk with Koesler.

"Okay," Tully said, "now do the same for the archbishop. Something about the man, about his job."

"This is another case," Koesler responded, "where I don't know all that much about him personally. We had our first, and, as it turned out, last, chat just yesterday."

"He's been here about a year, hasn't he?"

"Yes. So you're wondering why if he's been here all that time don't I know more about him?"

"That, and why you happened to have your first meeting just the day before he got killed."

"Lieutenant, I don't know how often you meet with the chief of police or the mayor, but I'll bet you stand a better chance of socializing with them than a priest does of hobnobbing with a bishop. So there isn't much explanation necessary as to why I had no personal association with him before.

"As to why I met with him yesterday? He invited me to visit him."

"The reason?" Tully hoped it would not be some sort of unrevealable secret.

"He had heard that I had some slight experience with the police and he wanted to talk to me about these murders. He had a premonition that Cardinal Boyle would be the next victim."

"He thought Boyle was going to buy it, and the next one on the list turned out to be himself!"

"Strange . . . I know it's strange. A turnabout of sorts. But that's how it was."

"Do you know anything about the man?"

"Sure. I was very much aware of his track record in Cincinnati."

"That where he was born?"

"No. Florida. He was just a little older than Cardinal Boyle. They studied in Rome at the same time, became friends. They used to vacation together. That is all common knowledge, at least among priests . . . and a few laypeople who have a special interest in this sort of thing.''

"Like Carson and Stapleton?''

"Yes . . . I suppose so. Anyway, Foley seemed to mellow over the years he was archbishop of Cincinnati—but then, so has Cardinal Boyle in the years he's been in Detroit. Some time ago Bishop Foley retired. He could have lived anywhere he wished. Odds were that he would retire to his native Florida. That he made his home in Detroit is a sign of the friendship he had with our cardinal.

"Which, I guess, brings us to what he did in Detroit. Probably one word describes it best—help. He, along with the auxiliary bishops, would visit parishes and confirm—that's a sacrament that normally is conferred by a bishop. He attended meetings. He spent a lot of time with his friend Cardinal Boyle. He didn't have to do anything he didn't want to do; he was, after all, retired.

"He had a substantial amount of dignity. He was an archbishop and there aren't all that many archbishops. In retirement he remained an archbishop. He had plenty of dignity still, but, in retirement, not much clout.''

"Did he close any parishes or schools in Cincinnati?''

Koesler smiled. "You're really building a case on these closings, aren't you? I've got to admit, the theme does seem to emerge, though I don't think I would have thought of it. But, no, as far as I know, he didn't. Of course, the situation probably is nowhere near the same in Cincinnati as in Detroit.''

"How about now? What do you think he would have advised the Cardinal?''

"Again, I don't know. But I guess we're dealing in speculation here. Only Larry Hoffer is on the record firmly in favor of the closings. I think—and I'm basing this on all that I've read and heard about Archbishop Foley—that left to his own devices, he would have tried to avoid closing any parishes or schools by executive order.''

"Executive order?''

"I think it unavoidable that some schools, some parishes, particularly in large and basically poor urban areas, will close by attrition, if nothing else. I don't think any bishop can prevent that no matter how he feels about it. But I doubt that Bishop Foley himself would have issued an order, in effect euthanizing these institutions. However, what he might have suggested to the Cardinal could be another matter.''

"Why's that?'' Tully's spirits took hope. Until this final caveat, he had visions of his new theory going down in flames as Koesler supposed that Foley would not advocate the closings. Now the priest seemed to be speculating on what the opposite side of the coin might be.

"Of the two choices—to close or not to close—the easier way to go is closure. As Larry Hoffer would argue, it makes perfect sense financially. In a society that practically lives by 'the bottom line,' no other persuasion is necessary; most everybody would agree there's no sensible alternative.

"In this context, some might object to closing institutions that are still able to survive, even if marginally. But few would insist on keeping the destitute alive. It would be like keeping a brain-dead patient in a vegetative state on a heart-lung machine.

"So you see, Lieutenant: Struggling to keep these schools and parishes going when they are beyond self-help would be unpopular as well as a losing battle. That's why I think it possible that, even though Archbishop Foley might choose martyrdom for himself, I don't think that his close friendship with the Cardinal would permit his advising this painful and frustrating course.

"Now, that's only a guess. But it's my best shot.''

"It's a help. It's a help.'' Tully proceeded to gather

his notes and pack away the tape recorder he'd had running. "Now, I'll have to see whether Carson or Stapleton is a better fit."

"Better fit?"

"Uh-huh. Which one of them would find the threat of closing schools and parishes a sufficient motive to commit murder."

"Do you really think anyone would find something like that a sufficient motive?"

Tully shrugged. "You tell me. Remember the guy in Florida last year who was a member of a church's building committee and got so upset at proposed renovations that he wounded two people, took a hostage for several hours, and ended up killing himself? And"—his eyes twinkled—"he wasn't even one of your Catholic zealots; as I recall, he was an Episcopalian." He grew serious again. "You gotta remember, Father, we're probably dealing with a psychopath here. It takes a crazy of some sort to get into serial killing. Something that might get a normal person upset enough to write an angry letter to the editor is the kind of stuff that gets mass murderers going."

"Well, if you put it that way, which one seems more likely to you?"

"From everything you've told me about the tensions in the Church . . . I guess I'd put my money on Carson. He's the one who wants to go back to a time before all the changes. Well, that's the time when Catholic parishes and schools were going gangbusters. I don't see Stapleton in the same frame of mind. But you never can tell. We'll look both of 'em over good in terms of what we've just discussed."

"There's one thing," Koesler said, as he retrieved Tully's coat from the closet, "whoever has done this knows the victims' routines exceptionally well. He'd have to know that Sister Joan regularly comes home late and that both Larry and the archbishop walk their dogs at about eleven at night."

"A bit of dedicated surveillance would disclose that. Neither one of them, by the way, has an alibi for the times of the crimes. Carson lives alone and claims he was home at the times in question. There's no one to say he was or wasn't. Stapleton claims he was en route to a meeting or returning home or at a movie, by himself, at the crucial times. Again, no one to corroborate.

"We even brought in the two dogs to get their reactions. Hoffer's mutt just sniffed each of them and sat down. Foley's dog went wild over both of them. So: nothing."

"If you brought in the dogs, Carson and Stapleton must know they're under suspicion."

Tully snorted. "They know okay. They've known for a while now. It's a very delicate balance," he explained. "Something like that series on TV—what is it—the cop with the antique raincoat . . . ?" He tapped his forehead trying to recall the character's name.

"Columbo?" Koesler supplied.

"That's the one. You know how he keeps coming back, driving the perp crazy? Well, this is something like that: These guys get angry when we keep coming back at 'em over and over again. Especially Carson; he's the type who yells 'police brutality' when a cop helps a little old lady across the street.

"The thing we don't want to do is get them so shook up that they call in their lawyers. We don't need that kind of headache. It's a very delicate balance.

"But I should tell you: These two guys are not our only suspects. They're just the leading candidates. Now we'll be looking through all the others for that thread we found this afternoon. There's someone out there who gets so worked up about closing Church facilities he's flipped. We'll get him," Tully promised as he stepped out into a cloudy but dry winter's day.

As he watched Tully hunch his shoulders against the cold, Koesler offered a brief prayer that the police would, indeed, get the person who was doing this be-

fore anyone else was harmed. Too many innocent people had been killed already. Please God, inspire the
police, and there would be no more.

Still, he reflected as he turned back into the rectory,
he had not "dived right in" to this investigation as both
Archbishop Foley and Cardinal Boyle had asked. He
was still only reacting.

He hadn't contacted Tully; the lieutenant had contacted him. He hadn't come up with any brilliant theory; he had merely answered Tully's questions.

It was enough, Koesler told himself, that he be no
more than an instrument in the solution of this mystery.
He would like to have fulfilled the commission of the
two bishops. But, quite frankly, he still had no clue as
to where to begin.

26 IT WAS STILL early, but people were already crowding into Blessed Sacrament. The cathedral would be filled by the time the Scripture Service for Archbishop Foley would begin.

Father Koesler stood in a long line of people moving almost imperceptibly forward to view the archbishop's remains. The line moved so slowly that he had plenty of time for his stream of consciousness to dissolve into myriad unconnected thoughts.

He looked about at those already seated, standing against the walls, or, like himself, waiting to pay respects at the coffin. Since his chat this afternoon with Lieutenant Tully, Koesler tended to regard many familiar faces as suspects. He was not eager to believe that either Stapleton or Carson had committed these murders. But somebody had. Who? Monsignor Young? Hardly. But until this case was solved, almost everyone could be a suspect.

Koesler's height enabled him to see the entire interior of the cathedral more easily than many others who also served by standing and waiting.

The sanctuary, formerly enclosed on three sides, had been transformed into the equivalent of a thrust stage, open on three sides. Thus, the altar, once so remotely situated near the rear wall, was now proximal to most of the congregation.

Directly in front of the altar was the archbishop's bier. Koesler could not see it in full view. It was as yet only

291

a flash of brilliant white revealed periodically as those in line ahead of him shifted from one foot to the other.

Above the bier, suspended from the cathedral ceiling, was the huge ceremonial red hat that had belonged to Cardinal Edward Mooney, Detroit's first Cardinal. It would hang there alone as long as the cathedral stood. By the time Mark Boyle was elevated to Cardinal, Pope Paul VI had done away with much of the ancient panoply of the office, including the *cappa magna*, a grandiose garment of watered silk and ermine, as well as the great red hat.

The hat was never actually worn. During the ceremony of installation it was held above, then touched to the Cardinal's head, not to be used again until the Cardinal died. Then it was suspended from the cathedral ceiling. According to Church wags, it would not fall until the Cardinal was released from purgatory. Which ensured a torture lasting centuries. If so, more recent Cardinals could be grateful the custom of the red hat had been abolished.

Koesler was nearing the coffin. Tomorrow morning Cardinal Boyle would be principal celebrant at the Mass of Resurrection. Many archbishops and prelates from neighboring dioceses would concelebrate. From Detroit the body would be shipped to Cincinnati, where another funeral Mass would be offered. Finally to Florida for the final Mass and burial.

There he was. Koesler had lost track of time and distance. He was surprised to find himself standing alongside the casket.

The vestments were sumptuously ornate. Moving upward from the polished black shoes there was a spotless, starched alb, then the white chasuble glittering with inlaid gems; white ceremonial gloves covered his hands; the *pallium*, emblem of an archbishop, crossed his chest; on his head was the white miter. Koesler judged the miter would have to be removed or they'd never get the casket closed.

Foley's face was the only body part not covered. In death his years had caught up with him. He appeared skeletal. Had it not been for the wrinkles, his face might have been mistaken for a bare skull.

A shiver shook Koesler. He could scarcely believe this was all that remained of the kindly gentleman with the musical voice who spoke so forcefully just yesterday afternoon.

Someone coughed. It startled Koesler. How long had he been standing there? It was not like him to be thoughtless of others. He was holding up the line. He moved from the bier quickly and was about to enter a nearby pew when he heard a muffled sob. He turned to see who had been so moved.

Third behind him in line was Sister Joan Donovan. A handkerchief was held tightly to her mouth. Tears flowed down her cheeks. Koesler waited as she viewed the body. Then, wordlessly, he led her to the pew and seated himself beside her. Soon the weeping stopped and she regained control.

"Excuse me, Father," she said. "I didn't intend to make such a fool of myself. I just couldn't stop crying once I got in that line."

"You know what they say," Koesler said, "there's no one as dead as a dead priest unless it's a dead bishop. I think Archbishop Foley would be very pleased that you were so moved." He amended himself. "The archbishop *is* pleased that you cared."

"It's just that he was so kind when Helen was . . . when Helen died. While I was worried whether she could have a Church burial, he called and volunteered to offer the Mass. And then at the wake, he was just like a father . . . or a grandfather. He was such a support. I hardly knew him before Helen died and, in a day, it was as if he'd been part of my life for as long as I could remember."

"Some people have the ability. I guess I should say

'charism.' It's rare. But, I agree, Archbishop Foley had it.''

Father Koesler and Sister Joan fell silent. He glanced at her. The tears had stopped flowing. She seemed at peace and lost in thought.

She was right, thought Koesler. The archbishop had excelled in humanity. Koesler had witnessed Foley participating in liturgical functions innumerable times. He always seemed distracted, constantly called back by a master of ceremonies from a private reverie. But present at all times was the hint of humor and a concern for others that was open and genuine. The two men had met personally only once. Yet it was as Sister Joan noted: It seemed as if Koesler had known him, and known him well, for a long time. He wasn't some remote dignitary lying in state, but a friend.

There was a rustle behind him; something brushed against the back of his head. "Sorry," a male voice said.

As Koesler halfway turned, he recognized two priests of roughly his vintage. They were about to be seated directly behind him. One of their coats had brushed him as they entered the pew. He nodded. "Ted . . . Harry."

Almost simultaneously, they replied, "Bob."

The two priests settled into the pew, making barely audible rustling noises as they shifted about in search of comfort, knowing all the while they would never find it.

After a few minutes, they began talking to each other in tones that shifted between normal speaking volume and a whisper. At any rate, they were a distraction, Koesler glanced at Joan, wondering if they were disturbing her. Apparently not; she seemed transfixed as she gazed steadfastly at the remains of the man who, in so brief a time, had made such a lasting impression on her. She was not disturbed by the conversation going on behind her.

He was. Koesler tried recollecting his thoughts in

prayer, but the conversation continued to distract him. He decided that living with it was an easier course than creating a small scene.

"Too bad about the old man." Koesler thought it was Ted, but was not going to turn around to make certain.

"Yeah. He seemed like a nice enough guy. How long's he been here . . . a year?"

"About. He could've lived in Florida, you know. That's where he was born and raised."

"I knew that, but I'd forgotten. Retired in Florida! And it's his home at that. Why in hell would he want to come up here?"

"The boss. They got along like brothers."

"I don't think I like *anybody* that much." They both chuckled. "Think the boss will go down now that Foley's gone?"

"Hard to tell. If I had a last buck I'd bet against it. What's there to do there now for him? He's not a golfer. For him it's just a long walk in the sunshine interrupted by hitting a ball with a stick."

Silence. Then, "When we goin' down?"

"Dunno. I was waiting for you to make up your mind."

"Lent comes early this year."

"When?"

"Sometime late February."

"Wow! We better get on the ball."

"A Titleist, preferably."

Another chuckle. "Got to get back before Ash Wednesday."

"It'll be great getting down there. Winter's just beginning here and already I'm tired of it." A pause. "It just doesn't seem right somehow."

"What?"

"That the boss won't be down. I mean with Foley gone and all. One thing you gotta admit: Nobody works any harder than the Cardinal. I didn't think I'd ever say that about any priest, let alone a bishop, but, dammit, the guy deserves some time off. Personally, I hope he does go down.''

"Yeah, it'd be nice seeing him relaxed. I'd even buy him a drink.''

"You? With the tightest pockets in the diocese, you'd buy him a drink? Somehow I got to get the message through to him. Then he'll go for sure.''

They laughed. Silence. Then: "Oh, I almost forgot: You wanna play a little cards tonight?''

"Tonight? Where?''

"The chancery.''

"The chancery? Clete Bash having a party?''

"Uh-huh. Some of the guys are from out of town. Here for the funeral tomorrow. Staying at the chancery overnight.''

"Sounds like it could be fun, despite Bash.''

"Why 'despite Bash'?''

"Guy's a prick.''

"What's he done to you?''

"Nothing. I'm just sick and tired of seeing his mug on TV all the time. Who the hell's he think he is, Walter Cronkite?''

"You got the wrong guy. Cronkite was anchor. Bash is a—whaddyacallit—a press officer—like that McLaughlin, the Jebbie, for Nixon. Besides, he doesn't like wild card games.''

"Who?''

"Bash. They're a lot of fun.''

"But not professional. Probably some of those out-of-town guys are sticklers: five-card stud, nothing wild, down and dirty.''

"Well, I don't know. It might be kind of fun meeting the new guys. Hmmm . . . I guess so. But I gotta leave early. I got early Mass at the convent tomorrow.''

"God! I forgot you've got a convent. Those are practically a relic of a bygone day. You may just end up having the last nun in captivity.''

"Hell, I don't have 'em. They just live in the old

convent. Five of 'em. Soon's the sun's up, they're off to the four winds doing God knows what. Social work, prison counseling, and so on and so forth. I can just barely remember when we had teaching nuns living there. By God, those were the days.''

"Gone forever. So, it's settled then. We can go downtown in my car. I'd just as soon leave early too. I got a hunch somebody in that bunch is a ringer and there's going to be a lot of local priests who are broke tomorrow. I don't want to be one of them.''

That did it.

Until this moment, Koesler was feeling left out. He hadn't been invited to the party and he felt certain that in such a cosmopolitan group of priests there would be at least a few who would want to chat. It was instructive for those living under the jurisdiction of Cardinal Mark Boyle to get a taste of what life could be like under the more rigid control of almost any other bishop in the country.

But Ted or Harry—whichever it was who said it—was correct: The poker probably would be unrelentingly serious; light conversation would be at a minimum. And Koesler had had enough poker the other night to tide him over until spring or summer at the very earliest.

The organ sounded. There was a rustling as people throughout the now crowded cathedral struggled to their feet. The procession entered from the cathedral rectory. With enthusiasm and heartfelt sincerity the congregation took up the hymn, "And He will raise you up on eagle's wings. . . .''

Cardinal Boyle, his dazzlingly white vestments set off by the scarlet-orange signs of office, halted at the bier. His tall, slender figure seemed bowed as he contemplated the remains of his old friend. He appeared able to remain standing only by clutching his crosier tightly with both hands. Clearly he was crushed by this senseless death.

Koesler's heart went out to the Cardinal, whom he

admired greatly. Cardinal Boyle had so many controversial responsibilities, and he obviously believed that the buck stopped with himself. He certainly did not need the grief he now bore.

These thoughts caused Koesler to consider the deep loss suffered by Mrs. Hoffer as well as the sorrow inflicted on Sister Joan, who now stood beside him. At sight of the Cardinal's sorrow, silent tears again coursed her cheeks.

It was all so senseless.

But that was the point, wasn't it: It wasn't senseless. To someone it made a lot of sense. Someone had a purpose in all this death and sorrow. What was it Lieutenant Tully had said? A thread. There was some kind of thread connecting these murders. If he, Koesler, could identify that thread, he—they—might be able to solve this case and possibly prevent further killings.

Koesler hoped that what he had told Tully had been of help. Maybe the whole thing was linked to the parishes and schools and whether they were to remain open or should be closed.

One thing was sadly certain to Koesler: He was not as actively involved in this investigation as two archbishops had asked him to be. He was not as involved as he wanted to be.

27 "THE CARDINAL WAS good today." Then, remembering that he was not allowed to have an independent opinion, Bob Meyer deferred to his boss. "Didn't you think he was?"

"I've been trying to get him to do that for years," Father Cletus Bash said.

"Do what, Father?"

"Why, speak extempore, of course."

Meyer reflected on that for a moment. "That's right; he usually types his speeches and then reads them verbatim."

"Always makes him sound like he's reading a goddam dull textbook."

"May I get you gentlemen something from the bar?" the waiter asked.

Bash wanted a Beefeater martini with a twist. Meyer ordered a Piesporter, an appropriate choice as they were lunching at the Pontchartrain Wine Cellars.

"I think," Meyer said after the waiter left, "the Cardinal is a shy man who doesn't want to show his emotions." As his mouth formed the words he again remembered that he was not supposed to think. Two blunders, and they hadn't even ordered lunch yet. He knew Bash was keeping score. One more and Meyer would either be reprimanded here in public, or he surely would get a scathing memo later this afternoon.

Bash paused to tally the blemishes on Meyer's current tab. "Of course it's not that. The Cardinal is a precise man. Too precise. That's why he writes everything out beforehand."

Careful now not to strike out, Meyer lobbed the conversational ball into Bash's court. "Why do you think he spoke without notes this morning?"

The waiter brought their drinks, took their menu orders, and left.

"Emotion got the better of him," Bash said. "They were close . . . very, very close, the Cardinal and Archbishop Foley. Matter of fact, I'm surprised the Cardinal trusted himself to speak without notes. He got carried away. Don't blame him."

Bash felt a firm loyalty to Boyle. Next to the Catholic Church—as Bash perceived it—and the army, Bash's greatest fealty was to his Cardinal. It was Boyle who had given Bash this job as director of communications, which, in turn, had freed him from the deadly monotony of a parochial ministry and offered the opportunity of becoming a big fish in an acknowledgedly very large pool. Which opportunity he had seized and made the most of.

No one would have accused Bash of having a particularly affectionate nature, nor even, for that matter, an affectionate bone in his body. But he felt . . . well, kindly, toward his benefactor.

When Bash had become a member of the "staff" because he headed his department, Boyle had been an archbishop. Since then he had become a Cardinal, a prince of the Church—short of being Pope, the highest dignity in the Church—and an elector of Popes. This dignity had rubbed off on everyone in the archdiocese of Detroit, not the least on Bash himself. He was official spokesperson for a prince of the Church. And Bash never let the media forget that fact.

Thus, when attempting to encourage the Cardinal to make comments off the cuff, Bash's recommendations were made with sincerity and reverence. And that, in Bash's life, was pretty much the extent of those virtues.

Bash was, in a word, selfish, with bottomless ego needs. As often as possible, he gorged himself on generous supplies of ego gratification.

Nothing was said for several long minutes. Bob Meyer sipped his wine. Bash had downed his martini in a few gulps and was enjoying the gin's magical warmth as it seemed to be carried by his bloodstream throughout his body. He ordered another martini, which he finished before the waiter brought their meal. As he began to eat, fortified by the double martini, he felt slightly more kindly to the whole human race, even Meyer.

In this expansive glow, Bash became somewhat uncomfortable with the silence between him and Meyer. Obviously the younger man was content to eat rather than talk.

In reality, Meyer had simply run out of ways to keep the ball in Bash's court.

"You know, Bob . . ."

That was a good sign, Meyer recognized. Bash seldom used Meyer's given name. But when it was used it meant that Bash was in one of his rare relaxed and good moods.

"You know, Bob," Bash said, "one of the good things—fringe benefits—of an occasion like this—the death of a priest or a bishop—is that the gang gets together to really let their hair down and relax. Last night, for example, we had a bunch of out-of-town priests spending the night at St. Al's." Bash thought about that for a moment, and added sadly, "All those rooms above the chancery. Used to be overflowing with priests. Now they're empty except for when something like this happens."

Then, as rapidly as he had become maudlin, his happy frame of mind returned. "One of the guys from Toronto was telling about a priest's funeral up there sometime back. The dead priest was lying in state in the rectory parlor. Some priests gathered to pay their respects. Then they went upstairs where there was a generous supply of booze. They all had a few drinks when this one screwball priest said, 'You know, Tony would like this.'—Tony was the name of the dead priest.

"Then this priest left. Everyone figured he had gone home. But after a bit they heard this sound. Someone was dragging something up the stairs. Something stiff and heavy.

"They all had the same idea at the same time: that the screwball was dragging Tony upstairs so he could enjoy the party.

"Well, they all went running out into the hallway—and there was the screwball dragging a statue up the stairs.

"And one guy had thrown up for nothing."

They laughed. Meyer 55 percent because he thought the story funny, 45 percent because it was the boss's joke. Bash laughed for the same reason he told the story: The martinis had done their job and he was expansive.

One story reminded him of another, and so Bash told stories throughout their luncheon. In Meyer's association with Bash this was a unique performance.

After finishing coffee, Bash pushed the check to his assistant. "Take care of this and take it out of petty cash."

Meyer knew that Bash would eventually check to see that nothing more was taken than the luncheon's tab plus a modest tip. Bash ran a tight ship.

Bash stood without swaying. All evident effect of the liquor was gone. "I'm going to stop off at my room before I go back to work this afternoon. If there are any calls from any of the media I'll get back to them later today."

The direction was unnecessary. Meyer knew there was one, and only one, spokesman for the archdiocese.

Bash bundled up and started off. He crossed Larned and turned onto Washington Boulevard. He began the slow ascent toward Michigan Avenue. At his back was Windsor, calling up a Detroit claim to fame of being the only city in the United States whence one traveled south to reach Canada.

This close to the riverfront was one of the coldest areas in the city. The wind whipped off the water, turning the already frigid air into a humid, bone-chilling force as it swept through the skyscraper canyons. Bash had not dressed particularly warmly. After all, he knew he'd be spending most of the morning in the cathedral at Foley's funeral. And, as anticipated, it had been very warm in there.

But that strategy had left him unprepared for this. The cold was so bitter he gave thought to hailing a cab. But it really wasn't all that far—a little more than four blocks. Besides, there weren't any cabs in sight. Practically nothing in sight. A combination of the early afternoon hour and the weather seemed to be keeping most cars and just about everybody off the streets.

God, it was cold! So cold his bones felt brittle—as if they would shatter any minute. Memories of Korea enveloped him. No matter how cold he had been before or since, nothing could match his experience in that wretched country.

MacArthur had been right, of course: You shouldn't fight a war unless you fight to win. Didn't learn it in Korea. Maybe learned it in Vietnam.

He squeezed his eyes nearly shut against the biting wind, as he tried to make his body crawl inside itself in search of an escape from the cold.

Once more, in memory, he was hunkered in a hastily dug trench. He had never been more terrified. The night was so black; no moon, no stars. His beard was frozen. He tried to keep tears from flowing. They were ice as soon as they left his eyes.

The soldiers with him in those trenches were so young, and more frightened even than he. He at least had a more untroubled attitude toward death. Not that he wanted to die. He wanted to live as much as anyone, but, as a priest, he had prepared himself for inevitable death any number of times in the past, an ingredient of spiritual retreats and missions. These poor kids, most of them had never seriously thought their young bodies could cease functioning. Not until now. All they wanted to do now was to go home and work in the family gas station. More urgently, they wanted to get out of their frozen clothing, get those boots off, and see if they could wiggle their toes—or if they still had toes. They wanted the noises of war to stop—the shrieking shells, the trip-hammer machine guns, the screams of wounded buddies.

Then there was the single sound Bash would never forget. It was the shell he instinctively knew was zeroing right in on his platoon. Then there was the explosion that cost him an eye.

Then there was the explosion on Washington Boulevard.

Cletus Bash pitched forward and fell to the pavement.

He was above the scene looking down at it. It didn't hurt. He could see people looking out their windows onto Washington Boulevard where his body lay stretched out on the pavement. None of the onlookers could see the figure running down the alley, tucking the gun into his coat pocket. The man who had been following Bash at a discreet distance since he'd left the restaurant. The man who had waited until Bash reached the alley. The man who, moving up quickly, had fired a single shot into Bash's head, turned, and dashed down the alley.

Bash, now drifting farther from his body sprawled on the ground, could see it all. He even recognized his killer. Somehow, now it didn't make any difference. He continued to drift away and became less and less interested in what was going on on earth.

Gradually, as people concluded that the gunshot was a solitary, not-to-be-immediately-repeated event, some cautiously emerged, but not before donning hat and coat. One helpful soul, when he realized Bash's condition, hurried back to call the police, which, oddly, no one else had thought to do, even after hearing the gunshot and seeing the prone figure. The others stood about, observing that it wasn't safe to walk around in Detroit, even downtown, even in broad daylight.

It was but seconds until a blue-and-white arrived. Once the uniformed police saw the head wound and that the victim was a priest, one of them called and alerted Zoo Tully.

28

IT WAS EARLY evening, but no one was counting.

At police headquarters, the Homicide Division was almost deserted. Some officers were investigating cases that demanded immediate attention. But most were out kicking the bushes on the Church-related serial murders. With the killing of Father Cletus Bash earlier in the day, all burners were on high. Shift times were disregarded, as, in many cases, were dinners. It didn't need to be said but the mayor said it anyway: This string of murders must be ended, and the perpetrator brought to justice.

Homicide didn't have to be specially motivated. The officers who worked this division were experienced and good at their job and they knew it. Beyond every other consideration, they were personally embarrassed by three—in effect, four—murders of members of the Catholic archdiocese.

In one of the squad rooms, Lieutenant Tully and Sergeants Mangiapane and Moore sat with Father Koesler around a couple of pushed-together desks. The silences—there were many—were awkward.

The common denominator of this group was Tully, who had invited Koesler to sit in at this meeting. Of course Tully also was Mangiapane and Moore's commanding officer. Neither of the sergeants knew precisely where the priest fit in, particularly at this stage of the investigation when it was expedient that things

306

run most smoothly and efficiently. As far as the sergeants could see, this was a time for the highest degree of police procedure. Not a time for bringing in a layman—in police terms—and an amateur at best.

But Tully, in inviting Koesler to attend, was following the same hunch he'd had throughout this investigation: That the priest could provide a Catholic insight that might elude the police area of expertise.

"Are we sure of the bullet?" Moore asked.

Tully nodded. "I just got the report from ballistics a little while ago. Just before you got here. A head wound; same gun."

"Wow!" Mangiapane exclaimed. "Record time."

"That's what we haven't got—time," Tully commented. "Father Koesler, is there any chance this Father Bash could have had a vital interest in the possible closing of Church schools or parishes?"

Koesler pondered the question briefly. The pause was largely pro forma; he was quite certain of the answer. He slowly shook his head. "Not to the best of my knowledge, Lieutenant. Oh, he undoubtedly had an opinion on the question, although I have no idea what that opinion might have been.

"But he would not be intimately affected in either event—whether the institutions were closed or allowed to remain open. He was not in the parochial ministry. By that I mean he wasn't attached to any parish. At most, he probably helped out at some parish on weekends. Again, if he did, I don't know where. His prime concern would have been in relaying the decision to the news media. In effect, I guess you could say he probably didn't care what decision was made as long as he had that decision in hand in enough time to dish it out to the media.

"As far as I can see, Lieutenant, that thread we had going to link the murders broke when Father Bash became a victim. Sorry."

"Don't be," Tully said. "It was my theory. You told

me what you knew of the first three and I came up with the idea. The problem is it puts us back on square one. And an added problem is that the perp seems to have changed his M.O.''

"His M.O.?" Moore said. "How's that?"

"The first three killings," Tully explained. "They all took place at night . . . with Donovan, early in the morning, actually. Both Hoffer and Foley were killed near eleven at night as each one was walking his dog before retiring. In each case the killer picked his time carefully. Of all the times and places he could have picked for Donovan, he struck late at night, 'cause she had a habit of doing a lot of her work in the evening and she frequently got home very late. Plus, at that hour, not only could he depend on her coming home alone but there likely would not be anyone around to witness the killing.

"He was right about everything but the victim. No way he could guess that one particular night would be the one and only time the nun loaned an outfit to her sister. So he got the wrong one. But it was a one-in-a-million chance. The important thing is that the perp had himself pretty well protected.

"The same in the next two killings. Both men had a steady, dependable habit of ending the day about eleven by walking their dogs. In both cases, that's exactly what both did. In both cases it was late at night on a pretty predictably empty street.

"In every case—in all three killings—his careful preparation paid off: All three were killed at his convenience. The victims were faithful to their schedules. It was most unlikely anyone would be around to witness the killings. If by chance he had spotted anyone coming home or passing by unexpectedly, he could just have walked away and done it some other night. None of the habits these people had were going to change. If anything prevented him from killing them when he originally intended, all he needed to do was come back another night."

"I see where you're headed, Zoo," said Moore. "The Bash killing doesn't have any of those elements."

"Not one," Tully continued. "How could the perp know what Bash was going to do today? According to his assistant . . . what's his name . . . ?"

"Meyer. Robert Meyer," Mangiapane supplied.

"Meyer. According to him, Bash suggested the Pontch Wine Cellars right out of the blue. Bash ate there frequently but by no means so regularly that it could be predicted. But the killer either followed him or waited for him in that alley. The more likely probability is that the guy was either in the restaurant or waiting outside. By the way, while I'm thinking of it, get some of our people to do as complete a make as possible on who was in the Pontch this afternoon. Joe Beyer knows his clientele pretty well. See if he recalls Carson or Stapleton—or if anybody can identify either of them as being there."

Both Mangiapane and Moore noted the instructions.

"To get back," Tully resumed, "the perp, as I figure it, followed Bash up Washington Boulevard. When he got to that alley, the perp checked out the area and when he didn't see anyone, he shot Bash and escaped down the alley.

"But just look at the difference: It's not at night; it's in broad daylight. The perp hasn't done his usual thorough surveillance; he's winging it for the first time. And he's taking a huge chance that someone—maybe looking out one of the windows—could be a witness, possibly even recognize or identify him. Now what does all this mean for us?"

A slight smile played at Moore's lips. "He's getting desperate. He's not being cautious. He's in a hurry."

Tully nodded. "Something like that. For whatever reason, he went against his M.O. And that's something we've got to figure out: Why? He improvised and still got away with it. We got to make sure if he improvises again, we're there to make sure he isn't lucky again. Or . . .'' One of Tully's worst fears in this case seemed to be coming true. At this point the only thing that made sense was that more than one killer was out there; that two—or more—crazies were operating, using the same gun, but, obviously, if one wanted to consider this latest killing, not the same M.O.

There was no help for it; they'd have to proceed on the basis that they didn't know which basis to proceed on: Was there one killer with two M.O.'s, or two or more killers with God knows how many M.O.'s?

Tully looked at the others, the three who had already invested so much time, effort, and brain work in this puzzle. He threw this latest ingredient into the pot. Koesler looked first startled, then thoughtful. Oddly, neither Moore nor Mangiapane changed expression. At first, Tully thought their lack of response was due to the newness of the hypothesis, but Mangiapane's low-keyed, ''Great minds run in the same channels,'' followed by Moore's smile of accord, gave him to realize that, in the words of countless comedians, the feeling was mutual, and that his two chief assistants had indeed been operating on the same channels.

''Well,'' Tully concluded, ''whichever, or whatever, or whoever is carrying out these killings, I repeat: We've got to make sure the perp isn't lucky again. And, speaking of luck, have our guys had any?''

''Some,'' Moore said. ''Talking to some of the friends and associates of Carson and Stapleton, it seems that both those guys have something going for them. We haven't found anybody yet who can be specific, but several acquaintances have said that Carson had been bragging about something he's been doing that will shake things up in the local Church. And, oddly, Stapleton has been doing somewhat the same. Only he doesn't seem to be bragging—maybe threatening is a better word. And whatever it is that Stapleton's doing

he claims is going to affect the whole damn Church—
worldwide.''

"It's not possible, is it," Koesler asked, "it's not
possible those two could be working together?''

"Anything's possible," Tully observed.

"Do they have alibis for this afternoon?" Mangiapane asked.

"They seem to have come up short again," Moore
said. "Carson is on suspension from the post office. He
claims he was home at the time of the shooting. Stapleton was driving to a meeting downtown, alone.
There's no way to substantiate either claim. It's just their
word. But, so far, that's it.''

"Okay . . ." Tully slapped the desk top, then stood.
"Let's get back on the street. Make sure everybody's
got the word about how the perp's M.O. has changed.
The planning from here on in . . . if there are any more
hits planned—and I feel there will be—from now on
he's liable to be sloppy. Or, if we're dealing with two
or more nuts, the M.O.'s liable to change totally. We've
got to hope for some kind of a break. Meantime, double
up the protection for the nun. And get on the possibility
that somebody at the Pontch Wine Cellars might identify either Carson or Stapleton.

"Let's hit the bricks.''

The three rose and prepared to leave, though Koesler
surely was not going to "hit the bricks.''

"Oh," Tully said in afterthought, "and Father Koesler: If you think of anything, call—doesn't matter when.
Call here. They'll know where to find me.''

Tully was still banking on Koesler's coming up with
some sort of Churchy insight that might break this puzzle open. In this, Tully was much more optimistic than
was the priest himself.

The walk home, from police headquarters to St. Joseph's, was not a great distance, but it was bitterly cold.
Gratiot Avenue was not that far removed from the De-

troit River and its icy breezes, and there was that unprotected overpass across the Chrysler Freeway.

As he walked, Father Koesler thought of Clete Bash,
and how, earlier this very day, he too had walked a
downtown street. He had had no way of knowing he
was heading toward his final moment on earth. When
it came right down to it, no Detroit priest or nun—or
anyone employed by the archdiocese—had any clue as
to whether they—any of them—were on this madman's
list.

There were no lights on in the ancient rectory when
Koesler let himself in. He went directly to the kitchen.
It was the warmest room in the old building. There he
found a note from Mary O'Connor telling him his dinner was in the oven and giving specific instructions on
how to heat it. He thought the instructions a bit much,
but then he remembered a time he had put a frozen
dinner including the cardboard box containing it into
the oven to heat. Over the years, Mary had come to
know him better than he knew himself.

He followed her instructions to the letter.

He felt frozen to the bone. So he mixed himself a
Scotch and water. The first sip sent a welcome wave of
warmth through his still-shivering body. He glanced at
the afternoon paper's front page. No mention of Father
Bash's murder. It must have happened too late for their
deadline. The story surely would be the top headline in
both morning and afternoon papers tomorrow.

To be followed by . . . whom? Sister Joan? Would
the killer, now in seeming haste, double back and pick
off the one target he seemed to have missed? Would all
the present police protection scare him off? Could anything frighten off a person that determined on a plan of
destruction?

Sister Joan . . . something rattling around in his
memory.

Sister Joan was the first intended victim . . . or so
the theory went. But her executioner failed, and so he

moved on to the second, then the third, then the fourth victims, never returning to the first failed effort.

Hadn't Koesler been thinking of something similar recently? Something in the liturgy?

Of course; it was the feat of St. John the Apostle and Evangelist.

Koesler dug out his copy of *The Oxford Dictionary of Saints*. John suffered "(according to ecclesiastical tradition) under Domitian's persecution, from which, however, he escaped alive and ended his days at an advanced age at Ephesus."

But legend had it that all the apostles died martyrs. Even though John did not actually die for his faith, the Emperor Domitian did his level best to try to make John a martyr. And despite his escape, the Church considers him a martyr.

Like St. John, Sister Joan escaped her executioner. Somebody who was well instructed in Christianity would be familiar with the St. John legend. And whoever was responsible for this series of murders very likely would fit that profile. So Sister Joan, if Koesler were correct, would no longer be a murder victim candidate. She hadn't been murdered any more than St. John had. But both had been handed "the palm of martyrdom"—*honoris causa*, as it were.

His first impulse was to call Lieutenant Tully and inform him of this new line of reasoning. Instead, he paused. He felt that he was on some sort of deductive roll. Now that he had a clear impression of how this still-living nun fit into the picture, he might be on the verge of identifying that elusive thread that tied this string of murders together.

Something . . . something . . . something. It was something someone had said. The clue was so close at hand, lurking just on the edge of his mind. He was sure that if he could just relax and let his mind take its own tour in a stream of consciousness, it would surface. He took another sip of his drink. He was relaxing and his mind seemed right on target.

Meanwhile, his dinner was not only badly overdone, it was on the verge of catching fire.

Sure enough, the front pages of both the *Detroit News* and the *Free Press* were full of Father Cletus Bash's murder at midday on Washington Boulevard. That was the lead story and it was amplified both on page one and on the jump pages by sidebars covering the brief history of these serial murders and reports on the progress and lack of same of the police investigation.

Buried somewhere in the midst of these stories was the announcement by Robert Meyer, acting spokesman for the archdiocese of Detroit, to the effect that, immediately following Father Bash's funeral, Cardinal Boyle would leave on a combined spiritual retreat and vacation. The Cardinal's doctor was quoted as saying there was no emergency, but that the prelate was in need of some rest and solitude. Recent events and the tragic attacks on Church leaders had taken their toll. As his doctor put it, the archbishop needed to recharge his batteries.

No specific destination or duration was mentioned, only that he would be sojourning in a warmer clime for as long as it took to get those batteries recharged.

29

CARDINAL MARK BOYLE lived in what was by just about anyone's standards a mansion. It was located in Palmer Woods, a square mile enclave just inside Detroit's northern limits. Mansions are plentiful in this luxurious section, but the former residence of Bishop Michael Gallagher and Cardinal Edward Mooney and present residence of Cardinal Boyle well overshadowed its surrounding homes.

Traditionally, the neighborhood is quiet, elegant. But with the market value of these homes, one could expect little else.

It was quiet on this beautiful winter evening. Clear skies, lots of stars; only a quarter moon that shed little light. The drowsy dark was pierced only occasionally by a streetlight.

The streets were empty, except for the occasional car that would creep over the slippery pavement and turn in at a driveway to be tucked into its garage for the night.

One such vehicle, a late model black four-door Taurus, inched along the street, but did not turn in at any driveway. Instead, it circled the neighborhood as if the driver were on a sightseeing tour of the mansions. It drew no attention; one would have to have been watching the streets for some time and with concentration to note that the same car had passed not once but several times. And no one was paying that sort of attention.

Finally, the Taurus pulled to a stop on Balmoral. The

315

driver got out of the car and opened the rear door. Out popped a Heinz 57 mutt with a stubby, furiously wagging tail. The man attached a lead to the pup's collar, which was devoid of any identifying tags or license.

He set off at a normal pace, pausing only when the dog investigated a tree or a fire hydrant. To anyone who might have paid him any mind in the dim light, he was a neighborhood resident, home from a day of wheeling and dealing, walking his dog after dinner. The dog was a perfect pretext for strolling through the neighborhood.

Man and dog turned onto Wellesley Drive. Still no one on the streets. No cars going home anymore. Lights on in most of the houses, but recessed into the interior, perhaps the dining area.

There it was: the mansion by which its neighbors were measured.

The man did not break his pace, but proceeded until he was enveloped in shadow. There he stopped and unhooked the lead from the dog's collar, stuffing the lead into his coat pocket.

Freed, the little dog pranced along happily, hoping to find a warm place to spend the night.

The man cautiously approached the mansion, careful to stay in the shadows. His black garb helped conceal him. He headed along the side of the huge house toward a room that showed a light from inside. He knew the room was a study.

Slowly he approached the lighted room. As far as he could tell, it was the only light on in the entire mansion. That was fitting. The occupant resided with no companion; the help lived in the distant interior. The occupant undoubtedly had finished dinner and was commencing an evening of reading and study before an early retirement.

The man studied the ground. There were no footprints. The sidewalk, as well as the walkways leading to and around the house, were totally cleared of snow. He had expected no less.

He drew nearer. The room lay behind lace-curtained French doors.

He stood looking into the room. He could not see clearly because of the filmy curtains, but he could make out the tall, slender, cassocked figure. This was the man he would kill. This was the man he had to kill.

His face was almost pressed against the door's glass. Still he was unable to discern details clearly. The lighting was indirect—and there were those damned curtains.

From an inside coat pocket he drew a many-bladed knife. One of the blades was a glass cutter. He would effect entry through an adjoining room. But first, just on the off chance . . . He tried the doorknob. It turned. Very, very careless. It certainly simplified his objective. But, very, very careless.

He opened the door quietly, just enough to step into the room. He closed the door behind him, again quietly, never taking his eyes off his target. Even in the dim light, no one could mistake the distinctive Cardinal-red of the wide cummerbund and zucchetto. The cassocked figure was standing at a table, his back to the intruder.

As the man took a cautious step, a board creaked.

"Hello, Quent. I've been expecting you." The cassocked figured turned slowly.

The Reverend Mr. Quentin Jeffrey gasped. His gasp was followed by another small sound of surprise. "Bob? Bob Koesler?" Jeffrey stepped in front of a large chair and lowered himself into it, burying his hands in his coat pockets as he sank into the upholstery.

His mouth hung ajar as he fought to conquer his astonishment. Koesler's expression was both inquisitive and kindly as he stood facing Jeffrey. The two men remained motionless, as if caught in one of television's freeze-frames for several moments.

"How . . . how did you know?" Jeffrey stammered

finally. "Was it the clue I gave you? Did you catch my hint?"

"Not right away, Quent." Koesler sat back against the table. "It began at Archbishop Foley's wake. A couple of the guys were talking about a lot of things: vacations, the Cardinal . . . and a party they were going to after the wake. They were going to play cards—poker. One of them complained that, with the out-of-towners who would be playing, the poker would be deadly serious and professional—no wild card games."

Jeffrey nodded, a small smile pulling at the corners of his lips.

"That was the seed," Koesler said. "Later, I thought about the game I sat in on the other night. Young and Bash and you and I.

"Now, nobody in the diocese is more famed as a serious and professional poker player than you. And yet, one of the times it was your deal, you called one-eyed jacks wild."

Jeffrey could not suppress a broad grin. Not unlike a teacher encouraging a pupil who was on the right track.

In fact, Jeffrey's reaction was encouraging Koesler as he continued. "That also was the night you remarked that Church law held all the cards.

"Then I thought about how I tried to explain the administration of the Detroit archdiocese to a policeman, and I remembered the part the—at that time three—murder victims played in it.

"Larry Hoffer: the money man; in charge of most of the financial transactions in the diocese—in charge of ten departments with offices in the chancery.

"A ten.

"Sister Joan Donovan: Holding the highest rank of any woman in the diocese.

"Like . . . a queen.

"Archbishop Foley: Retired. The title of Cardinal being largely honorary, there is no one more powerful, outside of the Pope himself, than an archbishop. But this one had retired; was responsible for nothing, save himself. Once extremely powerful, now but a figurehead, powerless. Very much like the present function of most . . . kings.

"But I doubt anyone could have figured the connection without Father Bash. It wasn't his title, job, or responsibilities. It was what the Korean War did to him. It took the vision in one of his eyes. Not only that, but Father Bash was thought by many—rightly or wrongly— to be a selfish, tricky person. In bygone days, he might well have been known as a knave. And knave is another name for the jack in playing cards. So, one could think of Cletus Bash as a one-eyed jack.

"So there we have it: a ten, a jack, a queen, and a king. Drawing to the only unbeatable hand in all of poker. Even if Church law does hold all the cards, nothing can beat a royal flush. Ten, jack, queen, king. All you lacked was the ace. The top card in the diocese, the Cardinal Archbishop . . that's it, isn't it, Quent?''

Jeffrey's only response was a nod.

"Did you," Koesler asked, "set up the two suspects—Carson and Stapleton?"

Jeffrey shook his head. "I didn't know about them at all until Bash started running off at the mouth during the poker game. I was, of course, delighted. Made contact with them immediately and encouraged them in their plans. Warned each of them that it was vital to keep their projects a deep dark secret."

"What were they trying to do?"

Jeffrey shrugged. "A million miles from killing anybody. Though, as I say, it worked to my advantage that the police thought they were. It was all innocent enough. Stapleton, along with a few other CORPUS members, is making preliminary plans for a duplication of sorts of the Vatican Council, to be held, like the earlier ones, in Rome. Only this one will be by and for all those who want to function as priests and can't. Resigned priests, married men; women; homosexuals.

Their hope? That the Church will not be able to withstand all the publicity and that the bishops who agree with their objectives will come out of the closets.

"Fred, by the way, couldn't understand why the cops got so excited about his aunt's bequest. He's known about the dotty old gal all the while. He also knew all along that the Donovans were distant cousins. When it comes, he won't turn the money down. But he doesn't need it."

"And Carson?"

Jeffrey snorted. "He's the flip side of Stapleton. They're opposites. I'm surprised they don't attract each other. Carson is trying to organize the extreme Catholic right wing into vigilante groups—first locally, then nationwide, finally global." Jeffrey chuckled. "They're going to infiltrate every parish. Gather evidence—photos, recordings, testimony—of abuse of liturgy, abuse of everything. He 'knows the Pope will act.' And he's probably right on that.

"If," Jeffrey continued, "they hadn't been so secretive about what they wanted to accomplish, they probably wouldn't have ended up as suspects. But, as I said, it worked to my advantage. I even encouraged them to go ahead and, above all, to be quiet about it. If anyone, outside of their comrades, learned what they were doing, I assured them, their plans would be sabotaged."

Koesler considered what he'd just been told. He pushed away from the table and stood looking down at Jeffrey. "Quent, why did you drop that hint during the poker game?"

"Oh, I don't know. The way the game was being played, I guess I thought it was unfair. I suppose I wanted to even up the odds a bit."

"A 'game'? 'Even up the odds'? Quent, how can you talk like that!? This wasn't a game! Human life is what we're talking about. Innocent human lives! Quent, you committed murder! How can you call it a game?"

Jeffrey's expression changed instantly, radically.

"You're right. How can we call it a game!" He appeared furious and deadly serious. "How can anyone call what the Church did to me a game!"

" 'What the Church . . .' " Koesler did not understand.

Jeffrey grasped Koesler's unstated question. "Made me a goddamn eunuch!"

"A 'eunuch,' " Koesler repeated. "You mean because as a widower you can't marry again? But Quent, you knew that from the beginning. Those were the rules of the game from the start. You knew that if you became a widower, without extenuating circumstances you couldn't marry again."

Jeffrey snorted. "See? Back to the idea of a game. Can you still wonder why I chose to take them on in a game of my own? My deal! Certainly I knew the rules of their game. What I did not know was how much their game was going to cost."

"But—"

"Let me finish, Bob. Maryanne was younger than I— ten years younger. When we married, I didn't think about either of us dying. But if I had, I would have figured I'd go first, of course. Women, on the average, live longer than men, and Maryanne was ten years my junior.

"Another thought I would have had, had I asked myself, was that if my wife somehow would precede me in death, I probably would marry again. But I didn't give either possibility any conscious thought.

"Not until I got involved in this deacon program. Then, as you say, they stated the rules of the game. Then I was forced to consider what I'd never consciously figured on before: the prospect of becoming a widower. Having considered it briefly, I dismissed it out of hand. Maryanne was not only much younger than I and likely to outlive me, but she was in excellent health.

"Then it happened. Cancer."

"I remember."

"I was devastated. But I had no idea when she died that it was going to get worse over the months . . . over the years. It was never going to get better. I was not made for a celibate life."

"People can accommodate—"

Jeffrey continued as if Koesler had not interrupted. "I thought dating might help. It made it worse. I was like a clumsy teenager fumbling with the problems of necking and petting, for God's sake, when I should have been able to live the quiet, fulfilled life I had with Maryanne." Jeffrey stopped. He seemed to have completed that line of thought.

"You could have gotten out," Koesler said. "You could have applied for laicization. You could have been dispensed from your obligations as a deacon."

"Been 'reduced to the lay state'?" Jeffrey almost spat the words. "I've never backed away from anything in my life!"

Suddenly it was clear to Koesler. Quentin Jeffrey had been locked in a vise, part of it his making. But a vise, nonetheless, that he'd found inescapable. He was trapped, and, in effect, by refusing to escape through, for instance, laicization, he trapped himself. It must have been an enormous, overwhelming pressure. How could he possibly have withstood it? Maybe that was it: Maybe he couldn't withstand it. Maybe he cracked. But if he had "cracked," could he be as rational as he seemingly was?

Something was happening. Koesler was aware something was happening, but what? Jeffrey shifted in the chair. But not as if he were going to rise.

Jeffrey looked at Koesler for what seemed to the priest a long while. His expression seemed serene. He appeared far more tranquil than he'd been actually only moments before. "Well, Bobby," he said, "you figured out the whole thing out, didn't you? More power to you. You also figured out that since I was drawing to a royal flush, I would not harm you. You are a lovely man, Robert, but you are no ace.

"Nevertheless, Robert, I doubt that you—that we— are alone. There must be police all over the place. Am I right?"

Koesler nodded. "Yes. This room has been wired to record our conversation and the police are here. . . ." He inclined his head toward the inner doors and the side windows, in turn. "I'm sorry," he said, "there was nothing else to do. But you can get help, Quent. We can see to that."

"And how will we do that, Bob? Bring Maryanne back from the dead? Change the laws of the Church? No, Bob . . ." He shook his head. "There are no answers for me. I've played my hand and lost."

His voice dropped to little more than a whisper. Only Koesler could have caught his words. "It's time to go, Bob," Jeffrey murmured. "Not you. Me." With that, his right hand emerged from his coat pocket, holding a gun. The hand had barely started to move toward Koesler when a volley of gunfire erupted with a deafening roar. Simultaneously, Koesler raised his hand as a shouted "No!" was torn from his throat. Jeffrey's body lurched every which way as it was buried more deeply in the chair.

Koesler instinctively made the sign of the cross over the dying man and whispered the words of absolution, not knowing whether they were needed, not knowing whether they did any good.

He would never be able to erase from memory the sight of Jeffrey's face the instant before his body was riddled with bullets. It was an expression of completely incongruous tranquility. As if he were being relieved of an intolerable burden.

It was no consolation to Lieutenant Tully that an autopsy revealed that his had been the fatal bullet. Quentin Jeffrey was only the second person Tully had killed. Both deaths had been in the line of duty. Both deaths sickened him to the core. Though he stayed on the job, it took a long while before he came to terms with what his duty compelled him to do.

The case was closed. The mayor, the police brass, the city's movers and shakers, the Catholic community—all were relieved. The bad press, for some; the ordeal, for others, was over.

A priest and a police lieutenant were devastated by the tragic and unnecessary loss of life—of both the victims and their killer. But there was nothing the priest or the police lieutenant could do about it.

30

Two weeks had passed since Quentin Jeffrey, having received a very controversial Catholic Church funeral, had been buried. Many had argued for, many had argued against, the granting of Christian burial. Some said he was no better than a cold-blooded murderer and a notorious sinner. Others contended he was clearly insane and thus not responsible for the devastation he had caused.

In the end, it was Cardinal Boyle who decided. Since one of Jeffrey's victims had been Boyle's best friend, and since the Cardinal himself had been Jeffrey's designated final victim, few could argue that Cardinal Boyle was motivated by anything other than a generous and forgiving heart.

As it turned out, Cardinal Boyle had not left for a well-deserved vacation; Father Koesler, at the Cardinal's insistence, was the one who traveled down to Florida.

Koesler visited with friends, cautiously absorbed some sun, rested, read a lot, and tried to relax. The one thing he hoped to do—forget—he failed to do.

Now he was back at St. Joseph's parish. All the snow was gone. Detroit's weather had been true to form; a bitterly cold December was being followed by an unexpectedly warm January. God, and God alone, knew what the dreaded February would bring.

Koesler had returned to Detroit quite late the previous night. This morning was his first weekday Mass after vacation. He had been surprised at the unexpectedly large turnout. He estimated a crowd of at least fifty. While that number hardly filled the cavernous ornate church, it was something more than the five or six he was used to.

Among the congregation had been Mary O'Connor, who was now fixing breakfast for the two of them. Neither of them had much of a morning appetite. It was cold cereal, fruit, toast, and coffee.

"Good to have you back, Father." Mary's back was to him as she prepared the coffee.

"Good to be back, Mary. It really is." He sat at the kitchen table and started in on the cereal. "Anything important or outrageous happen while I was gone?"

"Not really . . . at least nothing an exciting person like yourself would consider important." She was grinning. He couldn't see her face but he knew the smile was there.

"Well, thank God for the Jesuits. We're running out of parish-sitters. If it weren't for the Jebbies at Sts. Peter and Paul, I don't think I would have been able to get away. Father Untener must have done a masterful job judging from this morning's crowd."

Mary, carrying the coffeepot to the table, shook her head. "It wasn't Father Untener; it's you."

"Me?"

"Have you forgotten? You were in the papers a couple of weeks ago. Your people knew you'd be back today; they came to see the celebrity."

"That's my fifteen minutes." He looked up at her. "You think that's really it? Well . . ." He smiled. "It beats ringing doorbells. But," he added resolutely, "I've got to get back to that as soon as possible. Maybe all those Catholics hibernating in the high rises will recognize me for a little while. I'd better capitalize on that while it's still warm."

He noticed that Mary, holding her cup, was looking

directly into his eyes and smiling. "Something?" he asked, puzzled.

"Aren't you going to tell me?"

"Tell you what?"

"How you knew it was Quentin Jeffrey—and how you caught him?"

"You read all about that in the papers."

"Not all and not from the horse's mouth."

"Thank you for not thinking of another part of the horse's anatomy.

"There's not an awful lot to tell that wasn't in the papers. The most bizarre part of the story—building an unbeatable hand by killing people—that was reported."

"Yes, but not how you got to impersonate the Cardinal—and how you knew the deacon would come that night."

"That? Well, it wasn't easy getting to stand in for the Cardinal. As to the timing, that was more or less a lucky guess. The murders seemed to be accelerating. Father Bash was killed almost as Archbishop Foley was being buried. I had the impression that the killer was getting anxious, in a hurry. So I thought if we falsely announced that the Cardinal was leaving for an extended period for an undesignated place, the killer would act before his victim could get away."

"And impersonating the Cardinal?"

Koesler grimaced. "That was the hard part. Oddly, I had a far easier time convincing the Cardinal than I had with the police. The Cardinal and I are about the same height. Oh, I'm a bit heavier, but in dim light and in a cassock, that wouldn't be too noticeable. I told the Cardinal that if I was right—and I was certain I was—that he would be dead very soon unless we set the trap. Fortunately, he believed me when I told him that he was the only one in danger. I assured him the killer wouldn't hurt me because I didn't fit into his plan."

"But why you, Father? That's the question I've heard

most often these past two weeks. Why not a policeman in the cassock?''

''The very question that was uppermost in Lieutenant Tully's mind,'' Koesler said. He sipped his coffee as his thoughts leaped back to the fateful evening.

''Well,'' he said finally, ''it wasn't so much a 'question' as a very, *very* strong objection. The lieutenant and I argued—yes, that's the right word—we argued about it for—well, hours, I guess. He was totally opposed to a civilian's risking his life in a situation that he felt demanded a trained policeman.

''My argument was that we didn't have any evidence to try him on, or even hold him on. We had no proof of anything and the most they could come up with using a policeman stand-in would be circumstantial evidence. And no matter how strong that might be, it wouldn't carry as much weight in a court of law or be as strong as a confession. And that once Quent found he was dealing with a policeman, he wouldn't say anything. I was sure he'd talk to me. And he did.''

''And that argument convinced the lieutenant?''

''Not by a long shot. He absolutely refused to let me go through with it.''

''And?''

''I told him I was going to do it anyway, whether he went along with me or not. He was really angry—just short of furious, I think. But eventually, he said if I was determined to be 'a damn fool'—those were his exact words—he'd set it up.''

''But it worked.''

''Yes. And I'm pretty sure he's still angry with me. Even though it did work.''

''It was lucky he agreed to provide protection or you might be dead now.''

''I don't think so, Mary. I heard the words he murmured. I saw the expression on his face. He had no intention of harming me. Once he knew the police were there, he knew if he drew his gun they would kill him.

The poor guy had nowhere to go but into another life, where I pray God and Quent's victims forgave him." Koesler paused. "There was another reason I insisted on standing in for the Cardinal. I don't know that it would make sense to anyone but me. See, I promised Archbishop Foley I would jump right in and get actively involved in the case. And I made the same sort of commitment to Cardinal Boyle. The opportunity to stand in for the Cardinal was a gift from heaven. I had to do it. That was the argument that finally convinced the Cardinal to go along with my plan."

"It makes sense to me."

"Thanks, Mary. I needed that. Thanks."

Mary refilled their cups. "Such a weird plot." She shook her head. "Do you think he really was insane? And if he was, how could he have appeared to be so normal?"

"That puzzled me too. I couldn't figure it out. It got so bad that I phoned my friend Dr. Rudy Scholl from Florida. I gave him an account of the whole thing. He said it was a classic example of what psychologists call a borderline personality."

"Borderline? What does that mean?"

"Would you fill my cup one more time? I think that'll do it. Thanks. Well, if I understand Rudy correctly, it means that such a personality is living right on the edge—the border—between sanity and insanity."

Mary shuddered. "That's frightening. I mean it sounds like some sort of science fiction—or a horror movie."

Koesler sipped the hot coffee. It was excellent. He was convinced there was no special trick to brewing good coffee. "It *is* frightening. But it's strange: When we were in that room, together, just Quent and I, I got the overwhelming impression that he had been under enormous stress for a long, long time—ever since his wife died. I think he felt he was caged in a box he couldn't escape from.

"Rudy agreed. And added the word 'conflict.' It was, he said, a 'stressful conflict.' Quent felt he was intended to live a married life. That had been taken away when his wife died out of due time. He believed that any sexual relationship had to be restricted to marriage. According to Church rules, he could not marry again. And he felt compelled to comply with that law even though he detested it. He was not going to back away from this obligation. You could scarcely find a more clear example of stressful conflict.

"My problem was the same question you raised: How could he function so well in a normal daily life and then deliberately kill people? He would have had to be some sort of chameleon. One moment he would be a well adjusted, even dedicated man, a minister of the Church—and the next moment he would be a madman.

"But Rudy explained that this is the key to the borderline personality. They function at a high level of normalcy and then they decompose and go into a psychotic state."

" 'Decompose'! That seems an awfully strong word."

"I know. But that's the word Rudy used. He also said that Quent was the right age to have been in the Korean War. Isn't that odd: Quent and Clete Bash would have been in the same war. One emerged physically crippled, the other maybe emotionally. Anyway, Rudy said that if it were true, that Quent could already have been programmed to be violent as a result of that bloody war. As a soldier he would have to follow orders. Then as a successful businessman, he would have the power to make his own rules. So he was used to being in charge of his life.

"Then he becomes a deacon and once again he is subject to rules that he cannot bend. Another stressful situation.

"Rudy said it was completely believable that Quent could begin to see these laws that hemmed him in on every side as a kind of catch-22—a game. In his psychotic state, he would treat the situation like a game. Only it was his deal. And he was going to deal himself the unbeatable power hand—a royal flush: ten, jack, queen, king, ace of the same suit—Catholic leaders.''

They were silent for a few moments.

"I was just thinking,'' Mary said, "those married ministers and priests who are becoming Catholic priests—they may have to face the same kind of problem Quentin Jeffrey did.''

Koesler nodded. "Yes, that's possible—even probable. It will be a problem that the Catholic Church—at least the Latin Rite—hasn't had to face for about a thousand years. That, and, I suppose, divorced priests . . . priests who want to remarry after a divorce. I guess that's why the Pope is paid so well.''

They laughed.

"It certainly is a different Church from the one we grew up in,'' Mary said.

"I'll say. Some think that in the Third Vatican Council, the bishops will bring their wives along. And at Vatican IV the bishops will bring their husbands.''

Mary laughed. "That's too much for this old head to handle.'' She finished her coffee and left the kitchen, to busy herself in the office.

Koesler, alone in the room, cradled his cup and thought. In such a brief time, five, almost six, people dead. Four people he'd known quite well; one, Helen Donovan, he never knew. Four people who had no idea why they had been selected, who had no advance warning whatsoever that the end was at hand. One man the cause of it all. Yet, could a "borderline personality'' be fully responsible? Was he himself a victim of a different sort, and was it one rule that was the cause of it all?

Koesler did not know. He tried to visualize the five, the victims and their killer, in heaven. In heaven—and in heaven alone—would it be possible to find the understanding and forgiveness needed to heal these wounds. Like the two soldiers in Wilfred Owen's war poetry who had fought hand to hand, thrusting and parrying until they had slain one another. Now, one invites the other to come away from the field of slaughter, and rest.

He thought of the last letter St. Thomas More wrote to his daughter before he was executed. The last words of that letter, the last words that great man wrote: *"Farewell, my dear child and pray for me, and I shall for you and all your friends that we may merrily meet in heaven."*

Only in heaven . . .

Be sure to read all the
Father Koesler mysteries
by

William X. Kienzle

*Available in paperback from
Ballantine Books.*

William X. Kienzle

ASSAULT WITH INTENT

Four clumsy assassins stalk the seminaries of Detroit. Who's behind this quartet of killers? Father Koesler, clerical sleuth extraordinaire, had better find the answer quickly as he himself is now the number-one target.

DEADLINE FOR A CRITIC

The venomous critic Ridley Groendal is dead. Who did it? The playwright? The violinist? The author? The actress? Each had a dark, longtime link to the victim. And Father Koesler, who'd known Groendal since their school days, wants to know what happened.

DEATHBED

Father Koesler goes undercover as a hospital chaplain to follow the tracks of four people whose rancor toward someone is so great it could translate into violence. The object of their wrath: an indomitable, unsinkable nun who almost single-handedly keeps the inner-city Detroit hospital open.

William X. Kienzle

DEATH WEARS A RED HAT

The first one is recovered beneath a cardinal's red hat. The next few specimens are found perched on the shoulders of church statues throughout Detroit. They're all human heads, heads that once conceived the most monstrous crimes in the city. Father Koesler begins a terrifying quest into ancient rituals of revenge for the critical clue to these macabre murders.

EMINENCE

From the converted bank building in downtown Detroit, four religious brothers and a priest give sight to the blind and new health to the sick. Before long the afflicted throng to be cured. Fat donations enrich the spartan quarters of the make-shift monastery. Church dogmatists debate whether these faith healers can be hailed as miracle workers. But from the walls of St. Hedwig's flow not only good works, but some very foul deeds. Like embezzlement. Torture. And murder.

William X. Kienzle

KILL AND TELL

Father Koesler has heard some shocking news in the sanctity of the confessional: yet a new murder victim will soon breathe his last. The honor-bound Father can't breathe a word, but as the sleuthing priest, he steps into action.

MARKED FOR MURDER

The older prostitutes of Detroit are the victims. Mutilation and branding are the methods. A man in the black garb and white collar of a Catholic priest is the suspect. Father Koesler may never forgive himself for what he's about to uncover.

William X. Kienzle

MASQUERADE

A mystery writers' conference brings together an unusual collection of authors: a rabbi, a nun, a monk, and an Episcopal priest. They all write mysteries, but they also have something else in common: each of them happens to despise the sleazy televangelist who is also on the guest list. If Father Koesler had any misgivings about acting as a consultant at the conference, they disappear when murder upsets the entire agenda, and Koesler is faced with a very pious group of suspects.

MIND OVER MURDER

The Monsignor's Cadillac is found in the parking lot. Inside are traces of blood and a shell from a .32 automatic. All that's missing is the Monsignor. Father Koesler, clerical sleuth extraordinare, had better find his way out of this mystery.

William X. Kienzle

THE ROSARY MURDERS

It begins on Ash Wednesday, when someone pulls the plug on the hospital respirator of an elderly priest. Then a nun is brutally murdered in a bathtub. In swift, terrifying succession, men and women of the cloth fall prey to a savage killer who leaves a macabre calling card—a plain, black rosary entwined in the fingers of his victim. The introduction to Willian Kienzle's indominatable sleuth, Father Robert Koesler.

SHADOW OF DEATH

A cardinal is brutally murdered in his own church. Another is slain in the Vatican. On a trail from Detroit to Dublin to Rome, Father Koesler plunges back into his own haunted past—and becomes an unholy candidate for assassination.

SUDDEN DEATH

Hank "The Hun" Hunsinger, superstar tight end for the Pontiac Cougars, is murdered by ingenious and macabre means in his own shower. Himself a religious football fan, Father Koesler unearths a secret every bit as astonishing as a winning eighty-yard touchdown pass with three seconds to go.

WILLIAM X. KIENZLE